A *Sense* OF DANGER

JENNIFER ESTEP

A SENSE OF DANGER

Copyright © 2021 by Jennifer Estep

ISBN: 978-1-950076-08-6

Cover Art © 2021 by Tony Mauro
Interior Formatting by Author E.M.S.

Fonts: *Spy Agency* by Daniel Zadorozny for Iconian Fonts, used under Commercial License; *Times New Roman* by Monotype Typography, used under Desktop License; *Goudy Old Style* by Type Solutions, Inc for Microsoft Corporation, used under Desktop License. *Crosshair vector* by Pixxsa, used under Shutterstock Standard License.

Published in the United States of America

To my mom and my grandma—for everything.

To myself—because I always wanted to write a spy book.

ONE

CHARLOTTE

You could always tell the assassins by their suits. Jackets, shirts, ties. The garments were all extremely expensive and finely made, but also unrelentingly dark and depressingly monochromatic. Black on black, navy on navy, perhaps a dark gray on an even darker gray if someone was feeling particularly cheerful. It was as though the men and women who served as assassins for Section 47 had decided to kill the color from their wardrobes as easily as they dispatched the paramortal terrorists, criminals, and other dangerous magic wielders who wished to wreak chaos and calamity on the unsuspecting mortal world.

I eyed a couple of black-suited male assassins as they grabbed plastic trays and got in the cafeteria line. Of course, we didn't actually call them *assassins* at Section 47. At least, not to their faces. Not if you wanted to keep breathing. No, my secret government agency referred to those men and women as *cleaners*, as if that somehow masked their true, deadly purpose. They didn't clean up anything. They just created more bloody messes, in every sense of the word.

Just like my father had.

"Penny for your thoughts, Charlotte?" a light, feminine voice drawled, and a hand waved, drawing my attention away from the assassins.

I looked at the gorgeous woman with long, sleek red hair, hazel eyes, and rosy skin, sitting across the table. Miriam Lancaster, my office friend and lunch buddy, stared back at me, clearly expecting an answer. I wasn't about to confess how much the black-suited cleaners reminded me of my father, so I gestured at my laptop instead.

"Just thinking about how much work I still need to finish."

Sympathy filled her face. "Trying to get that big report done before you leave to work your diner shift?"

My fingers curled around the edges of the laptop keys at the mention of my second, unwanted job. I never should have told Miriam that I moonlighted as a waitress at a diner near the main Section building, but she had pried it out of me during one of our lunchtime chats after spotting the cheesy uniform sticking up out of my shoulder bag. Then again, Miriam *was* a charmer—someone who cozied up to and subtly extracted information from foreign spies, diplomats, and businesspeople—instead of just a lowly analyst like me.

In addition to her stunning good looks, Miriam was also gifted with charisma. Even though she wasn't currently using her power, wasn't trying to charm or beguile me, I could still sense the magic emanating from her body. The warm, soothing sensation always reminded me of a soft, fuzzy blanket straight out of the dryer. Miriam knew how to use that comforting feeling to its fullest extent, knew how to smile, nod, and draw people in until they confessed their deepest, darkest secrets. She might not kill people, as the cleaners did, but Section 47 had trained and molded her into a weapon as well, one who wielded friendly grins and smooth words instead of guns and knives.

"Yeah," I replied in a neutral tone, finally answering her question. "Something like that."

Miriam nodded, then leaned back in her chair, her gaze sweeping over every nook and cranny of the cafeteria, as if the area were fascinating instead of functional.

The cafeteria was like any other in the Washington, D.C., area—a large, cavernous space filled with gray plastic tables and chairs with cheap, framed black-and-white prints of D.C. landmarks covering the walls. One side of the cafeteria featured floor-to-ceiling windows that showed the hustle and bustle of the busy sidewalk and street outside, although the foot and motor traffic had died down a bit from the earlier frantic lunchtime rush. Even though it was creeping up on two o'clock, people still came in off the street, walked through the open archway, and headed for the food line along the back wall.

The cafeteria—also uninspiringly named Section 47— served decent food, and the menu included everything from typical burgers, fries, and pizzas to vegan deli salads, cold-pressed juices, and gluten-free cookies. Since it was open to the public, the cafeteria did a brisk breakfast and lunchtime business, although the regular mortals who strolled inside didn't realize they were sitting and eating next to dangerous people with magical abilities and deadly training.

Then again, that was true of most restaurants in D.C. You never knew if the woman in the boring beige pantsuit throwing back shots of celery juice was a personal assistant or the head of some black-ops department, or if the guy in the wrinkled shirt and stained tie stuffing his face with mac-and-cheese was a taxi driver on his lunch break or some foreign diplomat spying on American soil. Washington, D.C., purportedly had more spies—both mortal and paramortal—per capita than any other city in the world.

Miriam took a sip of her iced tea, somehow not smearing her perfect red lipstick. It wasn't a magical talent, but I envied her the ability all the same. My own plum lipstick had evaporated seconds after I had arrived at work this morning.

"What about Jensen's funeral?" she asked. "You going to that tonight?"

My fingers flexed and then curled around the laptop keys again. Gregory Jensen had been my direct supervisor and a passionate environmentalist who was always railing about Section's carbon footprint and how the cafeteria was killing the planet with plastic straws. Jensen had also been a devoted cyclist who thought he owned the road, instead of the cars and trucks whizzing by, and he had biked to and from work every day—until he'd been killed by a hit-and-run driver last week. Jensen had fought the traffic, and the traffic had finally won.

I felt sorry for his wife and daughter, but Gregory Jensen had been a royal pain in my ass, always barking orders and pointing out perceived flaws in my work. The day before his accident, he'd said that the staple in my latest report was crooked, before ordering me to yank it out and re-staple the papers together to his satisfaction.

He also had a nasty, infuriating habit of taking credit for my work. More than once, I'd been in an interdepartmental meeting where Jensen had presented *my* reports as his own, glossing over the fact that *I* had compiled the information, and laying out the conclusions I'd drawn as if he'd come up with them all by himself. I might just be an analyst, but I worked three times as hard as Jensen, who had been too lazy to do his own damn work, to take my reports and confirm and expound on them the way he should have, the way he was *supposed* to. Instead, he had been perfectly happy to coast along on my insights.

Jensen was *always* riding my ass, the way that so many unhappy, middle-management bosses did with their underlings. Miriam was the only person in our office who Jensen had liked, and only because she had occasionally stroked his ego about what important work we analysts and charmers were doing.

Like many other spy organizations, Section 47's main mission was to gather intelligence and then use that information to prevent terror attacks, mass-casualty events, and other serious, life-threatening catastrophes. Only instead of tracking and chasing regular mortal bad guys, Section went after those who used magic and enhanced weapons to commit their crimes. In the unfortunate event that an attack did happen, and some paramortals unleashed their powers to rain down death and destruction, Section then covered up and explained away the magical calamity as best it could before hunting down the perpetrators—and eliminating them. And so, there was truth and justice for all. At least, that was the idea, although the execution was far from perfect.

But Jensen's real problem had been the fact that I was a Legacy and he was not. My grandmother and father had both worked for Section, which meant that I had a guaranteed job here after college and grad school. In many ways, Section 47 was a family business, albeit one made up of dozens and dozens of different families, instead of a single entity or bloodline, and those folks in the know raised their children to become cleaners, charmers, and analysts the same way that regular mortal families produced generations of doctors, lawyers, and dentists.

Given all that long, storied family history, there was

naturally a fair amount of nepotism and soul-crushing pressure within the spy agency. If your mother had done well at Section, then you were expected to do even better. If your brother had flamed out in his first year, then it was up to you to right the ship and restore your family's honor and good name. And so on and so forth.

Your family's standing and, well, *legacy*, could either help or hinder your own prospects inside Section. Due to their family members' previous service, histories, and connections, most Legacies tended to climb higher and at a much quicker pace through the Section ranks than non-Legacies like Jensen, who had been stuck in the same post for five years. Hence his seething bitterness toward me, even though the Locke family legacy was far more tarnished than sterling.

"Hello? Earth to Charlotte." Miriam snapped her fingers in front of my face. "Are you going to Jensen's funeral?"

I shook my head. "No. I don't have time. I'm supposed to cover for another waitress at the diner tonight. Besides, I signed the office card and chipped in for the flowers. That's more than Jensen would have done for me."

Miriam shrugged her agreement. Her phone buzzed, and she looked at the message. Then she picked up the device and started texting, her thumbs flying over the screen.

"New boy toy?" I asked, using her preferred term.

"Oh, yes," she purred.

"Who is it? Pete from accounting? Hank from the weapons depot? Or did you finally land that mystery man you've been crushing on for the past few weeks?"

A sly smile spread across Miriam's red lips. "You know I don't kiss and tell. At least, not until it's over."

I snorted. Miriam was *always* in some sort of relationship, whether it was the early, tentative stages of flirting, the heady excitement of the first date, the boring routine of maintaining the status quo, or the inevitable harsh breakup. Perhaps it was part of her charmer magic, her ability to beguile others, but Miriam was one of those people who loved being in love—or at least lust—and she thrived on all the drama that came along with juggling a relationship inside Section.

Fraternization wasn't forbidden here, but it was definitely frowned upon. The higher-ups wanted their agents to be loyal to Section, not to someone else, and more than one career, even a Legacy's, had been ruined over an affair gone wrong.

"You're really not going to tell me who it is?"

"Not this time. I don't want to jinx it. Besides, I really think this guy might be the one."

I snorted again. "You say that about every man you date."

Miriam grinned. "That's because it's always true. At least, it always seems that way in the beginning. But I'm more hopeful about this boy toy than most. Actually, this one is a bit more mature than my usual type, so I should probably call him my *mystery man* like you always do." She thought about it for a second, and her grin widened. "Nope! Boy toy it is. Because I've definitely been having fun *playing* with him so far."

Miriam snickered at her own bad joke and kept texting. I shook my head in disbelief, even as envy sparked in my heart. I didn't know how Miriam found the time and energy for her serial dating, hookups, and breakups, in addition to her similar schmoozing work for Section, and I envied her carefree attitude and enjoyment of it all.

I hadn't been out with someone in more than a year, thanks to my grandmother's illness and then death a few months ago. Even before my world had crashed and burned, I had never been much for dating. I had a hard time trusting people, thanks to my grandmother's myriad moneymaking schemes and my father's notorious fuckups, and my own work for Section had made me even more jaded, paranoid, and suspicious about other people's desires, motives, and agendas. Better to be alone and trust in myself than take a shot on someone who would probably screw me over the second he got the chance.

Morose musings aside, I still needed to finish the Hyde report by the end of the day, so I gulped down some of my cookies-and-cream mocha to give my brain a much-needed boost of sugar and caffeine. The cafeteria served excellent drinks, and the rich chocolate brew coated my tongue, while the airy whipped cream melted in my mouth like a vanilla cloud.

I had just set my cup down when a splash of color caught my eye. A man wearing a powder-blue tie with a light gray suit walked through the cafeteria, skirting around the people, tables, and chairs and heading toward the food line. His head was held high, his shoulders were back and down, and his stride was long, smooth, and confident. Definitely an assassin, despite his shockingly bright choice of tie.

"Who's that?" I asked, discreetly pointing him out to Miriam. "I've never seen that guy before."

I kept mental dossiers on all the assassins, er, cleaners, so I could be sure to steer clear of them. We might work for the same agency, but they weren't the kind of people you wanted to annoy, piss off, or stand out to in any way.

Section 47 spent thousands of hours and millions of dollars training, housing, feeding, and honing its cleaners into the most lethal weapons possible. All that time, energy, and money made cleaners far more valuable to the Section bosses than the other agents, especially analysts, like me. Cleaners were definitely number one in the pecking order; I was guaranteed to lose if I ever had a conflict or picked any sort of fight with a cleaner, even if it was something as simple as who got the last blueberry muffin during our interdepartmental meetings.

Miriam lowered her phone and glanced in that direction. She leaned forward, and a sharp, interested gleam filled her hazel eyes. "I don't know who that guy is, but I'd certainly like to find out. *Hubba-hubba.*"

"What about your mystery man?"

"He's great, but I *always* have time to make the acquaintance of a handsome stranger," she said, letting an exaggerated Southern drawl seep into her voice.

She winked, making me laugh. Typical Miriam, but her incessant, bubbly enthusiasm was one of the things I liked about her. Plus, hearing about her dating exploits—good, bad, and ugly—let me escape from my own humdrum life for a little while.

Miriam's phone buzzed again, and she glanced at the message on the screen. "Anyway, I've gotta run. I've got my own work to finish before Jensen's funeral."

"Sure. See you later."

Miriam stood up, tucked her phone into the back pocket of her skinny jeans, slung her designer bag over her shoulder, and sauntered out of the cafeteria. More than one person watched her go, including Diego Benito, the IT tech she had broken up with last month. Diego caught me staring at him staring at Miriam, and he ducked his head, focusing on his laptop again.

I took another fortifying sip of my mocha, then started working on summarizing the latest bank transactions I'd been reviewing.

I clicked through various documents and spreadsheets, scanning the information for immediate, obvious mistakes.

I didn't find any, so I sat back in my chair and took in my whole screen, letting the words and numbers fill my field of vision and sink into my brain all at once.

The longer I looked, the more colors started to appear.

To anyone else looking at my screen, the words and numbers were still in plain black type. But to me, they morphed from that absolute flat black into varying shades of gray, along with some light pinks and even a few bold, bloody reds.

I followed the gradation of colors, starting with the words and numbers in black—the ones that were true, correct, precise. From there, I moved on to the light grays—the ones with small typos and addition errors. Next came the pinks— the letters and numbers with more significant faults. And, finally, the reds—the large, glaring errors where someone had either made a serious mistake or had deliberately entered the wrong information and committed an outright electronic lie.

My left index finger hovered over the laptop screen, following the shifting colors. With my right hand, I jotted down notes on a pad. Almost everyone at Section 47 had some magical ability, and mine was an unusual form of synesthesia. I could see typos, mistakes, and errors that people made, whether they had accidentally transposed digits and written down a wrong phone number, knowingly fudged their expense reports, or deliberately committed fraud by submitting false information to a financial institution. My synesthesia took other forms as well, but I mostly used it to make my work as an analyst a little easier.

Not that anyone cared. Thanks to Gregory Jensen's dislike of me, most of my reports were either solely attributed to his supposed brilliance or given cursory looks at best before being filed on the Section electronic databases, never to see the light of day again. Jensen wasn't the only one stuck in middle management. I was thirty-five and had been working at Section for roughly ten years, ever since I had finished grad school. I should have already been promoted to a senior analyst position, instead of keeping the general analyst designation that I'd had for the past five years.

Part of my lack of upward mobility could be attributed to my father's mistakes at Section, but Jensen hadn't done me any favors by giving me one poor performance review after another. He'd wanted to keep me under his thumb, if only so he wouldn't have to do any heavy lifting himself. I didn't wish ill on the dead, but maybe my new supervisor, whomever that turned out to be, would appreciate and take my work more seriously—or at least give me proper credit for it.

Either way, I needed to finish and file this report, so I clicked through a few more screens and documents.

"May I sit with you?"

I kept staring at my screen, following the trail of gray, pink, and red letters and numbers that only I could see...

Someone cleared his throat. "May I sit with you?" The words came out a little louder and more forceful than before.

For the first time, I noticed that someone was standing on the opposite side of the table. I looked up from my laptop.

Him. The assassin I'd spotted earlier. The one with the bright, daring powder-blue tie. He was holding a large mug and a newspaper and staring at me, an expectant look on his face.

Up close, he was far more handsome than I'd realized. He was around six feet tall, with dark blond hair that was somehow sleekly styled and artfully messy at the same time. Golden stubble clung to his strong jaw, making him seem as though he'd just tumbled out of bed, although I imagined that he took as much care with his facial hair as he did with the rest of his appearance.

His light gray suit was perfectly cut and tailored, showing off his broad shoulders and lean figure. He wasn't bulked up with muscle the way so many cleaners were, but an obvious, effortless strength radiated from his body. He also carried himself with supreme confidence, as if he knew without a doubt that he was the biggest badass in the room. That same confidence glinted in his eyes, which were the same light powder-blue as his tie. Miriam had been right. Hubba-hubba indeed.

"May I sit with you?" he asked for a third time, snapping me out of my stupefied reverie.

His easy tone and small smile were probably meant to be innocuous and disarming, as were his mug and newspaper props, but he still pinged my internal radar.

In addition to seeing mistakes, my synesthesia also warned me about threats to my own personal safety, often gilding those dangers in the same colors I would notice in typos in a document. A wet, slippery floor might register as a light gray for a minor hazard, while a car rolling through a stop sign would be a hot pink for a more serious risk. This guy? No colors currently surrounded him, but cleaners always merited a bright, bloody red on my spectrum.

My gaze cut left and right. It was after two o'clock now, so the cafeteria was largely deserted, except for a few late-lunch stragglers. There were plenty of empty tables where he could have sat and enjoyed his beverage and newspaper. So why did he want to sit with me?

He kept staring at me, clearly expecting an answer.

"Suit yourself," I muttered.

"Excellent. Thank you."

What was that faint accent in his voice? Not English, not

European, but...Australian. I had to hold back an appreciative sigh. Accents did me in every single time. Hence my unfortunate affair with a minor Spanish diplomat back before my grandmother had gotten sick. I'd liked the diplomat's musical accent so much that I hadn't noticed what a cheating scumbag he was until I'd shown up early for one of our dinner dates and caught him canoodling with another woman.

The cleaner set his mug and newspaper on the table and pulled out the chair across from mine, the one Miriam had vacated a few minutes ago. He unbuttoned his suit jacket, slid it down his arms, shrugged out of the garment, and draped it across the back of his chair all in one fluid motion. Underneath, he was wearing a vest, along with a silver pocket watch on a lengthy chain. The light gray vest and the matching shirt revealed even more of his lean, muscled body, adding to his appeal. In addition to accents, there was nothing I found sexier than a well-dressed man, and James Bond had nothing on this guy.

The cleaner stepped forward, sat down in the chair, and picked up his mug, once again all in one continuous, easy sequence. He seemed to have a natural, almost liquid grace, and I got the sense he did everything with that same smooth, effortless motion, as if one action just naturally, continually, inevitably flowed into the next, whether he was doing something as mundane as brushing his teeth or as brutal as bludgeoning someone to death.

Most people probably would have thought it elegant, but I recognized the graceful ability as belonging to a natural predator. No doubt he was the sort of cleaner who could sidle up behind you and snap your neck before you even realized he was within striking distance. Sometimes, when presented with a particularly serious threat, instead of colors, my synesthesia took the form of an inner voice, and right now, that voice kept whispering *danger-danger-danger* over and over again.

The cleaner fussed with his newspaper, then picked up the string attached to the tea bag swimming in his mug. He dunked the bag in and out of the steaming water for a few seconds before sitting back in his chair and taking a sip. A faint whiff of the tea tickled my nose, smelling warm, green, and citrusy. No doubt it was the sort of brew that was probably really good for you and really disgusting to drink.

"Nothing like a cup of hot tea on a cool fall day, eh?" he said in a pleasant tone, like he was just making conversation, although his sexy accent made the innocuous words seem to hold a multitude of hidden meanings.

I made a noncommittal sound and looked at my laptop.

I still had to finish my report, so I focused on the words and numbers, trying to pick up the trails of grays, pinks, and reds again. Even though I had been investigating and tracking this particular individual, Henrika Hyde, for more than three months, and filing reports all along the way, I felt like I was finally on the verge of discovering something big, something that would tell me exactly where all this money was going and what horrible thing it was financing...

"Say, I'm new in town," the cleaner said. "Do you have any tips on good restaurants?"

I kept staring at my screen, clicking and following the color trail from one document and spreadsheet to the next. "If you like barbecue, Mama Flo's on the next block is pretty good," I murmured, still trying to track the words and numbers to their inevitable wrong and sinister conclusions.

"Sounds great. How about I take you there for dinner tonight?"

A moment passed before his words penetrated my work fog and sank into my brain. My gaze snapped up to his. The cleaner still had a pleasant smile fixed on his face, but there was a tightness to his jaw and a watchfulness in his eyes that hadn't been there before.

Danger-danger-danger, my inner voice whispered, louder and more insistent than before.

As I sat there, digesting his unexpected offer, a faint snicker caught my attention. I glanced to my right to see Anthony from accounting looking at me, with his phone clutched in his hand. Anthony and I had gone out on one disastrous date back before my grandmother had gotten sick. We both realized we had zero in common and that neither one of us liked the other—at all. Ever since then, Anthony had been my office nemesis, always denying my supply requests, even if all I was asking for was a lousy ream of printer paper.

I focused on the cleaner again. He was gazing at Anthony, who stared right back at him. Suspicion shot through me.

"Did Anthony put you up to this?" I asked. "Is this another one of his lame practical jokes?"

Anthony also had an annoying habit of getting his office buddies to ask me out, even though they had as little interest in me as I did in them. For some reason, Anthony and his friends thought it was *hilarious* to pretend like we were all in seventh grade again.

The cleaner's eyebrows drew together, and he looked confused. "What? Who is Anthony?"

I kept staring at him, and he shrugged.

"I'm new in town. I'm trying to meet people. Make some connections. That's all." His words once again seemed innocuous, although his accent and the way he purred *connections* made it sound as though he'd just offered to indulge in a night of wild sex with me.

"So you thought you would hit on the first woman you saw in the cafeteria? Aw, how romantic," I drawled.

He had the decency to wince, but not the common sense to give up. "I just thought we might have some fun together."

I glanced at the clock on the cafeteria wall. I only had fifteen minutes left on my lunch break, and I wasn't going to let this idiot waste any more of my time.

"Listen, Crocodile Dundee," I snapped. "I don't care what Anthony or anyone else told you about me. I don't work in accounting, so I can't pad out your expense report or validate your parking or whatever it is that you really want."

He jerked back, as though he was surprised that I was speaking to him this way. Yeah, berating a cleaner for hitting on me—or whatever he was doing—wasn't my smartest move. Then again, I'd never been known for my diplomatic tact. If I had, I would have played the office politics a lot better and probably been much higher up on the food chain than I currently was. Unfortunately, my temper often got the better of me, a trait I'd inherited from my father.

Oh, yes. I probably should have made some excuse, grabbed my things, and gone back to my cubicle, but *he* had come over to *me*, so *he* should be the one to leave.

"If you don't work in accounting, then what do you do?" he asked.

This time, I jerked back. His question surprised me, although the fact that he was still sitting here wasting my time made even more anger bubble up in my chest.

"I write reports that no one reads," I snapped again. "And I have one to finish before the end of the day. So why don't you take your tea and your newspaper that you're not reading and go bother someone else."

Anger sparked in his eyes, making them flash an even brighter silver-blue, and a muscle ticked in his jaw. I'd pissed him off. Good. Maybe that would finally get him to leave me alone.

The cleaner shot to his feet, grabbed his suit jacket, and shrugged into it, once again doing all of that in one long, smooth, fluid motion. Then he scooped up his mug and newspaper, spun around on his heel, and strode away.

I watched him leave the cafeteria. The second he vanished from my line of sight, I should have relaxed. But even though the cleaner was gone, my inner voice kept right on whispering, as if my magic knew something important that I didn't.

Danger-danger-danger.

TWO

CHARLOTTE

I kept eyeing the cafeteria entrance, but the cleaner didn't return, so I forced my unease aside. Maybe he was just a creeper trying to pick up the first woman he spotted. Some cleaners were notorious for having a booty call in every Section station around the world. No way to know for sure, so I pushed him and his sexy accent out of my mind.

I typed in some more information for my report and saved my work. Then I drained the rest of my mocha, grabbed my laptop and shoulder bag, and left.

The Section 47 cafeteria was part of a three-story pedestrian mall housed in an old train station that took up an entire city block. Stone stairs were located in all four corners of the enormous rectangular space, with large escalators in the middle of the first and second floors. Several upscale restaurants, bakeries, and coffee shops were housed on the first floor, although their prices were much higher and their food was far inferior to what could be found in the cafeteria. Luxury shops selling everything from designer suits and handbags, to fine jewelry and expensive perfumes, to organic teas and gourmet chocolates, lined the two upper levels, which were ringed with low glass walls topped with silver handrails.

A steady stream of people flowed through the revolving doors at both the front and the back of the building and headed into the shops and restaurants on all three floors, walking side by side with Section agents. Most mortals had no clue that magic actually existed, or that certain people had amazing abilities that could be used to help or hurt others.

According to Section estimates, paramortals only made up about one percent of the world's population, and most folks smartly hid their powers so as not to be ostracized, ridiculed, used, abused, or worse. But it was pretty easy for paramortals to keep their magic under wraps. These days, everyone—mortal and paramortal alike—was focused on their phones, and people were far more likely to see someone using their powers in a supposedly fake online video rather than realize someone with magic was reading their thoughts—and stealing their credit card info—while they were standing in line at the grocery store.

Normally, I would have taken a moment to admire the gleaming gray stone as well as the black wrought iron chandeliers hanging from the high vaulted ceiling. I might have also done a little window shopping, which sadly was the only kind of shopping I could afford. But I needed to get back to my cubicle to file my report, so I ignored the glass-fronted stores and restaurants and headed toward the raised, round dais sitting off to one side of the first floor.

A sixty-something woman with cropped black hair, silver glasses, and ebony skin was sitting behind a curved marble counter on the dais, watching the monitors mounted in front of her as well as the nearby keycard reader and metal turnstile. Her stylish pantsuit showed off her tall, trim body, and the bright teal fabric was a welcome splash of color among all the dark-suited agents moving past her. Evelyn Hawkes had been manning the front desk for as long as I could remember, calmly directing traffic into Section 47 while gently steering away mortals.

Section might allow clueless mortals to shop and dine inside its building, but the pedestrian mall was as far as common citizens went. To the outside world, this building housed mindless drones for the Section 47 Corporation, which did very important government things, although no one could quite explain what those very important but deliberately vague things were. Still, it was just another office building, one of hundreds in D.C., and no one batted an eye at the paramortals scanning their ID cards, pushing through the metal turnstile, and heading toward the private elevators embedded in the wall.

I started to wave at and go right on by Evelyn. The cleaner and his unwanted conversation had put me behind, and I should have been hustling toward the closest elevator, but I thought better of it, moved to the side, and stopped. I leaned my elbow on the smooth, glossy counter, which was covered with tourist brochures, restaurant guides, and other slick, shiny things to distract the mortals.

"Hello, Charlotte. To what do I owe this honor?" Evelyn's voice was soft and deep, which my synesthesia often translated into cool blue musical notes floating around in my mind. One of the few more pleasant aspects of my power.

Normally, I would have asked Evelyn how she was doing, perhaps even brought her a coffee, which sadly was the only kind of bribe I could afford. But since I was running late, I decided to get right down to business.

"Do you know anything about a new cleaner being in the building?" I asked. "Blond guy, lean and muscled, slight

Australian accent. He was wearing a light gray suit with a powder-blue tie."

Evelyn bobbed her head. "Oh, yes. A transfer from the Sydney station, brought in for a special mission. His name is Desmond, although I don't think he has officially reported for duty yet." She winked at me. "Not that you heard that from me."

I pantomimed zipping my lips shut. "Of course not."

Evelyn Hawkes was like a spider sitting in the center of a web, with strands of shoppers and spies constantly flowing all around her. She saw everyone who came through the doors, and she picked up an enormous amount of gossip just by sitting out here in the open, doing her job. My grandmother had warned me to always be nice to Evelyn, and the advice had paid off. Evelyn had given me details on more than a few people and missions during my time at Section.

Evelyn grinned, but the expression slowly faded from her face, and her dark brown gaze locked with my blue one. "How are you doing? I know it's been a while, but I've been meaning to check on you."

My grandma Jane had passed away three months ago, after a lengthy battle with cancer. Evelyn was one of the few people who had attended my grandmother's small funeral, and she had also sent flowers and had even made me some casseroles, not that I had felt like eating them. Since I had hocked my refrigerator, I ended up donating the dishes to a homeless shelter. At least those folks had gotten some enjoyment out of Evelyn's tasty cooking.

I gave the older woman a bright smile, trying to disguise the ache in my heart along with my ever-present exhaustion. "I'm okay. Grandma Jane had a good, long life. She's in a better place now."

I spouted the usual platitudes in a calm, steady voice, and

Evelyn nodded in return. Sentimentality wasn't exactly encouraged in Section agents, not even the information desk manager. We all knew the horrors lurking out there in the not-so-dark-and-distant corners of the world and that there was little time to dwell on our own problems and especially our own fraught emotions. Not if we wanted to stay ahead of the terrorists and criminals and prevent even more bad things from happening.

"Anyway, I should get going. Thanks for the info."

"Why are you asking about that cleaner?" Evelyn said. "I thought you tended to steer clear of them. Especially given what happened to Jack."

My jaw automatically clenched at the mention of Jack Locke, my father, but I forced myself to smile again, as if her words didn't bother me. "No real reason. I saw the cleaner in the cafeteria and wanted to know who the new face was."

Evelyn nodded again, seemingly accepting my explanation, but her eyes narrowed behind her glasses. Time to go before she became any more suspicious.

I said goodbye to her, then moved forward, grabbed the long black lanyard hanging from my neck, held out the attached white plastic keycard, and waved it at the reader. The light flashed green, and I pushed through the metal turnstile, walked over, and stepped into one of the elevators.

Instead of going up, I rode the elevator down to Section's third floor. The old train station had seven sublevels, and each one housed a different Section department with a different personality.

Accounting was on one, while IT was on two. Both had pretty standard office setups, although the accountants loved their fancy espresso machines and hoarded their locked closets full of office supplies, while the IT folks were into more mellow herbal teas and building their own robots.

Analysts and charmers were housed on three, while cleaners were down on five. Both of those floors also had standard office setups, although the cleaners had a state-of-the-art gym and a pristine locker room to help with their training, while we analysts and charmers were lucky to have landline phones that didn't crackle with too much static and moldy showers with weak streams of lukewarm water.

The weapons depot with its racks of guns, walls of gadgets, and closets filled with glamorous gowns was down on six, while seven was a parking garage for Section surveillance vans, cars, and other vehicles.

And then there was level four, right in the middle of it all, which featured offices for some of the Section higher-ups, like Maestro, along with interrogation rooms and cells where persons of interest and prisoners were kept until they were either released or transported to a black site for further questioning.

Crocodile Dundee Desmond was probably lurking some-where on the fifth floor, ruthlessly plotting the best way to kill whatever paramortal target he'd been assigned to eliminate. Or maybe he was hitting on the unfortunate soul who'd been selected to be his liaison. Each cleaner was assigned one, and *liaison* was just a fancy name for a personal assistant. Some liaisons wrangled weapons and gadgets, while others saw to their respective cleaner's housing and transpor-tation needs. A liaison could even be called upon to go out into the field and help their cleaner execute certain mission objectives, sort of like a glorified superhero sidekick.

The elevator door pinged open, and I pushed away all thoughts of the cleaner and liaisons. He was someone else's problem, and I had plenty of my own to manage.

I walked down a long corridor with bland gray walls, waved my plastic keycard over another reader, and waited for a set of bullet-and-magic-resistant-glass double doors to buzz open. I pushed through to the other side and stepped into a bullpen, a large open space filled with cubicles partitioned off with clear plastic walls.

People of all ages, shapes, sizes, and ethnicities perched, sprawled, and lounged in uncomfortable, squeaky office chairs inside the cubicles, just as they did in other bullpens on this level. Each area had the same basic equipment—a monitor, a keyboard, a mouse, a landline, and a place to plug in a Section-issued laptop. However, folks had added their own personal touches to their spaces, including family photos, sports posters, and pet calendars. Collections of everything from ceramic tortoises to crocheted otters to goofy stress balls shaped like witches and wizards also adorned the desks and cubicle walls.

I headed over to my desk on the right side of the bullpen. Unlike the others, my desk was devoid of decorations except for one thing—a small crystal mockingbird that had been a gift from my grandmother the day I had started working at Section. The figurine had a lot of sentimental value, but it also served as a visual reminder that things—and people— were very often not what they seemed in this spy business.

More stuff used to clutter my desk—some beloved old books, silver-framed family photos, even a couple of collectible superhero figurines in their original boxes—but I'd hocked them all after my grandmother had died. It truly was amazing the things you could sell online. I missed my knickknacks, though. I missed a lot of the things I'd sold over the past few months.

Miriam was sitting at her cubicle, which was right next to mine. She had long ago shoved her monitor to one side to make way for a freestanding lighted vanity mirror, along with a clear plastic organizer tray bristling with lipsticks, eye-shadow palettes, and bottles of foundation. Miriam loved beauty products as much as she did dating, and she was always trying some new lotion or cream in hopes of making herself look even more stunning than she already was.

In addition to the mirror and the makeup, her desk also featured a tall wooden jewelry box shaped like a castle. Most of the drawers were at least partially open and brimming with necklaces, rings, and bracelets. The gems winked at me like colorful eyes, as though they were watching my every move. Maybe they were. Like all charmers, Miriam had tiny cameras and microphones embedded in most of her jewelry so she could record every secret someone whispered to her in crystal-clear, high-definition video and audio.

A couple of bright silk scarves were draped over the top of her cubicle wall, and everything from little black cocktail dresses to lacy lingerie was neatly folded and tucked away in her desk drawers. Miriam could have gone down to the sixth-floor depot to gear up for her missions like the other charmers did, but she had told me more than once that she preferred to use her own makeup, jewelry, and clothes. I would have too, if I'd had access to all the designer labels she did.

I had often thought that Miriam must charm samples out of the luxury boutiques upstairs in the pedestrian mall to be able to afford such fine things on her not-so-fine government salary. Or perhaps she had a sugar daddy, past or present, she hadn't told me about.

Miriam propped her elbow on the low wall that separated our cubicles and held out her hand, offering me a stick of gum wrapped in light pink paper. "Rosemint gum?" she asked. "It's supposed to be great for nicotine withdrawal."

Miriam was trying to quit smoking, a nasty habit that a Greek boyfriend had gotten her hooked on a couple of months ago, and all sorts of crumpled candy and lollipop wrappers littered her desk. The gum must have been her newest method to try to combat her cravings.

"No, thanks." I didn't care for the gum's flavor, which was a disgusting mix of cloying rose and tangy mint. Plus, the pink wrapper reminded me of the words and numbers I still needed to chase down to finish my report.

Miriam shrugged, unwrapped the gum, and popped it into her mouth. Then she focused on her laptop and started typing, working on her own report. During lunch, Miriam had revealed that she was currently undercover as Coco Livingston, one of her many Section aliases. Coco, a trust-fund baby and notorious party girl, was cozying up to the wife of a South African diplomat she'd accidentally-on-purpose befriended at an embassy party last week in hopes of picking up information about the woman's shady husband.

I glanced around the bullpen. Ronaldo, Helga, Mika, Kaimbe. The other analysts were dutifully typing away on their own laptops, so I looked past them. Two glassed-in offices were set into the back wall, one each for the analyst and charmer supervisors, with a large conference room nestled in the center, although all three doors were closed, and the lights were off in both offices. The cats were away, but the mice knew better than to play.

My gaze lingered on one of the offices, which was empty except for a bare desk with a single lonely chair sitting behind it. Gregory Jensen's things had been boxed up and sent to his family a couple of days after his death, although no one had taken his brass nameplate off the door yet. But at Section, life went on, and there was little time to mourn the dead, especially if they'd been killed as the result of a tragic accident like Jensen had. So I sat down at my own desk, pulled my laptop out of my bag, and plugged it into the Section network.

Section 47 got its name from the fact that paramortals had forty-seven chromosomes, compared to regular mortals, who only had forty-six, or two pairs of twenty-three. That extra piece of our DNA gave us all kinds of interesting abilities. At least, that was the current scientific theory. For an organization that dealt with the magical and the mystical, Section higher-ups tried to explain a lot of it away with science, as though cold, hard facts somehow made it easier to wrap our minds around the terrible things that some paramortals did with their powers.

I didn't particularly care where my magic came from or how it worked—just that I had it and that it continued to function at a high level.

Everyone in the bullpen had some sort of magical ability. Ronaldo and Helga were synth analysts like me who used their own unique types of synesthesia to comb through reports from undercover Section agents, looking for patterns and other actionable intelligence to pass up the food chain. Mika and Kaimbe were linguists, aka lingos, who could speak, read, and understand any language. They were responsible for interpreting and transcribing terrorist and criminal chatter, and trying to figure out the code words people used to communicate their dirty deeds to one another.

As a charmer, Miriam engaged in an active social calendar and kept track of the various foreign paramortals in town, both the legitimate diplomats and the ones who were really spies for their own countries. She was responsible for gathering personal intelligence—gossip, whispers, rumors, and information that came from the actual people she communicated with on a regular basis. A couple of other charmers also worked in our office, although they were all away on assignments right now.

Me? As a Section analyst, I, well, *analyzed* things. Banking, tax, and other monetary transaction records. Property sales. Biomagical patents. Purchases of art, jewelry, and other high-end, big-ticket items. Planes, trains, and automobiles. Even stupid cat videos on social media. Section referred to all those things and similar items as paper intelligence, as in anything that left a paper (or digital) trail that could be followed. So I watched, tracked, and analyzed dozens of bank accounts, businesses, modes of transportation, and social media accounts belonging to known paramortal terrorists and criminals to try to figure out where they were sending—and spending—their money and what bad, bad things they or their associates might be planning to do with it.

Basically, I was a numbers guru. Grandma Jane had also been a Section analyst, and she had taught me long ago that while people might lie, numbers never did. *The money always goes somewhere* had been one of her favorite catchphrases.

Ronaldo, Helga, Mika, and Kaimbe were absorbed in their own tasks, while Miriam was now on her landline, planning a girls' lunch and shopping spree with that diplomat's wife. I pulled my wireless earbuds out of my bag, synced them to my phone, and cued up some classical music to drown her out. Then I cracked open my laptop and got to work.

As an analyst, I was always checking up on one bad guy or another, but for the past three months, most of my time had been spent tracking the wheelings and dealings of Henrika Hyde. To the regular mortal world, Henrika was the founder and CEO of Hyde Engineering, a pharmaceutical company on the cutting edge of medical research in a variety of fields. But to Section 47, Henrika Hyde was a paramortal weapons maker who used her money, engineering degrees, and laboratories to create some truly horrific biomagical weapons.

Corrosive gases that melted human flesh and bones, but left wood, glass, and other objects completely untouched. Poisons that targeted specific bloodlines and genetic markers that would eliminate entire paramortal families at once. Powders and pills that would give people amazing highs, along with super speed and strength, even as the drugs melted their internal organs and turned their lungs into ice. Henrika Hyde had invented all those horrible things and many more.

A few months ago, an undercover Section agent had managed to infiltrate Henrika's inner circle and had swiped some information on her many businesses. The agent had been found dead a few days later, with his bones liquefied inside his own body, even though his skin was still smooth and intact and showed no signs of outward trauma. But the stolen information had eventually been passed down to me, and I had been following the trail of corporate shell companies—and the millions of dollars that flowed through them—ever since.

Most of it was pretty standard stuff. Plant and office locations, safety protocols, employee personnel records, payrolls, tax breaks from local governments. Henrika Hyde was smart enough to keep her books mostly legit, but I had found a small anomaly among the thousands and thousands of pages of electronic documents and spreadsheets. For some reason, Henrika had started making hefty donations to the Halstead Foundation.

The foundation funded various charities, but its biggest, most public project was renovating the historic building that housed the Halstead Hotel on the outskirts of D.C. The building and hotel were both owned by the Halstead family, known for its collection of art and antiquities as well as precious jewels, many of which were on display in their hotels around the world.

That last fact was the one that interested me. Henrika wasn't known to be a patron of historic buildings, but she absolutely *loved* jewels. She had bid on several rare gemstones at various auctions over the years, as well as designer necklaces, bracelets, and rings. I had never seen a photo of Henrika where she wasn't wearing several carats' worth of diamonds, emeralds, rubies, and more. I had often wondered if the jewels had something to do with Henrika's magic, although no one seemed to know exactly what paramortal powers she had. Or maybe she just liked shiny things. Hard to tell, without more information.

Either way, I could understand why the Halstead family's jewelry collection would interest Henrika, but her sudden benevolence in shelling out money to their charitable foundation mystified me. The donations had to be a bribe or payment for something. I just didn't know what that *something* was yet.

I had filed a short, preliminary report about two months ago, suggesting further investigation into Henrika Hyde. My longer, second report last month had offered up even more reasons why Henrika merited watching, along with suggesting that Section find a way to arrest, hold, and interrogate her about all the biomagical weapons she had in the works.

But of course Gregory Jensen had said that my reports and conclusions were amateurish before presenting them as his own brilliant ideas at a recent interdepartmental meeting. He'd even presented my plan to grab Henrika as if it were his own. Lazy bastard.

And of course I couldn't protest and claim it was all *my* work, not without coming off as being difficult and jealous, and having Jensen make my office life even more miserable. So I ground my teeth, kept quiet, and imagined stabbing my pen into Jensen's smug face over and over again like he was a voodoo doll.

Now, I was determined to finish a third, even longer, updated, and much more detailed report before the new analyst supervisor was named. I wanted to start with a clean slate, and I was hoping my next boss would give me proper credit for my work and judge me on my own merits, instead of on my father's reckless reputation.

I glanced through the documents and spreadsheets again, but I didn't get any further than I had at lunch, so I put a few final touches on my report and emailed it to Trevor Donnelly, the charmer supervisor and my immediate boss at the moment. I got a bounce-back message saying Trevor was out of the office until tomorrow, but at least I had filed the report. It was off my desk and out of my hands.

A glance at my phone revealed that it was past five. Everyone else had already left the bullpen, including Miriam, although her desk was littered with rosemint gum wrappers. I crinkled my nose at the strong, sweet, minty scent hovering around her cubicle and resisted the urge to sweep the pink wrappers into the trash. Instead, I packed up my things and left.

I might be done with Section, but unfortunately, my workday was far from over.

I rode the elevator up to the ground floor, said good night to Evelyn, pushed through the glass revolving doors, and headed home.

Grandma Jane had owned and lived in an apartment a few blocks from the main Section building. I had moved in a few months before her death to take care of her, and I had inherited the apartment after she was gone. I trudged up three flights of stairs, crossed the hallway, and peered at the front door.

In addition to seeing mistakes and errors in documents and spreadsheets and physical dangers and hazards in my surroundings, my synesthesia also let me sense things that were askew, out of place, or just plain wrong. I reached out with my magic, but the door looked exactly the same as when I had left this morning. No telltale scratches marred the metal, and since no pink haze floated around the lock, it hadn't been tampered with. I opened the door, then shut and locked it behind me.

I flipped on the lights, entered the alarm code, and stared out at the open, empty space. Two years ago, before my grandmother had gotten sick, cozy furniture and cute knickknacks had filled the kitchen and living room as well as the two bedrooms and attached bathrooms in the back. Now, all of those things were gone, and the only furniture, if you could even call it that, was a mattress on the floor in the back corner of the living room next to the windows, and an old, worn-out yoga mat in front of the living room fireplace.

Cancer was one of the few diseases that impacted mortals and paramortals equally, and Grandma Jane's battle had been a long and expensive one. Even Section 47 insurance only went so far, and my grandmother hadn't had any savings, thanks to my father's final and most spectacular fuckup. As the medical bills started piling up, Grandma Jane and I had gone through the apartment, selling off her fine china, silverware, and other things we didn't need nearly as much as we did cold, hard cash. A sofa we never sat on. A gold-framed mirror. Even some of her clothes, which I had taken to a local vintage shop. Piece by piece, we had sold and hocked everything we could, trying to keep ahead of the rising cost of her care.

We hadn't been successful.

I had eventually taken control of my grandmother's finances, so she had never known how truly bad it was getting—or how desperate I was becoming. I had barely managed to scrape together enough cash to cover her funeral and burial. After that, I finally swallowed my pride and got a private loan to pay off the medical providers and insurance companies, but I was just keeping my head above water when it came to meeting the monthly payments. Really, I had only switched my debt from all those companies over to a single individual—the weight and stress of trying to pay it back was still slowly crushing me.

I sighed into the emptiness, and the bare walls soaked up the soft, resigned sound. I slung my bag onto the kitchen island counter, then went over and rolled up the yoga mat. Once it was out of the way, I reached down, removed a couple of short, loose floorboards, and slid my laptop into the small, hollow space underneath, which also featured a couple of guns, several magazines of ammo, three passports with varying names and nationalities, and ten thousand dollars in small bills. My own private, personal stash of emergency supplies in case I ever needed to get out of town quickly and never return. Always a possibility in the spy business, even for a lowly analyst like me. Of course, I had been tempted to use the money to pay down my debt, but a lousy ten grand was nothing compared to the hundreds of thousands of dollars I owed, so I had kept it.

Every Section agent was supposed to store their laptop,

documents, and other work products in a secure home safe, but I'd sold my grandmother's freestanding safe for three hundred bucks. The money had helped pay for her casket. Besides, since no one besides Jensen ever read my reports, no one had any real reason to swipe my laptop. My hiding space was good enough for government work, as the old saying went.

Once I'd stowed my laptop away and returned the floorboards and yoga mat to their previous positions, I headed into my bedroom, which was as empty as the rest of the apartment, except for my clothes hanging in the closet and a few cardboard boxes of loose photos and other mementoes stacked up in the corner.

I glanced over at the boxes. Since I had sold all the picture frames, I had taped photos of Grandma Jane and my dad, Jack, to the sides of the cardboard, along with one shot of myself. We Lockes all looked alike, with our auburn hair, blue eyes, and pale skin, and the photos featured my grandmother and father standing in front of the main Section building on their first days of work. My grandmother had started the tradition, and she had snapped a photo of me outside the building too. One of the better, more normal legacies that she and my father had passed down to me.

Another box featured a picture of my mom, Josephine, with her dark brown hair and eyes and tan skin, holding up a copy of *Charlotte's Web* in the library where she had worked. It had been my mother's favorite book, and she had named me after the title character, the smart little spider who saves her friends. My mother had died in a car accident when I was nine, and I still re-read the book at least once a year, usually around her July birthday, as a way to remember her. I had also read the book aloud to Grandma Jane a few weeks before she died.

The bittersweet memories washed over me, and I sighed into the emptiness again.

I opened the closet and pulled out an old-fashioned waitress uniform of a short-sleeve polyester shirt with an oversize white collar and round plastic buttons and a knee-length pleated skirt. The uniform's powder-blue color reminded me of the cleaner Desmond's tie. I once again wondered what he wanted.

Maybe he'd just been looking for a hookup. Most of the cleaners thought they were hot stuff and that we should all swoon and drop our undies just because they killed people. Either way, I had more important things to worry about, so I shoved the cleaner out of my mind and shimmied into the waitress uniform, along with white tights and thick-soled sneakers. A gray fleece jacket completed my ensemble.

I grabbed my bag, left the apartment, plodded downstairs, and fell in with the flow of people moving along the sidewalks. It was mid-October, and the sun was already setting. The fall chill, which had been so crisp and refreshing earlier in the day, was quickly turning cold and frosty. I shivered, wrapped my arms around myself, and hurried on.

A few blocks later, I reached an old metal train car that squatted at the back edge of a large parking lot covered with cracked asphalt and littered with potholes. Over the front door, a sign burned a bright neon-blue, spelling out *Moondust Diner* one cursive letter at a time, along with a white half-moon and surrounding stars. Smaller, atomic-red signs in the windows glowed in the shapes of burgers, fries, and milkshakes. Despite the battered gray metal, grimy glass, and uneven front steps, the Moondust served great food. Even better, since I worked there, I got to eat for free. My wallet thanked me for that, even if my arteries didn't.

I pushed through the door and went inside. Dull chrome booths lined the front windows. Next came a wide aisle and then a long dining counter studded with equally dull chrome stools and topped with clusters of silver napkin holders, plastic ketchup bottles, and glass salt and pepper shakers shaped like half-moons and stars. Behind that was another counter bristling with burping coffeemakers, gleaming glass cake stands, and towering stacks of neon-blue ceramic coffee mugs.

An open-air service window was embedded in the wall behind the counter so that the cooks back in the kitchen could pass the waitresses plates of pancakes, eggs, bacon, and meatloaf. Those same delicious aromas curled through the air, making my stomach rumble. I was definitely getting the meatloaf special for dinner.

It was just after seven, so the dinner rush was in full swing, and several folks were eating turkey clubs, onion rings, and fries and slurping down chocolate milkshakes at the booths and along the counter.

A seventy-something woman with iron-gray hair pulled back into a tight, severe bun sat behind the cash register directly across from the front door. She was tallying the day's receipts, although her head snapped up as I walked inside. Her dark brown eyes narrowed, and her tan, wrinkled face crinkled in severe disapproval as I moved around her, stripped off my jacket, grabbed a clean white apron off one of the hooks embedded in the wall, and tied it on over my uniform.

Zeeta Kowalski, who had opened the diner with her late husband, Mel, way back in the day, made a point of looking up at the pie-shaped clock on the wall next to the cash register. "You're three minutes late," she snapped in her low, gravelly voice. "It's coming out of your pay."

"Sorry," I muttered, even though I wasn't sorry at all.

Except for her yearly Christmas vacation to visit her daughter, Penny, in Florida, Zeeta spent all her time at the diner, and she thought the cooks and waitresses should be as devoted to the eatery as she was. To me, it was just a paycheck, and I planned on quitting as soon as I could afford to. Which was probably never, given my current glacial pace at paying down my massive debt.

Zeeta gave me the stink-eye, then went back to her receipts, slowly sorting through each and every slip of blue paper and scribbling down the amounts on a yellow legal pad. I could have gone through the tickets much faster, as well as totaled them up on the cash register, but the one time I'd offered to help with the money, Zeeta had growled that she didn't need a young whippersnapper like me trying to cheat her. Paranoid old crone.

I walked over and peered through the open service window. The rest of the diner might look old and rundown, but the kitchen was a shining beacon of stainless-steel appliances. Zeeta might skimp on the décor out front, but the kitchen was all clean, sleek business.

"Hey, Pablo," I called out, my voice much more cheerful than before. "What's the dessert special?"

Pablo Suarez, a tall, skinny, twenty-year-old guy with thick black hair, dark brown eyes, and bronze skin, pointed to a glass cake stand sitting off to one side of the counter. "Peach pie with a vanilla-sugar crumb topping. I've got a dozen of them back here."

My stomach rumbled again. Like me, Pablo was only working here for the paycheck while he put himself through culinary school. He was a talented chef, and peach pie was one of his specialties.

"Save me a piece?" I asked in a hopeful voice.

He winked at me. "I already set some aside for you to take home."

"You're a saint." I blew him a kiss.

"Aw, now, don't be doing things like that. Enrique might get jealous." He winked at me again.

Enrique was Pablo's boyfriend, a pre-med student who often came into the diner to drink coffee and study.

I would have chatted with Pablo longer, but Zeeta was giving me that look again, so I got busy, taking orders, refilling coffee cups, and doing my best to stay out of her way.

The first two hours passed by in a blur, but around nine o'clock, business slowed down for the night, the way it always did. Soon, the only people in the diner were truck drivers and nurses who wanted a quick bite to eat before getting back on the road or returning to the nearby hospital to finish their shifts.

During my break, I stood at the back counter and gulped down my own dinner of Pablo's excellent, spicy cayenne meatloaf, buttery mashed potatoes, and roasted Brussels sprouts with smoked bacon and onion jam. The kid truly was an artist, and I was going to miss him and his food when he graduated from culinary school and moved on to a bigger and better restaurant.

I was scraping the last of the mashed potatoes off my plate when the front door opened, and a man stepped inside. His black hair was cropped close to his skull, and his ebony skin gleamed under the lights. He was a couple inches over six feet, with broad shoulders and a muscled chest poured into a tight, black, long-sleeve T-shirt. Black cargo pants and boots completed his minimalist ensemble. You could take the cleaner out of Section, but you couldn't put the color back in his wardrobe.

Gabriel Chase grinned at Zeeta, who tittered and batted

her eyelashes, despite the fact that he was a good forty years younger than she was. The old crone hated me, but she loved Gabriel. Then again, most women did. I might have too, if I didn't know how dangerous he was.

Gabriel sauntered over and took his usual seat in the corner booth, with his back to the metal wall, and stared out over the rest of the diner. I topped a piece of Pablo's warm peach pie with a large scoop of his equally excellent home-made vanilla-bean ice cream, then grabbed the freshest pot of coffee and headed over to Gabriel. I set the pie down on the table and filled his cup.

"Mmm. Peach pie. My favorite," Gabriel murmured in a low, silky voice.

He gestured for me to sit in the other side of the booth, which I did. Zeeta shot me a nasty look, but she didn't growl at me to get back to work. She might think Gabriel was gorgeous, but she also knew he wasn't the kind of person you said no to. Besides, Gabriel often brought his crew in here to eat, and Zeeta knew it was in the best interests of her cash register to keep him happy, even if that meant letting me, her least favorite employee, take an unscheduled break.

Gabriel took a couple bites of pie and ice cream and washed them down with some coffee. He sighed with contentment, then raised his light brown eyes to mine, finally ready to get down to business. "Your information panned out."

I arched an eyebrow. "Did you ever doubt it would?"

Gabriel grinned, his white teeth flashing in the middle of his trimmed black goatee. "Nah. I know how good Charlotte Locke is with numbers. Even when we were kids, you were always the smartest person around."

Gabriel's father, Leon, had worked for Section, making him a Legacy just like me. The two of us had gone to the same schools and parties and had basically grown up together. We weren't exactly friends, but we had been through a lot of mutual shit, thanks to our fathers, and Gabriel was the closest thing I had to a true confidant. He was also the only person who realized exactly how desperate my financial situation was. Miriam thought I was temporarily working at the diner to pay down a few final bills for my grandmother's medical care, but Gabriel knew I was roughly five hundred thousand dollars in debt and that I probably wouldn't be quitting my crappy diner job—ever.

Gabriel used to be a cleaner, just like his father, but a few years ago, he'd gotten embroiled in a scandal involving a general's daughter and had been kicked out of Section. Most people probably would have slunk away in disgrace, but not Gabriel Chase. Instead, he had started Chase Industries, his own private contracting firm. Kidnapping rescues, witness protection, security details, even the occasional heist to return stolen art to its rightful owner. Gabriel and his crew did all that and more, and they had a reputation for being professional, efficient, and invisible.

As a result, Gabriel's fortunes, and especially his bank balance, had astronomically risen since his departure from Section, while mine had fallen off a cliff. Sometimes, I envied Gabriel's freedom, and especially the riches that had come along with being his own boss.

"You were right," he said. "Ramirez was skimming from our petty cash accounts."

A couple of weeks ago, Gabriel had asked me to take a look at his books, since money was going into various accounts and then seemingly disappearing into thin air. It had taken me less than a day to figure out that Alfredo Ramirez, his business manager, was diverting funds into his own private account. I had spent another day double-checking my work, as well as tracing the funds, which Ramirez had used to pay down some of his outstanding child support as well as buy his current girlfriend a very nice diamond bracelet.

"I assume Ramirez is no longer in your employ?" I asked.

Gabriel grinned again and curled his fingers around his fork, casually holding it like a knife he was about to stab someone with. "You might say that."

Danger-danger-danger, my inner voice whispered.

Gabriel might look like an ordinary, albeit gorgeous, guy, but he was far stronger and faster than a mere mortal. He could break bones as easily as regular people broke bread and snap someone's neck with little more than a slight twist of his hand.

He also had the far more unusual and unique paramortal ability to walk through walls. Wooden planks, concrete slabs, steel vaults. Gabriel could slip through all those objects and more with ease. *Phasing*, some folks called it. When we were kids, I'd once seen him dissolve his hand into a cloud of gray smoke, stick it into a birthday party piñata, and pull out all the candy inside. I'd screamed, but Gabriel had just laughed and started shoving candy into his mouth before offering me some of his spoils.

Gabriel didn't take too kindly to folks stealing from him, and he tended to use his fists and magic to make examples out of those who wronged him. Alfredo Ramirez's bloody, beaten body was probably already floating in the Potomac, just waiting to frighten some poor unsuspecting fisherman.

"You didn't stop by just to say I was right. You could have texted me that."

He leaned back in his side of the booth. "You should come work for me, Charlotte. We both know your talents, and especially your magic, are wasted at Section."

At Section, I was on record as being a synth who saw mistakes and errors. Nothing more, nothing less. But Gabriel was one of the few people who knew about all the other things I could do with my magic, including the sense of danger that perpetually haunted me.

I arched an eyebrow at him again. "So I could be further indebted to you? No, thanks."

"You're already indebted to me," he pointed out. "My dad was the one who fronted your Grandma Jane the cash for your father, remember?"

As if I could ever forget. About fifteen years ago, when I was in college, my father's last mission had gone horribly, horribly wrong. His entire team had been ambushed and slaughtered, and he had been captured by the leader of a Mexican drug cartel, who had threatened to send bloody pieces of Jack Locke back to Section unless the cartel's ransom demands were met. Section 47 didn't negotiate with terrorists or criminals, not even to rescue their own people, but my grandmother had wanted to save her son, so she'd gotten a loan from Gabriel's father—three million dollars.

I loved my father. Truly, I did. But sometimes I hated him for being such a thoughtless, reckless bastard, getting captured, and putting Grandma Jane—and now me—in this situation. His ransom had been the start of our downward financial spiral. Thanks to her savings, generous Section pension, and especially her various moneymaking schemes, my grandmother had managed to repay most of the money in the intervening years, but then she'd gotten sick, which had added even more debt on top of what she had already owed. Now, I was left to pick up the pieces and work my fingers to the bone trying to repay the rest of it. Sometimes, I thought being in dire financial straits was my father's true legacy to me instead of working for Section.

Gabriel must have realized he'd hit a nerve because his face softened, just a bit. "You know I didn't mean anything by that, but my offer still stands. Come work for me, Charlotte. All you have to do is say yes, and I'll forgive your debt."

It was tempting—so very *tempting*. But my grandmother had taught me you didn't take favors you couldn't pay back in kind, unless you absolutely had no other options. I might not like it, but working at the diner was another option. Besides, the only thing I had to offer Gabriel was my magic, and since I'd already found his embezzler, he didn't have any real use for my skills. I didn't want his pity, and I was no one's charity case.

I shook my head. "No. We'll continue with our current payment schedule. Minus the money you recovered from Ramirez's secret account. That would be thirty-three thousand nine hundred and nine dollars and fifteen cents."

Gabriel waved his hand. "We can round it up to an even thirty-five grand."

"*No*," I snapped. "Thirty-three thousand nine hundred and nine dollars and fifteen cents. Not a penny more, and not a penny less."

His eyes narrowed at the bite in my voice, but I stared right back at him, despite the *danger-danger-danger* whispers still clanging in my mind.

Gabriel and I might not be best friends, but I knew he would never hurt me, not like he had probably hurt Alfredo Ramirez. Still, he didn't have to get physical to wound me. He could always get pissed off enough to sell my debt to someone else—someone who wouldn't take no for an answer when it came to my magic, my body, or my position at Section. I might only be a lowly analyst, but someone could easily find a way to use that—*me*—to their advantage.

Gabriel shrugged. "Fine. If that's the way you want it. Text me the amount, and I'll deduct it from your debt."

The tension between us eased, and I nodded. "Thank you."

He shrugged again. "Don't thank me. I didn't do anything. You're the one who's being a stupid, stubborn fool."

He was right about that, although I would never admit it.

Over at the cash register, Zeeta let out a loud, angry, pointed cough. My break was over.

I slid out of the booth, got to my feet, and grabbed the pot off the table. "I'll bring you some more coffee. And another piece of pie."

Before he could say anything else, I spun around and stalked away from Gabriel, wishing I could leave the rest of my problems behind so easily.

THREE

CHARLOTTE

few minutes later, Gabriel paid up and left. I went back to work, taking orders, refilling coffee cups, clearing tables, and wiping down booths under Zeeta's suspicious, disapproving glower.

The diner slowly emptied out for the night, with only a few people trickling in, which made it easy for me to spot the cleaner when she pushed through the door.

The assassin was around my age, mid-thirties, and was wearing a black suit jacket over a black shirt and pants. Naturally. Her dark brown hair was pulled back into a pretty but functional French braid, and her lips were painted a bright scarlet, as were her short fingernails, bringing out her lovely features and bronze skin.

The cleaner didn't look at me as she took a seat in the corner booth, the same one Gabriel had occupied earlier. She gave her order to Felicity, the other waitress, and calmly, quietly checked her phone and ate her BLT and sweet potato fries, which she washed down with an ice water with lemon. She might not have noticed me, but I kept an eye on her.

This wasn't the first time someone from Section, especially a cleaner, had eaten here while I'd been working. The Moondust Diner had great food, reasonable prices, and was open until midnight, all of which made it attractive to the Section 47 crowd, who often worked long, odd hours.

Despite the fact that my coworkers were spies, no one ever seemed to notice me bustling around the diner, fetching their food and drinks. Mortals weren't the only ones who got lost in their devices and ignored their surroundings. The cheesy waitress outfit seemed to transform my familiar features into a stranger's face, one that my fellow agents couldn't be bothered to glance at, much less recognize. That was the only perk of wearing the atrocious, old-fashioned uniform.

The one exception was Miriam, who had come in several weeks ago with her Greek boy toy. She claimed she had been craving a bacon cheeseburger and a chocolate shake, but that had just been an excuse to leave me a hundred-dollar tip. I *hated* that she knew how badly I needed the money, but I had slipped the bill into my pocket anyway. I might not want people's pity or charity, but I wasn't above taking it in certain cases when I knew it couldn't be used against me. Besides, I wasn't letting Zeeta sink her claws into my tips, not one single cent.

The cleaner finished her BLT and fries, then ordered some peach pie and coffee for dessert. Felicity deposited everything on the table, along with the order ticket. The cleaner still didn't look up from her phone and food, but I studied her from my position behind the counter, flipping through the mental dossiers I kept on everyone I came into contact with at Section. Sadly, this dossier was thinner than most. All I could recall was that the cleaner's name was Rosalita, and the only reason I remembered that much was because of her lipstick. Red lipstick for Rosalita. A simple word association.

Despite my unease, Rosalita ate her dessert, paid up, and left. I let out a quiet sigh of relief when she was gone. Looked like her visit had just been a coincidence, unlike Desmond, the Aussie cleaner. Once again, I wondered what he had wanted with me—

"I don't pay you to stand around daydreaming." Zeeta's snide voice cut into my reverie, and she made a sharp shooing motion with her hand. "Go clear that booth."

I bit back the retort dangling on the tip of my tongue and scurried over to do her barked bidding.

At exactly ten minutes before midnight, Zeeta turned off the neon signs, locked the front door, and flipped the placard over to *Closed*. Felicity helped me wipe down the dining counter and turn off the coffeemakers, while Zeeta stuffed the cash from the register into a long, skinny money pouch that she tucked into her purse.

When Zeeta was ready, the three of us headed into the kitchen to help Pablo clean up and put away the leftover food. We'd done this same routine a hundred times before, and we worked in quick, efficient silence.

After we finished, Pablo slapped off the kitchen lights, then handed me a white plastic bag that contained my promised piece of his amazing peach pie. Even though I was full from my meatloaf dinner, my mouth still watered in anticipation.

"Hope you enjoy it," Pablo said as we trooped out the diner's back door. "And don't tell the boss lady, but I slipped you two pieces."

I grinned at his conspiratorial wink. "And that's why I love you."

"There you go again," Pablo teased. "I'll have to tell Enrique that you're trying to steal me away."

"If only I could. A girl can dream, right?"

He grinned back at me, and we went our separate ways.

It was after midnight now, and the moon and stars were shining big and bright in the October sky. The air was quite chilly, and I tucked my hands into my jacket pockets. The wind whistled down the street, cutting straight through my thin white tights and swirling up under my skirt. I shivered and hurried on.

A few people were ambling along the sidewalks or curled up in building doorways, trying to get out of the worst of the wind. If not for my grandmother's apartment, I probably would have been one of them. If I'd had the money, I would have given those folks a few bucks, but I didn't have so much as a nickel to spare.

Still, despite the cold, the walk was pleasant enough. During the day, D.C. was a pressure cooker of a city, with mortals and paramortals alike always hustling for more power, money, deals, and information. All those folks spewing all those innuendoes, half-truths, and lies sometimes sent my synesthesia into overdrive, and I often saw gray, pink, and red clouds streaming out of people's mouths the same way that my own breath was currently frosting in the chilly air. The resulting haze cloaked the streets in a swirling miasma of colors, giving me a headache and making me feel as though I were walking through an abstract painting.

I much preferred the city at night, when the streets and sidewalks were largely empty of cars, people, lies, and colors, and everyone's frantic greed, ambitions, and agendas had been put to bed, at least for a few hours.

It had been another long, tiring day, so I quickly headed home. I had just stepped onto my block when I spotted a woman leaning up against the side of my apartment building.

For a moment, I thought it was Miriam, sneaking a late-night smoke, although as far as I knew, Miriam didn't know where I lived and would have no reason to visit me at this late hour.

The woman must have heard the soft, steady *swish-swish-swish* of my skirt because she glanced over at me. Dark brown hair pulled back into a thick braid, sleek black pantsuit, bright red lipstick. Rosalita grinned, her white teeth flashing like square opals in the moonlight. The smile of a predator who had finally spotted her prey. Rosalita pushed away from the building and sauntered toward me.

The second I recognized her, my inner voice started screaming. *Danger-danger-danger!* But I didn't need my magic to tell me how much trouble I was in. A cleaner lurking outside my apartment building in the middle of the night only meant one thing.

Rosalita was here to kill me.

I whirled around to run away, but three men were coming up on the sidewalk behind me. I hadn't heard their footsteps, and I didn't recognize their faces, but their black suits and sharp, thin smiles marked them as cleaners too.

My mind seized on the numbers, the way it always did. Four cleaners were coming to kill me. Not one, not two, not three, but *four*. What had I done that would prompt someone to send four cleaners to murder me? Didn't they realize that one probably would have been enough? This was most definitely *overkill*, in every sense of the word.

My head whipped back and forth as I searched for an escape route. There wasn't one, so I lurched to my right and darted into the narrow alley that ran between my building and the next one over. Of course, that was a mistake, since the alley was a dead end, but at least the cleaners couldn't surround and attack me from all sides at once in here. Not that it was going to make a difference, since I didn't have any weapons.

I thought longingly of the guns hidden underneath the floorboards in my apartment. A weapon would have at least given me a fighting chance, although the outcome—my death—probably would have been the same. Besides, one of the many reasons I became an analyst was so I wouldn't *have* to carry a gun and worry about people trying to kill me the way they had when my father was alive. But here it was, happening again, all the same.

I sprinted to the far end of the alley, then whirled around so my back was to the red brick wall. Rosalita stepped into the corridor and sauntered toward me at a slow, steady pace, with the other three cleaners trailing along behind her. They had me cornered and were taking their sweet time coming to kill me. No doubt terrorizing me was a fun, added bonus. Fucking cleaners.

I dropped my blue shoulder bag and the white plastic one with its precious pieces of peach pie onto the ground, then scanned the alley, searching for a makeshift weapon. A broken beer bottle was lying next to one of the overflowing trash cans, and I darted forward, grabbed the neck, and brandished the jagged, broken end. I might be outnumbered and outmatched, but I wasn't going down without at least trying to save my own miserable life.

Rosalita stopped a few feet away. She arched an eyebrow, then laughed. "Oh, come on, Charlotte. You know who I am, so you know I can take that bottle away and cut your throat with it before you can blink, much less scream."

"Who knows? Maybe I'll get lucky and you'll trip or do something else stupid, and then *I* can cut *your* throat."

Her dark brown eyes narrowed, and she studied me a little more carefully. "You almost sound like you know what you're talking about—and that you have the balls to actually do it. What would an analyst know about killing people?"

Plenty, thanks to my father, and my grandmother too, but Rosalita didn't need to know that. Besides, it didn't matter. I might get lucky and kill her, given how badly she was underestimating me, but the other three cleaners were still lurking behind her. I couldn't get them all with my pitiful weapon.

"Who sent you?" I asked. "Someone inside Section?"

Even though I worked for the government agency, it wasn't unheard of for the Section higher-ups to discreetly eliminate agents who broke the rules, caused problems, and attracted unwanted attention to the paramortal population. Like analysts who used their insider knowledge to make big, illegal trades in the stock market. Charmers who double-dipped and sold the personal intelligence they gathered to third parties. Or cleaners who went rogue and started killing people indiscriminately.

I wasn't stupid enough to do any of those things, so this was most likely about my father. It was almost *always* about my father. Jack Locke might have been one of the best cleaners that Section 47 ever had, but he'd also racked up a lot of enemies, both inside the spy organization and out of it. My father had been dead for fifteen years, but paramortals had long, long memories. Killing me now would be a petty form of revenge, but I supposed it would be revenge nonetheless.

I looked past Rosalita at the other three cleaners. They weren't from the D.C. station, and I wondered if they might be part of Gabriel's crew. But I had just ratted out a thief to Gabriel. He wouldn't kill me right after I'd helped him recover thousands of dollars...would he?

Sometimes I hated being a spy and all the paranoia that came along with it.

Rosalita gave me another amused look. "Do you really think I'm dumb enough to tell you anything?"

"If you're going to kill me anyway, then what does it matter? I'll be too dead to tell anyone you ratted them out."

She tilted her head to the side, thinking about it. Then another grin split her red lips. "Nah. I'm not getting paid to talk."

Rosalita flicked her wrist, and a slender silver butterfly knife slid into her hand. The blade popped open, and she whipped it up, around, and into position almost too quickly for me to follow. She was clearly skilled with the knife, and she obviously had some supernatural speed to augment her deadly Section training. Terrific.

"In case you were wondering, your death is going to look like a mugging gone wrong. Sadly, the perpetrator will never be caught." Rosalita clucked her tongue in false sympathy.

The three male cleaners remained silent and hung back, apparently content to let her do the dirty, bloody work of actually murdering me. I wondered why she had brought them along, since she was so confident she could kill me all by herself. Whoever had dispatched Rosalita must have desperately wanted me dead to send this many cleaners, and that person wasn't taking any chances on my getting lucky and surviving a single assassin. Smart of them, deadly for me.

I racked my brain again, trying to think who I had pissed off or what I had done to warrant such a certain execution, but I couldn't come up with an answer. Then again, the answer didn't really matter, since my death was all but assured. Still, despite my dire situation, I tightened my grip on the broken bottle. My father might not have been around much, but he had taught me a few things, as had my grandmother.

Rosalita spun her knife around in her hand again and marched forward. She probably expected me to lurch away or try to sidestep her, but I raised my bottle, firmed up my stance, and held my ground.

Don't mess around, and don't dance away. Always go in for the kill the first chance you get, my father's deep voice whispered in my ear.

Memories of our sparring sessions flooded my mind, but I couldn't focus on them. All I could see was the red haze pulsing around Rosalita's knife. Not only was my synesthesia not an offensive power, but it sometimes went haywire and highlighted the wrong thing. In this case, I could see the danger the knife represented far more clearly than I could see the actual blade itself. I grimaced and ignored the swirling color.

Rosalita grinned again, then surged forward and swiped out with her knife. This time, I did sidestep her, but I whirled right back around and closed the distance between us. She must have been expecting me to retreat instead of attack, because she hesitated, which let me lunge forward and lash out with my broken bottle.

I was aiming for her throat, but she used her speed to jerk to the side at the last second, and I only got her left cheek instead. Rosalita yelped with pain and surprise and slapped her hand up against the deep gash on her face.

She looked stunned that I had actually managed to injure her, but then her eyes narrowed, and her nostrils flared with fury. "You Legacy bitch!" she hissed. "You're going to pay for that!"

Rosalita surged forward again. One second, she was five feet away. The next, she was right in front of me. I snapped up my broken bottle, going for her throat a second time, but I was too slow, and she ducked the blow and lashed out with her knife.

I spun away, so that she wouldn't lay my stomach wide open with the weapon, but the blade still stabbed deep into my left side. White-hot agony exploded in my body, and I screamed and staggered back into the alley wall. My legs buckled, and my ass hit the ground. I glanced down.

My left side was wet with blood, which had already stained my blue waitress uniform a dark, sick brown. Pain pounded through my veins like a sledgehammer hitting me over and over again, and tears streamed down my cheeks. I gasped for air, but I managed to hold back the second scream rising in my throat. No use wasting my breath.

I might just be a lowly analyst, but Section work had often followed my father home, and I had been stalked, kidnapped, and injured by his enemies more times than I cared to remember during my tumultuous childhood. So I knew my wound wasn't immediately fatal, although I would bleed out if I didn't get medical attention. But it was a moot point, since the cleaners would finish me off soon enough.

Rosalita loomed over me, her bloody knife still clutched in her hand. "I expected you to put up much more of a fight, Charlotte. Kind of disappointing, given who your father was."

I kept gasping for breath, too focused on that to snarl out some pithy retort. Everyone at Section 47 *always* compared me to Jack Locke, and everyone *always* found me lacking. Story of my rapidly ending life—

Behind Rosalita and the three male cleaners, I spotted a sudden, unexpected flash of color. Maybe the blood loss was already making me woozy, but I could have sworn it was a single, vertical strip of light, bright blue shaped like…a tie.

Rosalita bent down and snapped her fingers in front of my face. "Charlotte! Pay attention. I'm assuming your laptop is in your apartment. Tell me the code to your safe, and this can all be over. I'll finish you off quick and painless. Promise."

If I'd had the breath for it, I would have told Rosalita exactly where to shove her empty promises, but then her words sank into my brain. What did she want with my laptop? What was this about?

Once again, I tried to come up with some answers, but another wave of pain crashed over me, and I gritted my teeth to hold back another scream—

One of the cleaners behind Rosalita let out a low, strangled sound.

"What was that?" Rosalita straightened up and whirled around.

She and the other two cleaners looked at the third man, who stared back at them with bulging eyes. A thin red line appeared on his neck, one that quickly widened into a jagged, bloody gash. The cleaner clutched his cut throat. He teetered on his feet, then crumpled to the ground, bleeding out from the gruesome wound.

Rosalita and the other two cleaners froze. I remained propped up against the alley wall, too injured to move, much less make a run for it.

A figure strode through the shadows and stepped into the center of the alley. A light out on the street beamed a golden glow into the narrow corridor and highlighted his features. Blond hair, blond stubble, tan skin, blue eyes.

Desmond.

He was still wearing his light gray vest, shirt, and pants, along with that rebellious powder-blue tie, although his jacket was nowhere to be seen. In one hand, he was holding his silver pocket watch, with the end of the attached chain in his other hand. Even from this distance, I could see the blood *drip-drip-dripping* off the thin links. The metal must have some sort of sharp, hidden edge. Not so much a pocket watch as a knife-like garrote. Either way, he looked like a golden angel of death standing in the middle of the alley.

Desmond stared at the other three cleaners. He tucked his watch into his vest pocket, then grinned and crooked his finger, silently daring Rosalita and the two men to come at him. Arrogant as well as deadly.

The other cleaners took the bait and charged forward.

Idiots.

My inner voice might have whispered *danger-danger-danger* when faced with Rosalita and her men, but as soon as Desmond had appeared, that voice had risen to a shrieking scream, and *DANGER! DANGER! DANGER!* pounded in my mind over and over again, matching the pulses of pain ripping through my body.

The three cleaners were already dead. They just didn't know it yet.

As they ran toward Desmond, the two men reached for the guns under their suit jackets. Desmond charged forward as well, then coolly, deftly spun to his right, moving past one of the cleaners.

The instant the man's back was to him, Desmond glided forward and closed the distance between them. With one hand, he yanked the man's right arm down and to the side, away from the gun hidden in the small of his back. With his other hand, Desmond plucked the man's gun out of its holster, snapped up the weapon, and pulled the trigger three times.

Thanks to the weapon's suppressor, the gunshots were little louder than pops of bubble gum. The cleaner yelped and tumbled to the ground, but Desmond was already turning to the second man. He shot that cleaner three times as well, and that man also dropped to the ground.

That left Rosalita.

Desmond spun around to face her, his movements still full of that smooth, unnatural, deadly grace. I didn't know what kind of magic he had, but it was impressive. I'd never seen anyone move and kill, and move and kill, that easily and effortlessly before, not even my father.

"Who the fuck are you?" Rosalita said. "Do you know what you're interrupting? And what will happen to you once they find out?"

A small, humorless smile lifted Desmond's lips. "Oh, I'm counting on that."

Then he crooked his finger at her in another one of those clear, cocky challenges. Oh, yes. Most definitely arrogant.

Rosalita snarled and surged forward, using her speed and not giving him time to get off any more shots. She lashed out with her knife, and Desmond wisely dropped his stolen gun rather than get his hand sliced open. Rosalita whirled back around to gut him, but Desmond spun away from her as coolly and easily as he had from the other cleaner.

In one fluid motion, he grabbed the silver watch tucked in his vest pocket, glided forward, and looped the attached chain around Rosalita's throat. Then he jerked the chain to the side, quickly and cleanly snapping her neck. All the motion in her body instantly stopped, and she looked like a puppet waiting for someone to pull her strings and bring her back to life.

Desmond unwound the chain from around Rosalita's neck and stepped back. She pitched forward, her body joining those of the other three cleaners on the alley floor.

It was one of the most impressive and brutal ballets of death I had ever seen.

Desmond studied Rosalita, then the other three cleaners, making sure they were all dead. Smart as well as arrogant. Then he strolled over, plucked a dirty rag out of the top of one of the trash cans, and used the cloth to wipe the blood off his silver watch and chain. His movements were calm and unhurried, as though this was a ritual he'd done a hundred times before. No doubt he had.

Once he was finished, Desmond dropped the rag into the trash can and tucked his watch back into his vest pocket. Somehow, despite all the death and violence, not a single drop of blood marred his perfect clothes. I snidely wondered if that was another one of his paramortal powers, along with that eerie, deadly grace.

I was still slumped up against the alley wall, slowly but surely bleeding out from the stab wound Rosalita had inflicted on me. Desmond walked over and crouched down beside me.

His gaze flicked to the broken beer bottle I was still clutching. I didn't know how much he had seen, or what he thought of my pitiful attempt to fight Rosalita, but he didn't try to pry the bottle out of my fingers. Then again, why would he? We both knew I wasn't a threat to him.

He leaned forward and tilted his head, studying the wound in my side. His lips puckered in thought, and I got the impression he was having some sort of internal debate. Probably about whether it was worth the effort to help me, although I wondered why he would even bother. Why was he here? And why had he killed the cleaners instead of letting them murder me?

Desmond lifted his gaze to mine. An inscrutable expression crossed his face, as though we were children engaged in a staring contest, and whoever looked away first would be the loser.

"I guess…I shouldn't have…called you…Crocodile Dundee," I rasped between waves of pain.

It was the first thing that popped into my mind, although as soon as I said it, I hoped it wouldn't be the last sentence I ever uttered. *What a cheesy way to go out, Charlotte.*

The corners of his lips twitched upward into a tiny grin. "No, you shouldn't have."

"What…do you…want?"

"You."

If I hadn't been bleeding out, I would have shivered at his dark, ominous tone.

Desmond glanced around, his eyes narrowing as he looked at first one cleaner, then another. I had no idea what he was doing. They were dead, so what did he hope to see? Disappointment flickered across his face, but then his head lifted, and he stared at the light out on the street. He nodded, as if something about the light pleased him, then focused on me again.

"Sorry, Numbers," he said. "This is going to hurt."

Numbers? Before I could ask about the impromptu nickname, Desmond leaned forward and clamped his hand on my side, right where Rosalita had stabbed me. I hissed with pain, although I once again managed to swallow the scream rising in my throat.

Maybe it was the blood loss, but I could have sworn that Desmond's eyes flashed a bright silver-blue, like live wires sparking in the night.

A wave of…of…*something* slammed into my body, and this time, I couldn't stop myself from screaming.

The pain crashed through me again, stronger than before, and I mercifully passed out, not sure what sort of oblivion I was heading toward—or if I would ever wake up from it.

FOUR

DESMOND

The analyst was not what I'd expected.

I thought she would be a bland, boring, average sort of person. Another one of Section's mindless office robots, dutifully going about her work, punching a clock, and counting down the days until she could either find a more lucrative job in the private sector or retire and collect her government pension. Intelligent enough, but with a vanilla sort of life, just like the dozens of other analysts I'd encountered over the years.

I should have known better. She was a Locke, after all. Nothing about that Legacy family was bland, boring, or vanilla.

I stared down at the analyst. I had grabbed the electricity from the nearby streetlamp and channeled the resulting energy through my body and into hers. The extra jolt of power had let me heal her deep stab wound and stitch her skin back together. She was pale and unconscious, but her chest rose and fell in a steady rhythm. She would be okay in a few hours.

I left her lying there, propped up against the alley wall like a broken doll, and got to work.

The first thing I did was rifle through the dead cleaners' pockets, but none of them was carrying IDs or phones. Disappointing, but not unexpected. Besides, I already had a pretty good idea who they had worked for and why that person wanted the analyst dead—to keep me from getting to her.

I pulled my own phone out of my pocket and snapped photos of the cleaners' faces, then used an app to scan and store their fingerprints. Perhaps the analyst could make use of the information later. Once that was done, I dragged the bodies behind some garbage bins and piled several trash bags on top of them, hiding them from sight. I'd properly dispose of the bodies later. Right now, I needed to get the analyst out of the alley before some homeless person wandered in here and started screaming bloody murder about all the actual murders I had just committed.

I went over and crouched down beside the analyst again. Still unconscious. I'd give her another jolt of energy when I got her upstairs.

I pried the broken bottle out of her fingers, then grabbed her under the arms, hauled her upright, and leaned her back against the wall. She didn't stir, so I bent down, hoisted her onto my shoulder, and stood up, holding her in a fireman's carry. When I was sure she was properly positioned and I wasn't going to lose my grip on her, I carefully leaned down and grabbed her blue purse as well as the white plastic bag she'd dropped earlier.

I carried the analyst to the end of the alley, then glanced up and down the sidewalk. No one was in sight, no headlights glowed in the distance, and no traffic or security cameras covered the street, so I stepped out of the alley and walked over to the side door of her apartment building, which I had scouted earlier today. The door was locked with an electronic keypad, but that was no problem. I put my hand up against the keypad, then reached out with my magic, feeling the crack, snap, and sizzle of the electrical current running through the box and its attached wires.

Just about everything either uses or gives off some sort of electricity, from your common cell phone to the most powerful supercomputer to the smallest spy camera. As a galvanist, I had the ability to sense that power, no matter what form it took, as well as to control, manipulate, and make it flow from one object to another. Basically, I was a human magnet for electricity, along with kinetic energy, chemical energy, and the like, and I could shove that power in any direction—or into any person.

So it was child's play for me to redirect the current running through the keypad long enough to get the door to buzz open. I stepped through to the other side, and the door automatically shut and locked behind me.

I took the stairs and got the analyst to her third-floor apartment without anyone seeing us. She was still unconscious, so I gently set her down on the floor. I used the keys from her purse to open the door, then flipped on the lights. An alarm box was located inside, but I redirected the current inside it until the flashing red light winked back to a steady green. Then I scooped up the analyst and her bags, carried her inside, and kicked the door shut behind me.

I turned around, fully intending to set the analyst down on the closest sofa or chair, but no furniture filled the apartment, not so much as the smallest table. What kind of person lived in an empty apartment? What had happened to all her things?

I moved forward, intending to deposit her on the mattress in the far corner, which seemed to be her bed, but she probably

A SENSE OF DANGER   63

wouldn't want her bloodstained clothes mucking up her sheets and blankets, so I changed direction and put her down on the yoga mat in front of the cold fireplace instead.

Her arms and legs flopped out to the sides, and I straightened her limbs before folding her hands on top of her stomach, trying to make her as comfortable as possible. I would have snagged one of the pillows from the mattress and put it under her head, but her shoulder-length auburn hair was as filthy as the rest of her.

The analyst still didn't wake up, although her eyebrows were drawn together and a worried crease ran across her forehead, as though her subconscious mind was churning, trying to make sense of everything that had happened.

I leaned back on my heels, reviewing everything I had read in her official Section 47 file.

Charlotte Jo Locke. Age thirty-five. Granddaughter of Jane Locke, the first member of her family to work for Section. Daughter of a librarian and infamous Section cleaner Jack Locke. Employed as a Section analyst ever since her graduation from university at the age of twenty-five. Stuck in the same position for several years now, thanks to her grandmother's illness, her father's reputation, and general office politics. On record as being a moderately powerful synth with a form of magical synesthesia that let her see mistakes other people made. A fairly common ability, but one that probably helped a great deal with her job.

Those were the highlights from Charlotte Locke's official Section 47 file, and they were all more or less exactly what I'd expected.

What I *hadn't* expected was how coldly and abruptly she'd dismissed me in the cafeteria earlier, her second job at that greasy-spoon diner, the dangerous man she owed money to, and how many cleaners had been sent to kill her. I glanced around, adding the depressingly empty apartment to that growing list of unexpected things about Charlotte Locke.

Seemed as if I wasn't the only one keeping secrets from Section.

Since it didn't look like the analyst was going to wake up anytime soon, I searched her apartment, but it was as empty as it appeared at first glance. No furniture to speak of, and only a few mismatched plates, glasses, and silverware in the kitchen cabinets. The only other thing in the kitchen was a small crystal bird perched in the middle of the island counter. I didn't know what kind of bird it was, but I didn't want to break it, so I scooted the figurine off to the side.

I upended her purse on the island and looked through the contents. Wallet, phone, lipsticks, tissues, pens, a small note-pad. Nothing unusual, so I stuffed everything back inside. The white plastic bag she'd been carrying contained a couple of generous portions of peach pie.

Since there was no refrigerator, freezer, or microwave in the apartment, I was guessing the analyst ate most of her meals at the Moondust Diner. No wonder I'd had to drain all the juice from the streetlamp to heal her. Food also contained energy, and the cleaner and healthier you ate, the more natural energy your own body absorbed and produced in response. It seemed as though all the analyst consumed were greasy, empty, sugary calories. Sure, those calories might light up her taste buds, but they weren't doing her body any favors in the long run.

Since I was finished with the kitchen, I headed into the back of the apartment. One of the bedrooms was completely empty, while the other seemed to be Charlotte's. No furniture back here either, although the closet did contain clothes.

Earlier in the cafeteria, Charlotte had worn a black cardigan over a gray T-shirt and gray cargo pants. Her sneakers had been the same hot pink as the broken heart on her T-shirt. Her closet contained more of the same—cardigans, T-shirts, cargo pants, sneakers.

Lots of sneakers.

More than two dozen pairs of sneakers were lined up neatly along the closet floor, running the color spectrum from white, light gray, green, blue, red, purple, and black. No other shoes. No heels, no sandals, not so much as a pair of ratty house slippers. Just sneakers. Odd.

I closed the closet door and stepped into the bathroom. Brushes, combs, and hair ties were lined up on the countertop, along with bottles of makeup, shampoo, and lotion. Nothing unusual in here either, so I returned to the bedroom.

Some cardboard boxes were stacked up in the corner, so I pried the lid off the top one and dug through the contents. Photos, mostly, of Charlotte with her grandmother. Her mother was also in several pictures, but her father wasn't in very many of them. Then again, if Jack Locke had been anything like my father, he hadn't been around for much of Charlotte's childhood.

The others boxes contained more of the same, along with old school papers, a few books, tickets to long-ago museum visits, and other mementoes. I restacked the boxes and returned to the main living area, surveying the empty space again. And that was all she had. There was seemingly nothing else of interest in the entire apartment.

Oh, her Section laptop had to be in here *somewhere*, since I'd heard the female cleaner asking about it earlier. Charlotte must have powered it down for the night because I didn't sense any energy radiating from the device, and I didn't have the time or patience to search for whatever cubbyhole she'd hidden it in. Besides, I didn't want her laptop.

She was going to need it for work in the morning.

I glanced over, but Charlotte was still unconscious on the yoga mat. I would have liked to stay until she woke up, but I needed to get rid of the cleaners' bodies. I didn't want to just dump her here with no explanation, so I decided to leave her a note.

I went back to the kitchen island and grabbed the blue notepad and a pen out of her purse. But what to write? I wasn't stupid enough to spell out everything that had happened, and there wasn't enough room on the sheet for that anyway. My gaze landed on the plastic bag with its container of peach pie. I grinned, leaned forward, and scribbled a vague yet polite and friendly note, then stuck it on the counter.

Of course, she could always wake up, read the note, freak out, and make a run for it, but I was betting she wouldn't do that. From what I'd read in her file, Charlotte Locke seemed like a very smart, very careful individual, and she would probably want to know *exactly* what was going on before she made any big, drastic, life-changing—or life-ending— decisions. Besides, thanks to the directional microphone I'd used to eavesdrop on her conversation with the man in the diner, I knew she didn't have the money to go anywhere.

No, I was betting that Charlotte Locke would report to work at Section 47 in the morning like everything was normal and nothing noteworthy had happened tonight. That was the smartest, safest play. And if she didn't, well, I would find her and make sure she did. I needed the analyst too badly to let her pull a vanishing act.

Still, as an added bit of insurance, I pulled a black fountain pen out of my pants pocket and dropped it into her purse. The pen contained a GPS tracker as well as a camera and a microphone, all of which I had synced to my phone. Hopefully, she wouldn't spot it before I had a chance to talk to her. If she did and disposed of it, well, I had other ways of finding her.

I walked over and crouched down beside the analyst again. Her face was still a bit pale, so I gently took hold of her left wrist. Her pulse thumped steady and strong underneath my fingers. I concentrated, feeling the electricity humming through the lights and the attached wires in the walls, then reached out and grabbed hold of that power.

It only took me an instant to transform the sharp, jolting pulses of electricity into soft, steady energy, like the heat radiating from a fireplace. Once that was done, I slowly, carefully fed the warm, healing power into Charlotte's body until the last of the sickly paleness left her face, and her features relaxed and smoothed out. Then I let go of her wrist and folded her hand on top of her stomach again.

"Sleep well, Numbers," I said. "You've got a lot of work ahead of you."

Charlotte's forehead creased again, almost as if her subconscious was suddenly worried about my words. I stared at her a moment longer, then got to my feet, left the apartment, and locked the door behind me.

FIVE

CHARLOTTE

I sucked in a strangled breath and sat bolt upright.

My hands clenched into fists, my eyes widened, and my head snapped from side to side as I tried to figure out where I was and what was going on. I wasn't sure what I was expecting, but empty space greeted me, along with a familiar quiet.

For one heart-stopping moment, I thought I was in some abandoned warehouse, but then I spotted the mattress, blankets, and sheets on the floor a few feet away.

My apartment. I was in my apartment.

I sucked in another strangled breath and slowly let it out, forcing myself to push out the rest of my panic and fear along with it. My head snapped from side to side again, as I searched the area, but the lights were on, and no one else was here. No cleaners lying in wait to kill me, and no sign of *him*.

I drew my knees up to my chest and slumped forward, hugging one arm around my shins. With a shaking hand, I wiped the cold, clammy sweat off my forehead. I stayed like that for several seconds until my heart slowed and my hand quit trembling. Then I forced myself to straighten up and take a clearer, calmer look at things.

I was sitting on my old, worn-out yoga mat, and I was still wearing my waitress uniform, along with my gray jacket, although they were both covered with my blood, as were my ripped white tights and scuffed sneakers. I gingerly lifted the blood-crusted shirt away from my side, dreading what I would find, but to my surprise, my skin was uninjured and whole, and the gruesome stab wound had vanished. Even stranger, I actually felt...good...*energized* even.

I slowly climbed to my feet, expecting my head to start spinning and a wave of lethargy to crash over me, but nothing happened, and I felt better, stronger, and more clear-headed than I had in weeks, months even, since before the worst of my grandmother's illness had begun.

What had he done to me?

I didn't have an answer, and really, all I wanted to do right now was get out of these horrible bloody clothes. So I shrugged out of my jacket, shuffled into the kitchen, and stuffed the ruined garment into the trash can under the sink. Once that was done, I headed over to the alarm box on the wall by the front door, but the light burned a bright, steady green, indicating it was working. I switched off the alarm, opened the door, and peered at the lock on the other side, but no faint scratches or other marks marred the metal, indicating that it had been picked or jimmied open.

I glanced up and down the hallway, but it looked the same as always. An empty corridor with a few old landscape prints hanging haphazardly on the beige walls. So I reactivated the alarm, then shut the door, locked it again, and leaned my back against it. I crossed my arms over my chest and studied my apartment with sharp, critical eyes. My mind kept whirring, as my inner analyst kicked in, trying to make sense of everything.

After the cleaner attack in the alley, Desmond had obviously healed me—or had me healed—and had brought me here. Sick realization flooded my stomach. He knew where I lived, which meant he had been watching me. I wondered if he'd trailed me here from Section or the diner, or if he had already been in my apartment, waiting for me to come home. No way to know for sure, but each option made my skin crawl.

Then there was the giant, glaring, obvious question: *Why?*

Why had he been following me? Why had he saved me from the cleaners? And why had he brought me back here and then vanished?

What...do you...want? My own raspy voice rang in my ears, followed by his low, ominous answer. *You.*

Our previous conversation floated through my mind, and a shiver skittered down my spine. If there was one thing working for Section had taught me, it was that no one *ever* did anything simply out of the goodness of their heart, especially not a cleaner like Desmond. You didn't kill people for a living and have some hidden altruistic streak.

Once again, my gaze roamed over the apartment, which wasn't quite as empty as I'd first thought. My blue shoulder bag and a white plastic sack were sitting on the island counter that divided the kitchen from the living room.

I hurried over and peered into my shoulder bag, scanning the contents. Phone, wallet, lip balms. Everything seemed to be there, but my gaze snagged on one of the items.

"Keys," I whispered.

Desmond must have used my keys to let himself into my apartment, although that didn't explain how he had avoided triggering the alarm system.

A bit of pink haze caught my eye, swimming in the blackness at the bottom of my shoulder bag. I reached down, grabbed hold of the item, and pulled out…a pen.

I rolled it back and forth in my fingers, examining it from all angles. The black fountain pen was nice, sleek, and expensive, but it wasn't mine. Otherwise, I would have hocked it long ago. The cleaner must have put it into my bag to…track me? Eavesdrop? Record everything I said and did?

I shuddered and dropped the pen back into the bag. If there was a camera or some other bug hidden inside it, then all Desmond—or whoever else might be watching—would see was the bag's black lining. I thought about snapping the pen into pieces and tossing them into the trash, but I didn't want him to realize I'd found his bug. Not yet. Maybe I could turn the tables and somehow use it against him.

I looked through the rest of the items in my bag, but the pen was the only thing that didn't belong, and I didn't see or feel any trackers tucked into the lining.

I turned my attention to the other bag and pushed the white plastic aside to find…two pieces of peach pie in a clear container. After the cleaner attack, Desmond must have retrieved the food, along with my shoulder bag, and brought them both here to my apartment.

Why would he do that? What did he want with me?

I spotted another flash of color and slowly tiptoed forward again to find…

A light blue sticky note.

I recognized it as coming from the pad inside my shoulder bag. Desmond had apparently used it and one of the pens to leave me a message, which he had stuck to the counter in between my shoulder bag and the one that contained the peach pie.

Looks good, although you know that sugar will kill you, right? See you tomorrow. ☺

Looks good? Sugar will kill you? See you tomorrow?

Well, that was weird, random, and strangely ominous all at the same time. And what kind of psycho cleaner put a fucking smiley face on his weird, random, ominous note?

Once again, I didn't have the answers to my questions, and part of me didn't want to puzzle them out. Crocodile Dundee Desmond might have saved me from Rosalita and the other cleaners, but I had a sinking feeling I was in more danger than ever before.

But first things first. I had to make sure I was truly safe, so I used my synesthesia to scan the rest of the apartment, searching for dangers, hazards, or anything that was new or out of place, but I didn't find any more bugs. Looked like he'd only dropped the one pen into my shoulder bag. I also peered out the windows, but no one was lurking on the street outside. Not Desmond, not more cleaners, no one. Seemed like the danger was over—at least for tonight.

So what was I supposed to do next?

I glanced over at my yoga mat, thinking of the passports, guns, and cash hidden underneath the floorboards. Part of me wanted to raid my escape stash, stuff some clothes into a bag, and run away as fast as possible. But a lousy ten grand wouldn't get me very far, and someone would eventually find me—Section 47, Desmond, or whoever had sent those cleaners after me.

Besides, if I ran, I would also be shirking my debt to Gabriel, which was something I didn't want to do. Gabriel had been good to me in his own way, and he might understand if I told him what was going on...or he might not. Either way, he wouldn't be getting any more of his money back if I left town and went into hiding.

Running was an option, but it wasn't the best or most feasible option. So what else could I do?

My thoughts circled back to Desmond. He obviously wanted *something* from me, and he wanted it badly enough to kill four other cleaners to get it. His needing me alive was better than someone else wanting me dead. Besides, my blindly running away and waiting for more cleaners to show up and kill me wouldn't solve anything.

My gaze kept roaming around the apartment, much like the various thoughts and scenarios kept spinning through my mind. A glimmer caught my eye, and I walked over and picked up the crystal mockingbird figurine sitting on the island counter. This bird was another gift from my grandmother and the mate to the matching figurine on my desk at Section. Just touching the smooth, clear crystal made me feel better, and the longer I stared into the mockingbird's black crystal eyes, the more I thought about Grandma Jane and everything she had taught me.

The best thing—the *smartest* thing—would be to go to work at Section in the morning as though everything were normal and no one had tried to kill me. Once I was at Section, I could start gathering information about Desmond as well as figure out who might want me dead and why. Then I could plan my next move. And if I didn't like what I discovered about Desmond, or if I couldn't determine who my enemy was, then I could always come back here, grab my emergency supplies, and run.

I set the mockingbird on the counter and nudged it back into place. If nothing else, Grandma Jane would have approved of my coming up with a plan.

I just hoped my decision to stick around didn't wind up getting me killed.

I couldn't implement my plan until morning, and I was still covered in blood, so I stripped off my ruined waitress uniform and tossed it into the trash with my jacket, then took a long, hot shower and put on my favorite fleece pajamas. I also grabbed one of the guns from its hiding place, along with an extra magazine of ammo and one of the few kitchen knives I had left, and laid them on the floor next to my mattress. Once that was done, I crawled into my makeshift bed and pulled the blankets and sheets up to my chin, as though the soft fabric would protect me from whatever horrible things might come crashing through the front door.

The tremors started the second my head touched the pillow.

Adrenaline, fear, shock, worry. My emotions finally caught up with me, and I gritted my chattering teeth and let them run their course, just as I had dozens of other times over the years when I'd escaped from a dangerous situation that should have killed me. I didn't cry, though. I'd wasted all my tears on my father long ago.

Once the tremors finally faded away, a dull, weary resignation swept over me, and I fell down into the blissful blackness of sleep. I woke up early the next morning feeling... well, not refreshed, but at least ready to face another day of secrets, lies, and superspies.

I got up, took another hot shower, and did some yoga to get my body moving. A few cat and cow poses. A couple of downward dogs. Several cobras. Even some warriors, lunges, and lizards to stretch out my legs. I flowed from one position to the next, focusing on my breathing and emptying out my mind.

Yoga almost always made me feel better, sharper, stronger, and it also helped me deal with the overwhelming sensations that my synesthesia often produced. On my mat, there were no bright, unwanted colors or loud, warning voices. Just the sticky feel of the rubber under my hands and feet, the steady *thump-thump-thump* of my heart, and the air gradually filling and escaping from my lungs. Quiet, calm, controlled, serene.

I needed all the serenity I could get.

When I finished, I slipped into gray cargo pants, along with a royal-blue T-shirt covered with gray musical notes; a soft, warm gray cardigan; and my favorite pair of gray sneakers.

I *always* wore sneakers. You never knew when you might have to run away from someone who wanted you dead. Another lesson I'd learned from both my father and my grandmother, and one that might be especially true today.

I ate both pieces of Pablo's excellent peach pie for breakfast, grabbed my laptop from its hiding spot underneath the floorboards, and stuffed it into my shoulder bag, along with the gun, the extra ammo, and the kitchen knife. When I was properly armed, I left my apartment.

I stepped outside into the chilly morning air and scanned the people hustling along the sidewalks. Everything looked fine, and I didn't see any bright red haze that would indicate someone was an immediate threat to me.

I stopped at the corner of the building, moved to the side, and bent down, as though I were retying my shoelaces. I discreetly glanced into the alley, but I didn't see the cleaners' bodies. If he was smart, Desmond would have gotten rid of the bodies last night, but I wasn't going to be stupid enough to go back there and look for them. I got to my feet and moved on.

It was just after seven when I stepped inside the Section building, almost two hours earlier than I typically showed up, but Evelyn was sitting behind the information desk as usual. She always seemed to work longer hours than anyone else, and I couldn't remember the last time she hadn't been in the lobby, overseeing the comings and goings.

I waved at her.

"You're in early," Evelyn said, eyeing me in return. "Couldn't sleep?"

A seemingly innocent question, but I had to hide my grimace. "Something like that."

I forced myself to smile at her, then scanned my keycard, pushed through the turnstile, and headed to the elevators. Since so many Section agents were issued guns, there were no metal detectors in the lobby to scream out the fact that I was carrying multiple weapons in my shoulder bag.

I rode down to the third floor and headed into the bullpen. I was the first one here, and the area was empty and quiet, so I went to my desk, sat down, and powered up my laptop.

Normally, I would have used my regular *CLocke* log-in and password to access the Section network and start my work for the day, checking on the financial transactions, transportation purchases, and cute dog photos that my assigned bad guys had made and posted overnight. But someone was *always* watching at Section, including who accessed what information, and a whole IT subdepartment was devoted to making sure that the analysts, charmers, and other agents were actually working instead of using company computers, time, and Wi-Fi to play games, shop online, and download porn. Spies spying on spies. Such was life at Section 47.

Since I didn't know who my enemies were, I didn't want anyone to realize I was investigating Desmond, especially not Desmond himself. As soon as I searched for his name, an electronic record would be created indicating that I had looked him up, and I had no idea if anyone had put any alerts or flags on his file. So instead of using my normal log-in, I entered a different one—*Mockingbird*—along with the appropriate password.

Mockingbird was something Grandma Jane had dreamed up years ago. Back when she'd been working as a Section analyst, she had sweet-talked a hacker who owed her a favor into building the code, and it had been her invisible back door into the Section network ever since. It was a ghost log-in, one that didn't trigger any internal alarms and left no trace behind in the system. Grandma Jane had been an avid birdwatcher, and she'd dubbed the code *Mockingbird*, since it mimicked what was already in the Section network, just like actual mockingbirds could mimic the songs of other birds.

Mockingbird had come in handy more than once over the years, especially when my father had been held hostage in Mexico. Back then, the Section higher-ups had frozen out Grandma Jane, but she'd still been able to see everything that was happening with the mission. Hence her knowing about the cartel's three-million-dollar ransom demand.

My index finger hovered over the laptop keyboard. Grandma Jane had warned me that Mockingbird was to be used sparingly, and only if I couldn't get the information I needed through some other legitimate channel. I had never used it before, so I was hoping it still worked. Only one way to know for sure, but learning more about Desmond, and potentially discovering who wanted me dead, was worth the risk.

I hit the *Enter* key.

My screen immediately went completely black. I winced and leaned back, expecting my laptop to burst into flames, red lights to start flashing overhead, or something else equally dramatic to happen. Instead, the screen abruptly turned white, and lines of black code flooded my monitor, forming a distinctive shape—a mockingbird.

The screen went black again, then a message appeared, along with the regular internal Section home page. *Welcome, Mockingbird.*

The tense breath stuck in my throat *whooshed* out in a sudden, relieved rush. I was in the system.

I pulled up the main search engine and typed in Desmond's name. For security reasons, cleaners were only identified by their first names in the internal Section databases, but there was only one Desmond in the system, and his photo appeared on my screen. Blond hair, blond stubble, blue eyes, smug smile. That was definitely him. I started reading through his Section personnel file.

Desmond. Age thirty-six. Six feet tall. Born in Sydney, Australia, to an Australian mother and an American father...

Desmond had apparently been groomed to be a cleaner his whole life, given all the military schools he had attended growing up, and I got the impression that he was a Legacy like me, although there was no mention of his last name or his family. Still, it was all pretty standard stuff, except for one thing—Desmond had majored in art during college. Not what I would expect, especially given how largely useless drawing, painting, and the like would be in his line of work. Or perhaps he wanted to sketch the faces of the people he killed. It wouldn't surprise me, given the psycho smiley face he'd put on that charming little note he'd left in my apartment.

Once I had absorbed his general background, I moved on to his official Section service record. Like me, Desmond had started working for Section right after college, at age twenty-five. Unlike me, he had quickly risen through the ranks and become a full-fledged cleaner by the time he was thirty.

Since then, he had taken part in missions all over the world and had more than fifty confirmed kills, which was impressive, even by Section's lofty, deadly standards.

Still, the more I read, the more I realized something was missing—his magic.

Other than a few notes talking about his above-average strength, speed, and pain tolerance, none of the files mentioned anything specific about his powers. Weird. Usually, cleaners' abilities were the most well-documented. The Section higher-ups wanted to know *exactly* who and what they were dealing with in case a cleaner went rogue and had to be eliminated.

In addition to Desmond's missing magic, I noticed one other discrepancy in his file—he was listed as being en route from Sydney, Australia, instead of being confirmed as currently in the D.C. area. Section agents were supposed to immediately check in upon arrival in their destination city, but it seemed as though Desmond didn't want to advertise the fact that he was here. But if that was the case, then why had he come over to me in the cafeteria yesterday?

I clicked through a few more screens until I found Desmond's last mission, code-named *Blacksea*, which had taken place about two months ago. Unlike everything else in his dossier, the mission file was locked and required top, level-seven clearance to access. My eyebrows shot up my forehead. Relatively speaking, very few people had level-seven clearance—the members of the Section board of directors; Maestro, the mysterious head of the D.C. office; the equally mysterious heads of the other major stations around the world; and the analyst, charmer, liaison, and cleaner supervisors here in D.C. and abroad.

I didn't know if the Mockingbird log-in had enough juice to unlock the file, but Desmond hadn't been on an operation since then. A note indicated he had been severely injured during the Blacksea mission and spent several weeks recovering. A few days ago, Desmond had finally been cleared to return to active duty and assigned to a new mission, although no details had been entered about what that mission was.

Still, despite his new assignment, I was willing to bet that Blacksea was the *real* reason why Desmond was here. Even the most callous, jaded, hardened cleaner would have a difficult time getting over an assignment that had almost killed him. Although I had no idea what connection *I* could possibly have to a two-month-old mission. Only one way to find out. I hit the *Enter* key.

My screen went black again...

And then...and then...

The file opened.

"Thank you, Grandma Jane," I whispered and started reading through the information.

Desmond and another cleaner, an American named Graham, had been sent to kill Adrian Anatoly, a Russian-born paramortal who was responsible for dozens of bombings, political assassinations, and other horrible acts all over the world. Anatoly was a truly nasty piece of work, a terrorist-for-hire who killed and maimed people for money and amusement rather than carrying out some personal vendetta or ideological agenda. He was known to have exceptional paramortal strength and was rumored to not be able to feel pain, which was perhaps why he delighted so much in inflicting it on others.

Anatoly was also rumored to be part of the Syndicate, a shadowy group of paramortal bad guys. Some were terrorists, others were criminals, but supposedly they all worked together on occasion to exchange information, sell weapons to each other, and increase their own fortunes. Sort of like an evil twin to Section 47. Most people in the intelligence community thought the Syndicate was nothing more than an urban legend, but my father had staunchly believed in the group's existence. He had tried to find out more about the Syndicate—especially who its members were—for years, although he'd never had much success.

I didn't have time to speculate about hypothetical boogeymen, so I moved on. Three months ago, Section agents had discovered that Adrian Anatoly was holed up on a small island off the Australian coast, and the Blacksea mission had been green-lit.

The report gave me all the details: *Desmond and Graham left their liaisons and other support staff on a boat and swam to the island under the cover of darkness. They hiked over to and infiltrated the target compound, only to find it empty. When they returned to the shoreline, several boats carrying Anatoly's men appeared. Those vessels surrounded and fired upon the support staff's boat, which exploded. All Section staff on board were killed in that initial contact.*

Anatoly and his men then steered their boats toward the shore. Using a cell phone, Anatoly detonated more than a dozen IEDs that had been buried in the sand. Anatoly and his men escaped, and Desmond and Graham were left for dead...

I'd seen enough after-action reports to read between the lines—it had been a trap. Adrian Anatoly had known that Section was coming for him, and all those agents had died for nothing.

Still curious, I clicked on Graham's name, and his photo popped up on the screen. Graham had been quite handsome, with short black hair, green eyes, bronze skin, and an easy smile. I scanned his service record, which was remarkably similar to Desmond's, although not quite as impressive. The two of them had been partnered on multiple missions, and together, they had killed a lot of bad, bad people.

I returned to the Blacksea mission report and clicked through some more documents. It was all pretty standard stuff, although no one seemed to know exactly *how* Adrian Anatoly had realized that Section was targeting him. This time, I didn't even have to read between the lines, since an internal memo spelled it out—*Section leak suspected. Further investigation requested.*

In other words, there was a mole.

Given how many agents had died, a team of investigators had been charged with ferreting out who inside Section had tipped off Anatoly. The investigators had been brutally thorough, questioning everyone who worked in the Sydney station, including Desmond, even though he had been gravely wounded in the attack.

I studied Desmond's after-action interview: *Graham is dead. My best friend is dead. Blown up on a beach because Adrian Anatoly knew we were coming. So quit wasting time asking me the same stupid questions over and over again, get out there, and find the bastard who sold us out...*

Even though I was just reading a transcript, I could still hear the pain in Desmond's voice as clearly as if I'd been in the room during the interview. More of my magical synesthesia at work. Even more telling, every word he said was a flat, stark black. Whatever else he might be, Desmond wasn't a mole, and he hadn't betrayed his friend and fellow agents.

I read through all the other documents, but nothing jumped out, so I reviewed them a second time, using my synesthesia to carefully examine the interview transcripts. Lots of grays, indicating mistakes and errors, but no bright pinks and no glaring reds that would indicate half-truths and outright lies. No conclusive evidence had been found, and no one had been accused of being the mole. The hunt was still ongoing, although the files hadn't been updated in more than a month, indicating that the investigators had hit a wall. If the mole had escaped such intense scrutiny for this long, then they most likely weren't going to be caught.

The investigators had focused their mole hunt on the Sydney station's personnel, but anyone in any Section station around the world could have leaked the information to Anatoly, including someone here in D.C.

Someone that *I* worked with.

I rocked back in my chair, turning that thought over in my mind. If Desmond was truly in D.C. because of the Blacksea mission, then he must think that the mole was here too, something the cleaner attack against me last night further supported. Although I still had no idea what I had done to threaten or piss off the mole enough for them to try to kill me.

Still thinking about the mole, I clicked through to another screen. Instead of more reports, a photo appeared on my monitor—Desmond cradling his friend's body.

Desmond and Graham were both covered with gruesome burns that had turned their skin a bright, and strangely shiny, neon-red. In addition to the unnatural color, their skin also looked like raw meat that had been shoved through a grinder and then stitched back together with the remaining shreds of their black tactical clothes. My stomach roiled at the sickening sight, but I forced myself to study the disturbing image.

Desmond was clutching Graham's body to his chest, as though he were trying to shield his partner from further danger, even though one of Graham's legs had been blown off below the knee, his eyes were fixed, and it was obvious he was dead.

From the angle of the photo, it looked like a still image from a body camera, and Desmond was glaring up at whoever had been wearing the device. His eyes burned like silver-blue suns, his lips were drawn back into a feral snarl, and his red, blistered face was contorted in a mixture of rage, grief, guilt, and agonizing heartbreak.

For the first time, a bit of sympathy sparked in my chest, although I ruthlessly extinguished it. Desmond had lost his partner, his friend, but that was hardly unusual. Section dealt with all sorts of unsavory people, and death wasn't so much a risk as it was an eventuality.

My father had taught me that.

I glanced around, but the bullpen was still deserted, so I grabbed my phone and took a photo of Desmond clutching Graham's body. It was against Section protocols to copy an image like this, but I did it anyway. My conscience elbowed me in the gut, but I ignored the sharp stab of guilt. Information was power, especially at Section, and Desmond seemed to know far more about me than I did about him. Maybe this photo would help level the playing field between us.

I had dug as deeply into Desmond as I could, but he wasn't the only cleaner I'd encountered last night, so I typed Rosalita's name into the search engine. Her personnel file was exactly what I expected, with one large, glaring error— Rosalita was listed as being on a covert assignment in Colombia.

I frowned and clicked through a few more screens, but they all said the same thing. As far as the Section databases knew, Rosalita was shadowing a cartel leader in Bogotá in hopes of figuring out how to kill him without anyone being the wiser. But perhaps the most worrisome thing was that the information burned a bright, bloody red in my eyes, indicating that someone had deliberately typed in the blatant lies. And not just on one document but on multiple files.

I glanced at the names of the other people who had recently viewed the file, but they all had legitimate reasons for accessing it, and none of their notes or requests for more information struck me as being obviously wrong or overtly suspicious.

Frustrated, I rocked back in my chair again, making it *creak* in protest. Despite everything I'd learned, I still had no idea what Desmond, Adrian Anatoly, Rosalita, or the Blacksea mission and subsequent mole hunt had to do with *me*.

I *tap-tap-tapped* my fingers on the keyboard, my mind whirring. After a few seconds, I started typing again. This time, instead of searching for information on Desmond, I typed in my own name and title: *Charlotte Locke, analyst...*

I made a point of scanning my own file at least once a month, so I didn't have to read through the information. Instead, I looked at all the *other* people who had accessed my file recently and all the reports and work requests associated with it.

Gregory Jensen, of course, overwriting my work and claiming several of my reports as his own, along with dismissing and saying that no further action needed to be taken on the reports he didn't care about. Miriam, linking to her own charmer reports, whenever her targets mentioned something having to do with one of my bad guys. Anthony in accounting, denying my office supply requests as usual. Keila, also in accounting, transferring my biweekly paycheck into my meager bank account. And so on and so forth.

I worked backward, clicking through the screens, and scanning each log-in, along with the relevant information.

It took me a few minutes, but I finally found something interesting.

Graham, Desmond's partner, had accessed my file roughly two months ago, three days before the Blacksea mission.

I reared back in surprise. I'd never met Graham or gathered intel on any targets he'd been sent to eliminate. So why had he pulled up my file?

I kept searching. Graham had viewed my personnel file as well as several reports I'd written about various terrorists and criminals, but he hadn't made any notes, so there was no way to know exactly what he'd been looking at or why—

"What are you doing?"

I managed to hold back my shriek of surprise, although I couldn't stop from jumping in my chair. Some spy I was, letting someone sneak up on me. I thought about minimizing my screen but decided against it. That would only make me look guiltier than the jumping already had.

Miriam leaned down, hanging her arms over our shared cubicle wall and making the thin gold bangles on her wrists *clink-clink-clink* together like wind chimes. "You're in early."

"So are you." I eyed her green silk blouse and dark jeans, the same outfit she'd had on at lunch yesterday. "Or is this just the end of your very late night?"

She grinned. "Something like that."

"Another lovefest with your mystery man boy toy?"

Her grin widened, and she straightened up, raised her arms over her head, and stretched like a cat. I half expected her to start purring in obvious satisfaction.

"Something like that," Miriam repeated, then dropped her arms and gestured at my laptop. "What are you doing?"

"Just checking on something."

She frowned. "But I thought you already turned in the Hyde report."

Had I mentioned that at lunch yesterday? I was always working on some report, but I didn't usually divulge the name to Miriam unless it dovetailed with something she was working on. Either way, I shrugged off her question.

"I just wanted to double-check something."

Miriam rolled her eyes, but she grinned again. "And that's the Charlotte I know—exceedingly thorough."

"Something like that." I parroted her earlier words.

Miriam's phone beeped. She pulled it out of her pocket and frowned at the screen.

"Problems?"

"Oh, the diplomat's wife is a bit clingier than I expected. She keeps texting me, whining about her scumbag husband," Miriam murmured in a distracted voice, her thumbs flying over the screen. "Anyway, I need to get showered and changed. Later."

She gave me a distracted wave and walked away, still focused on her phone.

I waited until she left the bullpen, then stared at my own screen again. It was almost nine now, which meant the other analysts would be coming in soon. Frustration filled me that I hadn't learned more, especially about who might want me dead and why, but at least now I had a better understanding of who Desmond was.

I started to log out of the Mockingbird account, but I hesitated and returned to Desmond's file—specifically the photo of him clutching Graham's body.

The longer I looked at the image, the brighter the burn of blue became in Desmond's eyes, like pinprick flames about to cause my whole screen to catch fire. I didn't know if the color was my synesthesia at work or just my own vivid imagination.

I shivered and closed the photo. Desmond might be a fellow Section agent, but I didn't want to gawk at his pain any longer. Still, I couldn't quite push the image out of my mind—or stop worrying about how the cleaner's rage might impact me.

SIX

CHARLOTTE

I spent the rest of the morning working. I might have finished the Henrika Hyde report, but I always had more bad guys to track. Besides, sticking to my usual routine was the smartest—and probably safest—thing to do.

Someone at Section might want me dead, but I doubted they would be bold enough to try to murder me at my desk. Despite his seemingly innocuous note, there had been no sign of Desmond, and no one had come to whisk me away to an interrogation room to question me about Rosalita and the other dead cleaners. In some ways, it was like last night's attack had never happened—

"Charlotte! Hey, Charlotte!" a low, masculine voice called out, startling me out of my troubling reverie.

I looked over my shoulder. Trevor Donnelly, the charmer supervisor, was standing outside his office at the back wall of the bullpen.

I wasn't the only one who perked up at his voice. Ronaldo, Helga, Mika, and Kaimbe all turned around in their seats and started glancing back and forth between the two of us.

"What does he want?" Miriam murmured, sitting at her desk beside mine.

"He's probably just checking on the report I sent him yesterday."

Trevor had seemed a bit more impressed with my work than Gregory Jensen, but Trevor was swamped trying to oversee his own agents along with Jensen's, and he would most likely just rubber-stamp the Hyde report and say that no further action needed to be taken at this time.

"Charlotte!" Trevor repeated. "In my office!"

He waved at me, then stepped back inside the glassed-in space. I stood up, grabbed a pen and a notepad off my desk, and headed in that direction. I strode past the other cubicles, but my coworkers had already returned to their own work, so they ignored me.

I walked toward Trevor's office at a steady pace, but my mind kicked into overdrive, as various worries, fears, and scenarios zipped through my brain. Trevor probably wanted to talk about the Hyde report, but what if this was about the cleaner attack? I wouldn't put it past the Section higher-ups to pretend like everything was fine in hopes of lulling me into a false sense of security before they dropped the proverbial hammer on my head. Even though I had been attacked, more often than not it was guilty until proven innocent here, and more than one agent had vanished into a deep, dark Section hole, never to be seen or heard from again.

Even though he had summoned me, I still knocked politely on the open glass door. Trevor waved me inside, and I sank into one of the two chairs in front of his desk. He had already taken his own seat on the opposite side of the desk, which featured several inches of papers haphazardly shoved into brightly colored folders.

Trevor Donnelly was in his mid-forties with ruddy, freckled skin, light brown eyes, and wavy black hair generously sprinkled with silver. He was wearing a dark gray suit with a matching shirt and tie. No surprise, given his status as a former cleaner. Both his jacket and his shirt strained to cover his chest, which was all hard, ropy muscle, thanks to his vigorous running regimen. Trevor might not be killing people anymore, but he was in as good a shape as any active cleaner.

He was also an enduro, a paramortal with incredible endurance. Thanks to his magic, Trevor could run for miles, fight for hours, or surveil a target for days without needing to stop, sleep, or take any sort of break. His magic also probably served him well in his current office job, given the mountain of paperwork cluttering his desk. My father had also been an enduro, and I had a touch of that magic myself, although it seemed to help me concentrate, more than anything else.

Despite the fact that he was only about ten years older than us, Miriam often referred to Trevor as a silver fox. I didn't see it, but he had an easy smile and a low, soft voice that gave him a likable, mellow vibe. He also wasn't a pompous, overbearing, know-it-all jackass like Jensen had been, and he didn't berate me and mock my work at every turn, which were two definite points in his favor.

"Give me a minute. I need to send one more email..." he murmured.

Trevor started typing, so I studied his desk. Grandma Jane had always said you could learn a lot about a person just by looking at their personal effects. In addition to the mounds of papers and folders, a framed photo was perched on his desk of Trevor with a beautiful woman I assumed was his wife and a teenage boy with a sullen expression who had to be his son. The picture surprised me, since office gossip claimed that Trevor was going through a nasty divorce. Maybe he hadn't gotten around to disposing of the picture yet—or at least cutting his soon-to-be ex-wife out of the image.

My gaze flicked over the other items on his desk. A wooden paperweight shaped like a giant sneaker. Pens jumbled together in a mug bearing a logo for a recent 10K run. A half-eaten protein bar sitting on a white napkin. A sports drink with condensation sliding down the side of the can. A round crystal candy dish filled with individually wrapped pepper-mints, chocolates, caramels, and sticks of gum. Nothing too interesting or exciting.

I clutched my pen and notepad on my lap and tried to look unconcerned, even as my mind churned. This was most likely about the Hyde report, but if Trevor sucker-punched me and started asking questions about last night, then I needed to be ready. The best course of action would probably be to play dumb and claim I had never seen Rosalita and the other cleaners. I doubted Section could prove otherwise, since there were no traffic or security cameras around the Moondust Diner or on the street outside my apartment building.

When in doubt, keep your mouth shut, Grandma Jane's voice whispered in my mind. *If you absolutely have to talk, don't be stupid enough to lie. Instead, tell just enough of the truth to keep yourself alive.*

Grandma Jane had excelled at Section mind games, office politics, and telling people *exactly* what they wanted to hear. Even though she hadn't had the charisma magic for it, I had always thought she should have been a charmer instead of an analyst. In some ways, Grandma Jane's lessons about how to deal with people had been far more useful than anything my father had taught me about how to physically defend myself.

Trevor clicked his mouse, then leaned back in his chair and gave me a sheepish smile. "Sorry about that. But you know how it is. Everyone wants everything done right this second."

"No problem."

"I'm also sorry we haven't had a chance to chat about your work, but I'm handling Jensen's caseload until they get another analyst supervisor in here, and things have been crazy." He swept his hand over the mounds of papers and folders on his desk.

"No problem," I repeated.

Trevor nodded. "But something's come up, and I wanted you to hear it from me first."

My stomach clenched. This was it. The start of all the questions about last night that I didn't know how to answer—

"You've been reassigned."

Surprise spiked through me, and I gulped down the denial dangling on the tip of my tongue. "Reassigned?"

He nodded again. "Yes. As of this morning."

"To which department?"

Trevor looked past me, smiled, and waved. Annoyance filled me that I didn't have his full attention because he certainly had mine. I started to glance over my shoulder to see who he was waving at, but Trevor fixed his gaze on me again.

"Downstairs. To the fifth floor. With the liaisons."

"Wait. What?"

I was an analyst. I had *always* been an analyst, and I should have been getting bumped up to a senior position here on the third floor, not transferred to a completely different level. Oh, it wasn't unheard of for analysts and charmers to be loaned out to other departments, but it didn't happen all that often, and it had certainly never happened to *me* before.

"Well, it's not my place to reveal the details," Trevor said in his mellow voice. "The folks down on five will fill you in. All I can say is that you've been reassigned to participate in an active mission."

I nodded, as though this was perfectly normal. But me? Participate in an active mission? Analysts, well, *analyzed.* They safely spied on bad guys from afar. They didn't usually do field work, which was one of the main reasons I'd decided to become an analyst in the first place. I had wanted to be as far away from the action—*danger*—as possible. Thanks to my father, I had been exposed to more terrorists and criminals during my childhood than I cared to remember. But now, despite all my efforts to insulate and protect myself from that world, it seemed as though someone had booked me a ticket on an express train right back to Dangerville.

A knock sounded on the open glass door behind me, drawing Trevor's attention. He smiled and waved again. "There you are. Come on in. I was just telling Charlotte about her new assignment."

"Good," a familiar voice sounded. "I wouldn't want to miss that."

His low, amused tone curled around my chest like a boa constrictor, squeezing the breath out of my lungs, even as it filled my heart with even more worry and dread.

Desmond strolled into the office, grabbed the other chair in front of Trevor's desk, and angled it toward me. Then he gracefully dropped into the seat and gave me a wide, knowing smile.

"Hello, Charlotte," he purred. "It's so nice to finally meet you."

Surprised. Flummoxed. Bamboozled. Incredulous.

No, I decided. *Stupefied.* That was the only word that adequately described how I was feeling.

Out of all the things that could have happened, Desmond strolling into Trevor's office and sitting down right beside me had not been on my exceedingly long list of paranoid worries.

But here he was, smiling like nothing was wrong and he hadn't killed four other cleaners last night. I thought of that sticky note he'd left in my apartment.

See you tomorrow.

Well, at least now I knew what he'd meant. I had been right before. He was most definitely a psycho.

Desmond's smile widened, and his silver-blue eyes actually *twinkled*, almost as if he could hear and was highly amused by my turbulent thoughts. His smug expression burned through my stupefied state, and anger exploded like a grenade in my chest. I didn't know what was going on, but I would *not* allow him to use or humiliate me, or jeopardize my position and career at Section.

He wanted to play mind games? Well, buckle up, Buttercup. Because I could throw down with the best of them, cleaner or otherwise.

"And you are?" I asked in a cool voice, matching his supposed politeness and pretending like I had never seen him before.

Surprise flickered in his eyes, although it vanished in an instant. "Desmond."

He held out his hand, and I had no choice but to shake it. His fingers were warm, firm, and strong against my own, which felt like brittle chunks of clammy ice. One wrong move, one wrong word, and my cool façade would shatter to pieces.

Desmond held on to my hand a few more seconds than was polite, although he didn't do the macho alpha thing and squeeze my fingers to prove how much physically stronger he was. If he had, I would have dug my nails into his skin in my own alpha show of strength.

He stared at me the whole time, and I did the same thing to him. Once again, I felt like we were engaged in some childish staring contest. Only this time, I had the small satisfaction of seeing him blink and look away first. He dropped my hand, and I resisted the urge to wipe the feel of his skin off on my cargo pants.

Desmond was once again wearing a light gray suit, although he had left his jacket somewhere, revealing the vest and matching shirt underneath. His wing tips were an expected glossy black, although his tie was once again that bright, rebellious powder-blue and patterned with small silver dots. I tried not to notice how perfectly the color matched his eyes. Instead, I focused on the watch nestled in his vest pocket. No blood stained the timepiece, and the silver links gleamed brightly, as though its chain had been recently polished. He probably shined it up after each and every kill. Oh, yes. Complete and utter psycho.

Trevor beamed at the two of us. "Excellent! I always think it's more comfortable for folks to meet like this before everyone gets down to business."

"What do you mean?" I asked, even though I had a sinking feeling I knew exactly where this was going.

Trevor gestured at the cleaner. "Well, again, I can't get into mission specifics right now, but, Charlotte, you've been assigned to be Desmond's liaison."

Even though I'd been expecting the words, they still punched me in the throat, and I had a sudden urge to vomit. My gaze snapped back to Desmond, who gave me another smug smile. A second, larger grenade of anger exploded in my chest, burning away my nausea. He thought he could just waltz in here and get me to do his bidding? Not a chance.

"Well, Desmond, as nice as it is to make your acquaintance, I think there's been some mistake."

He arched a golden eyebrow. "Really? Why is that?"

"Because I'm an analyst, not a liaison. Surely, there are other people at Section who are better qualified to assist with your...*mission*."

We both knew I was really talking about his twisted agenda regarding me. Trevor frowned and looked back and forth between us, not quite sure what was going on. Well, that made two of us.

"No mistake," Desmond chirped in a cheery tone. "I asked for you specifically, Charlotte."

"Yes, I got the email from your father a few minutes ago," Trevor chimed in. "Do me a favor, Dez, and put in a good word for me with old man Percy. I could really use a raise."

Trevor snickered at his lame joke, but Desmond was not amused. The cleaner frowned at Trevor, who winced, as though he suddenly realized he'd said something he shouldn't have.

I seized on the name Trevor had mentioned. "Old man Percy? As in General Jethro Pearson Percy? On the Section board of directors?"

Desmond grimaced and shifted in his seat, not nearly as smug as before. "Yes."

I kept my face blank, although I couldn't help but wish that the floor would open up and swallow me whole. This just kept getting worse and worse.

I might be a Legacy, but the Percy family was the closest thing Section 47 had to royalty. The Percy family had been one of the driving forces behind the formation of Section in the nineteen forties, and various members had been involved in its operations ever since. I thought of all those military-school records in Desmond's file. He hadn't been brought up to be just a common cleaner—he'd been groomed since birth to carry on the Percy family tradition at Section.

I eyed his blond hair, blue eyes, and handsome features. Not just any Percy. "You're Jethro Percy's son," I spat out.

"Yes." Desmond's face hardened at my cold, clipped tone. "And you're Jack Locke's daughter."

The words—and the old, ugly accusations that went along with them—landed in between us like a ton of invisible bricks. Our fathers had absolutely *despised* each other. Hatfields and McCoys, Montagues and Capulets, and other feuding families, both real and fictional, had gotten along swimmingly compared to Jethro Percy and Jack Locke.

More than once, my father had come home from a mission ranting and raving about how *that idiot Percy* had screwed up this or that, or how the General had put his political, financial, and other ambitions above what was best for Section agents and the innocent people they were supposed to protect. Not to mention everything that had happened on my father's last, ill-fated mission in Mexico.

And now here I was, sitting next to Percy's son, who seemed determined to screw me over just as badly as his father had mine.

"Listen, I know your two families have some…history," Trevor said, trying to play peacemaker.

Desmond and I both shot him icy glares.

Trevor cleared his throat and tried again. "But the fact is that this mission requires both of your expertise."

"And what expertise would that be?" I asked through clenched teeth.

He gave me an apologetic look, but he didn't answer my question. "Now that Charlotte has been informed of her change in assignment, the two of you need to head down to the fifth floor for the initial mission briefing. Dez, maybe we can catch up later? And raise a glass to Graham? One last toast for the Three Musketeers?"

A muscle ticked in Desmond's jaw, but he nodded. "Sure."

Three Musketeers? I suddenly remembered another tidbit from Desmond's file—that he, Graham, and Trevor had worked together on several missions, back when Trevor had still been an active cleaner. The three of them must have been much closer than I'd realized, although Trevor didn't seem to know that Desmond and I had met before or anything about the other cleaners attacking me. I wondered why Desmond had kept that info from his fellow Musketeer.

The two men got to their feet and shook hands, and Trevor leaned forward over his desk and thumped a friendly fist against Desmond's shoulder. I also stood up and took a step back, putting some distance between myself and Desmond.

"Okay, then," Trevor said. "See you later."

"Sure," Desmond repeated in a flat, toneless voice. "It'll be great catching up and talking about Graham and the good ole days."

Lie, my inner voice whispered. Not only did my synesthesia let me see errors and mistakes on papers and screens, but I could also hear them, and my magic told me that his dead friend Graham was the very last thing Desmond wanted to discuss. So he was a liar, as well as a manipulator. I would expect nothing less from the spawn of General Jethro Percy.

Desmond turned to me and held out his hand, gesturing at the open glass door. "After you, Ms. Locke."

"Oh, no. After *you*, Mr. Percy," I replied, my voice just as cool as his was.

He smirked at me, then strode out of the office. As much as I wanted to ignore him and storm back to my desk, I had been reassigned, and I had no choice but to follow Desmond Percy, most likely to my own doom.

SEVEN

DESMOND

Charlotte Locke hated me.

I couldn't really blame her, given the bad blood between her father and mine, which was mostly my father's fault, due to the General's ruthless tendency to use people for his own personal and political gain. Still, I had been hoping for mild dislike, at worst. What I'd gotten was a look of pure, utter disgust the second she'd realized who my father was.

I had been hoping to keep my family name out of things, but Trevor had slipped up and let the cat out of the bag, which wasn't like him. Maybe it was for the best. Charlotte would have found out I was a Percy sooner or later. It was probably better to get all the hate out in the open right off the bat.

Now, Charlotte was marching along behind me. Thanks to my galvanism, I could feel the waves of emotional energy surging off her, and the heat of her anger blasted against my back like a fiery furnace. Again, I couldn't really blame her, but I had been hoping she would take into account the fact that I had saved her life.

Apparently not.

We left the bullpen, walked down a corridor, and headed toward the elevators. I stepped into one of the cars and stuck out my hand, politely holding the door open. Charlotte eyed me, but she also stepped inside. The door slid shut, and we rode in tense silence down to the fifth floor.

The elevator door dinged open, and Charlotte stormed out into the gray corridor beyond. I followed her and started to head toward the bullpen for the mission briefing, but she latched onto my wrist and yanked me to the left. She was quite a bit stronger than I'd expected, probably from the energy I had fed into her body. Either way, I let her pull me over into a shadowy alcove close to the door that led into the locker room.

Charlotte stopped and released my arm. She glanced around, staring at the gray carpeted floor, the thick concrete columns, and finally up at the ceiling. After a few seconds, she nodded in silent satisfaction.

I glanced around as well, but I didn't see any telltale black domes or blinking red lights or hear any faint hums that would indicate there were any cameras or listening devices nearby. Of course, this was Section 47, so most of the cameras and bugs would be hidden anyway.

I also reached out with my galvanism, scanning the area for sparks, flickers, crackles, and pulses of electricity, but I didn't sense anything in this space, not so much as a voice-activated bug designed to pick up whispered secrets. This was a rare surveillance dead zone inside Section, a place where people could have a private, non-recorded conversation, something Charlotte seemed to know. Clever of her to bring me here.

Then again, Charlotte Locke was most definitely clever.

She crossed her arms over her chest, still clutching the

pen and notepad she'd had in Trevor's office. I wondered what she saw when she looked at me. Probably a younger, fitter, deadlier version of General Jethro Percy, the man who'd gotten her father captured and then killed during a Section mission gone horribly wrong.

As for what I saw when I looked at her, well, the headshot in her Section file hadn't done her justice. The photo hadn't revealed the red highlights in her shoulder-length auburn hair, or what a deep, dark blue her eyes were, or how she smelled sharp, clean, and sweet all at once, like limes mixed with sugar. The picture hadn't given me a sense of her soft Southern drawl, and it especially hadn't indicated how bright, steady, and strong her aura was.

People constantly give off energy, just like phones, computers, and spy cameras do, and I could see that power as easily as I could spot the physical glow from a bare bulb. Sometimes, people's auras appeared to me as colorful lights, a flare of green or a spark of gold centered on their hearts. Other times, it was more of a feeling, of hot anger or sweeping passion or slimy envy, emanating from their bodies. Whether it was a color, a feeling, or something else, as a galvanist I could manipulate that human energy, adding to it as I'd done by healing Charlotte, or turning it off completely and killing a person the same way I could snap off a light switch on the wall.

Charlotte's aura was the same deep, dark blue as her eyes, and it gleamed around her heart as though she had a sapphire brooch pinned to her chest. Even though she was angry, Charlotte's aura also radiated a crisp coolness, like the air on a brisk fall morning. The soothing sensation took me by surprise, as did how much I enjoyed it. Maybe this was just another one of my *flights of fancy*, as my father would snidely, brusquely say. Or perhaps I was just tired, after everything that had happened with Graham, and looking for any comfort I could find, even in this woman who so obviously hated me.

That must have been it. I was tired—so damn *tired*—but I couldn't rest until I'd found and killed Adrian Anatoly. I owed it to Graham and everyone else who had died on the Blacksea mission, and *nothing* was going to stop me from achieving my goal. Not my father, not Section rules and regulations, and especially not the angry woman standing in front of me.

"What do you think you're doing?" Charlotte hissed.

Once she'd gotten over her initial shock at seeing me again and realizing exactly who I was, she had been all ice in Trevor's office. I'd been impressed by how quickly she had switched gears. Most people probably would have started blubbering about how four cleaners had tried to kill them, but not Charlotte Locke. Instead, she'd matched me move for move and hadn't revealed anything to Trevor about our two previous encounters. But now that initial ice had cracked away, revealing the fire underneath—far more fire than I had expected.

Then again, I was rapidly coming to the conclusion that I should *always* expect the unexpected when it came to Charlotte Locke.

She kept glaring at me, clearly wanting an answer. I shrugged. She wasn't the only one who could be cool and inscrutable.

"I'm not doing anything."

"Other than following me, killing people, and not telling your buddy Trevor about either one."

"I think you mean watching out for and saving your life. You're welcome, by the way."

Her thumb curled over the pen still clutched in her hand, and I got the distinct impression she wanted to stab me in the eye with it. She could probably do it. She had almost cut down that female cleaner with a broken beer bottle. I'd have to be careful to stay out of range if she ever had a real weapon in her hand.

"I'll ask you again, Dundee—why are you here, and what do you want?"

"You heard what Trevor said—you're to be my liaison for an upcoming mission."

Her eyes narrowed. "What mission? Who's the target?"

This was the tricky part. There actually *was* a mission, and I really did need Charlotte's help with the target. But I also had my own private agenda that Section didn't—*couldn't*—know anything about.

Charlotte would learn the details at the briefing, but I decided to tell her a few pertinent facts right now. Perhaps sharing some information would get her to trust me, just a little bit.

"Henrika Hyde," I replied. "She's the target, and you seem to know more about her than anyone else here. That's why I asked for you as my liaison."

"Henrika Hyde *is* a monster," Charlotte muttered, a note of reluctant agreement in her voice. "She needs to be stopped before she creates some new biomagical weapon that's even more horrible than her current inventions."

"At last, something we both agree on."

Charlotte ignored my sarcasm. "I've been telling Jensen that for weeks now." She grimaced. "At least, I *told* Jensen that before his accident. He agreed with me enough to pass off my work as his own, but I doubt anyone else ever read my original reports."

Ah, but that was the problem and the reason I was here. Someone else *had* read her reports—Graham Walker, my cleaner partner and best friend.

Graham had always been a total geek for anything analytical, and he read reports from Section stations just for fun and to decompress after missions. When the two of us had first been tasked with finding and killing Adrian Anatoly, Graham had started reading even more reports, cross-referencing them and looking for every scrap of information on Anatoly he could dig up, anything that would help us hunt down and kill the terrorist.

And he'd finally found something.

A few days before the Blacksea mission, Graham had told me about a report from a D.C. analyst linking the United Corporation, one of Anatoly's known shell companies, to a biomagical weapons maker named Henrika Hyde. Before Graham could follow up on the report, we'd gotten intel that Anatoly was hiding on an island off the Australian coast, and Section had sent us after him.

Among his many, many crimes, Adrian Anatoly had bombed a tourist market in Sydney six months ago, killing more than twenty people and injuring dozens of others. After that incident, Section had dispatched Norris and Stinson, two other cleaners, to eliminate the terrorist, although Anatoly and his men had turned the tables and managed to kill the cleaners instead.

That should have been our first clue there was a mole inside Section, although my respect for and friendship with Norris and Stinson had blinded me to that fact. I'd just wanted Anatoly dead, but Graham had been a little more curious and far more cautious, the way he always was, and he had started investigating Norris's and Stinson's deaths, although he hadn't gotten far. Still, we'd both been happy when Anatoly was finally located, and our mission had been equal parts righteousness and revenge.

Until it had all gone horribly, horribly wrong.

Just thinking about the mission took me back to that day. In an instant, everything around me vanished, and I felt like I was wandering through the macabre museum of my own mind, staring at the garishly colored paintings on the walls, the gruesome images that were forever burned into my brain.

The pristine white sand melted into crunchy black glass from the force, fire, and fury of the IED explosions. The lower part of Graham's leg separated from the rest of his body and sticking up at an impossible angle. The whites of Graham's eyes standing out in stark contrast against the rest of his red, ruined face. My hands digging into Graham's shoulders, dragging him away from the worst of the flames, my fingers covered with bright, fat, red, raw blisters and burns that made them looked like stewed sausages.

There was sound too, as though I were wearing headphones and listening to a tour guide talk me through that museum of horrors. Only it was Graham, urgently whispering to me in between choked coughs and wheezing breaths.

It's okay, Dez. You'll get the bastard... Read the reports. Talk to Charlotte Locke... Work it from the other end. Anatoly can't hide forever, and neither can whoever sold us out to him...

More sounds filled my ears. The lingering buzz from the explosions. The faint *slap-slap-slap* of the ocean waves against the scorched shore. My own hoarse, raspy voice, telling Graham it was going to be okay, over and over again, even though we both knew it was a lie. That the support staff was dead and no one was coming to help us anytime soon.

But perhaps the thing I remembered most vividly was the absolute lack of energy. No electrical currents, no phones, not even the faint auras of the fish in the ocean. Everything close to shore had been decimated and blown away by the IEDs, and I had never experienced such utter *stillness* before. I felt like my magic had been blown off just as Graham's leg had been, and the cold, sickening knowledge filled me that I wouldn't be able to use my power to save us, not this time…

"Are you okay?" Charlotte's voice cut through my miserable tour of memories and snapped me back to the here and now.

I found myself focusing on the jeweled aura pulsing around her heart, and I swayed a little closer, just breathing in the cool blue of her.

Charlotte stared at me, clearly wondering what I was doing, but she held her ground. I got the feeling she didn't back down from anyone, not even a cleaner like me.

"So you've been assigned to go after Henrika Hyde," she said. "Why?"

"Because she's a menace, a biomagical weapons maker who delights in inventing new and gruesome ways to murder innocent people."

"No, that's why Section wants to go after her. Why do *you* want her so badly?"

I shrugged. "No other reason. It's a mission, pure and simple, the same as any other."

"Lie," Charlotte snapped.

I had always prided myself on being an excellent liar, especially when it came to Section business. As a cleaner, I spent a lot of time undercover, getting close to my targets, so lying was part of my job, a necessary skill that helped keep me alive. Even if I hadn't been a cleaner, I still would have been good at lying. The General had been giving me a master class in the arts of treachery and deception my whole life.

"Let's try something simpler. Why did you come over to me in the cafeteria yesterday?" Charlotte asked. "Why not just tell me what you wanted instead of hitting on me?"

I had no intention of revealing the fact that I had been fishing for information on Henrika Hyde. "It seemed better to ease you into the idea of working with me, especially given the history between our fathers."

"Lie," she snapped again.

I resisted the urge to grind my teeth together. How was she doing that?

Her eyes narrowed. "Is this some weird sex thing? Do you get your rocks off having women under your thumb? Some liaisons might offer a full range of *services* to their cleaners, but I'm not going to fuck you, if that's what this is about."

Anger shot through me, and I stepped forward. Charlotte held her ground again, glaring right back at me.

"First of all, I would *never* touch a woman like that without her express permission," I said in a cold voice.

Something flickered in her eyes, and she jerked her head in a short, sharp nod, as though she suddenly believed me, just like that.

"And second, don't flatter yourself. You're not my type, Numbers."

"Don't call me that."

"*Numbers?* Why not? I think it fits you beautifully."

And it truly did. Graham might have read Section reports for fun, but he had his favorite analysts the way that regular folks had fiction authors. He had raved about how detailed and thorough Charlotte's reports always were, along with being absolutely free of typos. I thought he even had a bit of an intellectual crush on her, even though the two of them had never met.

After Graham's death, I had read her reports too. Every single one from the past year. I didn't understand half of what was in them, especially not the pages and pages of spreadsheets and numbers, but it was obvious Charlotte Locke knew her stuff. And now, being face to face with her, I could *feel* the energy pulsing off that big brain of hers, and I could see the calculations going on behind her eyes as she analyzed, measured, and weighed everyone and everything around her.

"Listen to me, Dundee," she snapped. "You might fool your buddy Trevor Donnelly and everyone else at Section, but you will never, ever fool *me*. So either come clean and tell me why you're really here and exactly what you want, or I walk."

"You can't do that."

She arched an eyebrow. "Why? Because you're a cleaner? A Percy? Or because you mistakenly think you have some kind of power over me?"

"Because you've been assigned to be my liaison. It's a plum job. You turn that down, and we both know that you're done at Section. They'll boot you out on your ass before you even have time to pack up your desk. And given your empty apartment and that charming man you met with at the diner last night, I'm guessing you desperately need your Section job and the steady paycheck that comes along with it to get yourself out of whatever trouble you're in."

Something that looked like weary agreement flickered across her face, although her anger quickly drowned it out. "Fuck off, Dundee."

Her aura blazed an even brighter blue, and the hot energy blasting off her told me that she meant every word she said. Despite her troubles, Charlotte Locke was pissed enough to walk away, no matter what the consequences might be to her

Section career or her own personal self. I admired her for that, even if she was mucking up my plans.

She whirled around to storm away, but I reached out and caught the edge of her gray cardigan sleeve. Not touching her, just the fabric. She might be angry and stubborn, but I wasn't giving up. I would *never* give up until I had avenged Graham.

Charlotte jerked away, but she faced me again.

"You can't walk away," I repeated.

"Why not?"

"Because, in case you've forgotten, someone sent four cleaners to kill you."

A muscle ticked in her jaw at the unpleasant reminder, and she couldn't quite hide the worry that filled her face. She shook her head, as if pushing away the emotion. "And how do I know it wasn't *you*? That you saving me wasn't just some elaborate plot to lure me over to your dark side?"

I barked out a laugh. "Wow, you are really paranoid, aren't you? Even I'm not that devious and diabolical."

"Anyone can be that devious and diabolical, if they put their mind to it."

I didn't—*couldn't*—contradict her. Thanks to the General, I knew *exactly* how deceptive and dangerous people could be, especially your supposed loved ones. "Devious or not, the fact remains that someone sent four cleaners to kill you, so they'll probably try again."

More agreement filled her face. "Do you know who wants me dead? Or why?"

I chose my words carefully. "It probably has something to do with your reports on Henrika Hyde. That's the main thing you've been working on lately, right?"

It most likely had *everything* to do with her reports, and that tenuous connection she'd found between Henrika and Anatoly, but I didn't tell her that. Not yet. I didn't want to bias her with my own opinions, especially when I needed her to look for more connections between the two of them. I shouldn't have said as much as I did, but Charlotte nodded, and some of the anger and suspicion leaked out of her face.

"You think it's someone inside Section—a mole here in the D.C. station. It's the only conclusion that makes sense. Someone saw my reports. They didn't like what they read, and they tipped off Henrika. Then they—or Henrika—sent those cleaners to eliminate me." She paused. "And most likely Jensen too. He's the only other person who looked at my reports on a regular basis, and he was always taking credit for my work. The mole must have mistakenly thought that Jensen was the one on Henrika's trail, which means his bicycle accident probably wasn't an accident at all."

She seemed to be thinking aloud and talking to herself rather than to me, so I didn't interrupt her. Besides, I didn't know who Jensen was, and if he was already dead, then he didn't matter right now.

Charlotte stared at me, once again analyzing, measuring, and weighing me with her sharp, critical gaze. "Tell me you had nothing to do with the cleaner attack last night. Say the words, or I walk."

I didn't know why that was so important to her, but I said the words. "I had nothing to do with the cleaners who attacked you last night."

"Truth," she whispered.

Her shoulders sagged with something that might have been relief, or maybe disappointment. I couldn't quite tell, but she sighed and stared at me again.

"What, exactly, are you proposing?"

I had to stop myself from pumping my fist in the air in triumph. "It seems to me that you, Charlotte Locke, are in desperate need of a bodyguard."

"And you're volunteering for the job?" she asked in a snide tone.

"Volunteering? Why, I'd say that I've already passed the audition and landed the gig, given what happened last night."

She snorted, but she didn't disagree. Instead, her gaze dropped to my chest and locked on to the silver watch tucked in my vest pocket. My grandfather Percival's watch. I never went anywhere without it.

"You saw me in action last night. You saw what I can do. Deep down, I think you know you have a better chance of getting to the bottom of things and staying alive with me than you do on your own," I said, sensing an opportunity to sway her to my so-called dark side. "No matter what you think of me or my father, I will do my very best to keep you safe. You can count on that."

Even as I said the words, I couldn't help but think they were a damn, dirty lie. I hadn't saved Graham, my best friend, the person I trusted most in the world.

Instead, I had killed him.

"Truth," Charlotte whispered again.

She shivered and hugged her arms around herself. Charlotte realized I was watching her, and she dropped her hands to her sides, although her fingers were still curled around her pen and notepad, as though they were anchors steadying her.

"So I get your protection and cleaner skills. What do you get in return?" she asked in a wary voice.

I held out my index finger and made a circular motion with it. "I get that big brain of yours, Numbers. I get your expertise on Henrika Hyde and anyone and everyone she deals with. Plus, we both think that someone inside the D.C. station is dirty. So you watch my back, and I'll watch yours until Henrika is captured or killed, and we figure out who the mole is."

I didn't say anything about Graham, the Blacksea mission, or my search for Anatoly. Charlotte didn't need to know about any of that, especially not my failure to protect my best friend.

She kept staring at me, once again doing those mental calculations in her mind, like there was a gymnast frantically tumbling from one side of her brain to the other and back again. I didn't want her to think too long, especially not about the many holes in my story, so I held out my hand.

"Do we have a deal?"

Charlotte stared at my fingers like they were scorpions about to lash out and sting her. "A Locke willingly working with a Percy inside Section 47. I never thought this day would come," she muttered.

"Neither did I, but here we are. So do we have a deal or not?"

"One condition."

"What?"

"Don't lie to me. *Never*. Not the first time, not the smallest fib. I'll know if you do. Trust me on that."

Her aura pulsed a bright blue, indicating she meant what she said. I once again wondered how she seemed to know my outright lies from the half-truths I was telling her and everyone else.

"No lies. Agreed." I raised my hand a little higher. "Deal?"

She sighed again, but she put her hand in mine. "Deal."

Together, we shook on our bargain.

EIGHT

CHARLOTTE

Desmond Percy wasn't telling me everything.

He wasn't even telling me *half* of everything.

The cleaner probably thought he was being smooth, suave, and charming, complimenting my intelligence and flattering my ego by claiming he needed my help with the mission. Parts of what he was saying were absolutely true. But thanks to my synesthesia, I could see the half-truths dropping from his lips like pink diamonds spewing out of his mouth and clattering to the floor, and my inner voice kept whispering *danger-danger-danger*.

Oh, yes. Desmond Percy wasn't telling me everything, and he was definitely using me for something. I just didn't know what that *something* was yet.

Then again, I was using him too. Like it or not, Desmond was right. Someone had sent four cleaners to kill me, and it was just a matter of time before they tried again. He was also right about my having a far better chance of surviving with him than on my own, especially given how easily he'd dispatched my attackers last night.

So, like it or not, I was stuck with Desmond Percy, and him with me, until this thing—whatever it truly was—was finished one way or another. I just hoped it wouldn't be the death of us both. And that we managed to refrain from murdering each other in the meantime.

After we shook on our uneasy alliance, I followed him out of the dead-spot alcove, and we headed toward the operations hub in the center of the fifth floor. Desmond pulled a keycard out of his pants pocket, waved it in front of a reader, and held open the glass door.

He gestured with his hand. "After you, Numbers."

"Why, thank you, Dundee."

His eyes narrowed, and we glared at each other before I moved past him, and he let the door swing shut behind us.

We went down a short hallway, then stepped into another bullpen that was a carbon copy of the one on the third floor—clear plastic cubicles manned by a variety of people, a wide walkway running down the center, and a large conference room nestled in between a couple of glassed-in offices set into the back wall.

Cleaners in their ubiquitous dark suits sat at desks on the left side of the center aisle, while their liaisons were perched in their own spaces on the right side. Even assassins couldn't escape filing Section reports, and most people were typing away on their laptops, while a few murmured softly into their landlines.

I had only been down to the fifth-floor bullpen a few times during my Section career, and only then to personally deliver a file that someone wanted ASAP, so I'd forgotten about the perpetual hush that filled the air and the stiff tension that radiated off everyone. This was where missions were put into action and decisions were made about who lived—and who was eliminated.

"This way," Desmond said.

He strode over to the cleaners' side of the room, and I followed him to a desk situated in the back row of cubicles. An open laptop perched on the desk, along with several papers and folders, while a closed, light gray leather briefcase was sitting underneath on the floor next to a metal trash can. Draped over the back of an office chair hung a light gray jacket that matched the rest of his dapper suit.

Desmond's desk was even more barren and impersonal than mine was. The only truly interesting and unusual item was a small sketchpad, with a blue ink pen stuck through the spiral wires at the top, although he flipped the pad over before I could see what he'd been drawing.

He pointed at a desk directly across the aisle from his on the liaison side of the room. "That will be your workspace."

The desk was completely empty, and not so much as a stray paper clip or a wayward staple dotted its blank surface. I had been so angry and distracted when we had left Trevor's office that I hadn't thought to grab my laptop, so I set my pen and notepad down on the desk. Somehow, the two small items made the space look even emptier and more depressing.

Desmond futzed around his own desk, shuffling papers and folders back and forth. I didn't know what to do, so I just stood there next to him, shifting on my feet like an idiot.

A woman was sitting at the desk directly in front of mine. She must have sensed my awkward hovering because she swiveled around in her chair, stood up, and crossed her arms over her chest, looking me up and down.

The woman was quite pretty, with rosy skin and long, glossy black hair that was curled into loose waves. Smoky shadow accentuated her light blue eyes, while pale pink gloss coated her lips. She was wearing a stylish dark gray pantsuit, along with sky-high black heels that added a few more inches to her petite frame.

"So this is Charlotte Locke," the woman said in a cold, flat voice.

Desmond grimaced, but he set down his papers and folders, stepped into the aisle, and made the introductions. "Charlotte, this is Joan Samson, one of Section's top liaisons. Joan, this is Charlotte, an analyst from the third floor."

Joan and I had been in the same rookie class, so I knew who she was, and I flipped through my mental dossiers, trying to remember everything I could about her. The Samsons were another Legacy family, just like the Lockes and the Percys, and Joan had a stellar reputation. She made sure that the missions she was assigned to ran smoothly and that the cleaners she assisted eliminated their targets in efficient, timely manners. She was also a transmuter, someone who could transform the physical properties of an element or object, such as changing water into ice or turning a cotton ball as hard as concrete, with just a wave of her hand.

"Nice to see you again." I held out my hand, which she gave a short, perfunctory shake.

Joan shot Desmond a disgusted look, then spun around on her heel and strode away, leaving the bullpen without a backward glance.

"What's her problem?" I asked.

Desmond sighed. "She wanted to be my liaison for this mission."

"So why isn't she?"

Joan Samson *should* have been his liaison, since she knew exactly what she was doing, unlike me, who was floundering around in the dark.

A shadow passed over Desmond's face. "Because I promised a friend that I would keep her out of this."

Truth, my inner voice whispered. I wondered if that friend had been Graham. I made a mental note to dig deeper into the dead cleaner's background as well as Joan Samson's past. My grandmother had fully believed in the old cliché that knowledge is power, but in this case, my survival would most likely depend on my knowing all the players as well as the dangerous, duplicitous games they were playing with one another.

"So you didn't want to drag Joan into this, but you're okay with me taking part in it?" I didn't bother to keep the snide tone out of my voice. "Exactly how dangerous is this mission of yours going to be?"

Desmond opened his mouth, probably to give me some glib answer, but he stopped, as if remembering his earlier promise not to lie to me. "I told you before, Numbers. I need your help with Henrika Hyde."

Another truth, but also a vague statement devoid of any real specifics about what his agenda truly was—and he *definitely* had an agenda. Trevor had mentioned he'd gotten an email from General Percy, and from what little Desmond himself had revealed, it seemed as though he had pulled some serious strings to get me assigned as his liaison. You didn't go to that much trouble to take down some random bad guy. No, this had to be deeply personal, and I was guessing it had everything to do with the doomed Blacksea mission and his buddy Graham's death.

Desmond stepped back over to his desk and started shuffling papers and folders around again. A couple of the other liaisons and cleaners glanced over their shoulders, giving us both curious looks. I didn't want to keep standing there like an idiot, so I plopped down into the chair at my own barren desk, leaned back, and stared up at the black domed security camera embedded in the ceiling.

I sighed, put my feet on the floor, and pushed off, making my chair revolve in a slow, creaky circle, spinning around and around, and going nowhere fast.

Ten minutes later, Joan Samson strode back into the bullpen, followed by Diego Benito, one of the resident genius IT techs.

With his short brown hair, bronze skin, and dark brown eyes, I'd always thought Diego was among the cuter of Miriam's many office exes. Unlike Joan and everyone else on this floor in their power suits, Diego was dressed down in a light green button-up shirt, a pair of gray khakis, and gray sneakers. Ah, a man after my own heart. At least when it came to his footwear.

I stopped spinning around in my chair and nodded at Diego. "Hey. Did you get roped into this mystery mission too?"

Diego peered at me through his square black glasses and gave me a quick, nervous smile in return. "You could say that."

His hands were curled around his laptop, which he was holding like a shield in front of his chest, as if the thin device would somehow protect him from all the dangerous people here.

A woman strode into the bullpen behind Diego, and everyone, liaisons and cleaners alike, snapped to attention. In an instant, they all stopped what they were doing, sat up straight, and fixed their gazes on her.

The woman had golden skin and black hair styled in an attractive, tousled pixie cut. Only a few wrinkles fanned out around her dark brown eyes, although I knew she was in her sixties, the same age my father would have been, if he had still been alive. She was wearing a scarlet pantsuit, along with black heels, and her only jewelry was a small gold pendant shaped like the letter *G*. Red reading glasses were perched on top of her head, while a thick, red leather folder was nestled in the crook of her left elbow.

Gia Chan was the cleaner supervisor and one of the most dangerous people in Section 47, perhaps in the whole world. She had been a cleaner for years, eliminating scores of para-mortal terrorists and criminals before transitioning over to management. My father had often talked about her, especially her enduro magic, which was even stronger than his own, and they had been on several missions together. Gia was one of the few other cleaners my father had actually respected, and he had told me more than once how smart, skilled, and lethal she was.

Gia stopped in the center of the aisle and surveyed the bullpen like a queen staring out over her loyal, devoted, deadly subjects. Her gaze landed on me for a moment before moving on. "Percy, Samson, Benito, Locke. Mission briefing. Now."

Gia swept past everyone and headed into the conference room. Diego gaped at her, and Joan shepherded him forward. The IT tech clutched his laptop a little tighter to his chest and scurried into the conference room, with Joan trailing along behind him.

Desmond stood up and gestured with his hand. "Shall we?"

I grabbed my pen and notepad, got to my feet, and stepped into the conference room. Desmond shut the door behind us, which locked with a *click*. A soft *buzz* rang out, indicating that the room had also been soundproofed.

We all took seats at the long, rectangular table. Gia sat at the head, naturally, with Joan on her right. Diego sat across from Joan. I took the chair next to him, while Desmond dropped into the one across from mine.

Gia opened her red leather-bound folder and started pulling out papers. "For those of you who are just being read in on this mission, the code name is *Redburn*. Mr. Benito, if you will be so kind as to set up the display so we can get started."

Diego cracked open his laptop and started typing. The overhead lights dimmed, and a screen slid down from the ceiling and covered one of the walls. Diego hit a few more buttons on his laptop, then passed a small black clicker over to Gia, who nodded her thanks.

Gia hit a button, and several photos appeared on the screen, all showing the same person—Henrika Hyde.

I had been tracking Henrika for three months, so I had seen plenty of pictures of her, mostly bland, staged corporate headshots that accompanied the press releases her pharmaceutical company put out from time to time, touting its latest medical breakthrough or charity effort. But these photos were much more candid, showing the biomagical weapons maker at dinners, fund-raisers, and other business and social functions.

Henrika Hyde was forty-five years old, with a tall, toned, lithe body that could have belonged to a professional ballerina. In most of the photos, her light brown hair hung in loose, shoulder-length waves that perfectly framed her beautiful features. Her eyes were as bright and green as the emeralds she loved to wear, while her skin was pale and luminous, thanks to her own ingenuity. In addition to creating biomagical weapons, Henrika had also developed several popular anti-aging serums, creams, and lotions for her company's beauty division. She made almost as many millions from her skin-care products as she did from her horrific weapons.

Henrika Hyde was an actual genius, with a sky-high IQ and degrees in chemical engineering and several other scientific fields. The daughter of a single mother, she'd grown up with nothing in the coalfields of southwest Virginia and had built her company from the ground up. I admired her toughness, tenacity, and the fact that she was a self-made businesswoman, even as I despised the terrible things she had created with her talents.

Perhaps it was the fact she'd had so little as a child, but as an adult, Henrika was known for her enormous appetites and unabashed love for the finer things in life. Fashion, food, wine, cars, drugs, men, women. Henrika indulged in all that and more, proudly chronicling each new designer outfit, lavish party, and steamy Hollywood hookup on her social media accounts.

But her main love was jewelry. Henrika had a personal treasure trove of necklaces, bracelets, rings, and watches that was conservatively valued at more than fifty million dollars, and she collected rare gemstones the way some kids did comic books. She often posted about her jewelry and gemstones, sharing perfectly lit glamour shots of her wearing and clutching the items, along with long-winded descriptions about the carats, settings, and more. Those posts were far more enthusiastic and complimentary than the faint praise she occasionally doled out to her various hookups.

"You should all be familiar with Henrika Hyde, as she has been on multiple Section watch lists for quite some time," Gia began the briefing. "To the public, Henrika is a scientific genius and the CEO of Hyde Engineering, but Section knows her for what she truly is—a paramortal arms dealer who creates biomagical weapons that she auctions off to the highest bidder. As long as they can pay her outrageous prices, Henrika doesn't care whom she sells her formulas to, what those people do with them, or how many innocent civilians they kill. She has no known political or religious ideologies. All she cares about is lining her own pockets."

Gia's cold, clinical assessment of Henrika Hyde was the same one I'd formed in my own mind and had written about in my reports. I thought that Henrika's lack of ideologies made her even more dangerous and unpredictable than most paramortal terrorists and criminals. You never knew what greedy whim might strike her next.

"Our intel suggests Henrika has created a new biomagical weapon that is even deadlier than her previous efforts," Gia said. "We don't know exactly what the weapon does, or if it's a liquid, gas, solid, chemical, or explosive, but we're going to find out."

Once again, everything she said dovetailed with my own investigation into Henrika. Thanks to several unusually large purchase orders for chemicals and other supplies, I'd realized several weeks ago that Henrika had been ramping up production at her personal lab, which was located on the grounds of her luxe estate in the Virginia countryside. She was definitely developing some new formula, although I hadn't been able to tell whether it was an innocuous face cream or a deadly skin-melting serum.

I had been pestering Jensen for weeks to forward my suspicions to the Section higher-ups, which he'd finally done—along with presenting my conclusions as his own. I hadn't thought anything would come of my work, but now here I was, sitting in a conference room talking about finally taking action against the weapons maker. I eyed Desmond.

A SENSE OF DANGER

Unless I missed my guess, he was the one behind this sudden interest in Henrika Hyde.

Gia cleared her throat and continued the briefing. "Through various back channels, Henrika has contacted several known criminals and terrorists about her new weapon, which she is calling *Redburn*."

Hence the mission name, I thought.

"Henrika is paranoid about her security and travels with a large contingent of guards at all times," Gia said. "We've tried more than once to embed someone in her organization, especially among her private bodyguards, and we've been successful—up to a point. But the higher an undercover agent climbs in her organization, the more risk is involved. We've had several agents disappear without a trace. We assume those agents were discovered, questioned, and then eliminated."

Gia hit some more buttons on her clicker, and the photos of Henrika vanished, replaced by headshots of Section agents. I recognized several of the faces. Cleaners, mostly, along with a couple of charmers.

"Since we can't infiltrate Henrika's inner circle, we've decided to snatch her right out in the open."

Gia hit some more buttons on her clicker, and the photos of the presumed-dead Section agents vanished, replaced by several shots of a massive stone building surrounded by acres of lush, landscaped grounds. I blinked in surprise and recognition.

"Henrika is scheduled to attend a gala at the Halstead Hotel on Sunday night," Gia said. "The event is being sponsored by the Halstead Foundation to celebrate the completion of the first stage of the historic hotel's ongoing renovations. It's also a fund-raiser to help pay for the remaining work."

I frowned, my mind churning. The foundation was the same one that Henrika had sent those extremely generous donations to over the past several weeks. The money I thought was a payment or bribe for something, although I hadn't found any malfeasance among the foundation members or in the Halstead family's finances.

"Henrika's attendance has been publically announced on the foundation's website, so we're certain she'll be there. Given the other known criminals on the guest list, we think Henrika is going to use the gala as a cover to sell her new weapon and pocket even more millions. Supposedly, Henrika has a video of Redburn in action, something she is going to show prospective bidders to further whet their appetites and drive up the price for her weapon."

A video? That sounded ominous and indicated Henrika was much further along in developing her new weapon than I'd realized. Also, the name *Redburn* nagged at me, as though I'd recently seen or heard something about it, although I couldn't remember exactly what it was.

Gia gestured at Desmond. "For those of you who don't know, Desmond has a long-established undercover identity as Desmond Macfarlane, an arms dealer who buys weapons either to use in his own criminal activities or to resell at higher prices. Thanks to his cover and some Section maneuvering, Desmond Macfarlane has scored an invitation to the hotel gala, where he is scheduled to have a private meeting with Henrika to discuss her new weapon. During the meeting, Desmond will neutralize Henrika's guards so that a Section strike team can move in. Henrika will be quietly smuggled off the hotel grounds and transported to a local black site where she will be thoroughly questioned about the Redburn weapon."

So Section was going to kidnap Henrika, torture her for information, and then most likely kill her after they had squeezed every last drop of knowledge out of her. Standard protocols, but in this case, I didn't have a problem with them. If my work for Section had taught me nothing else, it was that the world would be much better off without certain monsters in it, and Henrika Hyde was most definitely one of those monsters.

To my surprise, Gia gestured at me. "Charlotte will accompany Desmond to the hotel as his plus-one for the gala and to help isolate, neutralize, and prepare Henrika for transport."

"What?" Surprise shot through me, and the word exploded out of my mouth like a bullet.

Gia raised her eyebrows. "Is something wrong, Ms. Locke? I thought you would want to be part of this mission. After all, you've been tracking Henrika for the past few months, and you had put in a request several weeks ago to be assigned to any action taken against her."

I bit back the curse dangling on the tip of my tongue. Gia was right. I had filed that request, back when I had been trying to get away from Jensen and into another department where I might be given a fair shake. But that request should have gotten me assigned to another analyst desk somewhere on the third floor—not down here in a fifth-floor conference room discussing my physical self actually taking part in a dangerous mission.

No doubt I had my new partner in crime, Desmond Percy, to thank for that. I didn't look at him, but I could feel his cool, calm gaze on my face. He was probably wondering whether I was going to rat him out, especially since Gia didn't seem to know about the strings Desmond had pulled with his good buddy Trevor Donnelly to get me assigned as his liaison.

But I couldn't do that. Desmond was right. This was a plum assignment, and I couldn't turn it down without torpedoing my already floundering career inside Section. Plus, protesting now would make me sound like I was scared and whining, which were two other things I couldn't afford to do inside Section.

"Gregory Jensen said my taking part in a mission might be a possibility," I said, lying through my teeth, throwing my dead supervisor under the proverbial bus, and going for some vague neutral ground. "But I didn't think it would actually happen. After all, I'm just an analyst, not a cleaner or even a field agent."

Gia's black eyebrows climbed a little higher on her face. She didn't like my questioning her decision. "Are you up-to-date on your marksman, combat, and other field-agent qualifications?"

"Of course."

Section 47 took its agents' training very, very seriously. Everyone from the newest rookie analysts to the mid-level charmers to the most hardened, seasoned cleaners had to undergo standard testing at least twice a year with basic firearms.

The firearms training was one of the few things that had always come easily to me, thanks to the hours I'd spent at the gun range with my father as a child. My magic also gave me a natural affinity for ranged weapons. My synesthesia always told me exactly where to aim, and I rarely missed my mark, no matter whether I was shooting a gun, throwing a knife, or hurling some other object toward a target.

Gia waved her hand, dismissing my concerns. "Then you'll be fine. All you have to do is smile and hang on to Desmond's arm for most of the evening. Once the two of you meet with Henrika, Desmond will neutralize her personal bodyguards, while you dose her with a sedative. It's a simple, standard, cleaner-liaison operation."

My gaze flicked to Desmond, who had the audacity to *grin*, as if this were all perfectly normal and he hadn't blackmailed, threatened, and hoodwinked me into putting myself in mortal danger. I didn't often long to be a cleaner, but at times like this, I desperately wished I had paid more attention to my father's lessons about how to kill people with everyday objects. Because right now, I had a burning desire to shove my ink pen through Desmond's right eyeball.

"Besides," Gia continued. "You're Jack Locke's daughter. I'm sure you know how to handle yourself."

That little tidbit got everyone's attention, and Joan and Diego studied me with a mixture of renewed interest and curiosity. Since I was a Legacy, everyone knew who I was and especially who my father had been. Oh, the Lockes might not have the money, power, prestige, and pedigree of the Percys, but we were still one of Section's most notorious Legacy families, and we Lockes had definitely left our mark on the organization over the years.

I sighed, giving in to the inevitable. "What's my cover for the gala?"

"You and Desmond have a personal relationship," Gia replied. "You've been involved for a few months, but the gala is the first time you've been seen together in public. It seemed like the best and most obvious way to establish your connection to him."

Personal relationship? I bit back a groan. That was Section code for *mistress*.

"You also work for Desmond as one of his money managers, which is how the two of you met. In addition to being his plus-one, you'll also be attending the gala to advise him on the financial feasibility of whatever deal Henrika wants to make for her Redburn weapon."

"So I'm a glorified accountant, whispering in my lover's ear about how much money he stands to make from either using or reselling Henrika's weapon."

"Yes," Gia said, ignoring my sarcasm. "You've been tracking Henrika's finances, so you can advise Desmond if something seems off about whatever deal she proposes."

Gia clicked a few more buttons, and the exterior photos of the hotel vanished, replaced by shots of the various ballrooms. "We're not sure exactly when or where Henrika will meet with the potential Redburn buyers. We think the meetings will happen in one of the hotel's private conference rooms, or perhaps one of the libraries, but we won't know for certain until Henrika actually summons the buyers."

More images appeared on the screen, showing the hotel's conference rooms and libraries. They were all fairly standard spaces, although the libraries were more like exhibit areas showcasing the art, antiquities, and jewelry from the Halstead family's private collections. Paintings, sculptures, figurines, furniture. Nothing terribly interesting or unusual, except for one thing—a stunning gold chandelier necklace studded with large teardrop-shaped emeralds and smaller princess-cut white diamonds.

"Wait. Stop." I stabbed my finger at the screen. "That's the Grunglass Necklace."

Gia nodded. "Yes, it belongs to the Halstead family, and it's currently on display at the hotel as part of an exhibit celebrating the renovations. Is there something special about it?"

I held back an exasperated sigh. People *really* needed to start reading my reports. "Henrika loves jewelry."

"So what?" Joan spoke up. "Everyone knows that."

I stabbed my finger at the picture again. "So Henrika especially covets the Grunglass Necklace. I don't know why, but the necklace has some special meaning for her, and she's been trying to buy it for *years*. I didn't realize the Halstead family still owned it. Anyway, Henrika will most likely meet with the buyers in that room, where the necklace is. So if you really want to capture her, then you should focus on that section of the hotel. Trust me."

Gia stared at me, a thoughtful look on her face, and Joan and Diego eyed me as well. Desmond smirked at me again, as if I'd finally done something he approved of. Arrogant psycho jackass.

"You're sure that Henrika is interested in the Grunglass Necklace? Specifically *that* necklace and not some other piece of jewelry on display?" Gia asked.

I shrugged. "Well, knowing Henrika, she wants it all, but she's been chasing the Grunglass Necklace for a long, long time. It's her white whale. She'll go to that room sooner or later, if only to set eyes on the necklace. She might even try to steal it during the gala, since she hasn't been able to buy it outright."

As soon as I said the words, I knew I was right. Maybe that was why Henrika had made all those donations to the foundation—so she could score a VIP invitation to the gala and get close enough to swipe the necklace. Either way, I couldn't imagine her being in the same room with the Grunglass Necklace and willingly leaving it behind.

Gia nodded. "All right. We'll focus on monitoring that section of the hotel."

"And what if Henrika doesn't want to meet there?" Desmond asked, a tense note in his voice.

Gia shrugged. "Then we'll snatch her from wherever she does decide to meet with you."

Desmond sucked in a breath like he was going to say something else, but then he looked at me again, shut his mouth, and leaned back in his chair. He must have realized that my so-called big brain had given him the perfect solution for how to get close to Henrika.

Gia clicked through some more photos and started droning on about the other agents and support staff that would be involved in the Redburn mission, along with the dozens of details that needed to be addressed in order to make it a success.

Eventually, she wound down and glanced around the table. "Anything else?"

Joan and Diego shook their heads, and she looked at Desmond.

"Like you said, it's a simple operation," Desmond replied. "Charlotte and I will make contact with Henrika and have our private meeting to discuss the weapon. Then we'll take out her security detail, sedate her, and turn her over to the strike team."

LIE.

The sheer, brutal force of his falsehood slammed into my mind like a red-hot poker stabbing into my skull. I grimaced and massaged my right temple, trying to ignore the sudden, pounding ache in my head. Desmond stared at me, a bit of worry flickering across his face. No one seemed to notice it but me, though.

"Problem, Charlotte?" Gia asked.

I forced myself to drop my hand, even though my head was still aching. "Of course not."

She eyed me a second longer, then clicked a few more buttons, talking about some other mission logistics. Joan and Diego turned their attention back to the screen. Desmond did the same, although I could have sworn he was looking at me out of the corner of his eye. Or maybe that was because I was doing the same thing to him.

I had already known that Desmond Percy was hiding things from me. I just hadn't realized he was hiding them from Section too.

NINE

DESMOND

Charlotte was pissed at me again.

I had known she would be, of course, especially when Gia revealed her cover as my money manager—and mistress. It had been stupid and selfish not to tell Charlotte more about the mission, especially those pertinent details, but I'd been afraid she would tell me to fuck off again.

She still might do that anyway. I wouldn't blame her if she did.

After ordering us to report to the sixth-floor weapons depot tomorrow morning for mission prep, Gia wrapped up the briefing. As soon as she finished speaking, Charlotte grabbed her pen and notepad, yanked the door open, and left the conference room without a backward glance.

Instead of returning to her assigned liaison desk, she strode out of the bullpen. I had to resist the urge to charge after her and...do what, exactly? Explain myself? I couldn't do that. Not without jeopardizing my chances to get my hands on Henrika Hyde, and eventually Adrian Anatoly.

Gia crooked her finger at Diego Benito, the IT tech, and beckoned him into her office to discuss some mission equipment. She closed the door behind them, leaving Joan and me to head back over to our desks.

It was just after noon, and everyone else in the bullpen had gone out to lunch. Joan glanced over, making sure that Gia was focused on Diego, then crossed her arms over her chest and glared at me. The aura around her heart flared a pale, icy blue, indicating how angry she was with me.

"What was that, Dez?" Joan snapped. "You're seriously going to use Charlotte Locke as your liaison? In case you haven't noticed, she hates you."

"Oh, believe me, I've noticed."

Joan didn't care for my self-deprecating humor. She glared at me again, then looked around. Once she was sure we were still alone, she sidled closer to me. "I thought you said we were in this together. That we were going to get Anatoly and all the other bastards who helped kill Graham."

Her voice cracked on the last few words, making fissures appear in my own heart. Ever-widening, ever-deepening chasms of guilt and grief that would never truly heal, but I was going to do my best to spackle them over—starting with Anatoly's death.

"And that's exactly what we're going to do. That's what the Redburn mission is all about. A mission you are still a very important part of," I said, trying to reassure her.

"Part of the mission?" Joan huffed, the sound full of derision. "Please. I get to sit in the van and watch the monitors while you do the real work of cornering Henrika Hyde."

I shrugged. Nothing I could say would convince her otherwise, especially when we both knew she was right.

"Why her?" Joan asked. "What can Charlotte Locke do that I can't?"

"You saw the reports, and you heard what Gia said. Charlotte has been tracking Henrika for months. She knows everything there is to know about Henrika, and she's the best person to help me capture her."

The words slipped easily off my tongue. They were mostly true, but of course I couldn't tell Joan the real, absolute truth—that I was going to torture Henrika until she told me everything she knew about Anatoly. The less Joan knew about what I was really up to, the more plausible deniability she would have if things went wrong.

"But *I* wanted to help you," Joan said in a much softer, quieter voice. "It's the least I can do for Graham after everything we…went through together."

Joan had been Graham's liaison on a number of missions, both here in the States and abroad, and the two of them had been… Well, I didn't know *exactly* what they had been. Definitely lovers, according to some hints Graham had accidentally dropped, which wasn't unusual. Liaisons and cleaners worked together in intense, high-pressure, life-and-death situations. Sex was a natural release in that sort of environment.

I'd suspected that Joan and Graham had a much deeper connection than just post-mission stress relief, something Graham had confirmed when he'd been dying on the beach. Graham had truly cared about Joan, and he'd begged me not to involve her in my hunt for Anatoly. I hadn't been able to save my best friend, but I would be damned if I wasn't going to honor one of his last requests. And that meant keeping Joan as far away from the action as possible.

"I appreciate that you want to help, and I know Graham would appreciate it too," I said. "But the best way for you to do that is by sitting in the van. Like you said before, Charlotte hates me, so I need someone on this mission whom

I can trust. Someone who will be watching my back, watching out for me. And that person is you, Joan. Okay?"

Her face softened, and the icy blue aura shimmering around her heart dimmed.

"Fine. Whatever. I'll sit in the stupid van." She stabbed her finger at me. "But when you and Charlotte Locke screw this up, I'm definitely going to say *I told you so.*"

I flashed her a grin. "You can say it to your heart's content."

Joan nodded, moved over to her desk, and started shuffling papers around. I let out a quiet sigh of relief that she had backed off. For now.

So you didn't want to drag Joan into this, but you're okay with me taking part in it? Charlotte's earlier accusation floated through my mind, along with something else she had asked me: *Exactly how dangerous is this mission of yours going to be?*

That, unfortunately, was the million-dollar question—and one that I couldn't answer.

I sat down at my desk and started reviewing the hotel blueprints for the Redburn mission. I expected Charlotte to return to the bullpen with her laptop and perhaps some files, but she didn't reappear. She must have been far more pissed than I'd realized because the minutes ticked by and turned into hours. I checked my phone, but the tracker pen I'd slipped into her purse indicated that she—or at least it—was still inside the building. Finally, at the end of the day, I gave in, packed up my things, and went looking for her.

I headed up to the third floor, but Charlotte wasn't at her

old desk. At least, I assumed it was her desk, although no framed photos adorned the space, just a crystal bird figurine that matched the one I'd seen in her kitchen. A hard fist of worry punched into my gut. Had she decided to renege on our deal?

"Hello, handsome," a soft, feminine voice drawled. "Where have you been all my life?"

A gorgeous redhead stood up at the next desk and leaned her elbows on the cubicle wall. Tall and lithe, with a body that had plenty of generous curves in all the right places, she was dressed in a pair of dark, skintight jeans, and a clingy, pink silk blouse that she'd unbuttoned just low enough to offer a tantalizing glimpse of her impressive cleavage.

Her hazel gaze slowly slid down and then back up my body in a frank, assessing way, and she raised her eyes to mine and smiled. Her aura pulsed a bright gold, letting me know she liked what she saw. Most women did. Some men too.

People might have thought me arrogant, but looks are just another weapon spies use to get whatever advantage we can over our enemies, and I wasn't above deploying mine on occasion. So I grinned, as though I was as interested in her as she was in me. "And who might you be?"

She toyed with one of the buttons on her blouse, moving it to the side and giving me a slightly better view of her cleavage. "Miriam. And you are?"

"Desmond."

She held out her hand, which I shook. I started to let go, but she squeezed her fingers around mine. "Charmed."

Her gold aura pulsed again, even brighter than before, and her hand grew pleasantly tingly against my own. A faint crackle of magic swirled in the air, heating the space between our bodies, and subtly inviting me to step closer to her tantalizing warmth. I recognized the sensations. Of course she would be a charmer, with those good looks and that stunning body.

"Yes, charmed," I murmured, then dropped her hand to break our connection and lessen the hypnotic feel of her warm charisma. "Do you know where Charlotte is?"

Miriam shrugged. "I think she left for the day." She toyed with her blouse again, showing me even more of her cleavage. "I was just about to leave myself and grab a drink. Care to join me?"

She gave me another winsome smile, then leveled her gaze on mine again. Her gold aura pulsed even brighter than before, and that crackle of magic around her intensified, making my fingers tingle even though I was no longer touching her. She was really giving me the full-court press, using her charisma to try to get me to say yes.

Normally, magical beguilement or not, I might have taken her up on her offer, which would probably lead all the way to her bed. Section's main branch was here in Washington, D.C., but it had offices all around the world. London, Paris, Berlin, Moscow, Tokyo, Beijing, Sydney. Some cleaners were notorious for having a woman or a man (or both) in every station, while some agents were equally notorious for hooking up with as many cleaners as they could. Dust bunnies, those agents were rather derogatorily called.

I enjoyed the pleasures of female companionship as much as the next man, and Miriam looked like she would be very good company indeed, but I was here to avenge Graham's death, not hook up with a random charmer. "Unfortunately, I have a meeting tonight, but maybe some other time. Will you do me a favor, though?"

"Anything for you, handsome," she purred.

"If you see Charlotte, please tell her that Desmond stopped by looking for her."

Something flickered across Miriam's face, and her aura

sputtered like a lit match in a strong wind. In an instant, all the tingly warmth of her charisma vanished, replaced by a still, noticeable chill. She seemed annoyed, although she gave me another smooth, sexy smile.

"Sure thing, handsome. And if you get tired of waiting for Charlotte, well, maybe I can help you with whatever you need." Miriam winked at me, then dropped her hand from her blouse, sat down in her chair, and started texting on her phone.

I left Miriam to her electronic conversation, got in an elevator, and rode up to the ground floor. The doors dinged open, and I stepped out into the lobby.

A familiar Southern drawl drifted through the air. "...don't know why my keycard isn't working..."

I stopped and looked to my right. A cool pulse of blue caught my eye, a flicker of soft, soothing color among the crush of auras and Section agents waiting to exit through the turnstile and leave the building.

Charlotte was standing at the front of the line, waving her keycard back and forth over the reader, which kept emitting loud, angry *beep-beep-beeps*. Evelyn, the front desk manager, was standing beside her, fiddling with the reader.

"Try it again," Evelyn said.

Charlotte did as instructed, and the light on the reader flashed green. Charlotte must have sensed my gaze because she glanced over her shoulder. I hoped that she would wait for me, but her mouth pinched into an angry frown, and she whipped back around, shoved through the turnstile, and marched out of the building.

Part of me wanted to call her name and ask her to slow down, but I'd be damned if I would chase after her like a schoolboy with a first crush. So I waited my turn in line, scanned my own keycard, and picked up her trail on the sidewalk outside. Which, in all honesty, made me feel like the worst sort of stalker, but she was the one who'd left the fifth-floor bullpen in a snit. I'd give her a few more minutes to cool off. She would come around eventually.

Except that she didn't.

Charlotte didn't glance over her shoulder, not once, and she marched all the way to her apartment building with stiff shoulders and a ramrod-straight spine that would have made any drill sergeant proud. She even marched up the three flights of stairs, although I noted with a bit of smug satisfaction that she was huffing and puffing by the time she reached the top.

I caught up with her just as she was getting ready to slide her key into the apartment door. I started to grab her hand, but then I remembered my earlier promise not to touch her, so I settled for reaching out and blocking the lock instead. "What are you doing?"

Charlotte finally deigned to glare at me. "Heading into my apartment, changing clothes, and going to work my shift at the diner."

I shook my head. "Did it ever occur to you that more cleaners might be waiting inside to finish what the others started last night?"

She rolled her eyes. "Of course it occurred to me. I'm not an *idiot*. But no one is inside my apartment. Trust me. I would know."

I reached out with my power, scanning the empty space behind the door. No buzzing phones, no crackling earbuds, no electrical heartbeats. Charlotte was right. No one was waiting inside, although I didn't understand how *she* could know that with such certainty.

"You should have come back to the bullpen this afternoon so we could get started on mission prep," I said, dropping my hand from the lock. "And you definitely should have waited for me to leave the building with you."

She rolled her eyes again. "I am not a child who needs you to hold my hand while I cross the street. I am thirty-five years old and more than capable of taking care of myself."

"Really? Like you took care of those cleaners last night?"

Her eyes narrowed, and her aura flared with anger. "Are you going to keep throwing that in my face? Because you playing that card has already gotten old. Yes, you saved my life. What do you want? A thank-you? Well, *thank you*, Desmond Percy, for showing me what a badass cleaner and sleek, beautiful, killing machine you are."

I grinned, strangely pleased by her words. "You think that I'm sleek *and* beautiful?"

Her right eye twitched, and her fingers tightened around her keys as though she were thinking about stabbing me with them. She shot me another angry glare, then shoved a key into the lock and opened the door. I half expected her to whirl around and slam the door in my face, but instead, she threw it wide open and strode inside. I followed her and closed the door behind me.

Charlotte entered her alarm code, then dumped her purse onto the island counter, crossed the depressingly empty space, and disappeared into the back of the apartment. I leaned against the counter, crossed my arms over my chest and my feet at the ankles, and waited.

She returned ten minutes later wearing a waitress uniform. Even though I'd seen it through the diner windows last night, I hadn't gotten the full effect. A short-sleeve, light-blue shirt with a wide white collar and oversize buttons marching down the front. A matching light-blue pleated skirt that stopped at her knees. White tights and sneakers.

It was truly *awful*, like something out of a cheesy, old-fashioned movie. But the longer I looked at the outfit, the more I started to appreciate it, especially how the skirt and white tights showed off her toned, muscled legs. I suddenly found myself wondering what the rest of her body was like under that awful fabric—

"Stop looking at me like that," Charlotte snapped.

"Like what?"

She flapped her hand at me. "Like *that*. Believe me, I know exactly how hideous the uniform is, but I have to wear it."

"I didn't say anything about the uniform."

"You didn't have to."

She glared at me again, then marched over, grabbed her purse, and slung it onto her shoulder. Then she headed for the door. I stepped in front of her, blocking her path.

"Are you seriously going to work?" I asked.

Charlotte gestured at her uniform. "I'm not wearing this for fun."

"You're a sitting duck in that diner. Whoever wants you dead obviously knows you work there, and if you go back tonight, then they can send more cleaners after you."

She sighed, the sound full of weary resignation. "I know that, but I need the money. Zeeta is already itching to fire me, and I can't afford to lose this job. The tips are surprisingly good. Now, if you'll excuse me…"

Charlotte started to move around me, but I stepped in front of her, blocking her path again.

"You stubborn fool," I hissed. "You're going to get yourself killed. And for what? Just to thumb your nose at me?"

Her eyes narrowed, and her aura flared with anger again. "Well, I have to do something to entertain myself, Dundee. Isn't that what *mistresses* do? Twiddle their thumbs while their menfolk are off conducting more important business?"

So she was still pissed about the briefing and especially

her cover. I scrubbed my hand through my hair. "Look, I admit that I should have told you exactly what the mission would entail."

"But?"

"But it doesn't change anything. Someone wants you dead, and you going to that diner by yourself is not a good idea." I gestured at her empty apartment. "And neither is coming back here tonight."

"Where else am I going to stay? I don't have the money for a hotel room." She grimaced and glanced away, as if the admission pained her, even though I already knew she was in financial trouble.

"You can stay with me."

The words slipped out before I had a chance to think about them. Then again, I had been so focused on getting Charlotte to agree to my scheme, I hadn't really thought about what would happen if she said yes. About the logistics of watching her back and hopefully convincing her to do the same for me. Graham had always taken care of such things. He got us close to our targets, and then I killed them. That had been one of the things that made us such a great team.

"Stay with you?" Charlotte laughed. "You've got to be kidding."

"I'm not kidding. I have a place nearby, and there's plenty of room. Besides, I'm not staying here."

Her face hardened. "Why? Is my apartment not good enough for you?"

I held up my hands in surrender. "I'm not trying to insult you. Believe me, I've stayed in far worse, but those cleaners were waiting outside your building. Whoever wants you dead knows exactly where you live. You should at least make it *difficult* for someone to find and kill you."

Reluctant agreement flickered across her face.

"Then there is the simple fact that you don't have any furniture. Care to tell me why that is?"

Her jaw clenched. She didn't respond, but I was willing to bet that she'd sold the furniture to help pay down her debts, whatever they were.

"I'm not sleeping on your yoga mat, and that mattress only looks wide enough for one of us. Unless you want to be bunk buddies, Numbers."

Once again, the words slipped out before I thought about them, and they hung in the air between us. Charlotte's blue gaze snapped to mine, and her aura pulsed with...*something*. It might have been annoyance, or perhaps even interest, but her face smoothed over, and I couldn't tell what she was thinking.

I cleared my throat, trying to push away the sudden, unwanted image of Charlotte Locke lounging on that mattress and slowly peeling those white tights off her toned legs. "There's plenty of room at my place, which is off the books. No one at Section knows where I'm staying, so it should be a secure location. Besides, it makes sense for you to stay with me until the mission is over."

Plus, that way I can keep an eye on you and make sure you don't derail my plans. I didn't dare voice the thought. She already knew far more than I wanted her to.

"Fine," she muttered through gritted teeth. "We'll have a sleepover at your place, Dundee. *After* I go to work."

I opened my mouth to once again argue that she should skip her shift, but she stabbed her finger at me in warning, and I shut my mouth. I had a feeling that was the best course of action around Charlotte Locke.

TEN

DESMOND

Charlotte disappeared into the back of the apartment again and returned a few minutes later with a couple of canvas bags bulging with clothes, sneakers, and toiletries. I offered to carry the bags, but she gave me another disgusted look and stomped out of the apartment. I shut the door behind us and followed her.

She once again did that stiff-as-a-board, drill-sergeant walk all the way over to the Moondust Diner. "I work from seven until midnight," she muttered as we approached the parking lot. "So I hope you like burgers, fries, coffee, and pie."

"Surely there are some healthier options on the menu. Perhaps some sort of fruit smoothie?"

She made a derisive sound in the back of her throat. "It's a mom-and-pop diner, not an organic juice bar."

"Point taken."

Charlotte trudged up the steps and yanked open the front door. She nodded to the old woman sitting behind the cash register, who I assumed was Zeeta, given the faded black nametag on her blue shirt. Zeeta grunted back, and her aura pulsed a sour, putrid green. She wasn't a fan of Charlotte Locke.

"You're late," Zeeta accused in a low, raspy voice. "Again."

A muscle ticked in Charlotte's jaw, and her hand curled around the strap of her purse like she wanted to swing it out and brain the older woman with it. I hid a grin. Good to know I wasn't the only one she not-so-secretly wanted to murder.

"Sorry. I had to stop and pick up my…friend." Charlotte jerked her head at me. "He's going to hang out for a while. I thought you might appreciate the extra business."

Zeeta eyed me, her aura still pulsing that same sour green. She sniffed. "Late is late, no matter how much *business* you supposedly bring in."

That muscle ticked in Charlotte's jaw again, but she didn't say anything else as she swept past the other woman, dumped her bags on the back counter, tied on a white apron, and got to work.

I slid into the back corner booth, one that gave me a view of the entire diner as well as the parking lot outside. I ordered an egg-white omelet with ham and spinach, plain whole-wheat toast, and an ice water with lemon. Charlotte took my order and handed it to the young guy in the kitchen, Pablo, according to the nametag on his blue work shirt.

"How was the peach pie?" Pablo asked in a friendly voice.

"Oh, it was great," Charlotte replied. "It really hit the spot after a…rough night."

Pablo nodded and smiled, apparently not hearing the slight hesitation in her voice.

Charlotte smiled back at him, seeming to have some genuine affection for the young cook. That one simple motion completely transformed her features. Her eyes brightened, her cheeks lifted, her shoulders relaxed, and her aura glowed a cool, soothing blue. In an instant, she went from ordinary to extraordinary. The change startled me even more than seeing her legs in those white tights.

Charlotte must have sensed my curious gaze because she glanced in my direction, and the smile dropped from her face like a stone sinking to the bottom of a lake. In an instant, she had morphed back into a cold, prickly analyst, despite the fact that she was still wearing the tacky waitress uniform. She stared at me a moment longer, then went over to refill someone's coffee.

She ignored me, but for some reason, I couldn't tear my gaze away from her, and I couldn't help but wonder what it would take to get Charlotte Locke to smile at me like that.

While Charlotte waited tables, I ate my omelet, which was surprisingly good. Then I plucked some files relating to Henrika Hyde out of my briefcase and read through them, prepping for the Redburn mission. I also kept an eye out for cleaners and other potential enemies, but a steady stream of people entered the diner, ate their food, and left, and no one showed any untoward interest in either Charlotte or me.

The evening passed by quietly until around nine o'clock, when a man strode inside the diner. He was tall and muscled with short black hair and ebony skin and was dressed in a tight, long-sleeve black shirt, black cargo pants, and black boots. Despite the casual clothes, he had *cleaner* written all over him, and I didn't have to feel the energy pulsing off his body or see his smoky gray aura to know he was just as dangerous as I was.

The man's head swiveled back and forth as he scanned the diner, looking for potential threats just as I had earlier. His gaze focused on Charlotte, then his head turned, and his light brown eyes locked with mine. Surprise and interest filled his face, and he sauntered in my direction, his long, confident strides eating up the distance between us.

"This seat taken?" he asked in a low, deep voice.

"It is now."

The man slid into the seat across from mine. He leaned back in his side of the booth and crossed his arms over his chest, studying me the same way I studied him. After several seconds, he tipped his head. "Gabriel."

"Desmond."

He didn't say anything else, and neither did I, although we both kept staring, silently sizing each other up. Danger recognized danger.

Charlotte finished with another customer and headed over to our booth. She glanced back and forth between the two of us before focusing on Gabriel. "What can I get you?" she asked in a wary voice.

"The usual," he replied. "Please."

She walked off and returned a few minutes later with a cup of coffee and a large piece of cherry pie topped with vanilla ice cream, which she deposited in front of him. Gabriel nodded his thanks, although he didn't make a move toward his cup or plate. Instead, he kept staring at me, his arms still crossed over his chest, his right fingers drumming out a slow, steady rhythm on his left elbow.

Below the table, out of sight, my hands clenched into fists, and I started thinking about how I would kill him. I'd start by snatching his cup and tossing the hot coffee in his face. Then, while he was screaming and flailing around,

I'd grab the fork on his pie plate, lunge forward, and ram it into his throat—

Charlotte let out a loud, derisive snort. "If the two of you are done puffing up your chests, maybe you can tell me what you want, Gabriel."

"I came to talk to you," he rumbled back to her, although he kept his eyes fixed on mine. "I thought you might want to know that four bodies got fished out of the Potomac this afternoon. The cops haven't identified them yet, but one of my guys was on the scene, and he gave me a heads-up." Gabriel paused. "My guy recognized one of the bodies as a Section cleaner. Rosalita."

Charlotte didn't react. Didn't blink, swallow, sigh, or shift on her feet. She didn't do anything to indicate that she already knew about the bodies, and her aura didn't so much as flicker with the faintest trace of worry or concern. It was an impressive show of seemingly bored impassivity. "So?"

"So I saw Rosalita last night. Spotted her lurking around the diner parking lot when I was leaving. Funny coincidence, don't you think? Her coming here last night and then turning up dead today?"

"What are you implying? That *I* killed her?" A merry little laugh tumbled out of Charlotte's lips. "Please. You know me better than that."

Gabriel finally fixed his gaze on her. "Oh, I do know you, Charlotte. You could kill a cleaner, if you had to. We both know you've done it before."

She grimaced, and the two of them exchanged a look I couldn't quite decipher. In that moment, they seemed to have some deep, dark, shared history, and I was surprised by how...*excluded* that made me feel. I shouldn't care what sort of relationship Charlotte had with this man, but for some reason I did. But that was only because I didn't want him messing up my plans for Henrika and Anatoly. Yes, that was it.

When Charlotte didn't respond, Gabriel's gaze flicked back to me. "Or perhaps your boy here did it. He could definitely kill a cleaner, or four."

She bristled. "He is not my *boy*."

Gabriel tilted his head to the side, still looking at me. "Really? Well, if the two of you aren't knocking boots, then why is he here?"

"Maybe I like the ambiance," I replied.

"Ambiance," he drawled. "Right."

Gabriel turned toward Charlotte. "If you're in trouble—"

"I am *not* in trouble," she snapped, cutting him off. "And even if I was, it wouldn't be any of your business."

"You're my investment, so that makes it my business."

Charlotte's jaw clenched, her eyes glittered with anger, and her aura blazed a bright neon-blue. Her fingers also clenched around the pen in her hand in that familiar, unconscious, I-want-to-stab-you-to-death motion. Gabriel grimaced. Even he realized that had been the wrong thing to say.

"Well, your *investment* has to get back to work." She ripped his order ticket off the top of her pad and slapped it down on the table. "Pay Zeeta on your way out the door."

Charlotte glared at him again, then whirled around and stalked over to take someone else's order. Gabriel watched her go, and his gray aura dimmed with regret.

"Fuck," he muttered.

We sat there in silence. I watched Charlotte out of the corner of my eye, but she was smiling and chatting with the other diners. If not for the color in her cheeks and the continued blaze of her aura, I wouldn't have known anything was wrong—

"You know, I've always thought that tacky waitress uniform is kind of hot."

Surprised, I jerked my gaze back over to Gabriel.

"I especially like those white tights," he continued. "Then again, I've always been a leg man. Seems like you are too."

I didn't respond, and the two of us studied each other in tense silence again.

"I know you're a Section cleaner, just like I used to be," Gabriel continued. "I don't know what you have going on with Charlotte, but you'd better treat her right."

I raised my eyebrows and smirked at him. "Or what? You'll come beat me up?"

"Nah. I'll just kill you."

His aura pulsed a vivid gray, burning as brightly as the neon signs in the diner windows. He meant what he said and had the confidence—and deadly skills—to back up his bravado.

"You might find that far more difficult than you imagine," I replied in an icy tone.

This time, Gabriel raised his eyebrows and smirked at me. "Well, I certainly hope there's more to you than just that slick suit and pretty face. Otherwise, I would be severely disappointed."

Before I could snap back at him, Gabriel leaned forward and speared me with a cold, hard look. "Charlotte is a good person. Stubborn as a mule, but truly good. I consider her a friend, and if there is one thing you should know about me, Slick, it's that I watch out for my friends."

"Really? All your friends? Or just the ones who owe you money?"

He stiffened at my insult.

"What *was* it that you called Charlotte?" I snapped my fingers together, as though the answer had just come to me. "Oh, that's right—an *investment*."

"That came out wrong."

"Did it?"

"Yes, it did." His eyes narrowed. "And you're in no position to point fingers at me, *Percy*."

This time, I stiffened.

"Oh, that's right. I recognize you. Desmond Percy, cleaner extraordinaire, the golden boy of Section 47. Tell me, is your daddy, the General, still around? Still running the show and screwing people over left and right?"

His words punched me in the gut. The General didn't merely screw people over—he *destroyed* them. Everyone, that is, except for Adrian Anatoly. Despite what Anatoly had done to Graham, to all those other Section agents, to *me*, my father had dismissed the situation as being beneath his notice and not worthy of calling in any favors to aid my mission.

Anatoly is just another terrorist, my father had barked at me over the phone while I was still in the hospital recovering from the Blacksea ambush. *Someone will get lucky and kill him someday.*

Well, that someone was going to be me, and that day was fast approaching. My father might not have helped me, but his name and the fake emails and orders I'd sent from his Section accounts certainly had.

Gabriel smirked at me again. "I'll take that as a yes."

I still didn't say anything, and his face slowly turned serious again.

"As for Charlotte owing me money, well, maybe you should ask your old man about that."

His words surprised me. "What do you mean?"

"You know about Charlotte's father, right? The Mexico mission?"

Every Section cleaner knew about *the Mexico mission*, even though it had happened some fifteen years ago. It was a painful reminder and a stark example that while we might work for a government agency, that same agency would disavow any knowledge and leave us to rot if we were ever captured—or executed, as Jack Locke had been.

Gabriel leaned forward and lowered his voice. "My old man was working for Section then. He was part of the support staff for the Mexico mission. Jack Locke and some other cleaners were sent to eliminate a drug cartel leader, a real nasty piece of work named Feliciano Salvador. But things went wrong, and everyone was killed, except for Locke."

"So what? Everyone knows that."

He leaned forward a little more, his eyes fixed on mine. "So, not everyone knows that Salvador made a ransom demand to Section, to your daddy, specifically. Fifteen years ago would have been back before your daddy was a general and on the Section board of directors. Back when he was still stationed here in D.C. and in charge of the cleaners. Maybe you remember that time?"

He was right. I had been in D.C. back then, spending a long, hot, unfortunate summer with my father, and I remembered all the tense, hushed calls about the Mexico mission.

"The ransom demand was three million dollars," Gabriel continued. "Of course, Section wouldn't pay it, since they don't negotiate with anyone."

"But?" I asked, even though I knew I wouldn't like his answer.

"But Jane Locke, Charlotte's grandmother, didn't want to lose her son, so she borrowed the money from my family, the Chases, and she asked my dad, Leon, to deliver it, which he did. But of course, things went bad," Gabriel said. "Your daddy wanted another crack at Salvador, so he secretly sent a team of cleaners to the exchange—but they screwed up. Salvador bolted, and Jack Locke was killed in the crossfire."

Gabriel's aura pulsed a bright gray again, and his voice rang with a truth I couldn't deny. His meaning was crystal-clear—that my father had put his own goals and ambitions above the life of a fellow cleaner and Section agent. I would have liked to claim that the news shocked me, but it didn't. Not in the slightest. I knew the General better than anyone, so I knew exactly how cold and calculating he could be.

Gabriel sat back in his side of the booth. "Here's another funny thing about the Mexico mission. The three million in ransom money vanished. As far as my father could tell, Salvador didn't get it, and my father didn't know where it went or who ended up with it. Then again, money has a tendency to disappear during missions."

Knowing the General, he'd had something to do with that too, although I didn't voice my thought.

"So that's how Charlotte and her grandmother first got into debt," I said, finishing his story. *Because of my father.* I didn't have to say the words. We were both thinking them.

Gabriel shrugged. "My father helped them with it the best he could, letting Jane pay back the money a little bit at a time. She had actually paid off most of the debt, but then she got sick, and her medical bills started piling up. So Charlotte took out another loan from me. And now, well, here we all are in this diner tonight."

"Why are you telling me this?" I asked.

He shot me another cold look. "Your family has already fucked over the Lockes once before, and a man died because of it. You fuck over Charlotte the same way, and I won't be lazy enough to dump your body in the river. No one will ever find so much as the smallest piece of you, no matter who your daddy is. That's a promise, Slick."

His deadly warning delivered, Gabriel slid out of his side of the booth, got to his feet, and strode away without a backward glance. His story lingered, though, along with the uncomfortable truths he'd revealed about my father—and myself.

All this time, I had been so focused on avenging Graham that I hadn't stopped to consider what impact my plan would have on Charlotte—namely, the danger I was putting her in. Oh, I imagined that someone would have tried to kill her sooner or later, but I'd probably accelerated the timeline by coming to D.C. and roping her into my scheme to take down Henrika Hyde.

Maybe Gabriel was right. Maybe I was just like my father and about to fuck over an innocent woman—and get her killed.

ELEVEN

CHARLOTTE

I n between helping the other customers, I watched while Gabriel and Desmond had their little macho cleaner tête-à-tête. Snatches of their back-and-forth conversation drifted over to me.

"…Mexico mission…"

"…everyone knows that…"

"…borrowed the money…"

"…why are you telling me this…"

"…a man died…"

I couldn't hear everything they said, but I got the gist of their conversation. Gabriel was telling Desmond what had happened to my father and why I was in such deep debt to him. Anger spiked through me, and my fingers fisted in the damp cloth I was using to wipe down the dining counter. My debt was personal, private, and strictly between Gabriel and me. Desmond had absolutely nothing to do with it, and I certainly didn't want his sympathy—or worse, his pity.

I also didn't blame him for what his father had done to mine. Desmond had been a college kid back then, just like me. He couldn't have changed what General Percy did, just as I'd never been able to convince my father to quit taking such dangerous missions and spend more time at home with Grandma Jane and me.

Gabriel finished his conversation with Desmond, slid out of the booth, and paid Zeeta for his uneaten pie and coffee. Then he stepped over to me.

"I don't know what's going on between the two of you, or why those cleaners are dead, but you need to be careful, Charlotte," he said. "I'm going to be busy the next few days on a new job, but if you need anything—anything at all— you call me."

"Don't worry. I'm not in trouble, so I won't need anything." My voice sounded weak even to my own ears.

Gabriel snorted. "Fine. Don't tell me what's going on, but don't let your stupid, stubborn pride get in the way of saving your own skin." He jabbed his finger at me. "Especially when a Percy is involved. You hear me?"

I gave him a short, reluctant nod. As much as I didn't want to accept his help, I would do it to save my own skin, just like he said. Survival was one of the few things more important than my own stupid, stubborn pride. "I hear you. Loud and clear."

"Good." Gabriel nodded back at me, then turned around, opened the door, and stepped outside.

I watched through the windows as he crossed the parking lot and got into the front passenger seat of a waiting black Escalade. The vehicle cruised away like a shark swimming across the pavement and disappeared from sight.

I looked over at the back corner booth. Desmond was staring at me, a thoughtful and vaguely guilty expression on his face. More anger spiked through me, and I spun away from him. Even though I had already cleaned off the counter,

I wiped it down again with harsh, jerky motions.

I wasn't quite sure why I was so upset. Gabriel was the one who'd blabbed about my troubles, so I should be pissed at him, not Desmond. Still, I didn't like the way the cleaner was looking at me, almost as if he was seeing me as a *person* for the very first time, instead of just as the lowly analyst he'd manipulated into doing his bidding.

I didn't want Desmond Percy to see me as a person. But even more important, I didn't want to view him as one either. That sort of thing led to unwanted feelings, conflicting loyalties, and twisted agendas that were almost certainly a one-way ticket to death for everyone involved.

Especially me.

The rest of my shift passed by quietly. Customers came and went, Pablo cooked in the kitchen, Zeeta gave me a sour look whenever I walked by, and Desmond sat in the corner booth, sipping a mug of hot green tea and reviewing files. Every once in a while, I would go refill his water and glance at the photos, documents, and blueprints, which were all related to the Halstead Hotel and the upcoming Redburn mission. Well, at least he was taking it seriously. That was a point in his favor. Maybe, just maybe, I would live through this after all.

At fifteen minutes before midnight, Desmond gathered up his things and grabbed his briefcase. He jerked his head to the side, indicating he would wait for me out front. I reluctantly nodded back. Like it or not, he was right. I couldn't return to my apartment where more cleaners might be lying in wait, so heading to his place was the best, safest option.

Desmond was the only customer left, and as soon as he paid up and stepped outside, Zeeta locked the front door and flipped the sign over to *Closed*. We went through our usual shutdown routine. I grabbed my bags of clothes, then headed into the kitchen, where Pablo handed me a white plastic bag.

I glanced inside to find a white paper box with a clear top. "A whole cherry pie? What's this for?"

"You and your friend." Pablo winked at me. "You both look like you could use a little sweetness tonight."

I barked out a laugh. If only he knew how true his words really were. "Thanks, Pablo."

He grinned. "No problem."

Zeeta shooed us outside and locked the back door, then she and Pablo left. I glanced around, but I didn't see anyone lurking behind the Dumpsters that lined the back of the diner. I also reached out with my synesthesia, scanning the midnight shadows, as well as the few scraggly trees in the distance, but my inner voice remained quiet. Everything was as it should be, so I drew in a breath, steeling myself, and headed around to the front of the diner.

Desmond was leaning up against the diner, his briefcase dangling from his hand, scanning the empty parking lot. The glow from the nearby streetlights added a gilded, golden sheen to his hair and made his eyes glitter like silver-blue stars in his handsome face. Despite the midnight hour, his suit was still impeccable, his tie was perfectly straight and centered, and he looked like a model waiting for some late-night photo shoot to begin.

Me? Well, several strands of my auburn hair had slipped out of its ponytail, my cheeks were still flushed from the heat of the kitchen, and grease, ketchup, and coffee stains covered my waitress uniform like blood spatter at a crime scene. The only modeling I could do right now would be for some public service announcement. *Stay in school, and get an education, kids.*

Desmond pushed away from the side of the diner and straightened up with that easy, enviable, elegant grace. "Ready?"

"Yeah."

He gestured with his hand, and we fell in step together as we left the parking lot and headed over to the sidewalk.

"My place isn't too far away," he said. "I'd rather walk than take a car."

Getting a car would leave an electronic record some-where, which would defeat the purpose of going to his safe house. I had tracked more than one bad guy because they'd been stupid enough to use a ride-share app.

I nodded. "Fine with me."

Desmond nodded back, and we strode along the sidewalk in silence, heading in the opposite direction from my apart-ment. I glanced at him out of the corner of my eye, but he didn't say anything about his conversation with Gabriel. Maybe he wouldn't mention it. I hoped not. I had no desire to talk about my father and how I was still paying— literally—for his mistakes.

"While you were working, I read through your reports on Henrika Hyde," Desmond said.

His choice of topic surprised me. "And?"

"And Graham was right. You are a very good, very thor-ough analyst." His mouth curved a little, but his smile was more sad than not.

Thanks to my snooping through the Section databases, I'd known that Graham had read my reports, but I was surprised that Desmond had done the same. Most cleaners didn't bother with such things. Section pointed them at a target, and they eliminated it, no questions asked.

I hesitated, wondering if he was just making awkward conversation, or if he was truly interested in my work. But I was stuck with him, so I might as well find out. "If you read my reports, then you know that Henrika Hyde is truly evil."

"That was never a doubt in my mind," he replied. "But you really did a deep dive and broke down all her businesses, associates, even that flashy jewelry she likes to show off on her social media accounts. I couldn't follow a lot of what you were saying, especially the financial stuff, but I could see how good you are at your job. Your reports were impressive, Charlotte. Truly."

Truth, my inner voice whispered. Desmond really did mean what he said, and he'd just shown me more respect than Gregory Jensen ever had in all the years I'd worked for him at Section. A warm, unexpected rush of feeling flooded my body, and some of my anger cooled. Perhaps this partnership wouldn't be as horrible as I'd thought.

We reached the end of the block. Once again, we both glanced around, but the area was utterly deserted. No one was trudging along the sidewalks, going home after a long shift, and no cars cruised by on the street, not so much as a single taxi in search of one more fare.

"Does this seem right to you?" Desmond asked in a low voice.

"No. There should be some foot and car traffic. Not this...emptiness."

He nodded, agreeing with my assessment. "Let's get out of here."

Desmond unbuttoned his suit jacket, probably so he could grab his pocket watch and its deadly, attached chain. I tightened my grip on the bags of clothes, pie, and more I was carrying in my left hand, then slid my right hand down inside my shoulder bag, my fingers curling around the gun still hidden inside.

We crossed the street to the next block and kept walking at a steady pace. Not running, but not dawdling either, and both of us still scanning our surroundings. This block was also devoid of people, although an anonymous sedan was parked at the corner. Farther up the street, an old junker car was pulled up haphazardly to the curb, as though its driver had drunkenly parked it there and then abandoned it.

We walked past the sedan. Desmond and I both glanced inside, but it was empty, so we kept going, heading toward the junker. The closer we got to it, the more something about both vehicles nagged at me.

I frowned. Wait. Why were two cars parked here? Wasn't this street a tow-away zone—

DANGER! DANGER! DANGER!

My synesthesia blared to life like a siren wailing in my mind, and a red haze enveloped the old junker car in front of us. For a moment, I thought the vehicle was actually on fire, but then I realized it was just my magic, warning me away.

"Stop!" I dropped the canvas bags in my left hand, reached out, and grabbed Desmond's arm. "Get back!"

I hadn't even finished speaking when Desmond whirled around, putting his back to the car, almost as if he sensed the same danger that I did. Then he surged forward, wrapped his arms around me, and pulled me up against his body, almost as if he were trying to shield me from whatever horrible thing he knew was going to happen next—

The car exploded with a fiery roar.

TWELVE

DESMOND

I dimly heard Charlotte shout a warning, and her hand clamped around my forearm, almost as if she was going to pull me away from whatever danger she sensed. But I was focused on the old car parked by the curb in the middle of the block.

No one was sitting inside the vehicle. No driver meant no engine running, and the car should have been completely cold, still, and silent, with no energy of any sort pulsing through or around it. But a faint, constant, electrical hum emanated from the vehicle, and a telltale series of *beep-beep-beeps* sounded, too soft for mortal ears to hear. Even I might have missed the hum and the beeps, if not for my galvanism. But I'd heard both sounds plenty of times in my nightmares, so I knew exactly what was going to happen next.

I immediately dropped my briefcase, whirled around, and wrapped my arms around Charlotte. She gasped, and her purse tumbled off her shoulder, but I ignored her surprise and churned my legs, forcing her back, back, back—

The car exploded. Hot, concussive waves of energy

slammed into my body and tossed me forward, along with Charlotte.

I tried to stop it, tried to reach out with my magic and pull as much of that raw, brutal energy inside myself as possible, but there was simply too much of it, and some of the power surged through me and zinged into Charlotte, like we had both been struck by lightning. She screamed. At least, I thought she screamed. Hard to tell above the roaring buzz in my own ears.

That all happened in an instant. In the next one, I was lifted off my feet, and Charlotte along with me, and we were both thrown backward toward the sedan parked at the corner. This hard, unyielding impact would be even worse than the force of the explosion, so I seized on the waves of energy still pulsing through me and used them to flip us around so my body would hit the sedan first.

My back slammed into the car hood hard enough to leave a dent, like I was a cartoon character. This time, I was the one who screamed. Charlotte's body rammed into my own, and she grunted, although I couldn't tell how badly she was injured.

More energy zipped through me, joining what was already raging through my body. The heat from the explosion and then the impact of hitting the sedan formed a wicked one-two combo, like I'd been sucker-punched by two giant, red-hot fists. My head spun around, and I gasped for air. Once again, I tried to contain the waves of power, tried to channel them, but there was simply too much energy, too much raw force, for my galvanism to handle...

I must have blacked out.

One second, I was holding Charlotte and getting slammed into the car hood. The next, I was flat on my back on the sidewalk beside the sedan, wondering how I had gotten there.

Those waves of energy kept burning and crackling like

liquid fire through my veins, once again making my head spin and stealing my breath. My eyes were twitching, my arms and legs were shaking, and sweat dripped down my forehead, but I rolled over and pushed myself up onto my hands and knees, even though all I wanted to do was slump back down to the cool, still pavement until the intense energy faded away. But I had to move. Whoever had triggered that explosion would come and make sure the job was done and we were dead.

"Charlotte?" I called out, my voice a choked rasp. "Charlotte!"

My gaze darted around, but I didn't see her lying on the sidewalk. Had someone already snatched her? If so, why had they left me behind? Did they mistakenly think I was dead?

Boots thumped on the pavement, and a shadow dropped over my body, blocking out the fire, heat, and light from the still-burning car. My head snapped up.

A cleaner loomed over me.

He was wearing a black suit and tie and holding a gun down by his side. Black hair, brown eyes, ruddy skin, square jaw. His name escaped me, but I'd seen him before, and he was definitely from Section.

"You should have died on that beach in Australia with your partner," the cleaner sneered. "But Adrian Anatoly sends his regards on your delayed death."

He lifted his gun and aimed it at my head. I raised my own hand, trying to focus through the waves of power still cascading through me, trying to find the electrical charge that made his heart beat and stop it cold—

A low wolf whistle sounded. Startled, the cleaner turned in that direction, and a figure darted around the front of the sedan.

Charlotte.

She hurried forward, closing the distance between herself and the cleaner. He cursed and lifted his gun to shoot her, but she was faster. With one hand, she grabbed his gun and shoved it to the side, away from her body. Then she growled, snapped up her other hand, and jabbed her fingers into his throat.

The cleaner wheezed and staggered away, but she followed him, ripping the gun out of his hand. The weapon skittered across the pavement, and Charlotte dove after it. The cleaner cursed again, leaned down, and stretched out his hand, like he was going to grab her short ponytail and yank her back toward him, but I crab-walked forward and kicked out with my foot.

The awkward, jerking motion made my head spin yet again, but I managed to drive the point of my wing tip into the cleaner's ankle, and he hissed, staggered forward, and crashed down onto his hands and knees. Charlotte scooped up the gun from the sidewalk, scrambled to her feet, and whirled back around to face the cleaner.

I thought she might hesitate, but she aimed the gun at the cleaner's head, and pulled the trigger as quickly, coldly, and calmly as I would have.

Thanks to the gun's suppressor, the shot was barely audible to my still-ringing ears. The cleaner's head snapped back, and he dropped to the sidewalk dead. Blood sprayed every-where, and a few drops stung my cheek, the coppery warmth soaking into my skin and mixing with all the other energy still pounding through my veins.

I grimaced, but I spotted two more cleaners hurrying along the sidewalk, racing in our direction, both with guns clutched in their hands. "Behind you—"

Before I could finish rasping out my warning, Charlotte

whipped around, as if she had somehow sensed the cleaners on her own. Once again, she didn't hesitate.

She fired six more shots in rapid succession, and the other two cleaners dropped to the ground, dead from the bullets in their chests. Where had she learned how to shoot like that?

Charlotte kept her gun up and pivoted back and forth, scanning the sidewalk, along with the street and the rest of the block.

By this point, the energy crashing through my body had died down to smaller, more manageable ripples, and I forced myself to stagger up and onto my feet. I took a step toward Charlotte, but my legs buckled, and I would have fallen on my face, if I hadn't reached out and latched onto the sedan's door handle.

Charlotte whipped around to me. "Desmond! Are you okay?"

Eyes wide in her pale face, Charlotte's aura pulsed a dark, worried blue, but her gun arm was rock-steady, and her finger curled around the trigger, ready to fire at anyone else who threatened her.

"I'm fine," I said. "We need to get out of here."

She nodded and slid the gun into her jacket pocket. Somehow, her purse had ended up at my feet, along with the canvas bags of her clothes, shoes, and toiletries, so I leaned down and scooped them all up, even though the motion made my head spin again. I also staggered over and grabbed my briefcase from where it had landed on the sidewalk.

Charlotte darted forward, wrapped her arm around my waist, and tucked her shoulder under mine. Together, we hurried down the sidewalk, moving away from the three dead cleaners and the still-burning car as quickly as we could.

Charlotte steered me to the first alley we reached. In the distance, police sirens started to wail, and red and blue lights swirled ominously in our direction.

"Hurry!" she urged. "Hurry! Hurry!"

I forced myself to ignore the many aches and pains in my body, especially those in my head and back, and move faster. We limped into the alley just as the first police car sped by us.

"This way! This way!" Charlotte hissed.

She helped me through that alley and out the far side. I pointed to the right.

"Touchstone Building," I rasped. "Safe house. Six blocks that way."

Charlotte nodded, put her shoulder under mine again, and guided me in that direction.

We kept to the alleys, staying off the main streets as much as possible. We passed a few people, mostly homeless folks wrapped in plastic trash bags and curled up in cardboard boxes, but no one gave us a second look. Everyone knew to mind their own business this late at night.

Our quick pace helped to burn off some of the excess energy coursing through my body. With every step, my head cleared, and the buzzing in my ears slowly faded. By the time we reached the block where the Touchstone Building was, I was feeling much more like myself. Up ahead, the building's bright lights illuminated the street, along with the security guard stationed at a desk behind the glass doors.

I started in that direction, but Charlotte tugged me back.

"Wait," she said.

"What?"

"You have blood on your face." She reached up and swiped her thumb across my cheek.

Her skin was soft and warm as it glided across my own. Her hand curled around my chin, and she vigorously stroked the stubble on my jaw. Even though she was scrubbing the blood away, her touch made me want to purr and lean into her like a tomcat getting its jowls scratched.

I swayed toward Charlotte, who froze, her fingers still curled around my chin. She cleared her throat and dropped her hand.

"I don't see any blood on your clothes, although your suit looks dirty and rumpled..." She tugged down my jacket and straightened my tie, smoothing her hands down my chest. "There. That will have to do."

She stepped back, and I was surprised by how much I wanted her to stay right beside me. How much I wanted her hands to keep sliding lower and lower. How much I wanted to gather her up in my arms, bury my face in her neck, and drink in her clean, tantalizing, sugar-lime scent, along with her cool, blue, soothing aura...

"You ready?" Charlotte asked.

I forced myself to straighten and hold my head up high, as though my thoughts hadn't been down in the gutter. "Yeah. You?"

She nodded, and together, we headed toward the building entrance.

The Touchstone Building housed several businesses, including a coffee shop, a cupcakery, and a bookstore, although they were all closed for the night. The security guard, Brent, perked up at the sight of me opening one of the glass doors and walking toward him, although he frowned at Charlotte, still in her waitress uniform and now carrying her bags of clothes. Not exactly the kind of woman I had brought here during my previous stays.

I slung my arm around Charlotte's shoulder, pulling her close to my side. She stiffened and drew her elbow back as though she was going to jab me with it.

"Just go with it," I murmured. "Act like you're utterly besotted with me. Think of it as practice for the hotel gala in a few days."

She huffed, although she somehow turned the annoyed sound into a pealing giggle, and leaned her head against my shoulder. Brent's frown smoothed out, and he waved as we strolled past his desk.

"Mr. Macfarlane, so nice to see you again," the security guard called out.

"You too, Brent. This is my friend Charlotte. She'll be staying with me over the next few days. Please let her come and go as she pleases."

Brent's lips twitched as he tried to hold back a knowing smirk. "Of course, Mr. Macfarlane. You two have a good evening."

I winked at him. "Oh, I'm sure we will."

Charlotte giggled again, although this time, her elbow did dig into my side, hard enough to make me wince.

We staggered through the white marble lobby, which was deserted except for Brent, and made our way to the back of the building. I headed over to a set of double doors with the words *Touchstone Gallery* stretching across the glass. I punched in the code on the keypad, and one of the doors buzzed open. Charlotte and I stepped through to the other side, and the door shut and locked behind us.

Lights clicked on in the ceiling, revealing the same blank white marble floor and walls as out in the lobby, but everything else in here was a riot of color, shape, and texture.

Oil landscapes of the Virginia countryside covered the walls, along with more abstract works in neon-reds and -blues that reminded me of the food signs in the Moondust Diner's windows. Stone statues of pyramids and obelisks perched on clear plastic stands, while larger metal and fiberglass sculptures of lovers embracing stood in the corners. But my favorite was the gallery's current centerpiece—a three-foot statue of a black bear cub perched in a nine-foot-tall maple tree. The bear was made of dead wood, but the maple was still alive and should continue to grow for years to come when properly planted. An interesting take on sustainable art.

"An art gallery?" Charlotte asked in a curious voice. "*This* is your safe house?"

"More like a front business and a safe house all rolled into one." I eyed her, wondering if she would mock me like the General so often did, but she simply nodded, as if my words made perfect sense. An unexpected bit of relief trickled through me.

The General had never approved of my interest in art, referring to it as a *tomfool waste of time*, but my mother loved to paint, draw, and sculpt, and she had passed those passions down to me. I wasn't as naturally talented as my mother was, and my work for Section left little time to dabble, so I'd bought the Touchstone Gallery as a compromise. A lovely woman named Julia ran the gallery, although I had a hand in picking the artists we exhibited.

"I like it," Charlotte said. "Especially since I can recognize most of it."

"Not an abstract fan?"

She shrugged. "If you're going to claim something is art, then you should at least make it recognizable to other people. Otherwise, what's the point?"

I grinned. I'd had the same thought myself on more than one occasion. "Something else we agree on. You know, Numbers, I'm starting to think we could be soul mates."

She rolled her eyes. "Let's settle for partners in crime for now, and see how that goes."

My grin widened, but I turned away from her and headed toward an elevator in the gallery's back wall. A blue velvet rope cordoned off the elevator, while a sign next to it read *Going Up? Going Down? Or Going Nowhere?* with colorful arrows pointing in different directions.

Charlotte frowned. "Is this another piece of art? Or an actual elevator?"

"Both."

I stepped around the velvet rope and punched in another code on a keypad on the wall. The elevators doors creaked open, and I stepped into the car. Charlotte hesitated, but she followed me inside. The doors slid shut, and the elevator started to rise.

A few seconds later, the doors slid back. I peered out into the small, white marble antechamber beyond, but it was empty. I also reached out with my magic, but I didn't sense any electrical hums, currents, or other energy that shouldn't be here. No one was lying in wait to kill us. A refreshing change from the rest of the night.

"We're clear," I said.

Charlotte followed me over to a thick wooden door and watched while I punched in yet another keycode, making the door buzz open. She stepped through to the other side, and I shut and locked the door behind us. More lights clicked on, revealing a spacious apartment.

Charlotte let out a low whistle. "Nice digs, Dundee."

It was rather nice. The front of the space was part living room, part kitchen. A door to the left opened up into the master bedroom and bath, while a door to the right led to a smaller bedroom and bath. Julia had decorated the apartment, so everything from the kitchen island barstools to the sectional sofa in the living room to the window seat in the far wall that overlooked the street below was done in her preferred palette of black, white, and gray, with splashes of color here and there, like the hot-pink pillows spaced along the sofa.

I walked over and set my briefcase on the kitchen counter, then faced Charlotte.

She gave me a critical once-over. "Are you okay?"

"Yeah. Just a little sore. A few scrapes and bruises. I've had worse. You?"

She shrugged. "The same. More or less."

"And what you did?" I asked in a soft voice, not quite sure how to broach the subject.

"You mean killing those three cleaners?"

I nodded.

Her face hardened. "I'm fine." Anger flared in her eyes and pulsed in her aura, making it burn like a blue star around her heart. "Tonight isn't the first time I've killed someone. And if the past two days have been any indication, it won't be the last time either."

To my surprise, I wanted to ask her about those other times. What had happened, who had threatened her, why she had killed them. But I kept my mouth shut. It seemed wrong to question her after she had just saved my ass.

I pointed to the right. "There is the guest bedroom and bathroom. Julia, the woman who runs the gallery for me, keeps it well-stocked. Help yourself to soap, towels, shampoo. The same thing goes for the food in the fridge or anything else you need. And don't worry. No one at Section knows about this place, so we'll be safe here."

She nodded, hefted her bags a little higher on her shoulder, and headed in that direction.

I hesitated, then called out to her. "Charlotte?"

She turned around. "Yeah?"

"Thank you. For saving my life."

She nodded, then gave me a grim smile. "I suppose we're even now, Dundee."

"Yeah. I suppose we are."

She stepped into the bedroom and shut the door behind her. I stood there and stared at the closed door, strangely wishing that she would return.

THIRTEEN

CHARLOTTE

Like the rest of the apartment, the bedroom was sleek, clean, and chic, and contained the usual furniture— a king-size bed, a nightstand, a freestanding armoire. The bathroom featured an oversize claw-foot tub-and-shower combo, along with fancy packaged soaps and several new bottles of expensive lotions, shampoos, and conditioners. A fluffy white robe wrapped in plastic was hanging on the back of the bathroom door, as though this were a hotel instead of a home. I wondered if the toiletries and robe got replaced every time Desmond brought a new woman here. Probably.

I sighed. The adrenaline from the fight was wearing off, and I sensed my body starting to crash. That was the reason— the *only* reason—why I was having such snide, petty thoughts about Desmond Percy's potential companions.

Part of me longed to curl up on the bed and pretend like the last hour had never happened, but if I did that, I wouldn't get back up. So I locked the bedroom door, then forced myself to go through my bags. To my relief, my laptop, phone, and clothes hadn't been damaged during the explosion and subsequent fight, so I plugged my electronics into an outlet to charge, then hung up the assortment of cardigans, T-shirts, cargo pants, and waitress uniforms in the armoire in hopes that some of the wrinkles would fall out of them. I also lined up my spare sets of sneakers in a neat row along the wall. Once that was done, I trudged into the bathroom and turned on the lights.

The sight of my reflection in the mirrored cabinets over the sink made me blanch. My face was pale and haggard, purple streaks of exhaustion gleamed under my dull, tired eyes, and my hair was a haphazard mess, half in and half out of its previously neat ponytail. Even worse, tiny brownish-red specks covered the front of my uniform, as though someone had flicked a paintbrush at me. Blood from the cleaner I'd shot at close range. More dark specks also covered my jacket, although they weren't as visible on the navy fleece.

I grimaced, shrugged out of my jacket, and let it fall to the floor. A soft *clunk* sounded as the cleaner's gun in the pocket hit the white tile. I grimaced again and scooted the jacket aside with my dirty sneaker.

My head dropped, and I reached for the white buttons on the front of my shirt, which were also speckled with blood. My fingers started trembling, and they slipped off the top button, smearing the blood. I gritted my teeth and tried again, and then again, but my fingers kept sliding off the button. The longer and harder I tried to undo it, the more my hands shook. Soon, tears were streaming down my cheeks, dripping off my chin, and hitting the front of my shirt, further staining the light-blue fabric. I hadn't cried after the first cleaner attack, but for some reason, I couldn't stop the waterworks tonight.

After my father died, I had thought I was finally *done*

with this—with all the violence, all the death, all the killing. But once again, I'd been thrust into a situation where it had been me or someone else, and I had chosen me the way I always did. Oh, I knew it was a normal, natural, human response, a survival instinct that everyone had, mortal and paramortal alike, but that knowledge didn't make the aftermath any easier to bear, especially since I couldn't get my fingers or that damn button to work. A sob rose in my throat, and I clenched my fist around the top button to tear it off, along with the rest of my bloodstained shirt—

A soft knock sounded on the bedroom door. "Charlotte? Are you okay?" Desmond's voice floated through the thick wood. Somehow, the faint note of concern in his tone made his Aussie accent deeper and even more appealing than usual.

I swiped the tears off my face and cleared my throat before answering. "Yeah. I'm fine."

The lie slipped off my tongue with ease, although I spotted a telltale red haze around my mouth in the mirror, as though I were wearing crimson lipstick. One of the side effects of my magical synesthesia. I couldn't speak a lie without seeing visible proof of it, even if no one else did.

I cleared my throat again. "I'm going to take a shower and then crash. We'll talk in the morning, okay?"

Silence. Several seconds ticked by. Desmond was probably hovering outside the bedroom door, wondering if the night's violence had broken me. If I'd had the energy for it, I would have told him not to worry. Thanks to my father and his enemies following him home, this latest attack wasn't even a minor chip in the cracked windshield of my life.

"Okay," Desmond said, that faint note of concern still deepening his voice. "If you need anything, come get me. See you in the morning."

More silence. Then his footsteps softly, steadily retreating. I waited the better part of a minute, making sure he wasn't coming back. Then I turned on the water in the sink, cranking it up as fast and loud as it would go.

My hands started shaking again, and this time, my legs joined the persistent, wobbly chorus. I put my back up against the closest wall and slowly slid down to the cold tile floor. Then I drew my knees up to my chest, buried my head in my arms, and let the shakes and the sobs sweep me away.

Five minutes passed. Maybe ten. My shakes and sobs slowly subsided, and I wiped my tears away, hoisted myself onto my feet, and started cleaning myself up. I stripped off the ruined waitress uniform and my torn tights and shoved them into the trash can, then took the hottest shower I could stand to wash off the cleaners' blood, along with the rest of the dirt and grime from the fight. One of the mirrored cabinets over the sink held medical supplies, and I popped a couple of aspirin and slathered some ointment on the worst of my cuts and bruises.

Considering how large, loud, and intense the explosion had been, I had gotten off pretty easily. My knees were badly scraped, and my body ached like I'd gone ten rounds with a professional boxer, but other than that, I was still in one piece.

Thanks to Desmond.

Somehow, he had used his smooth, effortless grace to spin us around in midair so that he was the one who had slammed into that car instead of me. He had clearly been rattled and shaken up, but a few minutes later, he seemed fine, as if nothing had happened. What kind of magic, what kind of paramortal power, let him walk away from what should have been a backbreaking blow? I didn't know, but I was even more curious about Desmond Percy than before.

But my many questions would have to wait until morning. Right now, I was too tired to do anything but put on my thin, worn-out pajamas and crawl into bed. I thought I might toss and turn, the way I had so many times before after other similarly traumatic events, but my eyes slid shut, and I was out as soon as my head hit the pillow...

A scream woke me.

I sat bolt upright in bed, my eyes wide, my heart galloping up into my throat, my hands fisting in the soft sheets. What was going on? Had more cleaners found us? Were they storming into the apartment and murdering Desmond at this very instant?

I tossed the covers aside, lunged toward the nightstand, and grabbed the gun lying there, the one that had been hidden in my shoulder bag all day. Then I snapped up the gun and aimed it at the door, expecting someone to burst through it...

Nothing happened.

No shots rang out, no crashes sounded, no footsteps *thump-thump-thump-thumped* in my direction. I strained to listen, but the apartment was silent, and my inner voice was quiet and not urgently whispering *danger-danger-danger—*

Another scream ripped through the air, although this one was a bit softer than before and quickly trailed off into a choked sob. I frowned. That sounded like...Desmond.

I bit my lip, hesitating to investigate, but my concern and curiosity won out, so I slipped out of bed and threw on the thick plush robe from the bathroom. Then I slid my gun into the robe's pocket, opened the bedroom door, and peered outside.

Moonlight streamed in through the windows, highlighting the kitchen and living room. I scanned the sectional sofa, the island counter, and everything else, but no one was crouching behind the furniture or lurking in the shadows, and the apartment was empty.

A third scream sounded, although it too quickly choked off into more of a low, snarling sob. I tiptoed across the apartment and crept over to Desmond's bedroom. The door was cracked open, and I slowly pushed on the wood so that I could see what was happening inside the room.

A small reading lamp on a nightstand was turned down low, casting the area in a soft, murky glow. Desmond was lying on his back in bed, his twitching eyes closed, his hands fisted in the gray sheet. He wasn't wearing a shirt, and the dim white light brought out the hard, muscled planes of his chest, along with the sprinkling of dark blond hair that arrowed down his stomach.

I sighed in appreciation. Cleaners were known for being exceptionally fit, but his body was even more glorious than I had imagined. I would have stood there and looked my fill, if not for the low, choked sounds rumbling out of his throat and the way his head lolled from side to side, even though his eyes were still tightly shut.

"Graham!" he mumbled in a low, hoarse voice. "The beach! It's rigged! It's rigged!"

He was obviously caught up in some nightmarish memory from the Blacksea mission, the one that had resulted in the death of his friend and all those other Section agents. Sympathy flooded my heart. I'd had more than a few bad dreams myself over the years.

"Desmond?" I called out, hoping the soft sound might ease him awake.

"Anatoly," he snarled, still caught up in his nightmare. "Gotta get that bastard. Gotta make him pay…"

"Desmond?" I asked again, a bit louder.

I crept up to the foot of the bed. I knew better than to try to shake him awake. Desmond might be confused and attack me, thinking I was part of his nightmare. Instead, I reached out and gently placed my hand on his ankle, which was peeking out from beneath the covers. A similar small touch had sometimes helped rouse my father out of his nightmares.

"Desmond?" I asked yet again.

My voice and touch didn't wake him, but he shuddered out a breath, and his body relaxed a bit, as though something had pulled him out of whatever horror he'd been reliving.

"Blue," Desmond rasped in a softer, calmer voice. "Breathe in the blue…"

I had no idea what that meant, but I didn't want to cause him any further distress, so I released his ankle and stepped back. He started mumbling again, mostly about the color blue and auras and other things I didn't understand. But he seemed calmer, so I crept out of the bedroom, hoping he would either fall into a more peaceful sleep or eventually wake up on his own.

I started to return to my own bedroom when a blur of pink caught my eye. I glanced to my left. One of the landscape paintings on the wall was a bit crooked, which had pinged my synesthesia, and an odd sliver of gray was peeking out from below the painting's bottom right corner. Curious, I walked over and hoisted the frame off its hook to reveal…

A large wall safe.

Now *this* was interesting. I glanced toward the bedroom, but Desmond had quieted, and his nightmare seemed to have passed. So I set the painting down on the floor, then clicked on a nearby lamp and took a closer look at the safe.

It was a standard safe, a thick metal shell embedded in the wall with an electronic keypad on the front. Probably locked with a three-digit code like the doors in the art gallery and the apartment one that Desmond had opened earlier. I leaned forward and reached out with my magic, staring at the numbers on the keypad. My synesthesia kicked in, and I screened out the numbers bathed in red. They weren't part of the combination, so I focused on the two black numbers that were. It took me a few tries, but I finally entered the right code—*007*.

"Seriously, Dundee?" I shook my head, but I turned the handle and opened the safe to find...

Files.

Since Desmond was a cleaner, I had been expecting a cache of weapons, along with some passports and a few stacks of cash. Maybe even another pocket watch with a deadly chain or some other seemingly innocuous yet extremely dangerous gadget. Not files. More curiosity filled me, and I grabbed the manila folders, took them over to the kitchen island, turned on the light over the stove, and sat down on one of the barstools. The first file was labeled *Blacksea*, and I opened it and started reading.

It was the same report I'd read on my laptop when I'd first gone into work, the one detailing Desmond's doomed mission to kill Adrian Anatoly. I scanned the information, but it was exactly the same as what I'd read before, so I set that file aside and looked through the next one. It too was about the doomed Blacksea mission, an after-action report that speculated how Anatoly could have possibly known Section was sending cleaners and a strike team after him. Lots of questions were proposed, but no real conclusions were drawn. I snorted with disgust. Of course not. The Section higher-ups would want to keep the fact that they had a mole in their ranks as quiet as possible.

I flipped through the rest of the folders, but they were all more of the same—until I got to the last file.

Initial Report on Henrika Hyde. Dated two months ago. With my name all over it.

I reared back in surprise. Why would Desmond have this file hidden in his safe? Even more curious than before, I flipped through and carefully scanned the document, but the report looked just as I remembered it, and none of the pages seemed to be missing. Finally, on the next to last page, buried half-way down, I came across a single line that had been high-lighted with a blue marker.

United Corporation—a known shell company of Henrika Hyde. Used to make supposed charitable donations to the Halstead Foundation.

A handwritten note had been scribbled in the margin beside the typed, highlighted line—*Anatoly connection.*

Henrika was connected to Anatoly? Of course. I should have realized it sooner. Desmond didn't want to take out Henrika just because her new Redburn weapon was a threat. No, he wanted to capture—and probably torture—Henrika in hopes of finding out where Anatoly was hiding, so he could avenge his dead partner.

And he was using me and my work to do it.

"Manipulative, lying bastard," I hissed.

I glared at the open bedroom door, but no more screams or murmurs rang out, and the silence indicated that Desmond was finally sleeping peacefully. He didn't care about protect-ing me. Not really. He was just using my *big brain*, as he called it, to get closer to Henrika and hopefully Anatoly in the process.

I thought about storming into his bedroom, dumping the files on top of his head, and waking his ass up. Then I would get dressed, grab my things, and…go where, exactly?

Four cleaners had tried to kill me last night, and then three more assassins had targeted me tonight. Oh, I had a suspicion the car bomb had been meant more for Desmond, to disrupt his magic, whatever it was, so that the cleaners could kill us both. Either way, someone still wanted me dead. Probably whatever mole—or moles—were inside Section, working for either Henrika, Anatoly, or both of them.

Like it or not, Desmond Percy was still my best chance of surviving these dangerous spy games. If he captured or killed Henrika and then Anatoly further down the line, then maybe the threat to me would disappear with their deaths. Either way, Desmond had backed me into a corner, one I couldn't escape without his help.

"Lying *bastard*," I hissed again.

But the longer I glared at the files, the more my gaze kept straying back to that one blue highlighted line about the United Corporation. The shell company was a new wrinkle in Henrika's financial holdings and something I'd been meaning to follow up on but just hadn't had the chance to yet. I glanced at the clock on the kitchen wall. Just after five in the morning. I wasn't going to get any more sleep, and there was no time like the present. So I slid off the stool and went into the bedroom to get dressed.

Besides, the sooner I helped Desmond get to Henrika, the sooner I could go back to my quiet, safe, normal life—and leave him to his dangerous, blood-soaked revenge.

FOURTEEN

DESMOND

The muttering woke me.

The low, almost musical sound was strangely pleasant. Certainly more pleasant than the nightmares.
Ever since the Blacksea mission, my sleep had been...well,
troubled was putting it mildly. And the car bomb hadn't
helped. The flash of fire, the scorching heat, the shock wave
of the explosion, the buzz in my ears, the overwhelming
energy zinging through my body afterward. The sensations
had been eerily similar to the IEDs that had exploded on the
beach around Graham and me...

I scrubbed my hands over my face, shoving the memories
away.

My hands dropped to my sides, and I glanced over at
the clock on the nightstand. Just after six a.m. Usually, I
tossed and turned all night, but the last time I remembered
looking at the clock was around two. I also felt...okay.
Like I'd actually gotten a few hours of decent sleep for a
change.

But the strangest thing was that I dimly remembered something intruding on my nightmares, something cool and blue that had soothed the fire and fear roaring through my mind. The more I tried to remember what it was, the faster the sensation slipped away. Soon, it vanished altogether, although muttered words caught my ear:

"...Hyde Engineering...

"...United Corporation...

"...Adrian Anatoly..."

The last name made me lurch upward. My head snapped from side to side, my heart rate spiked, and my hands fisted in the sweat-soaked sheet that covered my body. I was going to rip the sheet off the bed, twist it into a weapon, and strangle Anatoly and whatever men he'd brought here to kill me—

"Lying bastard."

Another mutter rang out, and the soft, feminine voice penetrated the fog of rage clouding my mind. Suddenly, I remembered that I was safe in my gallery apartment—and that Charlotte Locke was here. And apparently, very much awake. I frowned. But why would she be talking about Anatoly?

Worried, I climbed out of bed, threw on an old T-shirt over my pajama pants, and padded out into the living room.

Charlotte was perched on one of the kitchen barstools. She was already dressed for the day in a navy-blue cardigan over a white T-shirt with blue musical notes. Her cargo pants and sneakers were also both navy-blue.

A steaming mug of what looked and smelled like hot chocolate sat by her elbow, while reams of paper, piles of photos, and stacks of empty folders covered the island counter in front of her. Sprinkled here and there were neon highlighters and colored pencils that I recognized as coming from the stash of art supplies in one of the kitchen drawers.

She had definitely taken my advice to heart about making herself at home.

"What are you doing?" I asked, walking over to her.

Charlotte kept scanning a piece of paper, carefully highlighting one line after another. "Research."

"On what?"

"Henrika Hyde's connection to Adrian Anatoly," she said in that same distracted voice.

I froze, staring at the papers and photos spread out across the countertop. *Blacksea. Hyde. Anatoly.* My gaze snapped from one empty folder to the next, then over to the opposite wall. The landscape painting was sitting on the floor, and my safe was standing wide open.

"What are you doing?"

My harsh tone finally prompted Charlotte to look up from the papers. Her gaze flicked over me. I probably should have put on some real clothes before I'd come out here, but it was too late now, and I would be damned if I would retreat because of some flimsy pajama pants.

"You had a nightmare," she said. "You were screaming, so I went into your bedroom to see if you were okay."

Her voice was calm and even, with no hint of reproach or judgment, as though she were talking about the weather instead of something I desperately wished she had never witnessed. Somehow, her light, easy tone and steady gaze made me feel even worse. My demons were my own, and I didn't want anyone to suspect they even existed—much less hear the screams that rang in my mind and spewed out of my mouth night after night.

What had I been thinking bringing her to my apartment? I should have stashed her in another safe house, not here with me where she could see—and hear—just how weak I truly was.

But I couldn't change the fact that she had observed my latest nightmare, so I moved on to a different subject. "And the files?"

She gave an unapologetic shrug. "I got them out of your safe."

"How did you do that?"

She shrugged again. "*Double-oh-seven* might be amusing, but it isn't a hard code to crack. As for exactly *how* I did it, well, I suppose the same way you managed to absorb most of the blast from that bomb last night, as well as get up and walk away after being slammed into a car hood." Her eyes narrowed. "Care to tell me how you did all of *that*?"

I didn't respond. One of the handful of things my father and I had ever agreed on was that the fewer people who knew about my galvanism, the better. Even among paramortals, it was a rare, powerful ability, and the General didn't want to risk someone kidnapping and then forcing me to use my magic for their dastardly purposes. No, my father only wanted me to serve Section 47 and his own dastardly purposes.

"What's wrong, Dundee? You don't want to chat about your magic?" Charlotte asked. "Yeah, I didn't think you would like that any more than I would."

I ground my teeth and crossed my arms over my chest. The motion must have caught Charlotte's eyes because her gaze flicked over my chest again, then slid lower. Her aura spiked a bright, hot blue like a match flaring to life. Was she...checking me out?

I looked at her in return. I'd never thought that cardigans were particularly sexy, but the way the soft blue fabric clung to and yet hid her curves at the same time was very intriguing—and did some very surprising and rather uncomfortable things to my anatomy.

Charlotte cleared her throat and dropped her eyes, focusing on the files again. I uncrossed my arms and stepped around the island, putting it between us and hiding the evidence of her unexpected effect on me.

"Your files made for an interesting read," she said.

"How so?"

"Well, for starters, they told me that Henrika and Anatoly seem to be in business together. They both have access to a mutual shell company called the United Corporation. Henrika uses it to funnel charitable donations here and there, lately to the Halstead Foundation, while Anatoly dumps large amounts of money into the corporation's accounts, then takes most of it right back out again, I assume to finance his terrorist operations. But you already knew all of that, thanks to my report on Henrika and your own digging into Anatoly."

Charlotte raised her gaze to mine again. "Adrian Anatoly is the *real* reason why you're here. You're not planning to turn Henrika over to Section. At least, not immediately. You want to squeeze her for info on Anatoly so you can find him and avenge Graham."

Once again, she said it in a matter-of-fact tone with no reproach or judgment. And once again, it made me feel even worse than if she'd started screaming accusations. I opened my mouth, but Charlotte pointed her finger at me in warning.

"Don't bother lying," she said. "It will just make me even more pissed than I already am."

"Fine," I growled. "You're right. The Redburn mission is just a cover so I can get close to Henrika and pump her for information on Anatoly. There. I said it. Are you happy now?"

She leaned back on her stool and crossed her arms over her chest. "Do I *look* like I'm happy, Dundee?"

"I don't know, Numbers," I shot right back. "So far, all you've done is glower at me."

"And all *you've* done is dance around the truth and put me in danger," she snapped. "You *never* cared about protecting me. You just wanted to see what else I might know about Henrika."

"You're damn right," I snarled again, my hands clenching into fists. "If I have to choke the life out of Henrika Hyde with my bare hands to get the smallest lead on where Anatoly is hiding, then I will happily do that to her and anyone else who gets in my way."

"Even me?"

"Even you," I promised.

Charlotte glared at me, and I did the same thing to her.

The longer I looked at her, the more I worried about what she would do now that she knew my real agenda. That she might run straight to Trevor Donnelly and Gia Chan and ruin any chance I had of getting my hands on Henrika Hyde.

Charlotte's aura flared up, burning a bright blue, as if her anger and frustration matched my own. My fingers twitched, and I had a sudden, crazy urge to round the island, yank her into my arms, and... I didn't know what. Strangle her. Kiss her. Maybe both. The only thing I knew for certain was that Charlotte Locke was driving me absolutely *crazy*—

The lights flickered.

Startled, Charlotte glanced up. The second she looked away, I realized just how much electricity, just how much power, was pounding through my body, beating in time to the anger, frustration, and all the other unwanted feelings crackling back and forth between Charlotte and me.

I grimaced and forced myself to relax my hands and slowly release the electricity I had been unconsciously gathering up. I hadn't done something like this, hadn't lost control, in years. More proof that I needed to wrap up this mission and get far away from Charlotte Locke as soon as possible.

The lights quit flickering, and Charlotte looked at me again. Her eyes narrowed, and I could almost see the mental calculations going on in her blue gaze.

"You can do something with energy, with electricity. That's your power. Manipulating it is how you got up and walked away after being slammed into that car last night. I've heard of your ability. What's it called?" She snapped her fingers. "*Galvanism*. That's it."

I bit back a curse and opened my mouth to deny it, but she pointed her finger at me again in warning.

Her words sparked an idea in my own mind. This time, my eyes narrowed. "And your synesthesia lets you do more than see mistakes and typos in reports. You can tell when people are lying because you can *hear* it. I'm guessing your magic also warns you about danger. That's how you knew there was a bomb in that old car."

She blinked in surprise. Her pointed finger wilted, and her hand dropped to the counter. A tense, uncomfortable silence descended over the apartment.

I scrubbed my hand through my hair again, then down my face, trying to get my emotions under control. Charlotte and I might both work for Section, might both ostensibly be on the same side, but so far, all we'd done was lie to each other. I didn't want to lie to her—or to myself. Not anymore. That was something the General would have done, and I'd promised myself long ago I would not be the same sort of man my father was. Besides, Graham wouldn't want me to avenge him like this—by putting an innocent woman in danger.

I sighed, breaking the silence. "You're right. I'm here to use Henrika to track down Anatoly so I can kill him. But I didn't intentionally involve you in my plan, and I didn't knowingly put you in danger. I just wanted to get more insight into your report and pick your brain about Henrika.

That's why I came over to you in the cafeteria. Someone else sent those cleaners after you. Whether they would have done that if I hadn't approached you... Well, I don't know. But if I've put you in even more danger, then I'm sorry. That was never my intention."

"Truth," Charlotte said in an absent voice, staring down at the files again. "And they would have come after me anyway. Gregory Jensen dying in a cycling accident last week is entirely too convenient. They killed him before you ever came to D.C., most likely to get him to quit making noise about going after Henrika. I was probably scheduled to have a similar *accident* sooner or later, but you showing up probably accelerated their schedule."

She waved her hand over the files. "You know that this new mission is doomed, right? Because if Henrika and Anatoly are connected, then the mole is most likely leaking information to *both* of them, which means Henrika probably already knows everything about the Redburn mission—and us. And, of course, since we don't know who the mole is, we can't trust anyone else, not even Gia, Trevor, or the other supervisors."

"Of course I know that," I replied. "I also know we might not have the proper backup from Section during the mission and that Henrika will probably set some trap for us."

"But?"

"But if there is even the smallest chance I can get close enough to her to get information about the mole, or especially where Anatoly is hiding, then I have to take it. The risk is worth the reward." I straightened up. "Besides, I'm a cleaner. One of the best in all of Section. I can handle Henrika and her bodyguards."

"Careful, Dundee," Charlotte replied. "Your arrogance is showing."

I grinned. "It's not arrogance if you can back it up."

She rolled her eyes. "Is this all the information you have?"

I frowned at the abrupt change in subject. "What do you mean?"

She swept her hand out over the counter again. "Is this all the information you have on Henrika and Anatoly?"

"Yeah..." I replied, not quite sure where she was going with this.

"Can you get me more? From Section? Files that I can't normally access?"

"Yeah. I have level-seven clearance, thanks to the General. But why?"

"Because I need *more*—more reports, more files, every scrap of information Section has on Henrika, Anatoly, and every agent who ever had anything to do with you, Graham, the Blacksea mission, or could remotely access the mission info through the Section databases."

My frown deepened. "For what?"

Charlotte leaned forward, her eyes and aura both burning a bright, determined blue. "So we can pull off the Redburn mission, and I can help you get to Henrika."

Every word she said only confused me more. "Why would you want to do that? After everything I've just told you?"

She leaned back and shrugged. "Because the sooner we get to Henrika, the sooner we find out who the mole is inside Section."

Understanding flashed through me. "You want to know who sent those cleaners to kill you."

"Absolutely. You want revenge. Well, me too. And like it or not, we have a much better chance of getting revenge together, especially since you're the only one I can trust." Her face hardened. "Besides, they should have known better than to screw with a Locke. I might not be a cleaner like my father was, but nobody tries to murder me and gets away with it."

Ferocity was something else I hadn't expected from her, but I liked it—far more than I should have.

Charlotte's gaze flicked over my body again. Her aura burned even brighter and hotter than before, but it was nothing compared to the cruel grin curving her lips, one that did those very surprising and uncomfortable things to my anatomy again.

"Go get dressed, Dundee," she purred. "We have work to do."

FIFTEEN

CHARLOTTE

Desmond disappeared into his bedroom and emerged twenty minutes later, after showering and donning another light gray suit. His watch was nestled in his vest pocket as usual, and he was once again wearing a bold, rebellious tie, this one a beautiful royal-blue that brought out the lighter, more electric blue of his eyes.

He laid his suit jacket over one of the kitchen barstools, moving with that innate grace I found so strangely hypnotic. I was still sitting at the island, and the scent of his fresh, clean, pine-scented soap wafted over me. I couldn't decide which version of Desmond I found more appealing—all slick, coifed, and buttoned up, or how deliciously messy, rumpled, and casual he had looked when he had strolled into the kitchen earlier, his pajama pants slung low on his hips, his paper-thin T-shirt stretched tight across his chest, accentuating all those glorious, rippling muscles...

My heart quickened, as did other parts of me, and I had to shift around on my stool to ease the sudden ache between my thighs.

I was such an *idiot*.

Being attracted to Desmond Percy was one thing. I could easily handle that hormonal reaction and admire his gorgeous lethality from afar. But I was actually starting to *like* him, just a little bit, which worried me.

Despite the fact that we had agreed to work together, and the promises we had made to each other, we each had our own agendas and would do whatever it took to accomplish our own disparate goals. I couldn't let my emotions cloud my judgment—not if I wanted to survive.

"Find anything yet?" Desmond's low, husky voice sent a shiver zipping down my spine.

"Nothing so far," I replied, pushing away my lustful thoughts and gesturing at my laptop, which I'd cracked open while he'd been in the shower. "My work isn't classified, so anyone inside Section could have accessed my reports on Henrika Hyde. But your Blacksea mission *was* classified, so when I get to the office, I'm going to start cross-checking and see who looked at both files. Maybe that will at least give us a smaller pool of suspects."

"Good," Desmond said. "You do that, and I'll download every report and personnel record I can find about Henrika, Anatoly, and the agents involved in the Blacksea mission."

He strode over to the refrigerator, opened it, and started pulling out food—apples, carrots, pineapple chunks, even some spinach leaves. He carried everything over to a blender on the back counter, then grabbed a knife and started cutting up the fruits and veggies.

His knife work was as quick and skillful as a professional chef's, and I found myself strangely mesmerized by the way he maneuvered the blade up and down, and back and forth...

I shook my head. *Get a grip, Charlotte!* He was cutting

up produce, not offering to use those quick, skilled fingers on me.

"What are you doing?" I asked, mostly to distract myself from my continued lustful thoughts.

"Making my morning smoothie."

Desmond dumped everything into a blender, added some fresh-squeezed lime juice, along with diced ginger and a generous drizzle of honey, then turned on the appliance. A minute later, he flipped off the blender and poured the resulting dark green liquid into two glasses. He slid a jaunty, red-and-white-striped straw into one of the smoothies, then handed it to me.

"To our new partnership." He clinked his glass against mine, then downed his beverage in one long gulp.

I sniffed the green liquid, which smelled mostly of lime juice, then took a small, cautious sip through the straw. It tasted like a mouthful of grass that was somehow sweet and tart at the same time. *Blech.* I crinkled my nose and set the glass down.

Desmond eyed me. "I don't think I've ever seen a person's lips actually curl with disgust before. I suppose I can mark that off my bucket list now. You should drink up, Numbers. It's good for you, especially that big brain of yours."

I shuddered at the thought of willingly drinking more of that horrid green liquid. "Let me guess. You're one of those cleaner health nuts who doesn't believe in eating sugar, carbs, or anything else that actually tastes good."

He grinned. "My body *is* a temple."

Oh, yes, yes, it was. One that my hands and lips desperately wanted to explore. "Well, I learned a long time ago that life is too short to eat seeds and sprouts."

"Ah, so that's why you take home pie from your diner every night."

I silently cursed. I'd totally forgotten about the cherry pie Pablo had given me. I must have dropped it after the car bomb had exploded. What a waste. Cherry pie made for a great breakfast.

"Not *every* night," I said in a defensive tone. "Only when Pablo makes a flavor that I like."

Desmond arched an eyebrow. "Is there any flavor of pie you *don't* like?"

"Coconut cream. *Blech*. And pecan. Double *blech*. Pecans taste like dirt. So do walnuts. Why do people always insist on ruining sugar with nuts?"

Desmond kept staring at me, an amused expression on his face, and I actually found myself smiling back at him.

Despite the friendly, companionable silence, the smile slowly slipped from his face, and his eyes flashed a bright silver-blue. Something that almost seemed like a spark of interest, or perhaps even hunger, flickered across his face, although it quickly vanished.

Suddenly, the silence wasn't so friendly but rather charged with a current that hummed and snapped between us. At least, that's how it felt to me, and I didn't even have his galvanism magic. Then again, I'd just been mooning over him chopping vegetables, so there was no telling what I might be projecting. Desmond was probably about as interested in me as he was in a cactus.

Either way, I needed to concentrate on who wanted us both dead—not on how surprisingly charming Desmond Percy could be. So I nudged my smoothie glass a little farther to the side and focused on my laptop again.

"The mole has to be someone here in the D.C. station," I said. "Someone who knew I was digging into Henrika, and who wanted to bury my reports before anyone else besides Jensen paid too much attention to them or I discovered her connection to Anatoly. Henrika might be on Section's radar, but once it came out that she had dealings with Anatoly, well, that would put her at the top of Section's target list, especially given all the agents who died during the Blacksea mission. The Section higher-ups might not negotiate with terrorists, but they definitely make examples out of people who murder their agents."

Desmond nodded. "I agree. Then, when I came to town and showed an interest in you, the mole decided to try to kill both of us last night."

"The mole might even be someone involved in the current Redburn mission," I said, still thinking out loud. "A supervisor, a member of the strike team, even one of the IT techs. It could be anyone. But since the mole hasn't managed to kill us yet, their next move will probably be to sabotage the mission. To figure out some way to turn it to their or Henrika's advantage."

Desmond shrugged. "It's possible. Blacksea was the first time I ever even suspected there might be a mole inside Section, and everyone involved in that mission is dead, except for me." His voice took on a flat, hollow note, his eyes dimmed, and he dropped his head, as if he was remembering the horrible events of that tragic day.

Sympathy flooded my heart, and a strange urge seized me to reach across the counter and squeeze his hand, to try and...comfort him. My fingers flexed and stretched out, but I forced myself to curl them into a tight fist instead. I wasn't here to comfort Desmond any more than he was to soothe me. We had been thrown together by circumstance, bound by blood and our families' twisted, tangled legacies, and that was the extent of our relationship now and going forward for the duration of this mission.

Desmond let out a tense breath, then raised his gaze to

mine. "I'm sorry if I woke you last night. I suppose our run-in with that car bomb reminded me of...other things."

"The IEDs on the beach in Australia?"

His jaw clenched, but he answered me. "Yeah."

I probably should have dropped it, but my curiosity got the better of me. "How did you survive the blasts? Your magic?"

He shook his head. "No. I might be a galvanist, but there's a limit to how much energy I can absorb at one time. There were too many IEDs, and all that force and power would have overwhelmed my magic and burned right through me, along with the physical fire that would have scorched my body. But Graham..." Desmond had to stop and clear his throat. "But Graham was closer to the blast zone than I was. He realized what was happening, and he threw himself on top of me and buried my body in the sand an instant before the bombs exploded. Brave, stupid fucking *idiot*."

Yet more sympathy flooded my heart. I wanted to point out that Desmond had protected me the same way last night, but I kept quiet.

"Graham took the brunt of the blasts," Desmond said, his voice much lower and softer than before, although pain rasped through each and every one of his words. "Even though Graham shielded me, the fire and shock waves crashed over me too. Graham's leg was blown off, and we were both burned, blistered, and dying. Until..."

His voice trailed off, so I gently asked the obvious question.

"Until what?"

Desmond stared down into his empty smoothie glass as though the green dregs were tea leaves he was trying to read. "Until...Graham told me to take what little strength he had left."

My stomach dropped, and my mind spun at the awful implication of his words.

"All energy is different, you see. Electrical, chemical, kinetic. It all has different properties, different purposes, different reactions. I can manipulate any energy I encounter, but I can only use some of it in certain ways." Desmond stopped and cleared his throat again. "Human energy—the power in a person's blood, the electrical charge that makes their heart beat, the synapses constantly firing in their brain—that energy is the best for healing."

He paused again. "After the IEDs went off, there was no more energy, no more power or electricity, anywhere around us. Even the fish in the ocean were dead. The only things left were the faint sparks of life that Graham and I still had."

He drew in a deep breath, then let it out in a rush, along with his words. "So I took what little energy Graham had left and used it to heal myself. I used my magic to kill my best friend," he finished in a hoarse, broken whisper.

His confession hung in the air like an invisible thunder-cloud, crackling and sparking and spitting out bolt after bolt of guilt, grief, misery, and pain.

My heart clenched. Thanks to my father's work for Section, I'd been through a lot of bad things, but I'd never been faced with a choice like that—kill my friend to save myself or die right alongside him.

I couldn't help myself. This time, I did reach out, grab Desmond's hand, and squeeze his fingers tight. "I know it might not feel like it, but you did the right thing. Graham knew what he was doing, what he was asking. He knew there was no reason for both of you to die."

Desmond stared down at my hand on top of his, a dull expression on his face, as if he were a thousand miles away instead of standing right across from me. "Do you really think so?"

"Yes," I said in a loud, firm voice, squeezing his hand again. "And Graham knew something else."

He raised his weary gaze to mine. "What?"

"That if you lived, you would track down Adrian Anatoly and make him pay for what he did to the two of you as well as everyone else who died. I've seen your determination and skills firsthand. I don't doubt them, and neither should you, Dundee."

I added the nickname in hopes of lightening the mood, maybe even coaxing a small smile out of him. For a moment, it seemed to work, and his lips twitched upward. But then the expression dropped from his face, although his features turned more thoughtful than melancholy.

"Did you know that every person has an aura?" he said. "A color that reflects their moods, emotions, and personalities? I can see that color, that energy, with my galvanism, just like you can see mistakes with your synesthesia. Your aura is blue, Numbers."

Breathe in the blue. That's what he'd said when he'd been thrashing around on his bed, caught in the throes of his nightmare. When I had placed my hand on his ankle, and he had calmed down. Had my aura...soothed him? Could auras even do that? I didn't know, and I was suddenly too shy to ask.

Desmond kept his gaze steady on mine. I wondered what he saw. If he was staring at my aura, then it must have been pounding as hard and fast as my heart was right now.

"Blue, huh?" I drawled, once again trying to lighten the mood and ignore the treacherous feelings cascading through my body. "Good to know. I'll have to match my wardrobe to it."

"Blue definitely looks good on you," he said, nodding at me.

I glanced down. Somehow, I'd forgotten I'd thrown on my favorite navy cardigan this morning. *Real observant, Charlotte,* I chided myself. *Some spy you are. You can't even remember what color you're wearing.*

Desmond continued staring at me. My hand was still on top of his, and the heat from his skin began burning into my own. Or perhaps that was simply my imagination running away with me again. Either way, I gave his fingers another firm squeeze then removed my hand from his. The heat of him lingered on my skin, though.

"We should get going," I said. "Gia Chan sent out an email late last night. We have a mission briefing at ten."

Desmond nodded, turned away, and started cleaning up the kitchen. As I watched him, my inner voice started whispering *danger-danger-danger.*

But unlike before, Desmond Percy wasn't a physical threat. Not to my body.

No, my fragile heart was the thing that was suddenly, unexpectedly, in peril.

Desmond and I gathered up our things, then left the apartment and rode the elevator down to a sub-basement. Desmond led me through a variety of corridors, and we ended up in a parking garage two blocks over from where we'd started in the Touchstone Building. No one paid any attention to us, so we headed to work.

We stepped into the Section building and scanned our keycards. Evelyn Hawkes was sitting behind the front desk as usual, and I waved to her. She looked back and forth between Desmond and me. She winked, then waved back at me. She probably thought we had spent the night together and that this was our mutual walk of shame. To my surprise, I didn't mind the idea nearly as much as I would have yesterday.

Desmond and I stepped into an elevator, which floated down to the third floor.

"Be careful," he said as I got off.

"You too."

He nodded at me, then the doors closed, whisking him down to the fifth floor. I went into the third-floor bullpen and headed over to my desk to grab some more files I had on Henrika Hyde—

"Charlotte! There you are! In my office! Now, please!" Trevor Donnelly was standing in front of his glassed-in office. He waved at me, then retreated inside.

I frowned. What did he want? Had something happened overnight with one of my other bad guys? I put my shoulder bag down on my desk, grabbed a pen and a notepad, and stepped into Trevor's office. Miriam was already there, lounging in one of the chairs in front of his desk. She grinned at me, and I nodded and dropped into the seat beside her.

Trevor went around behind his desk and sat down. He looked at his laptop for a few seconds, then steepled his hands together and peered at me.

"There have been some new staffing additions to the Redburn mission," he said. "Miriam will now be going into the Halstead Hotel with you and Desmond. Gia thought it would be a good idea to have a charmer in the crowd to serve as an extra set of eyes and ears. To help you keep tabs on Henrika Hyde and especially her bodyguards."

I nodded. "That's smart."

And it was. Miriam could work a crowd like nobody's business. Thanks to her charisma, she could engage the most hardened, jaded spy in a brief, seemingly meaningless conversation and pry out their deepest, darkest secrets in five minutes flat. Dozens of rich, powerful, influential people were scheduled to attend the gala, and Miriam could potentially pick up loads of personal intelligence, in addition to helping me and Desmond with our mission.

"I'm always happy to serve," Miriam quipped.

She grinned at Trevor, who merely grunted in return. Miriam's grin turned into more of a pout, but she shrugged and rolled her eyes at me as if to say, *Can't charm them all.*

"You've got your assignment, Miriam," Trevor continued. "So head on down to the fifth floor for the briefing."

Miriam smiled at him again, winked at me, and left the office, shutting the glass door behind her. I started to get up and follow her, but Trevor waved his hand, indicating I should stay seated. Unease rippled through my stomach. What else could he possibly want to talk about? And why in private, with the door closed? Had he somehow found out that Desmond and I had been near the car bomb? That I had killed three cleaners?

Trevor stared at something on his laptop. He let out a long-suffering sigh, as though he were extremely annoyed by whatever was on his screen, then reached into the crystal candy dish on the front of his desk. He unwrapped a stick of gum and chomped down on it, his square white teeth tearing into the gum like it had upset him as much as whatever document he'd just read.

He politely nudged the candy dish toward me. "Gum? Chocolate? Caramel?"

The scent of his cloying minty breath blasted across the desk. I crinkled my nose and eyed the pink gum wrappers swimming among the peppermints, chocolates, and caramels in the dish. "No, thanks."

Trevor rocked back in his chair and laced his hands over his stomach, staring at me. "I have a secondary assignment for you, Charlotte. On the Redburn mission."

Secondary assignments weren't unusual, as many Section missions often had multiple objectives. Still, I didn't like the hushed tone in his voice or the conspiratorial gleam in his light brown eyes. "What is it?"

"Since you're going to be working as Desmond's liaison, I want you to keep a close eye on him and report all his movements leading up to the mission back to me. Who he talks to, who he calls and texts, anything and everything you hear and witness. I also want you to do the same during the mission itself."

He didn't come right out and say it, but I knew what he was really asking me to do. "You want me to spy on Desmond."

Just saying the words left a bitter taste in my mouth, especially after everything that had happened between Desmond and me in the past twenty-four hours.

Trevor shrugged. "Dez had a rough time on his last mission. A lot of agents were killed, including Graham, another cleaner who was a close friend to the both of us. I'm Dez's friend too, and I'm worried about him." He hesitated. "Plus, this is his first mission since then, and we all want to make sure everything goes smoothly and according to plan."

Truth, my inner voice whispered. Still, I couldn't help but ask the obvious question. "Who is *we*?"

"The *we* doesn't matter. All you need to know is that this is coming down from on high."

Truth.

Someone much higher up on the food chain than Trevor, someone he was reporting to, thought Desmond needed to be watched. But who? And why? Had someone guessed Desmond's plan to interrogate Henrika for information on Anatoly? But if that were the case, then why wouldn't that person launch their own preemptive strike and simply have Desmond taken off the mission?

More and more questions swirled through my mind, and all of them had potential answers that I didn't like.

Trevor must have realized I wasn't convinced because he leaned forward and gave me a hard look. "This is an order. This comes from the top, Charlotte."

Truth.

And once again, I heard what he wasn't telling me. "You're saying that *Maestro* wants me to spy on Desmond?"

Trevor flinched. *Maestro* was the code name for the head of the D.C. station. Only a few people actually knew who Maestro was, and their identity was a topic of much debate and discussion among the analysts, charmers, liaisons, and cleaners. The department supervisors like Trevor and Gia were more or less equals, so Maestro was the only one here who would have the clout and authority to order Trevor to order me to spy on Desmond.

"Yes," Trevor said, still chewing his gum. "This order is coming directly from Maestro."

LIE.

The force of the falsehood slammed into my mind like a sledgehammer, and I had to grind my teeth to keep from wincing, although Trevor didn't seem to notice my sudden discomfort. But even more worrisome than the pain his lie caused me was the order itself—and the murky motives associated with it. If this directive wasn't coming from Maestro, then who was behind it? General Percy? The mole? Someone else?

"Do we understand each other, Charlotte?" Trevor asked,

his tone once again smooth and mellow.

Instead of answering him, I dropped my eyes to the crystal candy dish, and my gaze snagged on the pink gum wrappers floating among the peppermints, chocolates, and caramels. For a moment, I wondered if it was some trick of my synesthesia, some weird reflection of my current worry, but no, the wrappers were pink all on their own. Hmm.

"Charlotte?" Trevor asked again. "Do we understand each other?"

A strange thought occurred to me, and I reached forward, grabbed a piece of gum, peeled off the pink wrapper, and popped it into my mouth. Blech. The cloying mint flavor tasted even worse than I expected, but it confirmed my suspicions, so I kept chewing, my mind whirring, trying to puzzle out what Trevor's lie really meant—and how I could keep from betraying Desmond.

I might have only known Desmond for roughly forty-eight hours, but he had saved my life, and I had saved his. We were bonded in a way I didn't quite understand, and the thought of violating that bond made me nauseous, especially given the private pain and anguish he'd shared with me this morning.

"I shouldn't have to remind you how important an assignment like this could be to your career," Trevor said, an impatient note creeping into his voice. "You pull this off, and your position at Section will greatly improve. Why, you might even get that promotion to senior analyst you've been angling for." He paused. "Unless you're not comfortable with such work. But if that's the case, then I'm afraid I'll have to recommend that you be taken off the Redburn mission and returned to your regular duties."

In other words, follow his orders, or slink back to my analyst desk and toil away in obscurity for who knew how long. Part of me was tempted to do just that—to forget about

ferreting out the mole and return to my safe, normal, humdrum life.

But I couldn't—*wouldn't*—do that. I'd promised Desmond
I would help him avenge Graham's death. Even more important, I had promised *myself* that I would find the people who
wanted me dead and make them pay for being stupid enough
to mess with me.

My mind kept whirring and whirring, but I quickly
reached a conclusion—that it was far better for me to spy on
Desmond than for someone else to do it. So I looked Trevor
in the eyes and nodded. "No, sir. Taking me off the mission
won't be necessary. I understand what I have to do."

"Good," Trevor rumbled, relaxing back in his chair. "You
will report your findings directly to me in this office every
morning. No written reports, and no paper trail. Understood?"

I nodded again. "Understood."

"Good. Now, let's get downstairs to the briefing." Trevor
stood up and grabbed some folders.

I stared at the crystal dish on his desk again, pretending
that all that candy and sticks of gum were puzzle pieces in
this dangerous game I was playing. If I put this piece
here…then that would happen. If I slid another piece over
there…then something else would happen.

"Ready, Charlotte?" Trevor asked.

"Absolutely." I got to my feet.

The charmer supervisor might have lied to me, but I
hadn't done the same to him.

I knew *exactly* what I had to do now—about spying on
Desmond, how to prepare for the Redburn mission, getting
the mole to reveal themselves, everything. The only question
was whether I could actually pull it off—or if my plan would
wind up killing me.

SIXTEEN

CHARLOTTE

I discreetly spit the gum into the nearest trash can, grabbed my laptop from my desk, and trailed Trevor into the elevator. We rode down to the fifth floor. He scrolled through screens on his phone, muttering under his breath about budgets, agents, and other things, while I stared at the elevator door, still sliding puzzle pieces around in my mind, fine-tuning the image they formed.

The elevator door pinged open, and we stepped out into the corridor.

Trevor looked at me, his face kind but serious. "Remember what I said, Charlotte. You report to me first thing every morning."

"Don't worry, sir. You can count on me."

"Glad to hear it. See you in there." Trevor strode down the corridor.

Instead of following him toward the bullpen, I stayed by the elevator, my mind still spinning and spinning, wondering how I was going to juggle all of this—

"That sounded ominous," a feminine voice drawled.

Startled, I looked to my right. Joan Samson was standing a few feet away from the elevator, lurking beside one of the support columns. She'd apparently been checking her phone and had obviously overhead my cryptic conversation with Trevor. A disgusted look filled her pretty face.

"Let me give you some advice," Joan said. "Some tips about being a liaison."

"Sure." I kept my voice neutral.

"Being a liaison is different from being an analyst. Upstairs, your duty is to the facts, no matter what they say or where they lead you. But down here on the fifth floor, it's different."

"How so?"

"Your job as a liaison, your duty, your loyalty, is to your cleaner, to Desmond and Desmond alone," she snapped. "You watch his back so he can focus on completing his mission. Nothing gets in the way of your duty, and nothing compromises your loyalty to him. That's what being a liaison truly means. Not spying on your cleaner and then reporting back to someone like Trevor Donnelly to help yourself climb the Section ladder. Am I making myself clear?"

Joan might not have heard Trevor order me to watch Desmond, but she could guess that he'd asked, no doubt thanks to her own time as a liaison. I wondered how she handled such requests from her superiors, and juggled her loyalty to her cleaner against disobeying orders and risking her own neck, but I didn't dare ask.

"Are we clear?" Joan snapped again.

"Crystal."

"Good," she replied. "Desmond is a friend of mine, and he's been through a lot. For some reason, he thinks he needs your help with this mission. Maybe he does."

"But?"

Joan stepped closer, somehow staring down her nose at me, despite the fact that she was a couple inches shorter than I was. "But if you betray or hurt Desmond, even in the smallest way, then you will have to answer to *me*. And that is something you will most definitely *not* enjoy—or recover from."

Magic flared in her pale blue eyes, giving them an icy sheen, and a similar chill surged off her body. Her gaze dropped to my right arm, as if she were thinking about reaching out, latching onto me, and using her transmuter power to turn my body into a lump of cold, hard concrete.

Danger-danger-danger. I tensed, ready to lurch away if she came at me.

Joan eyed me for a few more seconds, but she must have realized I'd taken her threat to heart because she spun around and marched away, her high heels stabbing into the gray carpet.

I stood there and watched her go, my mind still whirring.

First Trevor, now Joan. Different people, different agendas, but two very real and distinct threats. It wasn't even ten o'clock, and I was already hip-deep in trouble. At this rate, I'd be up to my neck in it by lunchtime, especially given my own plans.

I just wondered who at Section would carry out their threats and try to eliminate me first.

I shoved away my worries and headed into the fifth-floor bullpen. Then I strode over to the glassed-in conference room, stepped inside, and took a seat at the table beside Desmond.

"Everything okay?" he murmured.

I forced myself to give him a bright smile. "Everything is fine."

He frowned, as if he didn't quite believe me, and I was glad he couldn't hear the bald-faced lie in my voice the way I could with my synesthesia.

I turned my attention to the other people. Gia and Trevor were sitting side by side at the head of the table and were flanked by Joan and Diego, respectively. Next came Miriam, with Evelyn across from her. In addition to manning the front desk, Evelyn also took notes at mission briefings from time to time.

I was sandwiched in between Miriam and Desmond, while other cleaners, liaisons, and support staff occupied the rest of the chairs.

Gia stood up, and everyone quieted and looked at her. She picked up the clicker and began the briefing.

"By now, you've all been read in on the Redburn mission, so you know that our target is Henrika Hyde," Gia said. "Desmond, Charlotte, and Miriam will attend the Halstead Foundation gala on Sunday night. Desmond, posing as Desmond Macfarlane, has been invited to the event and is scheduled to have a private meeting with Henrika to talk about purchasing her Redburn weapon. Once he gets Henrika to a more isolated area, Desmond will take out her bodyguards while Charlotte sedates her. Then a Section strike team will come in, remove Henrika from the premises, and rendition her to a black site where she will undergo extensive interrogation about her new Redburn weapon and exactly what it does..."

For the next hour, we reviewed the hotel blueprints, the gala guest list, Henrika's security team, and more. I stared at the headshots and other pictures that flashed across the film screen, asked the appropriate questions, and chimed in with the right answers, but I wasn't focusing on the mission. As I'd told Desmond this morning, the mission was already doomed and guaranteed to go sideways at some point. No, I was thinking about all the things *I* needed to do in order to put my own plan into action to expose the mole—and ensure my own survival.

The briefing wound down, and everyone gathered up their things to move on to their assignments and other work for the day.

"Want to have lunch in the cafeteria?" Desmond asked. "So we can compare notes?"

Most people would have assumed he was talking about the mission, but I knew he was referring to our mole hunt.

I shook my head. "I'm not going to have time for lunch with all this mission prep. Besides, I haven't really had a chance to dig into things yet. Meet you in the lobby after work?"

Desmond frowned, as though he didn't like the idea of not seeing me again until late this afternoon. He probably thought he needed to keep an eye on me, in case I did something stupid. Oh, I was most definitely going to do a lot of stupid things, starting by lying to him.

"Sure," he replied. "I've got my own mission prep to do, and I need to head down to the weapons depot right now. See you after work."

I flashed him a smile. "Great. See you then."

I left the conference room, walked over, and dumped some files on my new desk. Joan gave me the stink-eye as she walked by and sat down at her own desk directly in front of mine.

Miriam came over and put her own stack of files down on the desk to the left of mine. "I'm so glad we're going to be working on this together."

"Me too," I replied. "It'll be good having someone watching my back inside the hotel."

"You want to grab lunch?"

"Nah. I need to go upstairs and get some more files from my desk. I'll just get something out of one of the vending machines."

"Suit yourself." Miriam picked up her purse and strolled out of the bullpen.

One by one, everyone else left as well, heading out to lunch or to get started on their mission prep, leaving me alone in the bullpen. After about thirty minutes of working on my laptop, I stood up and stretched. Then I grabbed my bag and left, as though I were finally taking my own lunch break.

After collecting some files from the third floor, I returned to the fifth floor. My next stop was the row of vending machines in the break room. Thankfully, not everyone at Section shared Desmond's love of foul, grass-tasting smoothies, and I bought a bag of chocolate, almond, and dried-cherry trail mix, along with a ginger ale. Not nearly as good as one of Pablo's desserts, but given the way my stomach was grumbling, it was the lunch of champions.

I sat in a chair, gulping down my snack while pretending to check my phone. A few other folks were also in the break room, and I waited until they left before exiting the room myself.

When I was sure no one was around, I slipped over to the dead-spot alcove, the one with no surveillance cameras or recording devices. Then I hit a number in my phone's speed dial. He picked up on the third ring.

"Yeah?" Gabriel's voice filled my ear.

"It's Charlotte. Remember when you offered to help me last night? Well, it turns out I'm not too stupid and stubborn to take you up on that. I need you to get me something."

I told him what I wanted, and he let out a low whistle. "Girl, what kind of trouble have you gotten yourself into at Section?"

"I'm not quite sure yet, but I plan to make it out in one piece. And if everything works out like I hope, then I'll finally be able to pay off my debt to you once and for all. So will you help me?"

"I can do it," Gabriel replied. "It's going to take me a couple of days, though."

"Fine."

"When and where do you want to meet?"

Today was Wednesday, but it would take me a few days to work out the final kinks in my plan before I left for the mission on Sunday evening. "The diner. Three a.m. Sunday morning."

"That's a fast turnaround time," Gabriel replied. "I might not be able to procure the quality you want by then."

"Quality doesn't matter. As long as it's close, that will be good enough."

"All right," he replied. "See you there."

"Okay. And, Gabriel?"

"Yeah?"

"Thanks."

He snorted. "For helping you put yourself in even more danger? You shouldn't thank me for that." He paused. "But you're welcome anyway."

We hung up. I stayed in the alcove, clutching my phone, reviewing the facts in my mind and once again wondering if this was the correct play. Gabriel was right. I was throwing myself headlong into even more danger, and if my scheme failed, then winding up dead would probably be the least unpleasant outcome.

If you see an opportunity, then you grab on to it with both hands, and you strangle it into submission, my grandmother's voice whispered in my mind. *And never, ever second-guess yourself.*

I'd put the first part of my plan into action and had just tossed a handful of knives into the air. Only time would tell whether I managed to keep juggling them—or if the blades would all come crashing down and cut me to pieces.

SEVENTEEN

DESMOND

Charlotte and I quickly established a routine. During the day, we both went about our regular jobs at Section 47, and we attended a lot of the same briefings regarding the upcoming mission. Then, after hours, we headed over to the diner, where I hung out in a booth and combed through files, hunting for the mole and prepping for the mission, while Charlotte worked her shift. Once she was finished, we returned to my apartment for the night.

Most of the time, when I woke from yet another nightmare of the beach explosion and Graham's death, Charlotte was perched on a stool at the island counter, drinking hot chocolate, eating some sugary diner dessert, and going through the classified files that I'd downloaded for her. Sometimes, she was in the middle of the living room floor, breathing deeply as she moved, stretched, and flowed from one yoga pose to the next.

After that first morning, she never asked if I wanted to talk about the Blacksea mission, and I was grateful for her discretion. Right after the mission, I had been paraded around to half a dozen Section shrinks, and I was all talked out. Besides, talking wouldn't change anything. Not really, not for me. No, the only thing that might—*might*—quiet my nightmares and bring me any kind of peace was using Henrika Hyde to find and kill Adrian Anatoly.

Charlotte might not ask me about Graham, but she was considerate in other ways. Inquiring about my childhood growing up in Australia with my mother, offering me bites of her diner desserts, teasing me when I said all that sugar was going to kill her. She did her best to try and take my mind off the fact that I'd woken up screaming and in a cold sweat yet again. Given my nightmares, I often wondered when she got any sleep, and she almost always seemed tired, as if something were weighing heavily on her mind, but she respected my privacy, so I did the same with her.

To my surprise, no more cleaners targeted Charlotte or me, and no one set any more car bombs or other traps for us. The quiet put me on edge. I wasn't an enduro like Graham had been, so I'd never been good at waiting. If there had been another attack, then I would have at least known we were on the right track, that the Section mole felt threatened by us, by our investigation. I would have preferred some danger to all of this...*nothing*.

Charlotte seemed to take the waiting in stride, and I would often catch her staring at a blank spot on the wall while she was doing yoga, her aura pulsing as her mind tumbled through those mental gymnastics, as though her thoughts were a tough routine that she was trying to perfect right alongside her triangle pose. I enjoyed seeing her like that, enjoyed just being near her, and especially breathing in the cool, soothing blue of her.

In another place, another time, I might have done more than just look. Might have asked her out to coffee or dinner and see if the evening led back to my place, to my bed. Sometimes, I thought that Charlotte was as attracted to me as I was to her, but I didn't broach the subject, and neither did she. As soon as I had a lead on Anatoly, I would be gone, off to chase him to the ends of the earth, if need be, and Charlotte knew that as well as I did. So it was better for both of us not to start something that would be all too brief.

Damn if I didn't want to, though.

Sometimes, when Charlotte was sitting at the counter, poring over files, I thought about going over, gently brushing her hair aside, and pressing my lips against her neck, so that I could feel her pulse, feel the blue of her, beating beneath my tongue. Then I would turn her around, lift her up, and lay her down on the counter, right on top of all of those reports...

And then reality would intrude, and I would have to excuse myself and retreat back into my bedroom until my dick calmed down.

I felt like a schoolboy with the worst sort of awkward, unrequited crush, and I didn't know what to do about it.

And so things chugged along until the night before the Redburn mission. We still weren't any closer to figuring out who the mole was, and Charlotte and I had agreed that our best bet was to wring the answer out of Henrika Hyde—one way or another.

Of course, we still didn't know exactly what kind of trap Henrika might spring on us during the mission, but I'd reviewed all the information on her bodyguards, and I was confident I could kill each and every one of them—and keep Charlotte safe. That had become increasingly important to me. It wasn't just about the deal we'd struck. Not anymore. No, for me, protecting her was now a driving *need*.

Charlotte had a rare evening off from the diner, so we'd called it a night around ten, since tomorrow was going to be a long day. Sometime later, I woke up. For once, my sleep had been free of nightmares, so I wasn't quite sure what had roused me.

It took me a long, drowsy minute to realize that I didn't feel Charlotte's aura.

Even when she was tucked in bed in the guest suite with the door closed, I could still sense her, but right now, I didn't feel the cool blue of her anywhere in the apartment.

I threw back the sheet, got out of bed, and padded into the living room, but she wasn't doing yoga, and the countertop was oddly clear of papers.

"Charlotte?" I called out.

No answer.

I knocked on her bedroom door. More silence, so I slowly cracked it open. She wasn't inside or in the bathroom beyond.

Where had she gone?

Beyond the front door, a soft *ding* sounded, indicating that the elevator had arrived on this floor. I reached out with my magic, and I sensed the elevator sliding down, down, down. Just for an instant, I also felt Charlotte's aura, bright sparks of worry shimmering through the usual cool blue.

I hesitated, torn between letting her go and seeing what she was doing. Surely she had a good reason for going out this late right before a mission, but I couldn't quiet the sudden doubts crackling through my mind. Besides, in the end, I was a spy just like she was, and trust wasn't something that came to me easily. Not after what had happened to Graham.

So I hurried into the bedroom to throw on some clothes so I could follow her.

I was out the apartment door in less than two minutes. Rather than wasting time waiting for the elevator to return, I went over to the emergency exit, punched in my *007* code, and hurried down the stairs.

The lobby was empty except for the security guard, who was sitting behind his desk as usual. Charlotte was nowhere in sight. If she'd gone out through the sub-basement, then she had a big head start, and I'd probably never pick up her trail, so I decided to take a chance that she'd just walked out through the lobby instead, given the late hour. So I plastered a smile on my face and hustled over to the security guard.

"Brent! My man! Can you do me a favor?" I waggled my keys in front of him. "Can you tell me which way my lady friend went? She forgot her keys."

Brent gave me a knowing grin. "You just missed her. She went that way."

He pointed to the left, and I hurried away. "Thanks, man."

"Anytime, sir."

I pushed through one of the glass doors and jogged in that direction, scanning the sidewalk up ahead for Charlotte as well as for cleaners and other potential threats. Just because we hadn't been attacked again didn't mean that the mole wasn't watching and wouldn't seize the chance to kidnap— or kill—Charlotte.

But no one was sitting in a parked car or loitering at the corner. Whatever was going on, Charlotte seemed to have left the apartment of her own volition rather than being lured outside, which made me even more curious—and suspicious—about what she was doing.

I reached the end of the block and scanned the surrounding streets. I didn't see Charlotte anywhere, so I reached out with my magic, searching for her aura...

There. She was over to my right, a couple of blocks away. I turned and headed in that direction, following the faint energy trail, the faint blue of her, the same way a bloodhound would run down a fox's scent.

Once I keyed in on her aura, I slowed my steps, easing up to the street corners, peering around them, and making sure to stay out of her immediate line of sight. Charlotte was a professional, and she would be checking for a tail, just like I was. I didn't need to physically see her to follow her aura, and I just had to hope that she couldn't sense me the same way with her synesthesia. It only took me a few blocks to figure out where she was going.

The Moondust Diner.

I frowned. Why would she go there on her night off?

I reached the block where the diner was located, but instead of walking down the street in full view of the neon lights and signs, I slipped into an alley, circled around, and came at the diner from a different direction. I stopped behind one of the trees marking the edge of the small, grassy park that butted up against the parking lot. From this vantage point, I could see the entire lot as well as the diner.

I checked my phone. Almost three a.m., so no cars were squatting on the cracked asphalt, and the diner was locked up tight for the night. So where was Charlotte?

A cool flicker of blue shimmered in the distance, and Charlotte stepped out from around the back of the diner, although she stayed in the shadows, hovering by one of the trash bins. Her sneakers didn't make a squeak of sound on the pavement, and I never would have spotted her, if I hadn't been so tuned in to her aura.

Charlotte checked her phone, then let out a soft, muttered curse. But she didn't move and neither did I. Who was she meeting? And why? I wasn't leaving until I found out.

I didn't have to wait long.

A few minutes later, a black SUV cruised into view. The

vehicle stopped at the opposite end of the parking lot. Charlotte stepped forward so that the person in the SUV could see her, and flashed her phone at them three times. The headlights flashed three times in return, and Gabriel climbed out of the driver's seat and sauntered toward her.

I frowned again. Why was she meeting him? Gabriel hadn't been at the diner since the night he'd called Charlotte his investment, and she hadn't so much as spoken his name in the meantime.

Gabriel stopped in front of Charlotte, who crossed her arms over her chest and gave him a flat look. I still didn't know why they were meeting, but it definitely wasn't a romantic rendezvous. Unexpected relief pulsed through me, but I pushed it away, straining to listen.

Gabriel spoke first. "...got what you wanted..."

"...let me see..."

"...sure you want to go through with this..."

"...no other choice..."

They talked back and forth, although their conversation didn't give me any clues as to what was going on. Finally, Gabriel handed Charlotte a padded brown envelope. She hefted it, but she must have been satisfied by the weight and feel because she tucked it into the back pocket of her cargo pants without opening it and looking at the contents. Then she pulled something out from one of her other pockets and handed it to Gabriel.

The object looked small and metallic, like...a flash drive. My eyes narrowed. What was on that drive? The classified files I'd given her? Section secrets? *My* secrets?

A sick, sinking feeling filled my stomach. All this time, I thought I had been protecting Charlotte. A few days ago, when this whole thing had started, she had asked me to swear that I had nothing to do with the cleaners who'd tried to kill her. I had been so busy trying to convince her I was a good guy that I hadn't thought to ask *her* the same question in return.

Had Charlotte been playing me this whole time? And who was she working for? Gabriel? Someone at Section? The mysterious mole? Henrika? Anatoly?

Graham had always claimed I had a white-knight complex. That I had this deep-seated need to protect other people, especially since my father had never protected me or my mother from anything, especially not his own greed and ambitions. Most of the time, Graham had played his words off as a joke, but right now, bitterness cascaded through me in hot, sour waves, making me feel like the biggest sort of blind, stupid fool.

"Good luck." Gabriel's voice drifted across the pavement, a little louder and clearer than before. "You're going to need it."

Charlotte shrugged. "We'll see. But if you don't hear from me in a few days, assume the worst."

Gabriel barked out a laugh. "I always do whenever Section is involved."

He snapped up his hand and saluted her, then headed back to his vehicle. He got inside, cranked the engine, and drove away.

Charlotte watched until Gabriel's taillights had vanished. Then she scanned the parking lot again, her gaze lingering on the trees where I was still hiding. I froze, not daring to move a muscle. For a moment, I thought she had spotted me, but her head turned, and she looked past me. Charlotte nodded, as if satisfied she was alone, and slipped back behind the diner.

I waited a few seconds to make sure she wasn't going to poke her head around the side of the diner again, then hurried back the direction I'd come. I needed to return to the apartment before she realized I had followed her. Still, as my long, quick strides ate up the distance, one thought kept pounding through my mind and churning in my stomach.

I couldn't trust Charlotte.

EIGHTEEN

CHARLOTTE

I made it back to the Touchstone Building without incident. My meeting with Gabriel had taken less than an hour total. I nodded to the security guard, who smirked at me as usual, then went through the art gallery and rode the elevator upstairs. I punched in the *007* code on the keypad, opened the front door, and eased inside the apartment.

Desmond wasn't sitting at the counter waiting for me, as I had feared, and his bedroom door was cracked open the same width as when I'd left. He probably didn't even realize I'd been gone. Good. Part of me hated sneaking around and lying to him, but this crazy, dangerous plan of mine seemed like the best way for everyone to get what they wanted and exactly what they deserved.

Especially Desmond.

His main focus might be using Henrika to get to Anatoly, but I knew he also desperately wanted to expose the Section mole, who was equally responsible for Graham's death along with the other agents who'd perished on the Blacksea mission. I didn't know how much I could truly help Desmond with

Henrika and Anatoly, but I was going to do my very best to give him the mole on a silver platter.

Either way, I couldn't change course now, and my plan would go into effect during the Redburn mission. Time would tell how successful my scheming turned out to be—and if I lived to see another day.

But for right now, I needed to get out of these clothes and back in bed before Desmond had another nightmare and woke up, so I tiptoed into my bedroom. I started to close the door behind me, but something made me look across the apartment.

For a moment, I thought I saw a shadow snake across the floor of Desmond's room, almost like he was up and moving around. I blinked, and the shadow vanished. I waited a few seconds, but the shadow didn't reappear. It had probably been some trick of the moonlight sliding in through the windows.

I pushed my unease aside and closed my door, cutting off my view of Desmond's room. Then I went to bed to get what sleep I could for the rest of the night.

Around eight a.m., I stepped into the kitchen to find Desmond leaning back against the wall. He was already dressed in his usual sleek shirt, vest, and pants, although his tie was a flat, plain black today, as were the rest of his clothes. He looked as gorgeous as always, but the lack of color was a cold, stark reminder of exactly who he was—and what he was planning to do to his enemies tonight.

Desmond was clutching one of his smoothies, although the glass was full, and it didn't look like he had taken a single sip. I glanced at the island, expecting to see another smoothie glass sitting there, but the surface was surprisingly empty.

It had become something of a morning ritual for Desmond to make me a smoothie and then for me to complain about how awful it tasted. Truth be told, the fruit-and-veggie drink was slowly growing on me, although I would never admit that, just as I would never tell Desmond how much I enjoyed his sexy accent and his wicked sense of humor and all the other little things that attracted me to him like a bee to honey. I didn't have time for such an intense attraction. No, today of all days, I needed to focus every ounce of my energy on the Redburn mission and making sure that I got through it alive—and that he did too.

"Did you sleep well?" Desmond asked, his voice strangely cold and flat.

"Well enough," I replied. "You ready for this?"

He shrugged. "It's just another mission. One of dozens I've been on. Although this one will probably be more eventful than most."

"Why is that?"

He stared down into the green depths of his smoothie, as if choosing his words carefully. "Because I'll finally find out who I can really trust."

Truth, my inner voice whispered. Still, something about him seemed slightly off, although I couldn't put my finger on exactly what it was.

Instead of drinking his smoothie, Desmond dumped the untouched liquid in the trash can, rinsed out the glass, and set it by the sink to dry. "We should go. We still have a lot to do before we leave Section for the hotel gala tonight."

He didn't wait for a response before striding back into his bedroom, probably to grab his suit jacket and the rest of his things. I stared at the open door, and I finally realized what was bothering me.

Danger-danger-danger.

My inner voice was whispering again, but not because of my own worries about the upcoming mission.

No, my voice was whispering because of Desmond—and the strange, unexpected tension now simmering between us.

Despite my unease, Desmond and I left his apartment and made it to the Section building without incident. We both scanned our ID cards and headed toward the elevators.

Evelyn was sitting at the front desk as usual, and she waved at me. "Good luck," she murmured, flashing me a smile.

I forced myself to smile back at her. "Thanks."

Desmond and I got into an elevator and rode downstairs to the fifth floor. The normally quiet bullpen was teeming with activity, and the rest of the day passed by in a series of final meetings, strategy sessions, and more. The hours and minutes steadily ticked down until it was time to get ready for the mission.

Just after six o'clock, I stared at my reflection in the mirror that ran along a counter in the fifth-floor locker room. The Halstead Hotel gala was a formal event, so I was dressed in a long royal-blue gown with a scooped neckline and cap sleeves. A slit in the side showed off my legs, and my feet were encased in black stilettos, instead of my usual sneakers. Section 47 spared no expense when it came to outfitting its agents in glamorous clothes, and the gown was easily the most expensive and gorgeous thing I had ever worn.

I'd pulled my hair back into a low, loose chignon to better display the stunning choker that ringed my neck. To a casual observer, the necklace would look like the real deal, a wide band of silver crusted with tiny diamonds, with a large, teardrop-shaped sapphire glittering in the center. But it was costume jewelry, and the fake sapphire featured a camera, along with a two-way microphone that would let me hear and talk to Gia Chan, Trevor Donnelly, and the rest of the Section staff observing the mission.

Normally, Gia and Trevor would have been stationed here at Section headquarters, watching the hotel's security feed and seeing the mission unfold on the monitors in one of the fifth-floor control rooms. But since Henrika Hyde was such a prominent, high-value target, Gia and Trevor were both going to the hotel, although they would be stationed in a van outside, along with the strike team and the rest of the support staff.

I let out a tense breath and planted my hands on the counter, letting the chilly tile cool my sweaty palms. Then I glanced over at the white satin clutch lying on the counter next to me. The clutch contained my fake driver's license, a burner phone, some cash, and a gun, along with a deep red lipstick nestled in a silver tube and a small silver perfume spritzer.

Section 47 wasn't as gadget-crazy as some of the other black-ops government agencies, but I had been outfitted with a few toys for the mission. A button on the side of the lipstick tube would release a needle on the bottom containing a powerful sedative that would knock out whomever I pricked with it, as would the liquid inside the perfume spritzer.

The official Section plan was for me to use either the lipstick needle or the spritzer liquid to incapacitate Henrika when Desmond and I had our private meeting with her. Once Henrika was unconscious and her bodyguards were neutralized, Desmond would hoist her over his shoulder and carry her to the extraction point while I watched our backs. Then the Section strike team would take over and remove Henrika from the hotel, leaving the rest of her security team none the wiser that she was gone.

Of course, Desmond had his own plans for Henrika, namely questioning—or torturing—her for information on Adrian Anatoly. I didn't know how he thought he was going to get her to talk, especially since we would only have a few minutes alone with Henrika before the strike team moved in, but Desmond had assured me he would get the job done.

And then there was the real wild card—Henrika's plans for us.

The mole had probably told Henrika about the Redburn mission from the very beginning, so she'd had just as much time to prepare as we had. Desmond and I had talked about various scenarios that might happen, but in the end, we wouldn't know what Henrika's trap was until she sprang it. Still, I trusted Desmond to keep me safe, and I was going to do everything in my power to watch his back in return.

Heels clattered on the tile floor, snapping me out of my thoughts, and Miriam sashayed out from behind a row of gray lockers, put her hand on her hip, and struck a pose.

"How do I look?" she asked.

"Stunning," I replied.

Miriam was wearing a long, sequined, forest-green gown with spaghetti straps that showed off her flawless skin, impressive cleavage, and muscled arms and shoulders. Her long red hair had been curled into loose waves, and dark, smoky shadow made her hazel eyes glimmer like gold stars in her beautiful face. She was holding a small green clutch and wearing the same red lipstick that I had on, although it looked completely natural and much more glamorous on her.

"Maybe you should be the one posing as Desmond's mistress," I said, only half joking.

Miriam preened at her reflection in the mirror and fluffed out her hair. "Well, I certainly wouldn't mind doing that, both tonight and in real life."

She winked at me. A bit of anger sizzled in my chest, and I had to remind myself that Miriam didn't know how I felt about Desmond...and neither did I.

Besides, if things went the way I thought they would, then Desmond would never trust me again after this mission. Oh, he might understand about my spying on him for Trevor, since that had been a direct order, but I doubted he would approve of all the other sneaky things I'd done. That made me sadder than I'd thought possible, but I shoved the emotion away. Tonight was about a lot of things, but my feelings were not my main concern—staying alive was.

Miriam's phone chirped, and she pulled it out of her green clutch. "Oh, I gotta take this."

"Another text from your mystery man?"

We had been so busy prepping for the mission these past few days that we hadn't had a chance to grab lunch, so Miriam hadn't been able to regale me with any tales of her latest fling.

A mischievous grin played across her face. "Something like that. I'll see you in the garage."

Miriam strode away, texting on her phone. She disappeared from my line of sight, although I heard her open the locker room door and step outside.

I turned back to the mirror, staring at my reflection again. I thought everyone else had already left, but another set of footsteps sounded, and Desmond rounded the row of lockers. I immediately turned to face him, like the proverbial moth drawn to a candle flame.

Desmond was wearing a classic black tuxedo with a twist— his usual vest, of course, done in the same black as his suit jacket and bow tie. I couldn't see his pocket watch, but I knew it was hooked to his vest. He never went anywhere without it, and he would want to have a weapon handy tonight. His blond hair gleamed under the lights, and his eyes sparked a bright silvery-blue that reminded me of the electricity he could wield.

I let out a low wolf whistle of appreciation. "You clean up good. James Bond has nothing on you tonight, Dundee."

He smiled a little at that, but the expression quickly dropped from his face, and he looked me up and down the same way that I had him. In an instant, my palms grew sweaty again, and I had to resist the urge to smooth them down the front of the gown.

"You look good too, Numbers."

His voice came out as a low, husky murmur that sent a shiver skittering down my spine, but his features seemed dark and troubled as he stared at me, as if he didn't quite believe—or like—what he was seeing. Once again, I got the sense that something had changed between us. Whatever it was, I didn't like this sudden, odd distance.

Desmond hesitated, then held out his arm. "Shall we go?"

I grabbed my clutch off the counter, then threaded my arm through his. We stared at each other, both of us seemingly trying to read the secrets in each other's eyes, then left the locker room together.

NINETEEN

DESMOND

I couldn't stop sneaking glances at Charlotte.

I'd lied to her before, although she hadn't called me out on it as usual. She looked more than merely good—she looked *amazing*. The dress's soft fabric perfectly hugged her curvy body, while the royal-blue color bought out her eyes and her aura. That pesky part of my anatomy started acting up again, and it was all I could do not to draw her into the shadows, kiss her red, red lips, and see if she felt and tasted as good as I imagined she would—soft and strong, and sweet and tart, like sugar mixed with limes.

Even more than her looks, Charlotte herself intoxicated me. She seemed cool, calm, and utterly confident, and her aura burned a bright, steady blue. Whatever she was plotting, she was determined to go through with it. I just wished I knew what it was—and whose side she was truly on.

Charlotte hadn't mentioned her clandestine meeting with Gabriel, and I couldn't ask about it without revealing I had spied on her. Which would probably cause even more problems between us.

The reminder that she had fooled me, that I couldn't trust her, was like a bucket of cold water dousing me from head to toe, but I welcomed the chilly sensation. I had come too far and lost too much to let myself be captivated by the intriguing, duplicitous Charlotte Locke. Tonight was about cornering Henrika Hyde and moving a step closer to tracking down Adrian Anatoly and finally avenging Graham.

Charlotte and I left the locker room, got into an elevator, and rode down to the seventh and bottom level. A parking garage housing a fleet of Section vehicles dominated most of this floor, and people were scurrying back and forth across the dull gray concrete, the way they always did during an active mission.

Gia was here, along with Joan, Diego, the rest of the support staff, and the members of the strike team. Trevor was also in the garage, standing next to a column, his arms crossed over his chest, surveying everyone moving through the area. Miriam, Charlotte's charmer friend, was standing a few feet away from him, texting on her phone.

Gia clapped her hands together, getting everyone's attention, and we all fell silent and faced her. "All right, people," she called out. "The Redburn mission is a go. Is everyone clear on their assignments?"

Everyone nodded to her.

"Good. Let's mount up."

Gia strode over to a waiting white van, opened the door, and climbed into the front passenger's seat. Diego got into the back of the van, clutching a laptop, along with the rest of the strike team members, who were wearing black tactical gear and multiple weapons. Joan was holding a tablet, and she gave me a pointed look before she too climbed into the van.

That left me standing in the garage with Charlotte. Miriam sashayed over to us, along with Trevor.

Trevor clapped me on the shoulder. "Good luck, Dez, Charlotte."

I returned the gesture. "Thanks, buddy. I'm glad you're here for this."

He grinned. "Me too. I'll see you on the other side."

Trevor nodded at Charlotte, who nodded back. Then he climbed into another waiting van.

Miriam grinned at the two of us. "Let's party."

She too walked away, heading toward the black luxury sedan that the three of us would be taking to the gala. Charlotte watched her friend go, a thoughtful look on her face.

"Well, I guess this is it," Charlotte murmured.

I got the sense she was talking about a lot more than just the mission, but I didn't ask for an explanation. I didn't want to watch her lie to me.

"Miriam's right," I said. "It's time to go."

Charlotte nodded again, and together we walked over to the sedan.

Miriam slipped into the back, while Charlotte slid into the front passenger's seat, and I drove. I'd memorized the route earlier in the week, and it didn't take me long to navigate through the city traffic and over to the Halstead Hotel. I steered the car into a long line of vehicles heading toward the hotel's front entrance.

"All right, guys." Joan's voice sounded in my ear. "Comm check."

My communication device and camera were hidden in my bow tie. "Check."

Charlotte and Miriam also murmured back to her, indicating that we could all hear and talk to one another.

"Diego has hacked into the hotel's security system, so we

will be able to see and track you guys," Joan said. "Several Section vans are already parked on the side streets, and we're all in position. The strike team will move in to transport Henrika on your mark."

"Roger that," I replied. "We are a go on this end."

I pulled the sedan up to the front of the receiving line, and a valet rushed forward to hand me a ticket and jump inside the vehicle. I went around to the opposite side, opened the door, and held my hand out to Charlotte. The gesture clearly surprised her, but she put her hand in mine, and I pulled her up and out of the car. Another valet hurried to help Miriam. Then together, Charlotte, Miriam, and I headed into the hotel.

Located on the outskirts of the city, the Halstead Hotel was a massive gray-stone building with two attached wings that gave it a giant *U* shape. The hotel's interior featured glossy, light gray marble floors and walls, while crystal chandeliers dangled down from the high vaulted ceilings, each one blazing with light to show off the paintings, sculptures, and other objets d'art that filled the common spaces. Tall windows were set into many of the walls, offering sweeping views of the wide, crushed-shell paths that wound through the landscaped lawns and gardens surrounding the historic building.

I had been to the Halstead Hotel many times, usually attending some fund-raising dinner or another with the General and my mother. Being dragged to such tedious events was one of the things that had sparked my interest in art. I'd always found the hotel's paintings and sculptures much more interesting and far more palatable than the predatory people who moved in the General's circle.

Charlotte, Miriam, and I wound our way through the crowd of people in the lobby. Bellmen taking coats and bags, waiters hustling back and forth with trays of champagne and hors d'oeuvres, men in tuxedos and women in glittering gowns trying to let everyone else know exactly how rich, important, and powerful they were. This event could have been any one from my childhood.

We reached the main ballroom where the gala was taking place. Art, people, egos. It was more of the same in here, although several people lurked around the edges of the room, scanning everything and everyone around them.

"Lots of security on site," I murmured.

"We see them." Gia's voice sounded in my ear. "Looks like every dignitary, politician, and businessperson brought a bodyguard or two. Diego is running the faces against the list of guests and known associates to see if anyone unexpected is here."

"Roger that," I replied.

"All right, guys," Miriam said, surveying the room. "Time for me to do my thing. Good luck."

"Good luck," Charlotte echoed, although her voice sounded a bit flat.

Miriam grinned at both of us, then grabbed a glass of champagne from a passing waiter and dove straight into the center of the closest group of people. The charmer hadn't gone three feet before she squealed and called out to some-one she knew. Miriam engaged that woman in conversation, although her head kept moving back and forth as she scanned everyone in sight.

Charlotte's hand tightened on my arm. "There's Henrika."

This was the first time I had ever set eyes on Henrika Hyde in person, and she looked exactly like the photos in her Section file—a tall, forty-something woman with bright green eyes and a lithe body that was poured into a green velvet cocktail dress. Her light brown hair was swept up in a high bun, all the better to show off the gold choker studded with emeralds that ringed her throat, along with her matching emerald earrings. Still more emeralds glittered on her wrists and fingers, and a thin gold anklet—also set with tiny emeralds—flashed around her right foot.

"You weren't kidding about her love of jewelry," I murmured. "I'm surprised she's not wearing a tiara too."

Charlotte shrugged. "She could have. She has plenty to choose from. She must have thought that a million dollars' worth of emeralds was a grand enough statement to make."

I wasn't the only one who'd noticed her jewelry, and several guests shot envious glances at her. To most people, Henrika Hyde probably looked like the very epitome of elegant sophistication, but her aura burned a dark, sickly green, with black flecks swimming in the soupy miasma. She was not someone you wanted to fuck with.

Henrika was clutching a glass of champagne and gesturing with it while she told some story to the folks gathered around her.

"Let's go say hello," I murmured. "After all, she did invite us here."

Charlotte's hand tightened on my arm again, but she nodded at me.

Together, the two of us headed toward the paramortal weapons maker. Henrika must have sensed us approaching because she glanced in our direction. To my surprise, a wide smile split her face, and she set her champagne glass aside and waved at us.

"Ah, you must be Desmond Macfarlane," she purred in a low, throaty voice. "It's so lovely to finally meet you in person. I've heard so many interesting things about you."

Her green gaze raked up and down my body, lingering on my groin, and her sickly green aura pulsed with putrid interest.

I had the sudden urge to shower, but I took her outstretched hand and gave it a polite shake. "Ms. Hyde, it's so lovely to meet you as well. I'm hoping we can finally work together, as discussed."

I started to drop her hand, but she reached out with her other one, clutching my fingers in hers. Henrika lightly dragged her gold-painted nails back and forth across my wrist. I wasn't quite sure whether she was caressing me or about to rip my skin open. The urge to shower grew stronger.

Even worse, Henrika's magic crackled against my skin with every stroke of her nails across my wrist. Her power had a hot, scalding burn to it, more like acid than fire, the kind of magic that would eat right through anything it came into contact with. The sensation was oddly familiar, as though I had sensed her magic before, even though we had never previously met. Forget a shower. I wanted a hazmat suit.

"Oh, I'm hoping that we can do all *sorts* of things together," Henrika purred again, her aura pulsing even brighter and her magic burning even hotter than before.

She clutched my hand a moment longer, then dropped it and turned toward Charlotte. "And who is this beauty?"

Henrika gave her the same frank, assessing once-over, and her aura pulsed again with interest. Charlotte had also been right about Henrika's sexual appetites.

"This is—"

"Charlotte Locke," Charlotte replied, cutting me off.

I had to hide my surprise. Section had set up a cover identity for Charlotte—aka Charlotte Black—just as they had for me, so I hadn't expected her to use her real name. Then again, thanks to the mole, Henrika probably already knew exactly who we were, so I supposed there was no point in Charlotte or me using fake names or sticking to our cover stories.

Sometimes, I thought being a spy was like playing chess. Both sides knew the rules, along with the moves and countermoves, but we all kept going through the motions of the game anyway, even if we realized it would inevitably end in betrayal, blood, and death.

Henrika's face remained fixed in that leering smile, and she reached out, grabbed Charlotte's hand with both of hers, and caressed it the same way she had mine. "I'm so very pleased to make your acquaintance."

"Yes, I'm sure you're absolutely charmed," Charlotte replied in a cool tone and wrested her hand away.

Henrika frowned, as though something about Charlotte's words bothered her, but she covered it up with another smile. "Can I get you anything?" she asked. "Perhaps some champagne? I assure you it's an excellent vintage. I made the selection myself. A small perk of being one of the foundation's new benefactors."

I could have said yes, and we could have gone on with this whole polite song-and-dance, but seeing Henrika's smug face made me remember Graham's burned, blistered one. I had spent the past two months trying to find Anatoly, and I wasn't going to wait any longer. Not when my quarry was right in front of me.

"We didn't come here for the champagne," I snapped, not bothering to keep the anger or impatience out of my voice. "We came to make a deal."

"Right down to business, eh?" Henrika arched an eyebrow at me. "Personally, I enjoy a bit more foreplay, but I can respect a man who goes straight for what he wants. Follow me."

Henrika raised her hand and made a small, circular motion with her finger, and three tuxedo-clad men detached themselves from the ballroom wall and headed in our direction. I recognized their faces from the mission briefings. The three men were Henrika's private security detail, loyal to her and her alone. They were all highly skilled, but none of them was as dangerous as I was, and I knew I could kill them if—or rather when—Henrika tried to turn the tables on Charlotte and me.

"You guys are clear," Miriam's voice sounded in my ear. "I don't see anyone else making a move to join your party."

I glanced to my left. The charmer was standing just inside the main ballroom doors, and she lifted her champagne glass to me in a silent toast.

"Miriam's right," Gia said in my ear. "Henrika has three bodyguards, as expected. We're still running facial recognition, but so far, no one unexpected is at the hotel. You are clear to proceed with the mission. I repeat, you are clear to proceed."

I kept my gaze focused on Henrika, not giving any indication I had heard Gia's order. Henrika smiled at me again and winked at Charlotte. Then she turned and strolled away, trailed by her three bodyguards.

"Here we go," I murmured to Charlotte.

"Straight into the lion's den," she agreed.

Together, we followed Henrika and her men deeper into the hotel.

TWENTY

CHARLOTTE

After three months of staring at photos, scrolling through social media, and watching video clips of Henrika Hyde, it was a bit disconcerting to actually see her in the flesh. But one thing remained the same between the images and the real, live woman in front of me—they both made my skin crawl.

I could still feel the hot, clammy, disgusting warmth of her hand against my own, along with the pointed tips of her nails scratching against my skin.

Desmond hadn't seemed to enjoy Henrika's ministrations either, and he kept glaring at her as if he wanted to yank out his pocket watch, drop the chain over her head, and snap her neck with it just as he had Rosalita's. I couldn't do anything about his anger, but I shoved my own away. Now was not the time for any kind of emotion.

We trailed after Henrika and her three bodyguards, moving from one area to another. All of the hotel's common spaces were filled with lovely, colorful art as well as crystal vases of freshly cut flowers, and if this had been a normal party,

I would have slowed down to admire the paintings and literally smell the roses. But nothing about this night was normal, and I needed to stay sharp, so I focused on Henrika and her men.

Every once in a while, Henrika would stop to shake hands or call out a greeting to someone she knew, but for the most part, she made a beeline toward the back of the hotel, heading exactly where I had expected—and wanted—her to go. Good. My plan depended on several things, but the first, and perhaps most important, element, was Henrika's lust for jewelry.

A few minutes later, Henrika passed through a pair of open doors and into a private library. Floor-to-ceiling shelves full of leather-bound books covered the walls, while dark green leather chairs and a long couch took up the center of the room. A large antique desk was situated along the back wall, which featured several glass doors that overlooked the hotel grounds. White stone pedestals stood here and there, each one topped with a thick, clear plastic case containing some sort of expensive knickknack.

Henrika gestured for Desmond and me to step into the library. We did so, and the three bodyguards shut and locked the double doors behind us.

"This is still a bit public for our meeting, don't you think?" Desmond said, continuing to play his part.

"Oh, we're not having any *meeting*," Henrika said. "I just had to stop and get what I really came here for tonight. I hope you don't mind the delay, but I've been waiting to do this for a very long time."

She sashayed over to a pedestal near the center of the room. Like all the others, it was topped with a display case, but instead of a first-edition book, an antique pen, or some other writing-related treasure, a stunning gold chandelier necklace dripping with emeralds and diamonds glittered behind the clear plastic.

The Grunglass Necklace.

Satisfaction surged through me. I had been right when I'd said that Henrika would come here during the gala, and she was doing just what I expected—and needed—for my own plan to work.

"Isn't it stunning?" A rapt expression filled her face, and a low, reverent note rippled through her voice. "I've had my eye on it for a long, long time."

"Why is it so important to you?" I asked, genuinely curious.

Despite all my months of research and tracking Henrika, I'd never been able to figure out exactly *why* she coveted this piece of jewelry above all others.

Henrika trailed her gold-painted nails over the plastic case, and the shimmer of the emeralds matched the greedy gleam in her green eyes. "My mother, Natasha Hyde, came from a dirt-poor family, but she was quite beautiful. She was working as a chambermaid in this very hotel when she caught the eye of my father, Hiram Halstead."

The revelation took me by surprise. That information had *not* been in Henrika's Section file. Of course I'd researched her family on my own to try to learn more about her, but I'd never found any mention of her father, and his name hadn't been listed on her birth certificate. Still, I'd never dreamed that he was someone as rich and powerful as Hiram Halstead.

Desmond glanced at me, clearly as surprised as I was, then looked at her again. "Hiram Halstead, as in the former head of the Halstead family?"

"One and the same," Henrika replied. "My mother was his mistress for more than a decade. Hiram took good care of us—for a time."

Desmond frowned. "Wasn't he killed in a bombing at his London hotel last year?"

"Yes, he was. That was the first initial test of my Redburn formula," Henrika murmured, although she never took her eyes off the necklace. "I was only planning to damage the hotel to prove my formula's worth to potential buyers, but my father was in the wrong place at the wrong time. Nevertheless, he was no great loss to me or anyone else."

I blanched. She had killed her own father? The news didn't particularly shock me, but the stone-cold tone in her voice indicated she had zero regrets about murdering him or all the innocent people who'd died in the blast.

"The Grunglass Necklace has been handed down for generations through Hiram's family, and he promised it to my mother. Payment for services rendered, you might say."

"What happened?" Desmond asked.

Henrika shrugged. "Petra, Hiram's daughter by his first wife, hated my mother for coming in between her parents. Plus, she wanted the necklace for herself. Eventually, Petra convinced our father to find a younger mistress, and she kicked my mother and me out of the apartment that Hiram paid for, cut off the credit cards, froze the bank accounts, everything. My mother had to go crawling back to her family just to make ends meet. But she told me all about Petra, my father, and his broken promises. So I decided I would become richer and more successful and powerful than my father and half sister had ever *dreamed* of being. And then, when I was ready, that I would finally make the mighty Halsteads pay for what they'd done to my mother, to *me*."

Henrika's face hardened. "The Grunglass Necklace should have been my mother's long ago. And now, it will be *mine*."

Despite all the awful things she'd done, and the fact that she was probably planning to murder us in this very room, I couldn't help but feel a smidge of sympathy for Henrika Hyde. My father hadn't tossed me aside like hers had, but I'd always had to share him with Section, so I could understand her desire to latch onto this symbol of her own father—and to control the necklace the way she'd never been able to control him.

"Once I amassed my fortune, I tried to buy the necklace from Petra, but she refused to sell it to me, and she blocked all my attempts to buy it at auction. I was going to dispose of her the same way I did my father, but she went into hiding after the London hotel bombing and denied me even that small pleasure. Scared, spiteful bitch."

Henrika's nostrils flared, and anger glinted in her eyes, but she kept staring at the necklace. "Petra entrusted the Grunglass Necklace to the Halstead Foundation, to be put on permanent display here in the family's flagship hotel. I suppose my dear half sister thought that would keep it safe from me. I tried to convince the foundation's board of directors to sell the necklace to me, more than once, but they refused, despite my very generous donations to the hotel renovation efforts."

My eyes narrowed. So that's why she'd made all those strange donations. I'd thought the money had been a bribe or payment for something, albeit an unsuccessful one.

"So why are we here?" Desmond asked.

"Because I've decided to do what I should have done all along, what I do best—take what I want."

Bright golden energy sparked to life and filled Henrika's hand, as if she were cupping a miniature sun in her palm, and I could feel the hot, burning flare of her magic all the way across the library. She stepped forward and pressed her hand and that energy up against the display case, making it shudder and ripple. And then it just...*melted.*

One second, the Grunglass Necklace was encased in two-inch-thick plastic. The next, the pane that Henrika was touching dissolved like it was made of water. The melted plastic bubbled and oozed down the front of the pedestal like clear liquid sugar, scorching the white stone.

Despite all my research, I had never been able to figure out exactly what kind of magic Henrika had, but based on this demonstration, she had to be a transmuter, someone who could transform an object's physical properties with a mere touch of her hand. Henrika might even be a combusto, someone with even stronger, more dangerous magic than your normal transmuter.

Beside me, Desmond shifted on his feet, and his eyes flicked back and forth between Henrika and the three bodyguards, who were standing off to the side, completely nonchalant and unconcerned by what had just happened.

Henrika plucked the Grunglass Necklace off its white velvet stand and held it up to the lights, admiring the bright sparkles and luminous flashes of the emeralds and diamonds. It truly was a stunning piece, and I would have been admiring it too, if the circumstances had been different.

I fully expected Henrika to hook the necklace around her throat, but instead she gestured at one of her bodyguards. That man stepped forward and held out a rectangular white box lined with white velvet. Henrika gently nestled the neck-lace inside the box, which the man closed and slid into the left pocket of his tuxedo jacket. My mind whirred, thinking about how I could get my hands on that box, and my fingers curled around the white satin clutch still in my left hand.

"Now that my business is concluded, we can get down to yours," Henrika said.

She stepped behind a long bar and strolled over to a liquor cabinet in the corner of the library. I'd thought the cabinet was another antique that was just for show, but she opened one of the doors and pulled out a bottle of whiskey, along with a crystal tumbler.

She poured herself a generous drink, then used the tumbler to gesture at Desmond and me. "Can I interest the two of you in a libation?"

Desmond and I both shook our heads.

Henrika shrugged, then tossed back the whiskey and smacked her lips in appreciation. "Suit yourself. But if I were you, I would have taken me up on my offer. Best to have a last drink before we get down to our nasty bit of business."

Desmond sidled forward, putting himself in between Henrika and me. "What do you mean?"

She poured herself another round, then eyed Desmond over the rim of her glass. "I don't see any reason to keep this charade up any longer, do you? I know you both work for Section 47, and that you're here to kidnap and take me to one of your black sites."

Desmond started forward to take out the bodyguards just as we'd planned, but the other three men were faster. They each drew a gun from a holster and aimed their weapons at him. Desmond jerked to a stop, but his eyes narrowed, and his hands clenched into fists. He might have seemed defeated, but he wasn't—and neither was I.

"Did you really think I didn't know Section was coming for me?" A cold light filled Henrika's eyes. "I've worked far too long and much too hard to get to where I am to let some outdated agency like Section 47 take everything away from me."

"You're a biomagical weapons maker who comes up with new and creative ways to slaughter people," Desmond said. "And Section *will* put you in a cage where you belong."

An amused chuckle erupted from Henrika's lips. "Wow.

I hadn't thought it humanly possible, but you're even more self-righteous than your father. Tell me, Desmond. How is General Percy these days? Still enjoying those pink sulfur smoke bombs I sold him last year? The ones that melt para-mortals' lungs into goo?"

Desmond's eyebrows drew together in confusion. "What are you talking about?"

Henrika let out another chuckle. "I do business with all kinds of people, including your supposedly respectable father. Jethro Percy might run Section 47, but he's not above using my expertise from time to time, especially when it benefits him and kills his enemies. It truly makes him the worst sort of hypocrite. Don't you think?"

A muscle ticked in Desmond's jaw, but he didn't respond. He didn't seem surprised by her claims, though. More like resigned.

Henrika smirked at him, then focused on me. "Although I have to admit it has been a great pleasure meeting *you*, Charlotte, the daughter of infamous Section cleaner Jack Locke. Did you know that your father tried to kill me a few times? He got closer than anyone else ever has." She paused. "At least until he got caught up in that awkward situation down in Mexico."

She was trying to make me angry, trying to piss me off and tear me down with her words like she had Desmond, but I was more intrigued than infuriated. "And what would you know about Mexico?"

A small smile played across her lips. "Everything."

TRUTH.

The smug certainty slammed into my mind like a tidal wave, but I didn't ask Henrika any more questions. That was exactly what she wanted, and I wasn't going to give the bitch the satisfaction of playing her game.

The silence stretched on and on. Henrika kept looking at me, and I stared right back at her, keeping my face calm and blank.

Beside me, Desmond shifted on his feet, then reached over and discreetly pushed a button on the side of his silver wristwatch to send out a distress signal, per standard mission protocol. The two of us might have knowingly walked into Henrika's trap, but the hotel was still surrounded by Section agents.

Desmond frowned and looked down, as if the watch weren't working. That's when I realized the communication device in my necklace had gone absolutely silent and that I couldn't hear Miriam, Gia, Trevor, or anyone else murmuring in the background anymore.

I glanced around the library, and my gaze snagged on a small black box sitting on the desk. A pink haze surrounded the box, indicating it didn't belong in here. It must have been some sort of jamming device, designed to knock out our communications, along with any alarms that might have been attached to the necklace's display case. It seemed like no one at Section could hear us, and I was willing to bet they couldn't see us on the security cameras either.

Desmond and I were on our own. This wrinkle in the mission wasn't terribly surprising, but Henrika had been a little more creative and thorough with her trap than I'd expected.

Desmond must have realized it too, since he removed his finger from his watch and curled his hands into fists again.

"Don't you want to know about your father?" Henrika asked. "And Mexico?"

Even though I desperately did, I forced myself to shrug. "Not really."

Her green eyes narrowed. "I don't believe you."

I barked out a harsh, humorless laugh. "What you believe doesn't matter to me. Just like I never truly mattered to my father."

Henrika frowned, as did Desmond. I ignored them both and stalked over to the bar. The three bodyguards tensed, their guns still aimed at Desmond, but Henrika waved them off. She didn't consider me, the lowly analyst, a threat. She was probably right about that.

I laid my satin clutch on the bar, then opened the same cabinet Henrika had, grabbed a crystal tumbler, poured myself some whiskey from the bottle she'd used, and took a large swallow. The liquid burned down my throat, but it didn't drown out the bitterness in my heart.

"What do you mean you never mattered to your father?" Henrika asked the obvious question.

I used my half-empty tumbler to gesture out at the library. "My father was always far more interested in *this*, in being a spy and spending his time with dangerous people like you, than he ever was in *me*. I gave up on my father a long, long time ago. Want to know a secret?"

"What?" Once again, Henrika asked the obvious question.

"I was actually *relieved* when he died, when the great Jack Locke didn't come back from that doomed Mexico mission. At least after his death, all the kidnappings, stalkings, and threats from his enemies stopped. For once in my life, I finally had some fucking *peace*."

I looked over at Desmond, who was staring at me with a thoughtful expression. "Truth," I said.

He grimaced, and a strange mix of agreement, under-standing, and sympathy flickered across his face. He knew what it was like to be fucked up and fucked over by your father, perhaps better than anyone else. Maybe that was part of the reason why I was so drawn to Desmond—his heart had been smashed to pieces by his father just like mine had been.

I focused on Henrika again. "So you stand there and keep all your smug secrets about the Mexico mission to yourself. Because you know what? I don't give a damn anymore."

I threw back the rest of the whiskey, letting it burn away the lie in my mouth. I set my empty crystal tumbler down on the bar right beside my clutch, but I kept my fingers curled around it. Desmond noticed the motion, and he shifted to his right.

Henrika pouted. "Well, you're no fun—"

I didn't want to hear another word she had to say, so I slapped the tumbler off the bar, aiming it straight at Henrika. She flinched and jerked to the side, darting out of the way, and her three bodyguards swung their guns around and aimed their weapons at me.

The second the guards were distracted, Desmond sprang into action. He plucked his watch out of his vest pocket, surged forward, and wrapped the chain around the neck of the closest bodyguard. Desmond yanked, and the razor-sharp chain sliced cleanly across the man's throat. He gurgled, then crumpled to the floor, blood pooling underneath his body.

I pulled my gun out of my clutch, aimed it at the second bodyguard, and pulled the trigger three times.

He toppled to the ground, blood spewing out of the holes the bullets had punched in his chest.

The third bodyguard, the one with the Grunglass Necklace in his tuxedo pocket, darted in front of Henrika and snapped up his gun, aiming it at me. I trained my own weapon on him in return. Desmond moved to flank me, still holding his deadly pocket watch and chain.

Henrika stayed behind her guard, but she raised her hand,

and a bright golden glow filled her palm again. I still didn't know exactly what kind of transmuter or combusto magic she had, but if she could melt plastic with her fingertips, then I definitely didn't want to see what she could do to my skin with her power.

"I'm pretty sure I can kill you before you can throw your magic at me," I snarled, not quite bluffing. "So drop your hand. Right now."

Hate burned in Henrika's eyes, but her magic vanished, and she slowly lowered her hand to her side. The bodyguard kept his gun raised, though, pointing it back and forth between Desmond and me. Given the previous talk about my father and his doomed mission, I found it sadly ironic that we were engaged in a sort of Mexican standoff.

"You okay?" Desmond asked.

I kept my eyes fixed on Henrika. "I'm fine. Ask your questions. Section will probably be here any minute to see why our comms went down."

Desmond nodded and eased forward, his pocket watch still clutched in his fingers. As he walked toward Henrika, the lights flickered, and silver-blue electricity started sparking and crackling along the watch chain. The bodyguard aimed his gun at Desmond, but the cleaner ignored the other man, his gaze locked on Henrika.

"Now, Ms. Hyde," Desmond said in a cold voice. "We're going to have a little chat. Answer my questions, and you and your guard just might live through the next few minutes. Keep quiet, and you both can join your two dead men on the floor."

Henrika gave him the same hate-filled glare she had given me, but for the third time, she asked the obvious question. "What do you want to know?"

"Two things—who your Section mole is and where I can find Adrian Anatoly."

A low, masculine voice jumped into the fray. "I'm right here."

Desmond spun around. I kept my gun trained on Henrika, but my gaze flicked to the left.

A man was standing just inside one of the glass doors at the back of the library, flanked by half a dozen armed guards. He was wearing a black tuxedo that highlighted his broad shoulders and short, thick, muscled body. His sandy-brown hair was slicked back and up from his forehead into a widow's peak, and a thin white scar slashed through one of his eyebrows, like a jagged arrow pointing down through his tan skin to his pale blue eyes.

Beside me, Desmond sucked in a sharp, horrified breath. I had never seen this man before in person, but I recognized him from the various photos I had viewed over the past few days.

Adrian Anatoly.

TWENTY-ONE

DESMOND

natoly was *here*. At the hotel. Standing right in front of me.

"Hello, Desmond," he said in his deep, cultured voice, the one that had haunted my nightmares for months. "So nice to see you again."

Rage boiled up in my veins, scorching through my stunned shock, and I started forward, lifting my hands toward the bastard's throat. Fuck the mission and Henrika and the guards with guns and everything else. I was going to kill Anatoly right here and now for what he'd done to Graham, for what he'd made me do to my best friend—

"*No*," Charlotte whispered, grabbing my arm and jerking me back. "Don't be an idiot. That's exactly what he wants."

She was right. Anatoly was just standing there, with a smirk on his face and his hands clasped in front of him, just waiting for me to attack. His six men had their guns trained on me, and they would kill me—and Charlotte—long before I ever got so much as a fingertip on their boss. So I forced myself to stop and hold my position. My fingers clenched around the pocket watch in my left hand. I'd lost my grip on my magic, so the electricity had dissipated, but the razor-sharp chain sliced into my palm. A small sting compared to the rage crackling in my heart.

Anatoly's smirk widened, and his dark, blood-red aura pulsed with amusement. "Smart man. You should listen to Ms. Locke more often. From what I've been told, she's quite clever. Far more clever than you, Desmond."

"Who's been singing my praises?" Charlotte asked.

"Some friends of mine," he replied. "No one you need to concern yourself with."

Beside me, Charlotte's aura flickered a bright blue, and what looked like satisfaction gleamed in her eyes, as though Anatoly had just revealed a great secret. I thought his answer was vague nonsense, but she must have heard something in his words that I hadn't. Then again, I wasn't exactly thinking clearly.

No, right now, all I could see was Anatoly standing on the deck of a boat out in the ocean, smiling, raising his hand, and showing me the phone clutched in his beefy fingers.

More fragments flashed through my mind. The faint hum of the IEDs buried in the sand. Anatoly pushing a button on his phone. The bright red flares of resulting explosions. The energy pounding into my body like a blacksmith's hammer, bringing heat and hurt along with it. Too much heat, too much hurt, too much raw energy, blasting over Graham and burning right through me too, no matter how hard I tried to protect us, no matter how hard I tried to hold it all back...

"Desmond," Charlotte said in a low, warning whisper.

Her voice snapped me out of my memories. Sympathy filled her face, and her aura pulsed with the same emotion. The cool, steady blue of her helped me slough off the sound of the screams echoing in my mind.

"You're a dead man," I snarled.

Anatoly shrugged. "Death comes to us all in the end. But I think tonight will be the end of you instead of me. It's a shame that you dragged Ms. Locke into your petty quest for revenge. She could have been quite useful to me, especially given her status as a Legacy."

His pale blue gaze focused on Charlotte again. "When I was told who your father was, Ms. Locke, I was quite surprised to find you working as an analyst. I would have expected a cleaner like Jack Locke to have molded his daughter in his own deadly image."

Charlotte gave him a thin smile. "Who said that he didn't?"

A loud, merry, mocking chuckle spewed out of Anatoly's mouth, and he held his hands out wide. "If he did, I don't think you would be in quite this dire a predicament."

"You're probably right about that," Charlotte replied. "I've always thought I take more after my grandmother. She's the one who truly raised me. My father was more of a weekend parent."

"Who cares?" Henrika said, striding over to stand beside Anatoly. "Let's kill them, and be done with things."

Anatoly nodded. "As much as I would love to stay and chat about fathers and their unexpected legacies, Henrika is right. We have a schedule to keep."

I expected him to order his men to shoot us, and I rocked back on my heels, preparing to dive toward Charlotte and shield her as best I could. If I was lucky, I might be able to latch onto enough kinetic energy from the bullets to send them spinning away from us.

Anatoly gestured at his men. "Bring them."

My hand clenched even tighter around my pocket watch and chain. As soon as they were in range, I'd take out the bodyguards, then go for Anatoly—

"Stop," Charlotte whispered. "Wait. Think."

Once again, her soft voice and steady aura cooled some of my rage. She was right. I couldn't attack Anatoly and his men. Not right now. They would gun me down in an instant. Plus, I had to think about Charlotte. As much as I hated to admit it, Anatoly was right. I had gotten her into this mess, and it was my responsibility to get her out of it—alive.

So I tucked my watch back into my vest pocket, then raised my hands. Charlotte sighed, then tossed her gun on the floor, although she discreetly swiped her small white purse off the bar.

Two of the guards clamped their hands around my upper arms, while the other four men kept their guns trained on me. The seventh and final man, Henrika's bodyguard, holstered his weapon and latched onto Charlotte's arm, jerking her forward and making her stumble up against him. After a few seconds, Charlotte drew back as far as she could and gave the man a cold glare.

I considered what she'd revealed regarding her father. About how his work for Section had so often put her in danger when she was younger. And now here I was, doing the exact same thing. The realization filled me with shame. But I could be sorry later—*after* I had gotten us out of this.

Anatoly and Henrika turned and stepped out the open glass door in the back of the library. Anatoly's men strong-armed me after them, with Charlotte and Henrika's guard bringing up the rear.

The door opened up onto a wide balcony that overlooked one of the lawns behind the hotel. Anatoly and Henrika glided down the stairs, with the rest of us following along behind.

Anatoly and Henrika stopped in the center of one of the crushed-shell paths that wrapped around the wide-open grassy space. Anatoly waved his hand, and his men shepherded Charlotte and me out to the center of the lawn. I expected them to force us down onto our knees so they could execute us, but instead the men let us go and scurried backward.

"What's going on?" Charlotte whispered. "Why are they leaving us out here?"

"I have no idea."

Anatoly waved his hand again. "I don't know about you, Desmond, but this scenario seems remarkably familiar to me. I thought I'd planted enough IEDs on that beach to kill you and your friend Graham, but you somehow survived. This time, I decided not to take any chances."

A sinking feeling filled my stomach. He was right. I *had* been in this exact same situation on the beach, and the outcome now was going to be even worse than it had been back then. This time, Charlotte and I would both die, and I would perish knowing that my vendetta had gotten an innocent woman killed.

Graham would have been so disappointed in me. I'd promised to avenge him, but instead, I'd just made everything worse.

"You bastard," I growled. "You sick, twisted son of a bitch."

A deep belly laugh rumbled out of Anatoly's mouth. "Sick? Twisted? Why, I think that it's quite poetic."

"What is he talking about?" Charlotte asked.

I shook my head. I couldn't force myself to say the words, to confirm that my greatest fear was going to happen all over again—and kill us both.

"It's too bad we won't be able to stick around and see the demonstration," Henrika said. "I'd love to see my improvements in action."

I frowned. "What demonstration?"

"I told you I used my Redburn formula to bomb my father's London hotel. That was my first test. I made some improvements to the liquid explosive and conducted a second test, the one you were involved in on the beach in Australia." Henrika shrugged. "But you survived, so I made yet more improvements to the formula." She glanced over at Anatoly. "Adrian wants to see my new, improved explosive in action before he finally agrees to buy it."

Her words punched me in the gut. Beside me, Charlotte sucked in a startled breath. We'd both known the mission was compromised, and that Henrika would probably try to kill us, but I had never expected anything as cruel as this.

"Redburn," Charlotte murmured, looking at me. "She named it *Redburn* because of the marks that the explosive leaves behind on the victims' bodies—just like the ones you and Graham suffered."

Her words punched me in the gut too. Not only had Anatoly bombed the beach, but Henrika had also used Graham and me as lab rats, to test her weapon and prove it could kill paramortals so she could demand even more money for the formula. And now she was going to do it again, and there was nothing I could do to stop her—or save Charlotte.

"Henrika's generous donations to the hotel renovations led the foundation's board of directors to give her unsupervised access to the grounds over the past few weeks." Anatoly gestured at the lawn. "A couple of days ago, I took advantage of that. In preparation for this moment, for tonight, I had my men plant a series of Redburn explosives all over the lawn."

He pulled a phone out of his pocket and hit a button on it. An instant later, a low, familiar, ominous hum filled my ears, along with a series of faint *beep-beep-beeps*.

"You two are now standing in a minefield," Anatoly called out. "Only I'm afraid there is no way out. There's no pattern, you see, no way for you to safely navigate through. Even on the off chance you do make it off the grass, the devices are set on a timer, one that I've just started. You have ten minutes to say your goodbyes."

Damned if we moved, damned if we didn't move. It was a clever trap, and one I should have expected.

I cursed, then reached out with my power, hoping he was lying and that I could sense where the bombs were planted and give us a fighting chance of navigating out of the minefield. But there were too many explosives, and their energy all bled together in one dull, collective hum.

Since I couldn't sense exactly where the bombs were, I reached out with my magic again. Anatoly had probably used the same setup on these bombs as he had on the IEDs on the beach in Australia, which meant that these bombs were most likely wired together with cell phones. If I could make contact with those devices, then I could use my galvanism to drain the energy out of the phones and disarm the explosives that way. But there was some kind of resistance, some sort of barrier between me and the phones. I could sense their energy, but I couldn't quite grab it.

"In case you were wondering, I also had my men scatter thousands of plastic green nails all over the lawn," Anatoly said. "Neither one of you has any sort of magic that will let you disarm the devices."

Plastic didn't conduct electricity, so I wouldn't be able to reach through it and grab hold of the phones' energy. He had trapped us like rats in a maze, and all I could do was stand still and glare at him. I had never felt so utterly *helpless*, not even on the beach the first time the bastard had tried to blow me up.

"Any last words, Desmond?" Anatoly called out in a mocking voice.

I didn't have a retort—but Charlotte did.

"You might want to think twice about blowing us up. Especially since I have this."

She lifted her hand. At first, I thought she was showing off the white clutch she'd been carrying all evening, but then I realized she was actually holding a white box—the one that contained the Grunglass Necklace.

Henrika whirled toward her guard. "You idiot! You let her pick your pocket!"

She slapped him across the face. That man staggered back and fumbled in his jacket pocket, but all he came up with was Charlotte's white purse, which was roughly the same size and shape as the jewelry box.

I glanced at Charlotte, a wide grin creasing my face. "Sneaky, Numbers. Very sneaky."

She grinned back and waggled the box at me. "A little trick I learned from my grandmother. I told everyone I took after her. Maybe now they'll believe me."

She focused on Anatoly and Henrika again. "What do you say? How about a trade? The necklace for our lives?"

Henrika opened her mouth, probably to bargain, but Anatoly put his hand up, gesturing for her to be quiet. Henrika glared at him, but he ignored her and looked at Charlotte.

"Why should I trade for a bauble I care nothing about?" Anatoly asked. "My men can shoot you where you stand, and I can simply retrieve the necklace that way."

"You do that, and my body will most likely drop on one of your hidden bombs," Charlotte said, her voice full of cool logic. "And then you'll walk away with nothing. Why, you might even blow yourself up, if Henrika's Redburn explosive is as powerful as she claims."

Anatoly's eyes glittered, and his aura flickered a dark,

dangerous red. "I suppose that's a chance I'll just have to take—"

Suddenly, in the distance, gunfire exploded, each shot cracking through the air like thunder. The Section strike team must have finally realized we were in trouble and were coming to help, even though they would be too late.

Anatoly snarled and took a step forward, as though he was going to cross the lawn and snatch the box out of Charlotte's hands. He might not care about the bauble, as he called it, but he despised losing, and Charlotte had outsmarted him.

Henrika grabbed his arm and yanked him back. "Are you crazy? You'll set off the bombs. I want the necklace, but I'm not stupid enough to die for it. Let's get out of here! Now! Hurry!" She yanked on his arm again, trying to drag him away.

Anatoly gave us another angry glare, then turned and ran, leaving Charlotte and me trapped in the middle of the minefield.

TWENTY-TWO

CHARLOTTE

I let out a tense breath and lowered the box containing the Grunglass Necklace to my side. I hadn't been sure my gamble would work. But the gunshots had driven away Anatoly, Henrika, and their men, which meant that Desmond and I still had a chance—however small—to escape before the bombs went off.

Desmond's hands curled into fists, and his foot edged forward, as if he was thinking about charging after Anatoly, despite the bombs. But he must have realized how suicidal that would be because his foot stilled.

"Can you sense the bombs?" I asked. "Figure out where they are?"

Desmond shook his head. "I can sense them, and they are buried all around us, just like Anatoly said. He must have realized that plastic interferes with my galvanism. That's why he scattered plastic nails in the grass—to keep me from figuring out exactly where the bombs are. And if there's no pattern to the minefield, then there's no way of knowing where to step. Anatoly's men could have spaced the bombs five feet apart, or three, or two. I just can't tell."

Anguish, guilt, and regret shimmered in his eyes. "I'm sorry, Charlotte. So sorry. This is all my fault."

"It's Anatoly's fault," I replied. "Not yours. You have *nothing* to apologize for. Do you hear me?"

Desmond gave me a short, sharp nod, although I could tell he didn't believe my words.

"All right," I said. "We have to do something or we're dead. I'd rather die trying to live than just stand here and accept my fate. Wouldn't you?"

"Absolutely." His jaw clenched. "But I don't even know where to start."

I glanced around. We were standing in the center of the lawn, and the grass was perfectly smooth, as far as I could see. Anatoly's men hadn't left behind so much as a bent blade of grass to divulge the bombs' locations. Still, we had to do *something.* So I tucked the box with the Grunglass Necklace under my arm so I wouldn't lose it. Then I removed my stilettos, gently set them down on the grass, and carefully slid my bare foot to the left.

Danger-danger-danger! my inner voice immediately screamed.

I stopped and moved my foot to the right. Nothing. Not so much as a whisper from my inner voice. Hmm. I repeated the process, just to double-check myself. The results were the same as before. To the left was danger, to the right was not.

"Maybe you don't have to locate the explosives," I said. "Maybe I can get us out of here with my synesthesia. It warns me about danger, and I can't think of anything more dangerous than standing here, waiting for the bombs to blow."

"What do you need me to do?" Desmond asked.

His immediate, unquestioning confidence and trust warmed my heart.

"Be quiet, follow my lead, and step *exactly* where I step." I flashed him a wan smile. "And maybe hold my hand, for luck?"

"Anytime, Numbers."

Desmond grinned and threaded his fingers through mine. After these past few days of aching to touch him, that one small sensation nearly undid me. I savored the warmth of his skin, soaking into mine, then dropped my head, focused on the lawn, and concentrated on what I needed to do in order to get us out of here alive.

Slowly—very, very slowly—I moved to my right, stepping onto the nearest patch of grass that didn't ping my synesthesia. I held my breath as I fully shifted my weight onto that spot of earth, hoping it was safe—

And it was.

No metal plates depressed under my feet, no ominous *beep-beeps* sounded, and no explosion ripped through my body.

A tense breath escaped my lips, and I slowly shuffled my foot to the right again…

Danger-danger-danger.

I immediately stopped and changed direction, moving forward…

Nothing.

I shifted my weight onto that patch of grass, and I was once again rewarded by not blowing us up.

Again and again, I repeated the process, reaching out with my synesthesia to sense where the bombs were hidden. Desmond held my hand and trailed along behind me, keeping quiet and stepping exactly where I stepped. Slowly, deliberately, we made our way from the center of the lawn toward the crushed-shell path that led back toward the hotel.

I didn't know how long it took. Two minutes, four, six, although I could have sworn I could hear the seconds steadily, relentlessly *tick-tick-ticking* down in my mind, as though I could actually hear the timers on the bombs. Or maybe the phantom sensation was just my synesthesia telling me to hurry up.

Finally, after what seemed like forever, my feet landed on the crushed-shell path. I eyed the walkway in front of me, but my inner voice didn't whisper any more warnings.

Desmond stepped onto the path beside me. "Are there any more bombs up ahead? Any buried under the path?"

"I don't think so."

"Good. Because we need to run. Now!"

He gripped my hand tighter and dragged me along the path. I picked up my skirt and hurried after him, struggling to keep up with his long strides and trying to ignore the crushed shells biting into my bare feet. We made it back to the hotel and sprinted up the steps to the library balcony.

Danger-danger-danger! my inner voice started screaming again.

Desmond must have sensed the danger too because he wrapped his arms around my waist and whirled me around, so that his back was facing out toward the lawn. Then he churned his legs forward, shoving us both through the open glass door and into the library—

Explosions ripped through the air.

Light, heat, fire, smoke. All those things washed over me, but the one that shocked and stunned me the most was the sheer force of the *noise*—the continued, unending roar of all those bombs going off one after another.

My ears *pop-pop-popped* like they were full of firecrackers, and a dull ache bloomed in my skull, but those sensations didn't even come close to drowning out the overwhelming noise of the explosions.

Somehow, I ended up lying flat on my back, close to the desk in the library. Desmond plastered himself on top of me, shielding me from the blasts. All that pure, raw force washed over him, and his body convulsed against mine. I wrapped my arms around his waist, wishing I could absorb some of the energy and ease his burden. But of course I couldn't do that, and I had to settle for gripping him as tightly as he was holding on to me.

Sometime later, the light, heat, fire, and smoke slowly dissipated, and that seemingly unending roar finally died down to a faint, annoying buzz in my ears.

Desmond stopped convulsing. His body went utterly still, and he rolled off me and thumped to the library floor, landing on his back. My heart froze, and I scrambled up onto my knees beside him.

"Desmond? Desmond!" I shouted.

He shuddered out a breath, then grunted, slowly raised his head, and sat up. His eyes burned like silver-blue stars, and energy crackled in the air all around him. I reached out, intending to comfort him, but hot blue sparks snapped against my skin when my fingertips brushed up against his scorched tuxedo jacket. I hissed with pain and dropped my hand.

Desmond blinked several times, and some of the energy leaked out of his eyes. He was channeling the raw force of the explosions, slowly but surely getting control of the insane amount of power that had blasted over him and was still pumping through his body.

"Are you okay?" I asked. My voice sounded unnaturally loud, or maybe that was just the roar of the explosions still buzzing in my ears.

"Yeah," he rasped. "You?"

"I'm fine. I'm just glad we made it off the lawn in one piece."

"Yeah. Me too." Desmond hesitated. "Listen, Charlotte, there's something I want to ask you about—"

A hand grabbed Desmond's shoulder, yanking him to his feet. That same hand turned Desmond around, then clenched into a fist that plowed straight into his face. Desmond staggered back into the desk hard enough to make it *screech* across the floor.

My head snapped up. Adrian Anatoly stepped around the desk, both of his hands bunched into tight fists, and a murderous look on his face. He must have doubled back to the library from some other direction to see if the blast had killed us.

"Well, it seems that the two of you are full of surprises," Anatoly growled. "I don't know how you managed to escape my minefield, but no matter. You're still going to die."

Desmond pushed himself away from the desk, raised his hands, and staggered forward. Anatoly shouted, lowered his head, and charged at him. The two men surged in my direction, fists flying, and I rolled to my left, trying to stay out of the way of their deadly duel.

I scrambled around the desk and staggered up and onto my feet.

Desmond and Anatoly were exchanging punches, and

Anatoly was winning the battle, given his paramortal strength. He clocked Desmond in the jaw, making him stagger all the way back into one of the bookcases. Desmond snarled, pushed himself away from the wall, and surged right back toward Anatoly. I dropped my head and scanned the broken glass, splintered wood, and other charred, smoking debris on the floor. Where was it? Where was it?

There.

The gun I'd dropped earlier was still lying on the floor in front of the bar. I hurried in that direction, scooped it up, and whirled around.

Desmond and Anatoly were locked together, their hands wrapped around each other's throats, each one trying to strangle the other. I didn't have a clean shot, so I rushed over, flipped the gun around, and slammed the butt into the back of Anatoly's head. He hissed in surprise, but the hard blow didn't even faze him. Too late I remembered his power—that he couldn't feel physical pain.

Anatoly head-butted Desmond, sending him staggering back into the bookcase again. Desmond bounced off the wood, but his feet flew out from under him, and he hit the floor hard.

Anatoly whirled around to me. "You want to play too?" he snarled. "Fine. I don't care which one of you I kill first."

Before I could move, he darted forward and locked his hand around my throat. I raised the gun to shoot him, but he used his free hand to slap the weapon away. It thumped to the floor, well out of my reach.

Anatoly forced me back and up against one of the bookcases. I dug my nails into his hand and kicked out with my bare feet, but nothing I did bothered him, and I couldn't break his crushing grip on my throat. Gray spots flashed in warning in front of my eyes. Desperate, I reached down, grabbed one of the books off the shelf, and slammed it into his face.

He growled, but he still didn't release me, so I drew the book back and hit him again. And then again. And then again—

The corner of the book sliced across Anatoly's cheek, drawing blood, and slapped squarely into his nose, breaking it. That was finally enough to get him to loosen his grip on my throat. I sucked down a breath and hit him with the book again and again, driving him away from me—and straight back into Desmond.

Desmond staggered to his feet, slid forward, and dropped his pocket-watch chain over Anatoly's head. Then he yanked the chain to the side, snapping the terrorist's neck.

Anatoly might not be able to feel pain, but even he couldn't survive a broken neck. All the anger, all the energy, all the motion in Anatoly's body abruptly ceased, as though a transmuter had turned him into a statue.

Desmond removed the chain, and Anatoly teetered to the side before slowly dropping to the floor, his pale blue eyes wide and glassy.

Adrian Anatoly was dead.

Desmond and I both stood there, breathing hard, and staring down at Anatoly's body. Even though I had seen it happen, even though I had seen Desmond kill him, I still couldn't quite believe the terrorist was truly dead.

"Charlotte! Are you okay?" Desmond started to reach out, as if to cup my cheek, but for some reason, he dropped his hand to his side instead.

"I'm...fine," I rasped through my bruised throat, still sucking down air. "You?"

His gaze flicked to Anatoly. "Better, now that he's dead."

He didn't look better. If anything, he seemed even more anguished than before. I opened my mouth to ask him what was wrong—

"Desmond! Charlotte!" a voice yelled.

Miriam rushed into the library and skidded to a stop. Her eyes widened and darted from me to Desmond to Anatoly and back again. "Are you all right?"

"Yeah," I said. "Just some cuts, scrapes, and bruises for me. Desmond?"

"I'm okay," he replied. "Nothing too serious."

Lie, my inner voice whispered. I eyed him, wondering where he was injured. The back of his tuxedo jacket was scorched, and his face had already started to bruise and swell from Anatoly's punches, but he looked more or less okay. Or maybe it was his heart that was still hurting, more than his physical body.

"What's that?" Miriam walked over and grabbed something off the floor. She straightened up, clutching the white velvet box. "What's in here?"

"The Grunglass Necklace," I replied. Somehow, I had managed to hang on to it, despite everything that had happened.

Miriam held the box out to me, but I waved her off. "You keep it."

She nodded and hugged the box to her chest. "Sure thing, Charlotte. The others should be here any second—"

Section strike team members dressed in black tactical gear stormed into the ruined library, their guns up and at the ready. They paused, making sure that Desmond and I were okay, then swept out the back of the room, heading toward the still-smoldering lawn. No doubt they were going to search the grounds for Henrika, but I could have told them not to bother. Anatoly might have been stupid enough to double back to try to kill Desmond, but Henrika was smart enough to be long gone, even without her precious necklace.

Gia strode into the library, followed by Trevor. Gia glanced at Desmond and me before looking over at Miriam, who handed her the box containing the Grunglass Necklace. Gia opened the box and stared at the necklace a moment before giving it to Joan, who had stepped into the library behind her.

Then Gia focused on Desmond and me again. "Mission report."

Desmond told her everything that had happened, starting from when Henrika had led us into the library, to the two of us surviving the explosions, to us working together to kill Anatoly.

Gia frowned, looking back and forth between the two of us. "But how did you two manage to get off the lawn and out of Anatoly's minefield without setting off the bombs?"

I opened my mouth to tell her about my synesthesia—

"Just lucky, I guess," Desmond said, cutting me off. "It seems like Anatoly's men didn't plant as many bombs as he claimed."

I glanced at him, wondering what he was doing, but Desmond kept his gaze fixed on Gia.

She nodded. "Well, however you did it, I'm glad you both made it off the lawn alive." Gia turned to Trevor. "Time for us to see how we can keep this whole mess as quiet as possible. Miriam, Joan, with us."

Gia and Trevor strode out of the room, with Joan following them. Miriam flashed me a smile before doing the same.

That left Desmond and me standing alone in the ruined library. He focused on Anatoly's body again, while I concentrated on him.

"Are you sure you're okay?" I asked.

He grimaced and rubbed his neck where Anatoly had grabbed his throat. "Yeah. I have a massive headache, but that's about the worst of it. You?"

"About the same." I drew in a breath and let it out. "Thank you. For saving us. For shielding me from the blast. I know how hard that must have been. How it must have reminded you of...other things."

Desmond's gaze darted to Anatoly's body again. His jaw clenched, but he lifted his head and stared at me. "You're welcome. I'm just glad that...the outcome was different this time. Better. For both of us."

"Me too."

Desmond gave me a small, grim smile. "I should see if Gia and Trevor need any help."

Once again, his eyes darted over to Anatoly's body, and a haunted expression flickered across his face. Desmond spun around on his heel and strode out of the library without a backward glance. He might have finally killed Anatoly and avenged Graham, but Desmond's demons would probably stay with him for a long, long time, just as my own would always haunt me.

I waited until the sound of his footsteps had faded away, then stared out through the yawning space where the glass doors used to be. Outside, the lawn was a smoldering mess of churned earth, with large chunks of grass still burning here and there like campfires. I shuddered and wrapped my arms around myself, once again realizing how close Desmond and I had come to dying.

Danger-danger-danger.

Even though I was alone in the ruined library, my inner voice started whispering again. Not because of any immediate physical threat, but because of what I'd set into motion during the mission.

Adrian Anatoly might be dead, but for me, the real danger was just beginning.

TWENTY-THREE

DESMOND

The Section strike team searched for more than an hour, but they didn't find any sign of Henrika, her bodyguard, or Anatoly's men. I hadn't expected them to, but the fact that Henrika had escaped without telling me anything about the mole infuriated me all the same.

At least Anatoly was dead—finally, finally *dead*—thanks to Charlotte. If she hadn't been there, if she hadn't distracted him, then he would have killed me, given how overwhelmed I had been by the energy coursing through my body. But she had saved me, and then, when I had realized that Anatoly was hurting her, that he was going to *kill* her... Well, I had never wanted to murder him more than in that moment, not even to avenge Graham.

But Anatoly was dead, and we were not, so Charlotte and I got into a Section van and left the Halstead Hotel. Miriam and the other charmers were already hard at work, spreading rumors to the hotel staff and guests about a gas leak and subsequent explosion, while Gia and Trevor were talking to the mortal authorities and doing their best to cover up the whole messy affair. Just like Section higher-ups had covered up Graham's and all the other deaths related to the Blacksea mission. And so I had come full circle, or so it seemed.

Three hours later, I was back in the Section locker room on the fifth floor. The entire Redburn mission team had met for a quick debriefing in the bullpen conference room, then everyone had been given a break to clean up before coming back for a more in-depth talk about everything that had gone wrong. I grimaced and peeled off my scorched, shredded tuxedo jacket, then my vest, tie, and shirt underneath, trying to work out some of the tightness and soreness that had already gathered in my muscles. I turned to the side and stared at my reflection in the mirror over the counter.

My back was a mottled mass of black and purple bruises from the explosions, and some of the glass from the library doors had pierced my skin, opening up several small cuts, along with a deeper one that sliced down my right shoulder blade. I sighed, knowing I wouldn't be able to reach the cut to clean it and that I was too tired to heal it with my galvanism. I'd have to go visit the medical staff—

A soft knock sounded on one of the locker doors, like someone asking permission to approach, and Charlotte walked over to me. She'd already showered and changed.

"Hey. I just wanted to check and make sure you were okay—" Charlotte caught sight of my back in the mirror. Her eyes widened, and she rushed over to me. "Desmond! You said that you weren't hurt! I *knew* you were lying about that!"

"I'm not hurt...much. All the cuts have quit bleeding. Besides, I'm a fast healer. I'll be fine by morning." And if I wasn't, then I would grab some juice from the Touchstone Building's electrical grid and give myself a little jolt of energy.

"Turn around," she said in a stern voice.

I was too tired to argue, so I did as she commanded. Charlotte disappeared behind a row of lockers, then returned a minute later carrying a plastic basket full of medical supplies. She made me face the mirror, then soaked a cotton pad in alcohol and started cleaning my back. I hissed at the sting and the burn of the liquid soaking into the cuts.

She winced. "Sorry."

"It has to be done."

Charlotte nodded and kept cleaning my back. Her gaze was focused on my wounds, but I was staring at her in the mirror. Sometimes, I thought I would never get tired of looking at her, especially at times like these, when her brow was furrowed, her lips were puckered, and she was deep in thought, doing all those mental gymnastics in her mind. My own mind kept going back over everything that had happened tonight, especially what she'd told Henrika and how bright and true her aura had burned at that moment.

"Did you really mean what you said in the library?" I asked, still staring at her in the mirror. "About your father?"

"About being glad when he was killed during the Mexico mission?" A shadow passed over Charlotte's face, and her aura flickered and dimmed. "Yeah."

"Why?"

She sighed. "My father was completely devoted to his work at Section. Even when he was home with Grandma Jane and me, he was still training, or making me train with him, or getting ready for his next mission. He was never really there with us, with *me*, and he could never sit still and just *be*. He was always looking ahead, like a shark that couldn't stop swimming toward the next wave of danger."

"My father is the same way," I replied. "The General has *always* been more concerned with his work, career, and ambitions than he ever has been with my mother and me. The only times he even noticed me when I was growing up was when he thought I could be useful in furthering his own goals."

Charlotte nodded. "So you know how it is. Or rather how it was, with my father. And it wasn't just that he was always preoccupied. His work from Section followed him home more than once." She let out a bitter laugh. "*Lie*. It followed him home *all* the time. I can't even remember how often I was kidnapped, or threatened, or stalked growing up. All because my father was a Section spy. And every time something bad would happen to me, my father would apologize and swear up one side and down the other it would never happen again. But I always knew it was a lie."

"Did you ever tell him that?" I asked. "Confront him about it?"

"Did you?" she countered.

"Many, many times—with no result." My voice came out harsher than I intended, but Charlotte's confession scraped against my own old wounds, ones that still hurt, all these years later.

I cleared my throat. "Eventually, I realized the General was a lost cause, at least where I was concerned. So I quit trying to get through to him, quit trying to make my father see me as anything more than a tool he could use to improve his own standing inside Section."

She nodded in understanding. "I talked to my father about it—once."

"What happened?"

Charlotte raised her gaze to mine in the mirror. "My father told me he understood how I felt, but that *I* had to understand there were bad people out there, people who needed to be stopped, and that it was his duty to make sure those bad people didn't hurt and kill innocent folks. I think I was about ten, maybe eleven, but I still remember how *awful* his speech made me feel. How *guilty*. Like I was holding him back from something important. How do you compete with that? Even as a kid, I knew that I couldn't, so I never mentioned it to him again."

I winced. "I'm sorry he hurt you."

She shrugged, trying to pretend it didn't bother her, but the sputtering flare of her aura indicated how very much it did. "In the end, I suppose all I really wanted was for my father to choose me over Section, to pick me over his mission. *Just once.* That would have been enough. That would have told me I was just as important to him as being a spy was."

Charlotte shook her head, making her auburn hair fly around her shoulders. "But he never made that choice. So yeah, a part of me *was* glad when he was killed in Mexico. I thought that meant all the danger had died along with him. And for the most part, it did."

"Until I came along and dragged you into this." I finished her unspoken thought.

She looked at me in the mirror again. Slowly, her tense, haunted features relaxed into a small smile. "Oh, it hasn't been all bad, Dundee. If nothing else, you've given me a new appreciation for smoothies."

"I thought you hated my smoothies. What did you say about them? Oh, yes. That sipping one of them was like drinking pulverized grass."

"What can I say? They've grown on me. Just like you have." She flinched and dropped her gaze to my back, as if she'd said too much.

I didn't say anything else, and neither did she, although I kept staring at her in the mirror. Charlotte continued cleaning my wounds, her cool, smooth fingers dancing across my back as she applied one bandage after another. The sensation was the most delicious sort of torture, one that made me think of other ways she could touch me—and I could touch her. I had to clutch the edge of the counter to keep from reaching for her.

"There," she said. "All done. I should let you get dressed. We have another debriefing in fifteen minutes."

Charlotte busied herself with throwing the used alcohol pads and bandage wrappers into one of the trash bins. I leaned my hip against the counter and watched while she washed and dried her hands. Charlotte gave me another smile, then moved away.

I watched her cross the locker room, and her soft, squeaky footsteps finally slapped some sense into me. What was I doing? We'd almost been killed, and Henrika Hyde was still out there, along with the mole, which meant we were still in danger. I had never been shy about going after what I wanted, and I desperately wanted Charlotte.

She reached out and grabbed the door handle to leave the locker room, but I strode over and put my left hand above hers. Startled, Charlotte stopped and whirled around, putting her back up against the door.

I put my right hand up on the opposite side of the door, so that she was standing in between my arms. Not touching her, not yet, despite how desperately I wanted to lean in, press my body to hers, and feel her soft curves molding into my harder angles.

"As long as we're baring our souls to each other, there's something I've been wanting to tell you for a while now."

"What's that?" she whispered.

"I like it when you touch me, Numbers."

Charlotte sucked in a ragged breath, and her tongue darted out to wet her lips. I held back a groan and resisted the urge to lower my head and devour her lips, along with the rest of her.

"I told you once I would never touch a woman without her permission."

Charlotte didn't say anything, but her eyes widened, and she sucked in another breath. Even more telling, her aura sparked up, burning brighter and hotter than ever before.

"But I want to touch *you*," I growled. "I've been wanting to touch you for days now. Ever since that first night you came to my apartment. And every night and day since then."

I thought about telling her how much I admired her. How strong she was. And smart. And witty. And funny. And sexy, even when she was wearing that ridiculous waitress uniform. But I bit back the words. I'd already bared too much of myself to her, and only one thing really mattered.

"So here I am, Numbers, asking for permission. May I touch you?"

TWENTY-FOUR

CHARLOTTE

RUTH.

TRUTH. TRUTH. TRUTH.

The force of Desmond's words slammed into my mind, along with my heart, which started pounding, pounding, pounding. Red-hot desire exploded in my veins, and my whole body hummed with anticipation.

Desmond really did want me just as much as I wanted him. And he looked so *appealing* standing there, his body inches away from mine, the muscles in his bare arms and chest rippling as he braced himself on the door, still not touching me, not yet, not until I gave him permission. That care and thoughtfulness made him even more appealing to me.

His silver-blue gaze locked with mine, silently asking me to agree to something we both desperately wanted. But there was more than just a physical attraction between us, and our coming together would be more than just sex. At least to me. I genuinely cared about Desmond, and I could see how much it had cost him to open himself up like this, how vulnerable it made him to say those words.

In that moment, I knew I couldn't hurt him any more than I was already going to.

"No."

Desmond jerked away as though I had slapped him. In an instant, he had dropped his arms from the door and stepped back, putting some distance between us and taking the delicious heat of his body along with him.

"I see," he said in a short, clipped voice. "I'm sorry I misread the situation. I didn't mean to offend you."

He took another step back, and it was all I could do to keep from lunging forward and reaching for him.

"No, you don't understand," I said. "It's not that I don't want to. I just…can't."

Desmond gave me a wary look. "Why not?"

I opened my mouth to tell him that the mission wasn't over, at least not for me—

Out in the hall, a loud voice rang out. "Where is she? Where is Charlotte Locke?"

So they had already discovered my little deception. Faster than I had expected, which meant my time had run out.

I looked at Desmond again, staring into his eyes. "Whatever happens next, I want you to know one thing—I *never* betrayed you."

He frowned, clearly confused. "What are you talking about?"

I gave him a grim smile, but I didn't answer his question. The less I explained, the safer he would be. "Goodbye, Dundee. It was fun while it lasted."

Then, before I could change my mind and confess my sins, I turned around, wrenched the door open, and left the locker room.

Several people were waiting outside. Gia and Trevor were standing at the front of the pack, with several members of the Section strike team lurking behind them. Joan, Diego, and Miriam were standing off to the side, and even Evelyn was there, a worried look on her face.

Trevor stepped forward. "Charlotte, you need to come with us."

Desmond slipped out of the locker room behind me. "Trev? What's going on?"

Trevor gave him a regretful look. "I'm sorry, but an issue has come up with the mission."

"What sort of issue?" Desmond asked.

Trevor's gaze flicked back to me. "It's the Grunglass Necklace that Charlotte recovered from the hotel. It's a fake."

The strike team members escorted me to a fifth-floor conference room. At least, that's what Trevor called it, but given the fact that it only contained a table, two chairs, and a one-way mirror, along with a black domed camera mounted in the corner of the ceiling, it was really an interrogation room. The official interrogation rooms were on the fourth floor, but Section had a couple of spaces like this on every level.

I knew they were all probably gathered around outside watching me, but I didn't care. The only thing that mattered was getting through this with all my secrets intact. I stared at the mirror, but not even my synesthesia would let me see past my own reflection. I wondered if Desmond was standing on the opposite side, looking back at me. I wondered if he believed what they were saying about me. But I had no way of knowing, and speculation was a waste of energy and brainpower, especially since I would need all the wits and wiles I had for what was coming next.

So I dropped my gaze to the table. In the corner, on the side, largely out of sight, someone had jaggedly carved letters into the wood, the way a kid might to their school desk. I traced my fingers over the deep cuts.

Charlotte was here.

I had played in this interrogation room more than once while I was waiting for my father to finish his work. And now here I was, sitting on the wrong side of the table. I wondered what my father would think of that. He'd probably approve. Jack Locke might have loved working for Section, but he hadn't been above breaking a few rules in service of what he'd deemed to be the greater good.

And neither was I—especially when it came to getting Desmond his final piece of revenge, and me getting all of mine.

The door opened, and Gia strode inside, along with one of the guys on the strike team. I removed my hand from the wood, straightened up in my seat, and focused on her.

The strike team member took up a position in the corner, while Gia sat down in the chair across from mine. She laid a thick stack of folders on the table, along with a white velvet tray that held what everyone had assumed was the Grunglass Necklace. The emeralds and diamonds sparkled and flashed under the lights as if they were real, but by now, everyone at Section knew that they weren't.

Gia opened her folders and shuffled some papers around. She didn't speak, and neither did I. The worst thing I could do was start babbling to fill in the tense silence.

Gia must have realized I wasn't going to make that rookie mistake, and she quit fiddling with her papers. "It has come to my attention that you are deeply in debt, Charlotte."

No preamble about how this was a routine follow-up interview regarding the Redburn mission. No lies about how we just needed to clear up a few things. No obvious opening for me to try to spin things and dig myself in deeper. None of that bullshit. Gia was going straight for my jugular. Good. Soft-pedaling things was a waste of time.

"Yes, I am in debt."

Gia waited, probably hoping I would elaborate and try to explain, but that would have been another mistake. I couldn't afford to make *any* mistakes. Not in here. Not right now. Especially since I didn't know exactly who was watching.

"According to our information, you owe roughly five hundred thousand dollars to Gabriel Chase. A former cleaner, who left Section 47 in scandal and disgrace and who now operates his own private contracting firm."

Gia pulled out a photo and laid it on the table where I could see it. The picture showed Gabriel and me sitting inside the Moondust Diner. Judging from the peach pie Gabriel was eating, the image had been taken from out in the parking lot the night those four cleaners had attacked me.

"Five hundred ninety-six thousand fifteen dollars and sixty-seven cents," I replied. "Not counting monthly interest."

Gia blinked. "Why so exact?"

"I just want to be precise. I know how much Section values that."

That last part was bullshit, but I did want to be precise. I *had* to be precise and choose every word I said very, very carefully, as though it were the difference between life and death. Because for me, it absolutely was.

In addition to the camera mounted to the ceiling, other sensors were hidden in here, devices that were measuring everything from my heartbeat to my breath rate to how many times I blinked per minute. Outside the interrogation room, in a nearby office, a couple of synth analysts were no doubt watching, listening to my words and reaching out with their magic, trying to determine whether I was telling the truth. Standard Section operating procedure when dealing with a potentially hostile agent.

Gia's eyes narrowed at my flippant answer. She didn't like me jerking her around. "And how did you become so deeply indebted to Mr. Chase?"

I shrugged. "My grandmother was sick. There were lots of medical bills."

I didn't mention inheriting my father's debt or the missing ransom money from the Mexico mission. No doubt Gia had done her homework and already knew all about those things.

Gia pushed aside the photo of Gabriel and me and replaced it with one of the Grunglass Necklace. She tapped her finger on the picture. "This is the Grunglass Necklace—the *real* necklace. Not the fake you handed over to Section at the Halstead Hotel."

I didn't respond. Instead, I waited for her to get to the accusation I knew was coming next.

"Here's what I think happened. You asked to be assigned to any mission involving Henrika Hyde. You knew Henrika had her eye on the Grunglass Necklace, and when you realized she might try to swipe it from the hotel, you saw a way to pay off your debt. Steal the necklace, give it to your friend Gabriel Chase, and blame Henrika for the whole thing. Sometime during the general confusion of the mission and the subsequent explosions, you swapped out the real Grunglass Necklace for a fake, which you handed in to Section as though it were the genuine item. We're reviewing the security footage right now, Charlotte. It's only a matter of time before we pinpoint the exact moment you swapped out the necklace."

Gia leaned forward, an easy smile on her face, as though we were friends commiserating and sharing a secret. "All you have to do is tell me where you hid the necklace. That's it, Charlotte. You do that, and you can walk out of this room right now."

"And straight into a Section black site," I replied. "Right?"

Gia didn't say anything, but agreement flashed in her eyes.

I barked out a harsh laugh. "Don't try to bullshit me. My father was a cleaner, remember? Thanks to the infamous Jack Locke, I grew up seeing your playbook in action."

Gia leaned back in her seat and crossed her arms over her chest. "Then you know what's going to happen if you don't cooperate. Things can get very bad for you very quickly, Charlotte."

TRUTH, my inner voice blared out loud and clear.

Gia meant what she said, and I knew what was waiting for me beyond the door. A trip to an interrogation room up on the fourth floor, where I would be tied down to a chair and more thoroughly, forcibly questioned using increasingly unpleasant methods, both magical and otherwise.

I needed to do my best to prevent that from happening, so I leaned forward and tapped my finger on the fake necklace. "*This* is the necklace I lifted off Henrika's bodyguard at the hotel, and *this* is the necklace I turned over to Section. If something else happened to the necklace tonight, then I don't know anything about it."

Every word I said was true in letter if not spirit.

Gia sighed. "I've always liked you, Charlotte. You should make this easy on yourself. Given the extenuating circumstances, I can probably work out a deal for you. A short sentence in a minimum-security Section prison. Not a black site. But I have to recover the necklace to make that happen. You know that Section never gives something for nothing."

I shook my head. "I don't know what you're talking about."

Another bit of bullshit, but my words made Gia sigh again. "Let's go over the mission from the beginning…"

TWENTY-FIVE

DESMOND

I stood in front of the one-way mirror and watched Charlotte's interrogation.

Gia hammered Charlotte over and over again, asking about her debt, Gabriel, the mission, and especially the Grunglass Necklace. But Charlotte remained cool, calm, and composed through the whole thing, claiming she didn't know what had happened to the real necklace. In a strange way, I was proud of her. Most people would have already cracked, but not Charlotte, and I knew that she wouldn't. Gia might be an enduro, might be able to question Charlotte for hours on end, but she was wasting her time.

I scrubbed my hand through my hair. "You really think Charlotte stole the Grunglass Necklace to pay off her debt to Gabriel Chase?"

Beside me, Trevor shrugged. "That's the working theory, and it's the one that makes the most sense. Besides Henrika and her bodyguard, Charlotte was the only other person who handled the necklace during the mission. We checked the security footage. Henrika and her guard left the hotel grounds without the necklace. Which leads us back to Charlotte."

Trevor and I were standing right outside the interrogation room. Farther down the hall, in an observation room, several synths and some other paramortal techs were examining Charlotte's vital signs and all the other information they were recording and leeching off her. The whole process disgusted me. Or maybe that was because an hour ago, I was begging Charlotte to let me touch her. And now, I had to deal with the very real possibility that she had been using me this whole time.

Just like you were using her, a snide little voice whispered in the back of my mind. I quashed that unwanted twinge of conscience and focused on Charlotte again.

For the most part, she kept her eyes focused on Gia, but every once in a while, her gaze would dart to the side, almost as if she knew I was standing out here spying on her. I was surprised how guilty that made me feel, like I was betraying her simply by watching Gia question her.

I never *betrayed you*, Charlotte's voice whispered in my mind.

Remembering how earnest she had been in that moment, how sincere and serious, and especially how brightly her aura had blazed, increased my own guilt, but I pushed that aside too. Even I couldn't help Charlotte out of this mess.

Trevor turned to me, a sympathetic look on his face. "I know you like her, Dez, but you know as well as I do that people are never what they seem, especially inside Section."

His words made me feel like an even bigger fool, but I jerked my head, nodding back at him. I didn't trust myself to speak.

Trevor hesitated, then stepped a little closer to me. He glanced up and down the hallway, but the two of us were alone, and everyone else was watching from the observation room. "Did Charlotte ever say anything to you, Dez? About how deep in debt she was to Gabriel Chase?"

I never *betrayed you*, Charlotte's voice whispered in my mind again.

"No. I knew she and Gabriel were friendly, that they grew up together, but she never said anything about her debt to me."

If Charlotte had been here, she would have immediately said, *Lie*.

"Okay," Trevor said. "What about the Grunglass Necklace? Did she ever say anything about it? During mission prep, did she ever seem more interested in the necklace than she should have been? Did she ever do or say anything unusual? Anything you found suspicious?"

I flashed back to when I followed Charlotte to the diner where she met with Gabriel. That padded brown envelope he gave her could have easily contained a copy of the Grunglass Necklace.

"No, she never said anything about the necklace to me."

That much, at least, was the truth. Charlotte hadn't told me what she was planning, which was something else that made me angry. If she'd told me, I might have helped her. Or tried to talk her out of it. Or just given her the money myself to pay off her debt. *Anything* to keep her safe.

"Well, if you think of anything else, you'll tell me. Right, buddy?" Trevor asked.

I stared at Charlotte through the glass again. "Absolutely."

LIE.

Gia questioned Charlotte for more than an hour before getting to her feet, stepping outside the interrogation room, and closing the door behind her.

"She's not saying anything useful," Gia said to Trevor and me. "She keeps sticking to her story about not knowing anything about the necklace being a fake."

I peered through the glass. Charlotte had her left elbow propped up on the table, resting her head in her hand, while she idly ran her right fingers over one corner of the wood. She seemed completely calm and unconcerned about her dire circumstances. Charlotte had encased herself in ice, and Gia's interrogation hadn't so much as chipped the surface.

"What are you going to do with her?" I asked.

"She'll spend the night in one of the holding cells on the fourth floor, and then we'll try again in the morning," Gia said. "In the meantime, we'll review the security footage, every single second. Henrika knocked out some of the hotel cameras, but we have enough footage, angles, and witnesses to piece everything together and build a timeline of who had the necklace, when, and for how long. If Charlotte did steal the necklace, then we'll figure out how she did it and where she hid it. Once we know where the necklace is, Maestro will take over and decide Charlotte's fate. Stealing anything from Section, even evidence, is a serious crime. She'll definitely spend some time in either a Section prison or a mortal one. For her sake, I hope that it's a mortal prison."

"And if she's innocent?" I asked.

Gia looked at me as if I'd just sprouted another head. "I'd prepare yourself for the worst, Desmond. I've already told Charlotte to do the same."

My stomach clenched, but I didn't say anything else. I couldn't, not without revealing how much I cared about

Charlotte, even after she had seemingly betrayed Section and apparently played me for a fool.

Gia summoned a couple more strike team members, who went into the room, grabbed Charlotte's arms, and hauled her to her feet. The men escorted her out into the hallway, and Charlotte's gaze immediately locked with mine.

Even though I knew it was against protocol, even though I knew it was a mistake, I stepped forward, stopping right in front of her.

"Did you do it?" I asked in a low, strained voice. "Did you steal the necklace?"

Charlotte's aura flickered, but her face remained calm. "I don't know what you're talking about."

We both knew it wasn't a real answer. Gia waved her hand, and the strike team members fell in step around their prisoner.

I watched while they marched Charlotte to the end of the hall and escorted her into the waiting elevator. She turned around to face front, her gaze once again locking with mine. My chest squeezed tight again, but I couldn't help her. Right now, I didn't know if I even *wanted* to help her.

But I couldn't tear my eyes away from hers, and she stared at me until the elevator doors closed, cutting us off from each other and leaving me with nothing but questions.

TWENTY-SIX

CHARLOTTE

My interrogation lasted a week.

At least, I thought it was a week. It was hard to tell. During the day, I was shuffled from one interrogation room to another, and questioned by person after person about everything I had ever done before and during my time at Section. Gia, Trevor, and several other enduros all took cracks at me. They even sent Miriam in to try to charm the answers out of me, but I told her the same story I had told everyone else. Consistency and reasonable deniability were the keys to my survival.

Then, at night, I was stuffed back into a holding cell on the fourth floor. I was given the bare minimum of food and water, but there was no torture, which surprised me. Then again, they had no real proof I had done anything wrong.

It was harder than I expected it to be, mostly because I kept thinking about Desmond and the disbelief, doubt, and devastation on his face when he had confronted me outside the interrogation room that first night. I'd wanted to reassure him, but of course I couldn't do that. Not with so many eyes and ears on us. So I'd given him a vague answer, just like all the ones I'd given to Gia. Then I'd walked away from him, forcing myself not to look back.

I didn't see Desmond after that, but I could have sworn I felt his energy, his aura, hovering around, as if he were just out of sight but still watching over me. Sometimes, when I was getting bored with the constant questioning, I would daydream about him standing in front of me in the locker room, when he'd been inches away, asking for all the things I wanted to give to him.

Then my current interrogator would ask me another stupid, pointless question, interrupt my fantasy just when it was getting to the good part, and drag me back to the here and now.

Despite the bit of enduro magic I had, the endless, circular questioning quickly wore me down, and more than once, I thought about confessing my scheme. But if I did that, then the mole would get away scot-free, and I had suffered through too much to let that happen. And so had Desmond.

So every time I got tired, every time I wanted to give up, I forced myself to picture that image of Desmond I still had on my phone, the one of him clutching Graham's lifeless body to his chest. I also thought about the anguish that flickered in his eyes every time he talked about his best friend's death, and I especially thought about his screams and choked sobs ringing out when he was thrashing around in bed, caught in the throes of his latest nightmare.

And just like that, my resolve would harden, and I would keep on chugging along, talking in nonsense circles just like I'd been doing all along.

Finally, one day when I was bracing myself for yet another round of questioning, the door to the fifth-floor interrogation room opened, and Trevor strode inside.

"Congratulations, Charlotte," he said in a neutral voice. "You have been cleared to return to active duty. Effective immediately."

I blinked. "What?"

"You heard me. You are to report to your desk on the third floor as usual this morning. That is all."

Trevor exited the room, as did the guard in the corner, who left the door open behind him. I sat there staring at the open door, my mouth gaping, and my mind whirring with this new development. But this was exactly what I'd been hoping would happen, so I slowly pushed back from the table, got to my feet, and shuffled outside into the hallway.

A clock on the wall said it was just after nine in the morning, and people were streaming from the elevators to the bullpen to get started on their day's work. A few folks gave me cold looks as they walked by, including Joan Samson, but no one spoke to or tried to shove me back into the interrogation room.

Section 47 was really letting me go—or so it seemed.

I hadn't had a shower since the night of the Redburn mission, so the first thing I did was head to the fifth-floor locker room. I turned the water up as hot as it would go, scrubbed myself from top to bottom three times, and washed my hair twice. When I was clean, I opened the locker I had been using before the mission. A fresh set of clothes was sitting inside, right where I had left them. I eyed the garments, knowing that Section had probably embedded some microtrackers in my cardigan, T-shirt, and cargo pants, but I put them on anyway and threw my other clothes in the trash. I never wanted to see them—or smell their sour, sweaty stench—ever again.

Once that was done, I went up to the third floor and walked over to my usual desk in the analyst-and-charmer bullpen. For a few seconds, no one noticed me. But then Ronaldo looked up, then Helga, Mika, and Kaimbe. In an instant, everyone was staring at me. I ignored the curious and angry glares and headed over to my desk.

My shoulder bag and laptop were perched there, along with my crystal mockingbird figurine. But there was a new addition to my meager possessions—a white dry-erase board propped up on a small metal stand.

TRAITOR, someone had written in bold red letters with a giant red arrow pointing at my chair.

As far as psychological warfare and insults went, it was pretty tame, but a hush dropped over the bullpen, and everyone stopped what they were doing and stared at me. Miriam shot me a nervous, concerned look, and even Trevor came out of his office to see how I would react. My esteemed colleagues were all too chickenshit to actually stand up and tell me which one, or more, of them had placed the sign on my desk. But that was okay because I had my own message to send right back to them.

I grabbed the red pen from the ledge along the bottom of the board. I used the eraser on the top to wipe out *TRAITOR* and then the pen to scrawl a new word.

HYPOCRITES.

I stepped back, eyeing my masterpiece. There. That should add more fuel to the office gossip. Let my coworkers puzzle over my message. No doubt some of them wouldn't understand what I meant, but I imagined a few people would.

Especially the mole.

I glanced around the bullpen. Everyone looked back at me, then slowly returned to their phones and laptops, while Trevor disappeared back inside his glassed-in office. The only one who gave me any sort of encouragement was Miriam, who nodded.

"It's good to have you back," she whispered before concentrating on her monitor again.

I nodded back at her, then sat down in my seat and opened my laptop.

I had work to catch up on and reports to write.

The rest of the day passed by quietly. Actually, it was stone-cold silent, given the fact that no one so much as grunted at me, but that was okay. There was only one person there who I cared about.

Desmond.

Just before quitting time, I went down to the fifth-floor bullpen. All the cleaners and liaisons gave me nasty looks, just as they had this morning, particularly Joan, who looked as if she wanted to leap up out of her chair and strangle me with the cord on her landline phone. But I only had eyes for Desmond, who was standing by his desk, stuffing items into his briefcase.

He looked up at my approach, but his face remained impassive, and I couldn't tell what he was thinking—or, more important, what he was feeling.

"Can we talk?" I asked, once again aware of all the eyes and ears on us.

He snapped his briefcase shut, then stared at me, his gaze cold and remote. For a moment, I thought he might brush by me, but he jerked his head in agreement.

I retreated back to the front of the bullpen. Desmond finished gathering up his things, then followed me out into the hallway. I went over to the dead-spot alcove, the same place where we had had our first real talk all those days ago.

I glanced around, but I didn't see any red hazes, and my inner voice didn't whisper to me. Still a dead zone, although I had to be very careful about what I said to him.

"Thank you for talking to me," I said. "You must have a lot of questions."

Desmond shrugged. "Why bother with questions that you're not going to answer?"

Ouch. He had a point. I had to wait and see how things played out, and I wasn't sure how he would react if I told him what I was really up to.

Desmond kept staring at me, that dispassionate look still fixed on his face. The man I had gotten to know over the past couple of weeks, the one I had come to care so deeply about, seemed to be gone, and in his place was the remote, arrogant cleaner who'd first approached me in the cafeteria. My heart twinged, but I had no one to blame for the distance between us but myself.

"What do you want to say, Charlotte?" he asked in a cold, clipped tone. "I have things to do."

For the first time, I noticed he was holding a duffel bag along with his briefcase. "What's going on?"

"Section has picked up some chatter that Henrika has been spotted in London," he replied. "I'm going to check it out."

Realization punched me in the gut. "You're leaving."

"Yes."

I was surprised by how much the information hurt. Then again, I had always known that he would leave. Even if we had gotten both Anatoly and Henrika at the hotel, Desmond was still a cleaner, one of Section's best, and he would always be jetting off to some far-flung locale on the trail of yet another bad guy. This would probably be the last chance I ever had to speak to him, but now that the moment was here, I didn't know what to say. I decided on the truth. Or at least most of it.

"I'm sorry. I never meant to hurt you."

He arched an eyebrow in disbelief. "Is that all?"

"Yes."

LIE. The force of my own falsehood slammed into my mind, but I ground my teeth and didn't wince.

Desmond's eyes narrowed, and I willed my aura to be as calm and clear as my features were. If you could even do that to your aura.

"Well, then, I suppose there's only one thing left to say." Desmond stared at me, his eyes searching mine. Then he abruptly turned away, as if he couldn't stand to look at me any longer. "Goodbye, Charlotte."

He stepped out of the alcove and headed to a waiting elevator. He didn't even glance at me as he stepped inside and punched the button.

The door closed, cutting off my view and whisking him away from me.

TWENTY-SEVEN

DESMOND

I couldn't figure out how she had done it.

Try as I might, I just could *not* figure out how Charlotte had stolen the Grunglass Necklace right out from under Section's nose, much less where she had hidden it afterward. But I knew she had taken it. I could *see* it in her aura, a faint flicker that almost seemed like regret to me.

But the strangest thing was that I thought she must have had a good reason for stealing the necklace. Despite what Gia, Trevor, and everyone else at Section claimed, I didn't think Charlotte had stolen the necklace to pay off her debt to Gabriel. If she had wanted to do that, she could have easily slipped him some insider info about upcoming missions, or people in need of protection, or a dozen other things he could have turned into a hefty payday for his contracting company.

No, Charlotte had some *other* reason for stealing the Grunglass Necklace, although I couldn't imagine what it was. But she wasn't my concern anymore. Tracking down Henrika Hyde was. Still, I was having a hard time forgetting about everything that had happened between us, which was why I was currently sitting in a bar a few blocks from the main Section building, nursing my sorrows and stupidity over a glass of bourbon.

"I wouldn't have taken you for a bourbon drinker," a low, familiar voice rumbled.

Gabriel Chase slid onto the stool beside me. He glanced at me, as though he was worried I was going to protest. Or punch him in the face. Tempting as that last idea was, I merely shrugged. I didn't care that he was here. After all, he wasn't the one who'd fooled me.

Gabriel ordered his own bourbon, purchasing an entire bottle of liquor that was far more expensive than what I was drinking.

"Feeling flush tonight?" I asked in a snide voice.

He grinned, his teeth glinting like pearls in his face. "Something like that. Cheers, Slick."

Gabriel clinked his glass against mine, then downed his bourbon and poured himself another round. We sat there in silence, drinking, for the better part of five minutes. Finally, I couldn't stand the quiet any longer.

"Why are you here? Come to rub my face in how clever you and Charlotte are?"

"Nope. I came here to tell you to quit being an idiot."

"About what?"

He gave me a look, like it was patently obvious. "Charlotte, of course."

I grunted. "And here I would argue the problem is that I've been a complete idiot about Charlotte ever since I met her. She pulled a fast one on me, on all of Section. And you helped her do it. I'm surprised they haven't hauled you in for questioning."

"Oh, your friends Gia and Trevor tried to bring me in, but my lawyer told them in no uncertain terms that I have more than enough dirt to bury some of the Section higher-ups, so they have decided to let me be. Except for the watchers, of course."

Gabriel jerked his thumb over his shoulder at a woman sitting in the corner booth. She was nursing a drink and trying not to stare at him. "They've been up my ass all week. I guess they think I'll be stupid enough to lead them to this necklace that everyone is so hot to get their hands on."

"Don't you have it?"

"Nope. I don't have it, and I never sold it, if that's what you're thinking. I never made a dime off that necklace, and neither did Charlotte."

I couldn't automatically tell whether Gabriel was lying, not like Charlotte could have, but his aura remained a bright, steady gray, and his voice rang with conviction and just a touch of righteous indignation. Best guess? I thought he was telling the truth. About this, at least. Then again, I hadn't been the best judge of character lately.

I downed the rest of my bourbon, then turned the empty glass around and around in my hands. "It doesn't matter anymore. Charlotte Locke is someone else's problem now. I'm supposed to leave in the morning."

"New mission?"

"Yep. Related to an old mission. The one that got Charlotte into so much trouble."

Gabriel nodded. "So there's a personal element to it then. Something you can't let go."

Graham's burned face flashed before my eyes, along with his fading green aura. Saying that the Blacksea mission was personal for me was putting it mildly. But Gabriel was right. Adrian Anatoly might be dead, but the Section mole was still out there, and Henrika Hyde was my only lead as to who had sold out me, Graham, and all those other murdered agents. I wouldn't rest until both Henrika and the mole were as dead as Anatoly.

"Charlotte didn't tell you all my dirty little secrets?" I asked in a snide voice.

"You should know by now that Charlotte doesn't kiss and tell about *anything*. She plays her cards closer to the vest than anyone I've ever met." Gabriel paused. "It's going to get her in trouble."

Something in his voice made me take a closer look at him. "Are you saying that she's in trouble now?"

"Charlotte works for Section," Gabriel replied. "That means she's in trouble *all* the time. I'm surprised nothing serious has come up before now, especially given who her father was." He paused again. "But I guess you have your own set of daddy issues."

I snorted. "You could say that."

"I knew Charlotte's old man. He helped train me when I was first starting out as a cleaner. She would never admit it to anyone, but she's a lot like him—stubborn, determined, tenacious. Section might not realize it, but she's far more dangerous than Jack Locke."

"And why is that?"

Gabriel shrugged. "Because Charlotte is a whole lot smarter than her daddy ever was."

I thought of all those mental calculations constantly going on behind Charlotte's eyes, and the way that she carefully examined other people, as if she were seeing all their secrets, all the dark things they wanted to hide from everyone, including themselves. She hadn't even had to do her mental gymnastics on me. I had stupidly told her everything there was to know, which was probably the thing that rankled me the most. I had trusted her, laid myself bare, and she had left me out in the cold.

"Clever Numbers," I muttered.

Gabriel frowned. "What?"

"Nothing. Never mind."

He downed another bourbon, then pushed the bottle across the bar to me. "Consider this a going-away gift. If you're still going somewhere."

"What do you mean?"

His eyes locked with mine. "Just because Section sends you off on a mission doesn't mean you have to go. You're a Percy. You could pull some strings and stay in D.C. if you really wanted to."

"Why would I do that?"

Gabriel chuckled. "If I have to tell you that, Slick, then you really are an idiot." He gave me a hard look. "I guess you have to decide who and what you believe in more—Section 47 and your mission, or Charlotte. Good luck either way, whatever you decide."

He held out his hand, and I shook it. Gabriel dropped some money on the counter, winked at his watcher in the corner booth, and left the bar. The woman quickly paid her tab and followed him outside.

I could have told her not to bother. That Gabriel Chase wasn't going to do anything to incriminate himself. But the watcher wouldn't have listened to me, so I didn't even bother trying to flag her down. Besides, this fine, mostly full bottle of bourbon wasn't going to drink itself.

So I poured myself another round and tossed it back. As the liquor slid down my throat, I kept turning Gabriel's words over and over in my mind.

Obeying Section orders, or listening to my own instincts. Avenging Graham, or getting to the bottom of what Charlotte was really up to. Following my father's legacy, or creating my own.

I sighed and poured myself another drink. I was going to need a lot more alcohol to answer such lofty questions.

TWENTY-EIGHT

CHARLOTTE

Life slowly returned to normal.

Well, as normal as it could get, given the fact that Section 47 was spying on me. Someone was watching me from the moment I left my apartment building in the morning until I returned there late at night, after my diner shift ended.

After my week-long interrogation, I had returned to my normal routine, crappy waitress job and all. The only reason Section had let me go was because Gia and Trevor thought I would be stupid enough to lead them to the Grunglass Necklace. Or that I would try to run. Or both.

But I wasn't going to do either one of those things. No, I was going to wait for the mole to make a mistake. And they would make a mistake, sooner or later. I didn't have anyone to answer to but myself, but Henrika Hyde still desperately wanted the necklace, and she wasn't the kind of person you disappointed without incurring some serious consequences.

And never, ever second-guess yourself. My grandmother

had told me that long ago, so I stuck to my plan, just as she would have done.

A week after the end of my interrogation, I was working my usual shift at the diner. It was getting close to midnight, and the place was empty. Business had been much slower than usual, so Zeeta closed up early, and we all went our separate ways for the night.

Pablo gave me a strawberry pie to take home. Sadness filled me as I stared down into the plastic bag with its familiar box. The pie reminded me of Desmond. So many things reminded me of him, but he was long gone, off on his mission to hunt down Henrika.

Despite how badly things had ended between us, I wished him well. Henrika was a monster who needed to be eliminated, and I hoped Desmond found her and cut her throat with his pocket-watch chain. Oh, yes. I hoped that Anatoly's death, and Henrika's impending one, would bring Desmond the peace, satisfaction, and closure he was searching for, but I would probably never know one way or another.

I was so wrapped up in my thoughts about Desmond that I was almost to the front door of my apartment building when I noticed the figure loitering outside. But it wasn't one of the watchers who had been not-so-discreetly shadowing me over the past week. No, this was someone new, although I had been waiting for him to show up for days. I was surprised it had taken him this long to approach me. He'd been much more patient than I had expected.

I slowed my steps and glanced up and down the street, but the black SUV that had been parked outside my building when I'd walked to the diner earlier had vanished, along with my regular watchers. Of course they were gone. He wouldn't want an audience for this.

He stepped out into the light where I could clearly see him, an easy smile on his face, as though he wanted to be my friend. He probably did want to be my friend in hopes that I could pull him out of the mess he was in. He didn't realize I was the one who'd jammed him up in the first place. And that I was just getting started.

So I plastered a matching smile on my lips and headed over to him, as though I was genuinely pleased by this unexpected visit. His smile widened, although the streetlight cast part of his face in shadow. Appropriate, given the double life he was leading.

I was holding my phone in my hand, and I called out a single word, a voice command I had programmed into the device the morning of the Redburn mission.

"Mockingbird," I said.

My phone let out a soft *beep*, indicating that my command had been executed and my plan had been put into motion. I slid the device into my jacket pocket. Then I lifted my hand and fiddled with the black fountain pen nestled in my shirt pocket, making sure it faced outward toward the man I was approaching. The one who I'd once thought of as a colleague, but had realized some time ago was truly an enemy.

Trevor Donnelly. The mole.

I stopped on the sidewalk a few feet away from Trevor, who sidled forward and gave me another easy smile. The streetlights brought out the glints of silver in his black hair and the desperation in his eyes. Or perhaps that was just my own smug satisfaction coloring my perception of the charmer supervisor.

"Hello, Charlotte," Trevor said in a friendly tone. "I'm sorry to be lurking out here, but I wanted to discuss something with you, and I thought it best not to do so at the office. Too many eyes and ears. You know how it is."

I arched an eyebrow at him. "Oh, I know *exactly* how it is—and how awful you and everyone else have made it for me at Section these past two weeks. But let's be honest. You've been targeting me ever since Desmond came to town."

His smile faltered. Most people probably wouldn't have spotted the slight waver, but both my father and especially my grandmother had taught me to notice little things like that. The devil wasn't in the details—my survival was.

"I'm not sure what you mean," he replied.

"Oh, cut the song and dance, Trevor. I know that you're the mole."

His smile faltered again. Trevor Donnelly wasn't nearly as good at this game as he thought he was—and I was much, much better.

"You're the one who sent Rosalita and those other cleaners after me. You used to be a cleaner yourself, so it was probably easy to convince them to target me for money, or perks inside Section, or whatever else you promised them. Or maybe you blackmailed them into trying to kill me. It doesn't really matter," I said. "Once you realized that Desmond had killed Rosalita and the others, you rigged that car bomb and sent three more cleaners to take out the two of us. Only your plans kept backfiring, and we kept escaping your traps."

Trevor didn't say anything, so I kept talking.

"I've been around Section agents my whole life. In my experience, middle-management types like you only send cleaners to kill people when they have something big to hide. So I think it's safe to assume that *you* were the one who leaked intel on the Blacksea mission to Adrian Anatoly, which means that *you* are the reason why Graham and all those other Section agents are dead."

Trevor still didn't say anything, but his left eye twitched in another tell.

"After all, you had high enough clearance to access all the mission files, and no one would question you looking at them. Even on the off chance that someone did, you could always claim you were just checking on your good friends Desmond and Graham. Some loyal Musketeer you are."

Trevor flinched at my harsh words.

"You probably wanted Desmond to die too, just to tie up all the loose ends, but he survived. And then he did something even worse. Desmond started sniffing around Henrika Hyde, trying to figure out how she was connected to Anatoly, and he came to D.C. to see if I could help him put the pieces together. And, well, you just couldn't have Desmond talking to me about any of that, lest he discover how you had set him up."

Trevor's eye twitched again, and the smile melted completely off his face. "Fuck," he muttered, then yanked a gun out of his coat pocket. "You just had to make this difficult, didn't you?"

Instead of scaring me, the sight of his gun only made me angrier. "I've been thinking about you a lot over these past two weeks. Mostly, I've been trying to picture your face when you realized that the Grunglass Necklace that Section recovered from the Halstead Hotel was a fake, especially since you were probably going to switch out the real necklace with a fake of your own. That must have been quite a shock and a very bitter pill for you to swallow." I tilted my head to the side and studied him. "Tell me, Trev, did you curse? Hit something? Both?"

"Shut up," he snarled. "You think you're so clever, don't you, Charlotte? Always prying into other people's business, tracking their comings and goings, and writing your little reports from the safety of your cubicle. Well, you're right. I have been working for Anatoly *and* Henrika for months, right under your nose, and you didn't notice. And neither did anyone else at Section."

Oh, I was pretty sure someone else had noticed— Maestro, the mysterious head of the D.C. station. Time would tell whether I was right about that.

"Now," Trevor said, taking better aim at me, "you're going to tell me what you did with the real necklace."

"Or what? You're going to shoot me dead on the side-walk? Please tell me you're not *that* stupid." I sneered at him. "You need me to take you to the necklace. That's why you're really here, isn't it?"

"Yes," he replied. "I want the necklace. Now where is it?"

I shrugged. "I forget. So much has happened over the past two weeks. I've had to answer *so* many questions from *so* many people. Why, it's all just a big blur."

Trevor stepped forward and shoved his gun up against my stomach. The sharp motion made me lose my grip on my shoulder bag, as well as on the plastic one that contained the pie, and they both tumbled to the ground.

"Tell me. Right now," Trevor demanded. "Or I'll put a bullet in your gut and watch you bleed out all over the sidewalk."

"Go ahead," I snapped. "Shoot me. I still won't tell you a damn thing."

His eyes narrowed to thin slits. "Maybe I won't shoot you in the gut. Maybe I'll put a round in your shoulder. Then your other shoulder. Then your knees. Your feet. And every-where else I can think of until you tell me what I want to know. Trust me. You'll talk when the pain gets bad enough. Everyone does."

I laughed in his face. Trevor looked genuinely surprised that I wasn't more intimidated by his threats, and anger sparked in his eyes.

"Really?" I said when my laughter died down. "You're going to shoot me right here on the sidewalk multiple times and not expect anyone in any of these buildings to wake up and call the cops?"

He shoved the gun even deeper into my stomach. "That's what the suppressor is for. And I can always stuff something in your mouth to silence your screams."

He had a point, although I would never admit it. So I kept talking, trying to shake his confidence and stall for more time for my plan to take full effect.

"Forget about shooting me. You've already made far too many mistakes to get away with it, starting by dismissing my watchers." I gestured out at the empty street where the black SUV had been parked. "What do you think will happen if I show up murdered? Section will launch an investigation, and someone will realize that you told the watchers to stand down. And then *you* will be the one sitting in an interrogation room, trying to answer questions about where you were and what you were doing the night I was tortured to death. And once Section starts digging into you, well, we both know they won't like what they discover."

"That's assuming they find your body," he snapped.

Another valid point, so I changed the subject. "Let's make a deal."

He blinked. "What?"

"I give you the necklace, and you let me live."

His eyes narrowed again. "What kind of trick is this?"

"No trick. I want to live more than I want to bust you for being the mole. Besides, I'm assuming you're not planning to stick around Section after tonight."

Trevor didn't say anything, but his jaw clenched, and agreement flashed in his eyes. We both knew that getting his hands on the necklace and then disappearing was the only move he had left. I had figured out he was the mole, and it was just a matter of time before someone else did too, especially considering the Mockingbird voice command I'd given to my phone earlier.

"What do you say, Trev? I take you to the necklace, and you let me live. It's the best deal you're going to get."

Trevor's gun never wavered, never moved from my stomach, and I could almost see the wheels spinning in his mind as he debated whether to forget about the necklace and just go ahead and kill me. But he must have realized he couldn't escape both Section *and* Henrika Hyde and that he needed the necklace to appease Henrika so she would help him disappear. That was the logical conclusion, and I desperately wanted him to be logical.

Trevor slowly lowered the gun to his side. "All right, Charlotte," he said. "You take me to the necklace, and I'll let you live."

LIE.

The force of his falsehood slammed into my mind, and I had to grind my teeth to keep from wincing. Even without my synesthesia, I still would have known he was lying. I knew far too much for him to let me live.

"So," Trevor said. "Where did you hide the necklace? Where are we going?"

"Back to the place where it all started."

He frowned and raised his gun again. "I'm not in the mood to play word games."

I shook my head. "No word games. I hid the necklace the last place anyone would think to look for it."

"And where would that be?"

"Inside Section."

Trevor's eyes bulged, and shock filled his face. "You have got to be kidding me."

I shrugged again. "Why would I kid about something this serious? We both know that Section 47 is one of the most secure buildings in D.C. Besides, where else could I hide the necklace? I couldn't exactly stick it under a loose floorboard in my apartment. You would have already found it by now."

Trevor studied me for a few seconds, but he must have believed me because he let out a soft, muttered curse and yanked his phone out of his coat pocket.

"Don't move a muscle, or I will shoot you in the face," he growled. "Necklace be damned."

Keeping an eye on me, he sent a short text, then slid the phone back into his pocket. He gestured with his gun again. "Move. Now. Before I change my mind."

I slowly stepped in front of him and started down the sidewalk, heading toward the Section building, wondering if my scheme was going to work—or if I had just signed my own death warrant.

TWENTY-NINE

CHARLOTTE

I t didn't take us long to reach the Section building.
Trevor made me stop at the corner, and we both stared
up at the stone structure.

"What's the matter?" I taunted him. "Don't want to go
inside and get your prize?"

He knew as well as I did there was no sneaking inside
Section and that cameras would be recording our every move
once we stepped through the doors. Once Trevor made me
take him to the Grunglass Necklace, there would be no
explaining things away and pinning everything on me as
he'd tried to do before.

"Shut up and move," Trevor ordered, sliding his gun into
his coat pocket. "And don't try anything cute once we get
inside. I was a cleaner for a long, long time. I can kill you
before you take three steps."

He didn't have Desmond's smooth grace, but he was
right. He could most definitely kill me before I could warn
someone that he was holding me hostage.

I nodded, then stepped in front of him. Together, we crossed the street, headed down the sidewalk, and stopped in front of the main entrance. It was after midnight, so the pedestrian mall was long closed, and the glass double doors were locked, but Trevor used his keycard to open them.

He jerked his head at me. "Inside. Now."

I did as he commanded and pushed through one of the doors. The lobby was empty, all the shops and restaurants were locked up tight, and the overhead lights had been turned down low. The building seemed completely deserted.

"Move," Trevor snapped. "Through the turnstile and over to the elevators."

Once again, he scanned his keycard, clearing the way, and I did as commanded. As I neared the turnstile, I glanced over at Evelyn's desk. Her chair was pushed up to the counter, but the surveillance monitors were still on, and I spotted my and Trevor's images on the screens. Most of the Section security cameras were video only, with no sound.

Everything on Evelyn's desk had been put away for the night, except for one thing—a mug sitting off to one side, tucked away under the counter, almost out of sight. I slowed down, eyeing the steam wisping up out of the *World's Best Grandma* cup.

"Move," Trevor barked out, shoving me forward. "Quit stalling."

I pushed through the turnstile, and we got into an elevator. I expected him to ask me where I'd hidden the necklace, but instead he pushed the button for the third sublevel.

"Do you have to make a pit stop first?" I asked.

"Something like that," he grunted. "Now shut your mouth."

I did just that. We rode down to the third floor in tense silence. The doors pinged open. Trevor motioned for me to stay put, while he peered out into the space beyond. The coast must have been clear because he gestured for me to step outside.

"Move. Now."

Once again, I did as commanded. "Where are we going?"

"To the bullpen," he said. "I need to get something from my office. Then you're going to take me to the necklace."

We walked down the hallway. Trevor scanned his keycard yet again, and we stepped into the bullpen. My gaze flicked back and forth, but I didn't see anyone sitting in a cubicle, typing away on a laptop, and burning the after-midnight oil—

The sound of someone humming cut through the air, and Miriam entered the bullpen from one of the side doors.

Trevor and I both froze.

The charmer must have been out at some party, club, or restaurant because she was wearing a dark green jumpsuit covered with sparkly black sequins, along with black stilettoes. She didn't see us standing in the middle of the aisle, and she went over to and sat down at her desk as though nothing was wrong.

Trevor cursed and pushed me forward. I stumbled into Helga's desk, and my feet flew out from under me. On the way down to the ground, I swiped out with my arm, sending all the items on the desk flying through the air. I landed right in the middle of the mess, and I managed to wrap my hand around a pair of scissors, which I quickly, discreetly palmed and shoved into my jacket pocket.

"Trevor? What's going on?" Miriam's voice floated over to me, although I couldn't see her from my position on the floor. "Wait. What are you doing? Why do you have a gun?"

With every word, her voice rose a little higher.

"Stay right there!" Trevor hissed. "Don't move!"

He reached down, grabbed my shoulder, and hauled me

to my feet. I let him, although I clutched my pocket up against my side so that the scissors wouldn't fall out. Scissors weren't much of a weapon, especially when Trevor had a gun, but no matter what happened to me tonight, at least Desmond would learn the truth about his supposed friend.

I'd already made sure of that.

Miriam was standing beside her desk, having pushed her chair back and surged to her feet. Her face was pale, and her hazel eyes were wide with fear.

"What—what's going on?" she asked in a low, trembling voice.

Trevor shoved me forward again. "Get over there. Now."

I did as he commanded and went to stand beside Miriam, although I made sure to keep a couple of feet in between the two of us.

"What are you doing here?" Trevor snapped to the charmer. "You're supposed to be out at one of your stupid parties, chatting up that diplomat's wife and pumping her for information about her dirtbag husband."

"The wife got food poisoning, so I left early," Miriam replied.

She didn't ask him again what was going on, although her wide gaze kept flicking back and forth between Trevor and me. I didn't say anything to try to comfort her. Nothing I could say would help this situation.

Trevor leveled his gun at me again. "Tell me where the necklace is. Now."

"Necklace?" Miriam asked. "What is he talking about?"

I kept my gaze focused on Trevor. "He's the one who gave Section that fake Grunglass Necklace, not me. He's been working for Henrika Hyde and Adrian Anatoly for months, leaking info to them about Redburn and other missions. He's a mole and a traitor."

Miriam sucked in a ragged breath and swayed on her feet. Trevor swung his gun over to her, and she let out a squeal and raised her hands. He eyed her a moment, then trained his gun on me again.

"Tell me where the necklace is," he repeated.

"Why? So you can shoot me after all? No, thanks. I'm not telling you anything."

"We had a deal!" he hissed.

"Deal? Please. You were *never* going to let me walk away. No, you were going to put a bullet in my head the second you got the necklace. I might be a lot of things, but stupid isn't one of them."

Anger and frustration filled Trevor's face, and an ugly red flush swept up his neck. Then his eyes narrowed, and he studied me a little more closely. "Well, if you won't tell me where the necklace is to save yourself, then maybe you'll do it to save your friend."

He swiveled his gun over to Miriam again. She sucked in another breath, her hands still hoisted in the air. "Tell me where the necklace is, or I'll put a bullet in Miriam's pretty face."

I didn't respond. Trevor glared at me, and I stared right back at him. Several seconds ticked by in utter silence, the tension growing thicker and more palpable all the while.

Miriam glanced over at me, her hands raised, and her eyes still wide. "What are you waiting for? Tell him what he wants to know before he kills us both!"

I shrugged. "He's going to do that anyway. So why should I tell him anything?"

"Charlotte!" Miriam wailed. "You can't be serious!"

"Oh, I am very serious." I glared at Trevor. "He might kill us, and he might even get out of the building, but he'll be on the run for the rest of his miserable life, whether it's from

Section for being a mole, or from Henrika for failing to get her the necklace."

"And the two of you will still be dead in the meantime," he warned.

I shrugged again. "Yeah, but it won't be too long before someone tracks you down and puts a bullet in your head. Or maybe Desmond will snap your neck with his pocket-watch chain. He's very handy with it. Either way, that's all the incentive I need to keep my mouth shut."

Trevor stepped a little closer and took even more careful aim at Miriam. "I'm not bluffing. You either tell me what I want to know, Charlotte, or I'm going to kill your friend. I'm going to splatter her blood and brains all over your face."

"Well, it won't be the first time that's ever happened to me. So go ahead, pull the trigger." I held my hands out wide. "I hate this waitress uniform anyway."

"Charlotte!" Miriam squealed. "Do what he says! Please! I don't want to die!"

"Neither do I, but that's the risk we take working for Section."

Her eyes bulged even wider. "But I'm just a charmer! I go to parties and flirt with people! That's all!"

"Sorry you got mixed up in the middle of this. I guess this just wasn't your lucky night."

"Sorry?" Miriam hissed. "You're *sorry*? He's going to shoot us! Why won't you just tell him what he wants to know? Do it! Now! Before he kills us both. Please! Please, just tell him what he wants to know…"

She started blubbering, and tears spilled out of her eyes and streaked down her cheeks. As far as these sorts of things went, it was a truly impressive effort, and I was exhausted just looking at her. Who had the energy to cry that much?

In addition to her unending torrent of tears, magic also

blasted off Miriam's body. The soft, warm sensation wrapped around my chest and squeezed tight. It also tickled my tongue, as though her charmer power wanted me to reveal the necklace's location just as much as she obviously did.

"Shut up," Trevor snapped. "Just shut your mouth, and stop talking."

Miriam sucked in another breath. She stopped wailing, although her whole body was trembling, and she looked as if she might faint or vomit, or both, at any second. The invisible force of her magic pressed up against my body again, trying to prompt me to talk, but I ignored the warm, ticklish sensations.

"Wow," I drawled. "Your face gets really red and splotchy when you blubber. You're not very pretty when you cry, Miriam. I would think a charmer like you would practice bawling in front of the mirror."

She reared back as though I had slapped her. I stared at her a moment longer, then looked at Trevor again.

"You want to kill her?" I asked. "Well, go ahead. Shoot the bitch. She's a traitor, just like you are."

THIRTY

CHARLOTTE

My harsh words bounced off the plastic cubicles and quickly dissipated in the cool office air. Miriam and Trevor both blinked, as if they were trying to process my accusation.

"What are you talking about?" Trevor stepped forward, his gun still in his hand. "I'll shoot her dead right here and now—"

Miriam huffed, rolled her eyes, and waved her hand. "Forget it, Trev. She knows."

Trevor blinked again, but he slowly lowered his weapon to his side. I focused on Miriam. Even without a gun, she was far more devious and dangerous than he was.

Miriam sighed, then dropped her hand and palmed a blade that was hidden up her jumpsuit sleeve—a silver butterfly knife just like the one Rosalita had stabbed me with. From one moment to the next, Miriam's demeanor completely changed. Gone was the terrified, blubbering woman I'd considered a friend, and in her place was a cold, confident spy, one who was looking at me as though I were a high-school lab frog she was about to slice open so she could peer at my guts.

"How did you figure it out?" she asked.

"That Trevor was your new mystery man boy toy? That you were fucking him and getting him to be another mole inside Section for Henrika and Anatoly?" I shrugged. "The two of you weren't quite as discreet as you should have been."

"What do you mean?" Trevor asked.

Miriam ignored him the same way that I was doing. We both knew this was between us now. "And how did you figure out that I was fucking him?"

"It was a lot of little things."

"Like what?"

"You were the only one at Section who knew I was working at the Moondust Diner, so you were the only one who could possibly know I was in debt to Gabriel," I replied. "After Desmond killed those four cleaners outside my building, I started to wonder why they didn't just break into my apartment in the middle of the night, and how they knew that I was out and exactly what time I would come home. You were the only one who knew any of that."

"That could have been a coincidence," Miriam said. "People from Section eat at that diner all the time. Anyone could have seen you there and started spying on you."

"True," I agreed. "But it was the first domino that started falling in a long chain that led straight back to you."

Miriam and Trevor both kept staring at me.

"The two of you were very careful to keep things strictly professional around the office. No eating lunch together, no overt flirting, no quickies in the fifth-floor locker room. But I still knew you were sleeping together."

"How?" Trevor growled. "How did you figure it out?"

I gestured at Miriam's desk. "May I?"

She waggled her knife at me. "Slowly."

I shuffled in that direction. Miriam's desk was a mess, just like always, but I spotted a sturdy-looking metal stapler sitting among the candy wrappers and other debris. I made a mental note of exactly where the stapler was, then leaned forward and reached past it. I grabbed a small item off the desk, then turned around and held it up where Miriam and Trevor could both see it.

"A pack of gum?" Trevor said. "What does that have to do with anything?"

"Not just any old pack of gum—rosemint gum." I looked at Miriam. "The gum that Miriam has been chewing for weeks to try to help her stop smoking. It's a pretty unusual kind of gum, one I doubt that many people have even heard of, much less actually chew."

"So what?" Trevor snapped.

"So when you told me to spy on Desmond, I immediately became suspicious that you were the mole. Then I noticed you had several sticks of rosemint gum in the crystal candy dish on your desk. Everyone at Section knows what a health nut you are, Trevor. You rarely eat sugar, and you only have those mints and chocolates in that dish to offer to visitors. The gum was a new addition, and I started wondering why you would have the exact same flavor as Miriam. Combine you having the gum with her having a mysterious new boy toy, and the two of you sleeping together made the most sense."

I paused, but neither one of them said anything, so I continued.

"Of course, I didn't know for sure until I was accused of stealing the Grunglass Necklace. Everyone was so focused on me they forgot that Miriam also handled the necklace at the hotel. Not for long, not for more than a couple minutes, but that would have been enough time for you to swap it out for a fake." I gave her a thin smile. "I would have *loved* to have seen the look on your face when you realized that the necklace you had stolen from me was also a fake. I bet that really put a kink in your plans."

"How *did* you steal the necklace?" Miriam asked. "I haven't been able to figure it out."

"That's because I didn't steal the necklace—Gabriel Chase did."

Surprise filled Miriam's and Trevor's faces. They—and everyone else at Section—had been so focused on how *I* had stolen the necklace that it had probably never occurred to them someone *else* might have swiped it from the hotel.

"Remember all the prep work we did for the Redburn mission? All those blueprints we looked at? Well, I gave that information to Gabriel," I said. "With that intel and his ability to phase through walls, it was easy for him to slip into the hotel the night *before* the mission and switch the real necklace for a fake."

Miriam's eyes narrowed. "But he gave the real necklace to *you*, and you brought it *here*."

I shot my thumb and forefinger at her. "Winner, winner. I brought the real Grunglass Necklace to work the next morning, and I hid it before we ever even left for the Redburn mission. It's been here ever since."

"And you put all that together just by seeing a couple of pieces of gum? Clever," Miriam murmured. "It's too bad you're not one of us. I'm sure Henrika could find a use for someone as smart as you, Charlotte."

"Is that an invitation to join your little cabal?"

Miriam leaned against one of the cubicle walls, that long, sharp butterfly knife still clutched in her manicured hand.

"First of all, we're not a cabal. We call ourselves the Syndicate. I'm sure you've heard of us."

Of course I'd heard of the Syndicate. Like most people, I thought the alleged bad-guy collective was more of an urban legend than anything else, a scapegoat for Section and other agencies to blame when the true perpetrators of a crime or terrorist attack couldn't be found. But Miriam saying the name chimed a bell in the back of my mind and sent a chill zipping down my spine.

I'm finally going to discover exactly who is in the Syndicate. My father had said that to me right before he left for his doomed Mexico mission.

And what would you know about Mexico? My own voice whispered in my mind, along with Henrika's smug response: *Everything.*

I didn't believe in coincidences, and I was starting to think that the Syndicate was very, very real—and far more responsible for my father's death than the cartel leader he'd been sent to eliminate. But that was a mystery for another time.

"The Syndicate?" I said. "That sounds a bit pretentious."

"No more pretentious than Section 47. That sounds like something out of a rule book, and I've always hated following the rules." Miriam let out a small, mocking laugh, but then her face turned serious again. "And why *shouldn't* you join us, Charlotte? What has Section ever done for you? *Nothing.* They disavowed your father and left him to rot in Mexico. And then, when they thought you had dared to steal from them, they stuck you in a cell and interrogated you for a week. That's not the kind of organization I would give my loyalty to."

"That's because you don't have any loyalty to anyone, not even your boy toy."

Miriam didn't say anything, but agreement flickered across her face. Trevor eyed her, taking note of her silence. No honor among thieves, and most definitely no trust among spies.

"Enough talk," Miriam said, flashing her knife at me again. "Tell me where you hid the necklace, or I'll start cutting off your fingers. And believe me when I tell you that I won't hesitate like Trevor did."

TRUTH.

She meant every word, and she would carve me up like a wheel of cheese for a charcuterie board until I was begging to tell her where I had hidden the necklace. My time had officially run out.

I gestured at Miriam's desk again. "May I?"

Her eyebrows drew together in confusion, but she nodded her head. I stepped back over to her desk, tossed the gum down, and pushed aside some of the candy wrappers and other trash. Then I scooted the castle-shaped box that contained her costume jewelry to the edge of the desk. I opened one of the drawers, reached into the very back, and drew out the item I had wedged inside a couple of weeks ago.

I turned around and held out my hand. The Grunglass Necklace dangled from my fingertips in all its sparkling, shimmering, emerald-and-diamond-encrusted glory.

"It was in your desk this whole time? Right under your nose? You idiot!" Trevor hissed at Miriam. "How could you not think to look in your own desk?"

"Oh, Miriam *never* looks in that drawer," I drawled. "It's where she stuffs all her old, broken jewelry, along with all the ugly, unwanted baubles her boy toys buy her. Out of sight, out of mind, and all that."

"Shut up," Miriam snapped and held out her hand. "Give me the necklace, Charlotte. Now."

I stepped forward. Miriam snatched the necklace off my fingertips and stared at it with a reverent expression. She didn't notice that I had palmed the stapler off her desk.

"Henrika will be very pleased to see this," she murmured in an appreciative voice. "It's just the thing to get me back into her good graces."

"You mean she might not kill you once you deliver the bauble that you had already promised her, lost through your own stupidity, and couldn't find with all your Section resources?" I clucked my tongue in mock sympathy. "I wouldn't count on that. Henrika doesn't strike me as the forgiving type."

Miriam reached up and hooked the necklace around her throat. "Oh, don't worry about me, Charlotte. I'm a survivor. I can't say the same thing about you, though."

She opened her mouth, probably to order Trevor to shoot me, but her phone buzzed in her jumpsuit pocket. A second later, Trevor's phone buzzed in his coat pocket.

"The two of you are going to want to look at your notifications," I said.

Miriam and Trevor each stared at me, suspicion filling their faces, but the temptation was too strong, and they both pulled out their devices.

Trevor was quicker, so he got the bad news first. "There's been a transfer on my Swiss account..." He scrolled down the screen. He blinked a few times, as if he couldn't believe what he was seeing. "My money...it's all...*gone*."

Miriam cursed, staring down at her own phone. "My money's gone too." Her gaze snapped up to mine. "*You* did this."

I grinned at her. "Guilty as charged."

"But—but *how*?" Trevor sputtered.

I stabbed my finger at my cubicle. "I sit at that desk and

track terrorists' and criminals' money all day long. How hard do you think it was for me to find your slush funds? The secret Swiss bank accounts that Henrika and Anatoly funneled your payments into? You really shouldn't have put the account in your son's name, Trev. It was ridiculously easy to find."

He kept blinking at me, stunned by what was happening.

I turned my attention to Miriam. "Yours was a bit more difficult to locate, but then I remembered how fond you are of using the name Coco Livingston as one of your aliases, and *voilà*! There was your account. After that, well, it was just a matter of figuring out your passwords. Something else that was pretty easy to do."

I'd actually used the Mockingbird program to get their passwords, but I doubted they cared about that. No, all the two of them cared about was the fact that their money was long gone, along with the safety and escape it could have facilitated.

"This transfer was made five minutes ago," Trevor said. "There's no way you could have done that."

"As soon as I spotted you outside my building, I knew I was going to be indisposed, so I sent a voice command to my phone. That alerted Gabriel, who was more than happy to crack open his laptop, use the info on the flash drive I gave him before the Redburn mission, and hit a few buttons for me."

"You bitch!" Miriam hissed. "You duplicitous little bitch!"

"Temper, temper," I taunted her. "You shouldn't get so angry. It makes very unattractive wrinkles on your forehead."

"All my money is gone." Trevor looked at Miriam, a desperate note in his voice. "How are we supposed to run now? I have nothing left. *Nothing.*"

"Don't worry. The Syndicate will take us in. We'll get rid

of Charlotte, leave Section, and go to one of the local Syndicate safe houses. Everything will be fine. You'll see." Miriam tightened her grip on her knife and started toward me, but I held up my hand.

"Don't you want to know what else I did?"

Her eyes narrowed, but she stopped. "What?"

"Not only did my voice command alert Gabriel and tell him to drain your accounts, but it also triggered a series of emails."

"What emails?" Miriam snapped.

I grinned. They still might kill me, but I was going to savor this moment. "I sent all the information I compiled on the two of you, including your secret bank accounts, to several people at Section, including Gia Chan. Why, I think it's the best report I've ever written."

Miriam cursed, but I turned my attention to Trevor.

"I also sent a copy of the information to Desmond. He might be pissed at me right now, but sooner or later, he'll open the email and read the files. Then he'll know *exactly* how you sold out him, Graham, and all those other dead Section agents."

Trevor's eyes widened, and his face paled. "Dez—Dez knows?"

"He will soon enough. And I think it's safe to say there is no place on this green earth that you can hide where Desmond Percy won't find you, especially since your precious money is gone." My grin widened. "Consider this my payback for all the times you've tried to kill me over the past few weeks. Not to mention all those tedious hours you spent interrogating me when you knew I hadn't done anything wrong."

Trevor stared at me, worry, fear, and horror quickly flooding his features. He wet his lips and actually swayed on his feet, as though he was going to faint, and unlike Miriam's earlier histrionics, it wasn't a performance.

"Oh, snap out of it, Trev," Miriam said. "We have the necklace. Shoot her, and let's get out of here. We can figure out the rest later."

Trevor kept staring at me, his eyes wide. A sheen of sweat covered his forehead, and he yanked at his tie, as though it was suddenly strangling him. Trevor Donnelly might have been a cleaner, might have killed people for Section, but his whole world was crumbling to dust, and his confidence right along with it.

"You should have stayed in your cubicle," he growled and raised his gun.

I tightened the grip on the stapler still hidden in my hand. My plan was to throw it at him, and hope that my synesthesia would kick in, correct my aim, and help me knock his gun away. Then I would grab the scissors still tucked in my coat pocket and try to kill Miriam before she stabbed me with her knife. After that... Well, I was still working on the rest of my plan—

"Actually, no one is going to be shooting Charlotte," a low voice drawled. "I'm her bodyguard, you see, so it's my job to make sure nasty things like that don't happen to her."

A shadow detached itself from the wall, and a man stepped out into the light in the middle of the aisle.

Desmond.

THIRTY-ONE

DESMOND

Charlotte whispered my name like it was the answer to her most secret, fervent prayer.

The sound made my heart clench, but I focused on Trevor. He was the one with the gun, so he was the biggest threat to Charlotte. Nothing else mattered but making sure she stayed alive.

"You—you're supposed to be in London!" Trevor spit out, his voice growing higher and sharper with every word.

"I went to the airport, but I didn't get on the plane. I had some unfinished business here." My gaze flicked to Charlotte. "And I had a promise to keep."

She grinned at me. I winked back at her.

"How—how much of that did you hear?" Trevor asked, wetting his lips.

"Everything." I nodded at Charlotte. "I see you found the pen I dropped in your purse a couple of weeks ago. The one with the hidden camera and microphone."

She reached up, plucked the black pen out of her waitress shirt pocket, and tossed it down onto her desk. "I found it the very first night. Glad it finally came in handy. And that you were still monitoring the feed."

I hadn't been monitoring the feed. At least, not at first. No, I had been lurking outside the Moondust Diner, and I had followed Charlotte home, just as I'd done every night for the past several days, instead of being in London like everyone at Section thought. When I'd seen Trevor waiting outside her apartment, I'd known something was wrong.

I'd just never expected him to pull a gun on her.

I had thought about charging out of the shadows right then and there, tackling the bastard, and beating him until he was nothing more than a bloody smear on the sidewalk. But I knew Charlotte was up to something, given how cool she had been to him, and I wanted to know what she was doing.

Then I'd gotten an alert on my phone saying I had an email from her, and the app connected to the spy pen had also dinged. So I queued up the live footage and streamed it on my phone.

Hearing Trevor's confession that he was the mole, that he'd been working for Henrika and Anatoly, that he'd sent Graham and all those other people to their deaths, made me sick and furious. Once again, I had almost charged out of the shadows, but I trusted Charlotte, and I knew she must have some plan in mind.

She always did.

So I trailed the two of them to the Section building, then slipped inside after them and crept down the fire stairs to the third floor. For a third time, I had almost erupted out of the shadows, especially when Miriam had been sobbing and begging Trevor not to shoot her, but I'd seen the calculations going on in Charlotte's eyes, and her blue aura had remained bright and steady. She knew exactly what she was doing, so I had let it play out.

And now here we were, with not one but two moles exposed. A woman I had never suspected and a man whom I'd considered a friend and a confidant.

"You bastard," I snarled, my hands clenching into fists. "How much did Anatoly pay you to sell us out?"

Trevor's mouth twisted, but he didn't respond.

"Trevor got half a million," Charlotte said. "Miriam had more than a million in her account. I assume because she had the added task of fucking him, luring him over to the Syndicate dark side, and then keeping him in line."

"Shut up," Miriam hissed. "Just shut your mouth."

She brandished her knife at Charlotte, who gave her another one of those cool, unconcerned looks. I focused on Trevor again.

"After everything that we went through together over the years. All the training, all the missions. You, me, and Graham. The Three Musketeers. Why did you do it?" I asked, hating how much my voice cracked. "Why did you betray us?"

Trevor gave me a disgusted look. "Just wait until you have a few more years on you, Dez. When Section benches you from active missions for the sin of being closer to fifty than forty, and you have a bitch of an ex-wife who keeps asking for more alimony, and a brat of a kid who hates you for working so much but is all too happy to spend every dime you make."

"You did it for the *money*?" I asked.

"Divorces are expensive," he said. "I was drowning in debt. Charlotte knows how that is."

Charlotte let out a low, harsh laugh. "Drowning in debt? *Please.* You were a lousy five grand in the hole. All you had to do was cut back on those expensive, organic lunches and overseas trips to run marathons in London and Paris, and you would have been fine in six months. You don't know anything about life-altering, soul-crushing *debt*. The kind you know you'll *never* pay off, no matter how many jobs you have or how long and hard you work."

He grimaced, as though she had caught him in yet another lie.

"So what was the real reason, Trev?" I asked. "Why did you sell us out?"

A disgusted sneer twisted his face. "You're a Legacy, Dez. And not just any Legacy, but a fucking *Percy*. Your father pretty much runs Section, and he's turned you into his own personal assassin. You're Section's golden boy, and everything *always* comes easily to you—fighting, training, killing. And if that wasn't good enough, women throw themselves at you like you're made of chocolate, puppies, and ice cream. You've had everything handed to you on a silver platter your whole life. But I'm not a Legacy, and I've had to fight and claw and scrape for everything I have, both inside Section and out. Every mission, every promotion, every damn dollar and measly yearly raise. Well, guess what? I'm sick and tired of risking my life and watching Legacies like you get everything while the rest of us fight for your table scraps."

"Truth," Charlotte murmured.

I didn't need her to confirm his words. Hate, rage, condescension, and conviction rippled through Trevor's voice along with his golden aura. From one instant to the next, he had morphed from one of my closest friends into a stranger I had never really known.

"You disgust me," I snarled.

Trevor glared right back at me. "Ditto, Dez."

"If he's here, then more Section agents are probably on their way," Miriam cut in. "We need to get out of here. So shoot him, already!"

She didn't have to tell him twice. Trevor lifted his gun and fired at me.

"Desmond!" Charlotte screamed.

I ignored her cry and focused on the kinetic energy of the bullets as they erupted out of Trevor's gun. As the projectiles zipped through the air toward me, I concentrated on and grabbed hold of those tiny yet distinct waves of energy. Then I spun to my right and flicked my hand, redirecting that force and motion. The bullets veered away from me, slamming into one of the cubicle walls and cracking the plastic.

Behind Trevor, Miriam lunged at Charlotte, who snapped up her hand and tossed a stapler at Miriam. Her aim was true, and it slammed into the charmer's face. Miriam yelped and staggered back. Charlotte let out a low, angry snarl, yanked a pair of scissors out of her jacket pocket, and charged at Miriam, knocking her down to the floor.

The second that Trevor's gun *click-click-clicked* empty, I put my shoulder down, lunged forward, and plowed into him, shoving my elbow into the bastard's gut as hard as I could. He grunted with pain but quickly recovered and brought the butt of his gun down onto my spine. The force of the blow zipped through my body, but I used the sudden spike of pain and energy to churn my legs forward and ram him into the closest cubicle wall.

We crashed through the plastic and tumbled down to the ground. I landed on top of Trevor, and I rose up and drew my arm back to punch him, but he shoved his foot into my stomach and kicked me off him. I flew backward across the aisle and smashed through another cubicle wall. My head clipped the side of one of the desks, and red-hot pain exploded in my temple.

I scrambled back up to my feet, but my head spun, and I could tell that I was moving slower than usual—too damn slow.

Trevor struggled to his feet as well. He yanked another gun out of the small of his back, then snapped it up and aimed it at me. My head was still spinning, and I wasn't sure if I would be able to redirect the bullets with my galvanism as I had before.

Trevor must have realized how woozy I was because he sneered at me. "Not so golden now, are you? Goodbye, Dez."

He took a little better aim and started to squeeze the trigger—

Charlotte hurried forward, raised her arm, and stabbed him in the shoulder with that pair of scissors. Trevor screamed, whirled around, and punched her in the face. Charlotte's head snapped back, and she groaned and fell to the floor.

Rage exploded in my body that he had hurt her, that he had dared to lay one finger on her, and I lurched forward, closing the distance between us.

Trevor swung back around to fire at me, but this time, he was the one who was too slow. I chopped down with my left hand, knocking the gun out of his grip, then brought my right hand up and drove my fist straight into his jaw.

I put all the energy coursing through my body into the blow, and his teeth shattered like glass beneath my knuckles. Trevor mumbled out a low, strangled sound, and blood spewed from his mouth. He staggered and started to fall to the floor, but I grabbed his tie and hauled him back upright.

Maybe I should have looked into his eyes. Maybe I should have said something witty. Maybe I should have punched him in the face over and over again until he was hurting as much as I was inside. But all I could think about was Graham lying on the beach, using his last, raspy, dying breaths to tell me it was okay and that I would get the people who had set us up.

Well, this was one way to keep my promise to him.

So instead of hitting Trevor in the face again, I slammed my palm into his chest, directly over his heart. As soon as I made contact with his body, I reached for my galvanism and grabbed hold of the electrical charge that made his heart beat.

And then I stopped it.

Trevor let out a shocked, strangled gasp, and I shoved him away. He teetered on his feet, staring at me. Then his eyes rolled up into the back of his head, and he dropped to the ground. He would be dead in a few more seconds, just as soon as the rest of his body quit working.

I grabbed his gun from the floor, then whirled around, searching for Charlotte, who had gotten up onto her feet. She was swaying from side to side, but she looked at me, this wonderful smile on her bruised face.

She started forward, but Miriam darted up behind her. Before I could shout a warning, Miriam hooked her arm around Charlotte's shoulders and pressed her knife up against Charlotte's throat.

"Stop!" Miriam yelled. "Or she dies!"

THIRTY-TWO

CHARLOTTE

Desmond immediately stopped, although his free hand clenched into a tight fist, while his finger curled around the trigger of the gun he was clutching in his other hand.

I tried to jerk away from Miriam to give Desmond a clean shot, but she tightened her grip on me.

"Don't even *think* about trying to squirm away," she hissed in my ear. "You're my ticket out of here, Charlotte. You brought all this down on me, and you're going to get me out of it." She jerked her head at Desmond. "Back up! Now!"

Desmond's eyes narrowed, and he was clearly debating whether or not he could kill her before she killed me.

"You're not the only one who knows how to hurt people," Miriam hissed again. "Step back, or I start skinning Charlotte alive."

She dug the point of her knife into my neck, deep enough to draw blood. I grimaced, but I kept my mouth shut. I wasn't going to beg—not for Miriam to spare my life and not for Desmond to save it.

"Here's what's going to happen. You're going to back up, step aside, and let me walk out of here with Charlotte," Miriam said.

"Don't you *dare* let this traitor go," I said. "Kill her. Now."

"Desmond can't kill me before I cut your throat," Miriam snarled. "Now stop talking."

She was probably right about that, but she would kill me the first chance she got anyway, so I might as well go down fighting. I tensed, preparing myself to reach up, grab her knife, and try to shove it away from my neck before she cut me again—

"Drop the knife, Miriam. It's over." Another voice sounded, and Miriam spun around, turning me along with her.

Gia Chan strode into the bullpen, along with several strike team members. Evelyn came in behind them, hovering in the background as usual. The strike team members spread out, blocking all the bullpen exits.

Gia looked at me. "I got your email, Charlotte. It made for some interesting reading."

"I thought you might find it enlightening." I tilted my head to the side. "As you can see, Miriam stole the Grunglass Necklace from the hotel, not me."

"That's a lie!" Miriam screeched. "You stole the necklace!"

"How could *I* have stolen the necklace when *you're* the one wearing it?" I pointed out, not even bothering to keep the smug tone out of my voice.

Miriam let out a soft, muttered curse and adjusted her grip on me. "Here's what's going to happen," she repeated. "You're all going to let me walk out of here, or I will cut Charlotte's throat."

Gia shook her head. "You know Section doesn't negotiate with terrorists, Miriam. Not even to save our own agents." She looked at me again. "Sorry, Charlotte."

I didn't say anything. It was standard Section protocol and exactly what I had expected her to say.

Miriam sucked in a breath, and her fingers dug even deeper into my shoulder. I tensed, thinking that she was going to make good on her threat and kill me after all—

"I know things," she declared. "*Lots* of things. About Henrika, the Syndicate, more moles inside Section."

Everyone stared at her, except for Desmond, who was still looking at me.

"Truth," I said.

"What do you know about Henrika and the Syndicate?" Gia asked. "Tell me. Now."

Miriam laughed. "Please. I know better than that. You let me walk out of here with Charlotte, and then I'll tell you what I know. And not a moment before."

Gia stared at Miriam, a thoughtful expression on her face. Section didn't negotiate with terrorists...unless they had something Section wanted. And Gia and the rest of the higher-ups most definitely wanted Henrika Hyde's head on a platter, especially after the Blacksea and Redburn missions. And if Miriam knew something about the Syndicate too, well, that would be an added bonus.

"Stand down," Gia said.

The strike team members lowered their guns, but Desmond kept his raised and aimed at Miriam.

"Desmond," Gia barked out. "Stand down. That's an order."

Anger and frustration shimmered in his eyes, and a muscle ticked in his jaw, but he slowly lowered his gun. Even though I'd been expecting it, even though I knew it was a direct order, my heart still sank.

"What do you want?" Gia asked.

Behind me, Miriam relaxed, just a bit, although she kept her knife at my throat. "A helicopter on the roof, and guaranteed safe passage to an airstrip of my choosing. Once I'm at the airstrip, I'll release Charlotte and tell you everything I know."

LIE.

I didn't bother saying the word aloud. Miriam wasn't going to let me go. No, she would dispose of me the second she didn't need me anymore. I had outsmarted and humiliated her, and she couldn't—wouldn't—let that slide.

Of course, Desmond, Gia, and everyone else knew it too, but Gia kept staring at Miriam, as if she were already thinking about how to best use whatever information Miriam might reveal.

I had never wanted to end up like my father, but at this moment, I couldn't escape the irony that I had followed in his footsteps far more closely than I had ever intended to—and that I was about to die on a mission gone wrong, sacrificed for what a Section higher-up deemed to be the greater good.

"Do we have a deal?" Miriam asked.

Gia's gaze flicked around the bullpen. The strike team members. Desmond. Me. And finally Evelyn. She looked at everyone in turn before focusing on Miriam again. "Deal."

"Good. Then get out of my way," Miriam snarled.

Gia waved her hand, and the strike team members retreated, standing up against the walls and leaving a clear path down the center aisle to the main bullpen exit.

"Let's go," Miriam hissed in my ear. "And don't try anything stupid, or I will gut you where you stand, and screw the consequences."

She was once again telling the truth. We both knew she had nothing left to lose.

With Miriam's knife still at my throat, I moved forward, slowly heading toward the exit. Everyone watched while Miriam walked me out of here. No one moved, and no one spoke.

Except for Desmond.

He stepped out into the aisle, blocking the path, that gun still clutched in his hand and down by his side. "Forget the deal. Tell me what you know about Henrika and the Syndicate. *Now.*"

He didn't say anything about me, didn't try to negotiate for my release, for my life. Maybe he was pretending like he didn't care about me. Or maybe he wasn't pretending and he truly didn't care whether I lived or died. Either way, hurt still flooded my heart.

Miriam let out a low, ugly laugh. "Oh, no. That information is going to cost you my freedom." She glanced over at Gia. "Get your dog back on his leash, and let's get on with things. I have a helicopter to catch."

"Just tell me what you know, and you can still walk out of here," Desmond said. "I will personally guarantee your safety. I'm a Percy. You know I can do that."

Gia shot him an angry glare, but Desmond ignored her. He was right. He was a Percy, and he could get Miriam out of there, despite the fact that it would break about a dozen Section rules. But his father, General Percy, would smooth things over, especially to get information about a dangerous organization like the Syndicate.

"Maybe you can do that," Miriam said. "But I'm the one with a hostage, so I'm the one in charge. Now get out of my way."

"No," Desmond growled back. "I'm not letting you leave without telling me what you know about Henrika and the Syndicate."

For the second time, he didn't say anything about me. Miriam tensed, and I once again got the impression she was seconds away from cutting my throat.

"Get out of my way, Percy," she sneered. "Or watch Charlotte bleed out."

"You hurt her, and you die a second later," he threatened.

Miriam shrugged. "And then you'll have nothing. Not me and my intel, and not your new pet analyst either."

He didn't respond, although a muscle ticked in his jaw.

"Don't be an idiot," Miriam said. "You'll never get to Henrika without my help."

Desmond glanced at me.

"Truth," I said.

He kept staring at me, a silent debate raging in his eyes. He wanted to keep his promise to Graham, wanted to finish avenging his friend, wanted to find and kill every single person who'd had a hand in the doomed Blacksea mission. Miriam's information would help him track down Henrika and perhaps even dismantle her organization, along with the mysterious Syndicate.

"It's okay," I said. "I understand. I would do the same thing."

And I truly would. If our positions were reversed, and I had been through everything he had, then I would have done whatever was necessary to pry the information out of Miriam, even sacrifice another agent, no matter how I might feel about that person. And it wasn't just my life that was on the line. Desmond could potentially save dozens, perhaps even hundreds, of innocent lives in the future by eliminating Henrika.

Desmond stared at me a moment longer, then slowly stepped to the side, moving out of the center of the aisle and once again giving Miriam a clear path to the bullpen exit.

More hurt flooded my heart, but I kept my face blank. Desmond had made his choice, and I would just have to figure out some way to save myself.

Behind me, Miriam relaxed. She knew as well as I did that Desmond was the most dangerous person here, and the one real threat to her escaping.

"Move," she muttered in my ear again.

She shoved me forward, and I had no choice but to start walking. Thirty feet, twenty, fifteen...

We crept down the main bullpen aisle, getting closer to the exit. Gia, the strike team members, Evelyn, Desmond. No one moved or said anything, although I could almost see the tension hanging in the air like a thick gray blanket, spreading throughout the bullpen and leeching the color out of everything else.

We kept walking. Still using me as a human shield, Miriam turned me around, so I was facing out toward everyone and her back was to the exit. We were almost to the glass doors when Desmond shifted on his feet and stepped back out into the center of the aisle.

"Before you go, there's something I need to say to Charlotte," he called out.

"What?" Miriam growled.

Desmond's gaze locked with mine. A wry smile curved the corners of his lips, and his eyes flashed a bright silver-blue.

Danger-danger-danger.

"Fuck the mission," he snarled.

Desmond snapped up his gun and fired.

THIRTY-THREE

DESMOND

Miriam's head jerked back, and she dropped like a stone, dead before she even hit the floor.

Charlotte staggered away. She was clear of the cubicles, and her momentum took her all the way over to the wall at the front of the bullpen. Charlotte caught herself before she slammed into it, then turned around and put her back to the wall, as if she needed something to help support her.

I knew the feeling.

Gia started barking out orders, telling the strike team to make sure Miriam was dead, but I ignored the commotion and strode forward. I only had eyes for Charlotte.

I was by her side in seconds. "Are you okay?" I asked in a low voice.

She stared at me, her blue eyes wide, and her aura sparking, crackling, and flickering with emotion. Miriam's blood had spattered all over her bruised face, making Charlotte look like she was the one who'd been hurt. My heart twisted in my chest. I had come so very close to losing her that it took my breath away.

I wanted to reach up and wipe the blood off her face, but I didn't dare touch her, not even to do that. Once I started, I didn't know if I would be able to stop, even though I was painfully aware of Gia, Evelyn, and everyone else watching us. Instead, I settled for bracing my hand on the wall beside her and stepping in just a little closer, so I could better feel her energy, her aura, pulsing all around me, so that the lizard part of my brain would know she was still alive, still here with me, and not lying dead on the floor like Miriam was.

Charlotte stared back at me. Her shock wore off a bit, and her face creased with confusion. "Why did you do that?" she whispered. "You should have let Miriam drag me out of here. You should have waited until she let her guard down, and then found a way to disarm her, to take her alive. So why did you just shoot her like that?"

Because I couldn't risk losing you, I thought.

But I couldn't tell her that. Not with everyone watching. Even if they hadn't been watching, I still don't know if I could have said the words.

"We can talk later," I said. "Right now, I just want to stand here with you. Okay?"

Charlotte seemed startled by my confession, and her aura flickered again. "Oh," she whispered. "Okay."

And so we stood there, both of us against the wall, staring into each other's eyes, with so many unspoken words hanging in the air between us, while the rest of the Section agents swarmed through the bullpen.

Two hours later, I was sitting in Gia's office on the fifth floor. The strike team members were still up on the third floor, cleaning up the mess that had been left behind from the fight.

I had been sitting here for the last thirty minutes, alternately listening to Gia chew my ass out for disobeying a direct order by killing Miriam and explaining to her why I hadn't gone to London as planned. Evelyn was perched in the corner of the room, scribbling down notes on a legal pad.

"You should have told me you thought Charlotte was up to something," Gia said.

I shrugged. "I didn't know exactly what Charlotte was planning, but I wanted to let it play out. I trusted that she knew what she was doing, and it turns out I was right to trust her. Charlotte got you the Grunglass Necklace *and* exposed two moles. I would say that's a big win for Section."

Gia's eyes narrowed, and she rocked back in her chair. She was still pissed at me, especially for disobeying her, but she couldn't deny that Section had come out ahead tonight, thanks to Charlotte's scheme.

The door opened, and Charlotte stepped inside the office. She'd showered and changed out of her ruined waitress uniform and was now wearing her usual cardigan, T-shirt, cargo pants, and sneakers. She took the seat next to mine. I stared at her, and she looked right back at me. Together, we both turned to face Gia.

"Well, you two have made quite a mess of things," Gia said. "Ms. Locke, do you care to explain yourself?"

Charlotte sucked in a breath and told Gia almost everything that had happened over the past few weeks. How we had been attacked by cleaners twice, how she had figured out that Trevor and Miriam were working together, and how she had come up with a plan to get them to expose themselves and clear her name. Charlotte left out a few pertinent details, though, such as the fact that Gabriel had stolen the necklace from the hotel and that he had drained Trevor's and Miriam's secret bank accounts.

When she finished, we all fell silent, absorbing her words.

"Why didn't you tell me about Trevor?" I asked.

"I didn't know if you would believe me," Charlotte replied in a soft voice. "Especially since I didn't have any real proof. I also knew how close you were to Trevor, and I couldn't take a risk on you confronting him."

She was right. If she had told me, I would have gone straight to the bastard's office and started hitting him until he had told me what I wanted to know. And then we probably never would have killed Anatoly or exposed Miriam.

I nodded, telling her I understood, and some of the tension eased out of Charlotte's face.

She looked at Gia again. "As for people taking matters into their own hands, I think we should ask Evelyn about that. After all, she's the one who set me up with Desmond in the first place. Then again, I suppose such things are part of her job."

I frowned. "What do you mean? What does Evelyn have to do with anything?"

Charlotte shrugged. "Evelyn is Maestro."

Shock jolted through me. "What?"

She gestured at Evelyn. "She's Maestro, the puppet master who pulls our strings. Yours, mine, Gia's, and everyone else's here at the D.C. station."

I thought that Evelyn might deny it, but instead she quit scribbling notes and leaned back in her seat, and Gia went very still behind her desk. Evelyn gave Charlotte a cool, assessing look, and I realized it was true.

"*You're* the head of the D.C. office?" I asked.

Evelyn nodded. "I am. And I would like you to keep that

fact to yourself. Not even your father knows who I really am, and I would prefer it remain that way."

My mind spun, trying to make sense of everything.

Evelyn looked at Charlotte, a wry smile creeping across her face. "How did you figure it out?"

Charlotte shrugged again. "Everyone knows about my father and his history with Section, but people forget that my grandmother worked here too. Grandma Jane was an analyst, like me, and she told me all sorts of things about Section. But she tended to say one thing more than others."

"What was that?" Evelyn asked.

Charlotte grinned. "Always be nice to secretaries and janitors, especially Evelyn."

The older woman snorted. "I always thought Jane knew my secret, although I could never really tell for certain."

"My grandmother never revealed your secret to me. As for how I figured it out? Well, it was a lot of little things," Charlotte replied. "You knew Desmond's name the first day I asked about him after he came up to me in the cafeteria. Nobody at Section even realized he was in town yet, but you already knew exactly who he was. Then there was the fact that my keycard wouldn't work when I tried to leave Section the next day. At least, it didn't work until after Desmond showed up in the lobby. You delayed me so he could follow me home. You've been subtly pushing us together this whole time. You knew there was a mole inside Section, and you wanted us to work together to figure out who it was."

Evelyn let out a small, pleased laugh. "Guilty as charged. Your grandmother always told me you were even smarter than she was. Seems like she was right about that."

Gia scowled. "A little too smart for her own good, for Section's own good. You almost got yourself killed tonight, Charlotte."

"It was an acceptable risk to clear my name and expose the moles," she replied. "I just wish we could have pried more information out of Miriam about Henrika Hyde and the Syndicate."

Charlotte shot me a regretful look.

"It's okay," I said. "You were right when you told Trevor there was no place he could hide where I wouldn't find him. The same will be true for Henrika and whoever else works for the Syndicate."

"And everyone else at Section will make sure of that," Gia said in a grim voice. "We will hunt those bastards down and put them in the ground for killing our agents and staging that attack at the hotel."

The harsh promise in her voice rang through the office.

"So what happens now?" Charlotte asked.

Gia glanced at Evelyn, who nodded.

"First, we clean up the mess that Trevor and Miriam left behind, see how deeply their betrayals went, and figure out how many more moles there are, along with how badly our operations have been compromised," Gia said. "In the meantime, the two of you will be extensively debriefed over the next few days. But for right now, we're done. Go home, and get a few hours' sleep. I expect you both back in the building at nine a.m. sharp."

Charlotte and I both nodded and stood up. We left the office and walked through the empty bullpen. I jerked my head, and Charlotte followed me over to the dead-spot alcove.

"Are you okay?" I asked.

"I'm fine, thanks to you." She smiled, although the expression quickly faded away. "Thank you for saving my life."

"You saved your own life. You're the one who exposed the moles."

"But you kept your promise. You were my bodyguard, all the way to the end." She hesitated. "I know how hard it must have been for you to kill Miriam. Henrika was just as involved in the Blacksea mission as Anatoly was. I know how much you want to make her pay for what happened to you and Graham and everyone else."

"Henrika won't be able to hide for long. I'll get her eventually."

Charlotte grinned. "Truth."

I grinned back at her, and we stood there, staring into each other's eyes. Charlotte stepped closer to me. I reached out with my power, once again drinking in the beautiful blue of her aura.

"Desmond, I—"

"What are you two still doing here?" Gia barked out.

Charlotte and I both turned. The cleaner supervisor was standing in the hallway, her hands on her hips.

Gia stabbed her finger toward the elevators. "Go home, and get some sleep. I need you both back here fresh in a few hours. That's an order. One you shouldn't disobey if you know what's good for you."

Charlotte gave me a regretful look and headed toward the elevators. After a moment of wondering what might have been, what she might have been about to say, I followed her.

Our mission was over.

THIRTY-FOUR

CHARLOTTE

hree days later, everything had more or less returned
to normal. *My* normal, at least. I was back at my old
desk on the third floor, catching up on the work I'd
missed during the past few weeks.

Word had quickly spread through the building that Trevor
and Miriam had been the moles, and the dry-erase board had
been removed from my desk. The other charmers and analysts
actually nodded and smiled at me again, and everyone treated
me with an air of respect. I was the current shining star of
Section 47, although I knew it wouldn't last for long.

I had spent the past three days being debriefed by Gia and
Evelyn, as well as writing report after report, detailing all the
information I had uncovered about Trevor, Miriam, and
Henrika. For once, I was certain that people were actually
going to read my work, take it seriously, and give me credit
for it, which pleased me more than I would have thought
possible. Sometime during all of this craziness, I had realized
something important about myself—I actually *liked* working
for Section 47.

Oh, I still had no desire to be a cleaner like my father, but Jack Locke had been right when he had said Section did important work. The organization and the people who toiled for it might have their flaws, but they did far more good than harm, and I wanted to keep being a part of it.

So I answered questions and went to meetings and wrote reports. All while trying *not* to think about Desmond.

He was in many of the meetings, especially the ones regarding Henrika. Sometimes, he would even sit next to me, but we never had more than a minute alone together. Certainly not enough time to talk about us, or if there even was an *us*.

Desmond had his own questions to answer, meetings to attend, and reports to write. We were like two proverbial ships passing in the night, but perhaps that was for the best. It wouldn't be long before Desmond was sent on another mission, while I would stay here in D.C., and it was foolish to start something that had an expiration date, no matter how much I might want to.

I also kept my crappy job at the Moondust Diner. I might have paid off my debt to Gabriel in full, but I still needed money to replace everything I'd hocked. Not to mention the new waitress uniforms I needed to buy, since I'd gotten so many covered with blood over the past few weeks.

I was two hours into my usual shift when the diner's front door opened. My head lifted, and my heart leaped up into my throat, hoping it was Desmond, but Gabriel strolled through the door and took a seat in his usual corner booth.

My heart deflated like a popped balloon. Of course, Desmond wouldn't come here. He probably never wanted to see this place again.

I sighed, but I grabbed Gabriel's usual piece of pie— apple, tonight—along with one of the coffeepots. I placed the pie plate on the tabletop and filled his cup before sitting down in the booth across from him.

Gabriel took a couple of bites of pie and a few sips of coffee before getting down to business. He scanned my body, then leaned to the side, looking at my legs. "No white tights tonight? Isn't that against the strict dress code?"

"I ruined all the ones I had, and I haven't had a chance to buy any new pairs yet."

He grinned. "I bet Zeeta *loves* that."

I glanced over at the owner, who was sitting behind the cash register and scowling at me as usual. "Yeah. Zeeta has threatened to fire me multiple times, especially since I didn't show up for work while Section was interrogating me. But we've been too busy the past few days for her to actually go through with it. Well, that, and I think she actually likes glaring at me."

Gabriel chuckled. "Well, despite the missing tights, you're looking good, Charlotte. Much better than the last time I saw you. A lot less stressed."

I laughed. "Yeah, you might say that. Then again, after being attacked multiple times and interrogated by Section, ignoring Zeeta's nasty looks is a whole lot easier than it used to be. Besides, I finally settled my debt to you. That has been a huge weight off my shoulders."

"Speaking of that, this is for you." Gabriel reached into his pocket and slid a small flash drive across the table to me.

"What is it?"

"A bank account in your grandmother's name that you can access. When I checked it this morning, there was one million, three hundred thousand, thirteen dollars, and eighty-four cents in there." Gabriel grinned. "I know how you like to be precise about such things."

I rolled my eyes at his teasing, but I didn't have to ask where he'd gotten the money. It had obviously come from what he had drained out of Miriam's and Trevor's accounts. Still, the longer I looked at the flash drive, the more shock bubbled up inside me, along with a sensation I hadn't felt in a long time—hope.

I shook my head. "I gave that money to *you*. To settle my debt and for the risks you took stealing the necklace."

"You're the one who found the money, so I'm giving you what you earned."

I frowned. "Why?"

He shrugged. "You like to be precise, and I never take more than I'm owed. Besides, you're the one who did all the hard work of planning the heist and dealing with the aftermath, so you should reap most of the rewards."

I opened my mouth to protest, but Gabriel wagged his finger at me.

"You *are* going to take this money, Charlotte. You're going to need it sooner or later, especially if you keep working for Section and digging into people like Henrika Hyde and whoever else is part of the Syndicate."

He was right, and he was giving me a gift—from one friend to another—with no debts owed on either side. I wasn't going to insult him by protesting anymore, so I nodded my thanks, grabbed the flash drive, and tucked it into my apron pocket. "I've been meaning to talk to you about that."

"About what? Terrorists?" Gabriel arched an eyebrow at me. "Girl, we need to work on your conversational skills."

"You're probably right about that. But more specifically, I wanted to talk to you about coming back to Section."

He blinked in surprise, then snorted out a laugh. "You can't be serious."

"I'm absolutely serious. I'm sure Gia Chan would be happy to welcome you back, especially given your recent help in exposing two moles."

Gabriel leaned back in his side of the booth and crossed his arms over his muscled chest. "Maybe she would, but I don't want to come back. I'm quite happy being my own boss."

"Lie."

He scowled. "You know I hate it when you do that."

I grinned. "But, seriously, you should think about it. You were great at being a cleaner, and I know how much you loved it. Face it, Gabriel. You're a Legacy like me—stuck in the Section family business for better or worse."

Gabriel scowled at me for a few more seconds, then shrugged a shoulder. It wasn't a yes, but it wasn't an outright no either. It was definitely a start, and I would have to satisfy myself with that for tonight.

"Speaking of cleaners, how is your Aussie supermodel?" Gabriel asked, deliberately changing the subject.

"Desmond is not my anything, and he's fine, as far as I know. He's getting his new assignment tomorrow, so he'll probably be leaving D.C. to track down Henrika."

Gabriel threw his hands up in the air. "Then why are you still sitting here? Go and be with your man on his final night in town."

I rolled my eyes again. "Desmond Percy is not *my man*."

"Lie," Gabriel crowed, much the same way that I had earlier. "I've seen the way the two of you look at each other."

"And how is that?"

He gestured at his plate. "The same way I look at a piece of pie—like I want to devour it all at once." He shoveled another bite into his mouth to prove his point.

"I am not a piece of pie, and neither is Desmond."

"No," Gabriel replied. "You are both idiots who are too stubborn, paranoid, and uptight to just kick back, relax, and enjoy each other."

I didn't have a response to that, mostly because his words were all too true. Gabriel gave me a smug look, knowing he had made his point yet again. He finished his pie and drained his coffee, then got to his feet.

"Think about what I said about Desmond," he rumbled. "And, Charlotte?"

"Yeah?"

"Now that you have a little money in the bank, do yourself a favor and get some furniture for that empty-ass apartment of yours."

Gabriel grinned at me, then sauntered over to Zeeta to pay his tab. I watched him go with a smile on my face, knowing that things were finally good between us.

I worked until midnight as usual, then left the diner. I stood at the edge of the parking lot, debating which way to go. Left would take me home to my apartment, while right would take me in the direction of the Touchstone Building.

I let out a tense breath, then turned right.

It didn't take me long to reach Desmond's building. The security guard recognized me, and he hurried to open one of the doors. I nodded to him and stepped inside. For a moment, my steps faltered, but I crossed the lobby, opened the art gallery doors, and headed back to the elevator. Then, before I could change my mind, I stepped into the car and punched the button.

A few seconds later, the elevator door slid open. I walked

through the foyer and over to the front door of Desmond's apartment. I stood there, staring at the blank slab of wood. Then I let out another long, tense breath, raised my hand, and knocked.

The only sound was the soft echo of my knock rattling through the foyer. I strained to listen, but I didn't hear anything on the other side of the thick wood. Was he home? Had he already left on his assignment? Did he have company?

That last thought made me step back, but before I could hurry over to the elevator, the door opened, and Desmond appeared.

He was once again dressed in his usual light gray shirt, vest, and pants. His tie was the powder-blue one with the silver dots that was my personal favorite. Seeing him looking so sleek and polished reminded me that I was still wearing my horrible waitress uniform. I could have smacked myself upside the head. I should have gone home and changed first, but it was too late now.

Desmond seemed surprised to see me, but his face quickly smoothed out.

I cleared my throat. "May I come in?"

He stared at me a moment, then opened the door. I stepped through to the other side, and he closed and locked the door behind me.

The apartment looked the same as always, except for one thing—several suitcases were sitting outside Desmond's bedroom door. It looked as if he had already packed in preparation for his new assignment the next day.

My heart sank a little, but I put my shoulder bag on the island counter, along with a white plastic bag. I gestured at the box sitting inside the plastic. "I know you don't eat sugar, but I brought you some dessert anyway."

"What did Pablo make tonight?" Desmond asked.

"Apple pie."

He nodded, and the two of us stood in the kitchen, close to the island, staring at each other. I sucked in a breath, then let it out, along with the words I had been wanting to say to him for weeks now.

"Do you remember the question you asked me in the locker room the night we came back from the Redburn mission?"

Desmond's eyes sparked like live wires in his face. "I could never forget it."

"I wanted to tell you yes that night. I would have said yes, if I hadn't known what was coming next."

"So?"

I gathered up my courage and stepped even closer to him. "So now I'm going to ask the same question of you, Dundee. May I touch you?"

We both knew what I was really asking. In an instant, those sparks in his eyes coalesced into bright, hot flames. The heat of his gaze washed over me, sending a shiver down my spine, even as my stomach clenched with anticipation.

"Permission granted," Desmond said.

THIRTY-FIVE

DESMOND

I couldn't believe that this was real. That Charlotte was here. That this was finally *happening*.

But she was real, she was here and standing in front of me, and her aura was burning as bright, hot, and blue as I had ever seen it.

Charlotte shrugged out of her fleece jacket and threw it onto the counter, then stepped in close to me again. She stared up into my eyes, reaching out and carefully plucking my watch out of my vest pocket. She set it aside and undid the buttons on my vest.

"I don't think I ever told you how sexy I find this vest of yours," she murmured. "I've wanted to peel it off you for days now. Especially since I know exactly what's underneath it."

"It's not nearly as sexy as that uniform you're wearing," I replied.

She arched an eyebrow in amusement, but she didn't stop undoing the buttons. She made quick work of them, then moved around behind me, sliding the vest off my shoulders.

I let her, and she carefully laid it on the counter next to my watch.

She undid my tie, slowly loosening the knot and pulling one end of it down so that it slipped around and off my neck. She laid the tie aside too. My shirt was next, and I noticed with satisfaction that her fingers were trembling as she undid the buttons. Charlotte might seem cool, but a fire was raging inside her—the same one burning inside me.

She worked the last button free, then moved around behind me, pulling the shirt down my arms. I let her, and she tossed it aside, not bothering to pick it up when it fell short of the counter.

Charlotte came back around to my front again. She reached for my belt, but I stepped forward and put my hands on top of hers.

"Let me." I reached around to my back pocket and grabbed my wallet. I pulled out a condom, then tossed the wallet aside.

She nodded her approval. "I use protection too."

"Good."

I undid my belt, yanked it off, and threw it aside. She watched while I unzipped my pants and stepped out of them, along with my boxers. I peeled off my socks, then straightened up so she could see all of me, laid bare for her.

Her blue gaze tracked up and down my body, lingering on my stiff, throbbing erection. She let out a low wolf whistle. "Not bad, Dundee. Not bad at all."

"Oh, Numbers. You ain't seen nothing yet."

I covered myself with the condom, then moved forward. Charlotte sucked in a breath, and I grabbed her around the waist, picked her up, and set her on the edge of the counter. Her eyes widened, and her tongue darted out to wet her lips.

I leaned forward and placed my lips on the pulse in the hollow of her throat. More satisfaction filled me to feel it hammering, just like mine was. Then I breathed in the blue of her, drawing her aura, her energy, deep into my lungs.

Charlotte tangled her fingers in my hair and nuzzled my face just as I was still doing to her neck. "You smell so good," she murmured against my skin. "Like pine and soap mixed together."

"And you smell like sugar and limes, sweet and tart at the same time," I replied.

I lifted my head. She leaned forward to kiss me, but I drew back. She stopped and frowned, wondering what I was doing.

I stepped forward, so I was standing in between her legs. She sucked in another breath, and her eyes burned a little hotter and bluer than before. I eased her thighs apart, then reached forward, moving my hands under the skirt of her waitress uniform.

Charlotte hissed as my fingers stroked her bare thighs, then slowly started gliding higher and higher. That first soft touch of her, the first feel of her warm, smooth skin against my own, almost made me lose control, but I kept going all the way up, until I hooked my fingers in the top of her silky panties. Then I started sliding them down, first one side, then the other, a little bit at a time, doing the same sort of slow, deliberate striptease that she had done to me.

She lifted one of her legs, then the other, and I pulled her panties the rest of the way down and off her legs and tossed them aside. Charlotte toed off her sneakers, which clattered to the floor. She wasn't wearing any socks. Then I leaned forward, bracing my hands on the counter on either side of her.

We stared into each other's eyes, both of us breathing hard.

"I fantasized about you on this counter so many times," I growled.

"Me too," she whispered. "So why don't we make it a reality?"

She didn't have to tell me twice. I picked her up again, holding her high for a moment, then slowly slid her down my body. Charlotte shivered and looped her arms around my neck, even as her legs locked around my waist.

Then I moved forward, set her back down onto the counter again, and thrust into her.

We both groaned, then Charlotte grabbed my face, leaned forward, and crushed her lips to mine. Her tongue slammed into mine, and I rocked my hips back and surged forward again.

And then again, and then again.

Charlotte met me thrust for thrust, and we quickly found a rhythm. She tangled her fingers into my hair, digging her nails into my scalp, even as her lips and tongue kept crashing into mine.

Her soft lips and the lingering trace of apple pie on her tongue. Her sugary-lime scent. Her tight, wet heat. Being with Charlotte was everything I had ever imagined, and every soft groan and breathy sigh she let out made me want to give her as much pleasure as possible, so I pumped my hips faster, going deeper and deeper inside her with every quick thrust.

"Ah!" she moaned. "Yes! Desmond! Yes!"

Her eyes fluttered shut, her fingers dug into my shoulders, and her head lolled back as the first orgasm pulsed through her body. Her aura burned even brighter and hotter, the blue so intense it seared my eyes.

I pushed into her a final time. That was all it took for me to explode with her. Pleasure crackled through my body, and I groaned, joining her in that amazing burn of blue.

THIRTY-SIX

CHARLOTTE

When it was over, Desmond and I stayed locked together, his hands on my hips, mine gripping his shoulders, our foreheads touching, both of us breathing hard.

"Did that…live up…to your fantasies?" I asked, gasping for breath. "Because…it certainly…did mine."

"And…then…some," he replied.

Desmond leaned forward and kissed me again, then drew back. I braced my hands on the counter. My legs were trembling like they were made of jelly, and I wasn't sure I could stand without falling.

Desmond prowled toward me again. I was still a puddle of goo on the counter, and he scooped me up into his arms and carried me back to his bedroom. He set me down on my feet, his hands settling on my waist.

"You are wearing entirely too many clothes, Numbers."

"I agree." I fumbled for the first button on my waitress uniform, but he put his hand over mine.

"Let me," he rasped.

I dropped my hands to my sides. Desmond made fast work of all the buttons on my uniform, then slowly pushed the sides of my shirt apart, his hot, hungry gaze locked onto my breasts. I was suddenly very glad I had worn my one good lacy blue bra tonight.

Desmond moved around behind me and slowly peeled the shirt off my shoulders, just as I had done to him in the kitchen. He also unhooked my bra and slid it down my arms. I yanked it off and tossed it aside.

His hands settled on my waist again, then slid lower and undid the zipper on the back of my skirt. The garment puddled at my feet, and I stepped out of it and turned around to face him.

We were both naked now, and I looped my arms around his neck and kissed him again, soft and slow, gliding my tongue against his. Desmond gently trailed his fingers up and down my back, making me shiver.

We broke apart, and he walked over and sat down on the edge of the bed. He looked up and held out his hand to me. I took it, stepped forward, and lay down on the bed with him.

I kissed Desmond over and over again, flicking my tongue against his, even as my hands explored all of his warm, rippling muscles. A low, satisfied growl rumbled through his chest, and his hands traced down my body, following my curves.

"I love the way you feel," he murmured against my lips.

"Right back at you, Dundee," I whispered.

We kept kissing and caressing, taking it slow, figuring out what the other liked, and doing all the things we hadn't had the patience for the first time around.

I stroked Desmond's thick, hard erection, and he hissed with pleasure and started pumping his hips. I stroked him harder, faster, and he groaned, his hands fisting in the sheets.

"You drive me crazy," he gasped.

I leaned forward to kiss him again, but he grabbed my waist and flipped me over onto my back. Then his hand eased between my legs, and he started stroking me the same way that I had him. I writhed against him, but it wasn't enough.

"Condom," I whispered. "Now."

Desmond rolled away from me, and I heard the nightstand drawer slide open, then a rip of foil. He rejoined me a moment later, and our mouths, hands, and bodies melded together. I locked my legs around his waist again.

"Ah," I groaned, digging my nails into his back, enjoying the sensation of him filling that deepest part of me.

Desmond groaned as well, and we started rocking back and forth.

For once, my synesthesia was completely silent, and all I could see, taste, touch, and smell was him, and all I could feel was our bodies moving, striving to reach newer, sharper, higher heights of pleasure—together.

Afterward, we lay in bed, our limbs tangled up, both of us basking in the afterglow. Desmond's arm was curled around my shoulders, his fingers sliding over my skin, while my head was pillowed on his chest, with his heart beating against my ear.

"Why did we wait so long to do that?" I asked.

"I have no idea, Numbers. If I'd known how good it would be, I would have offered to be your bodyguard the moment I met you."

I laughed, and we fell into an easy, companionable silence again. I could have lain here all night next to him, pretending this moment was going to last forever, but I could already hear the hours *tick-tick-ticking* down in my mind. There was no point beating around the bush.

I braced myself. "I saw your suitcases outside. Getting ready for your next assignment?"

His fingers stilled on my shoulder. "Something like that. You?"

I shrugged. "I'm supposed to see Gia in the morning. She says she has something else she wants me to tackle in addition to my usual analyst duties."

Desmond drew back, staring down at me. "Are you happy?" he asked, his eyes searching mine. "Working for Section? If you wanted to, you could leave now. If anyone has earned the right to walk away from Section and their family's legacy, then it's you."

I got the sense that he was talking about something else, something more, although I didn't know what it was. "I was never *unhappy* working for Section. But, yeah, I will be much happier now that people are taking my work seriously. And I want to help stop Henrika, and the Syndicate, and all the other bad people out there."

"Just like your father?" Desmond teased.

"Just like my father." I paused. "Although I've always thought that I was more like my grandmother."

"You mentioned her before when we were talking to Gia and Evelyn. What kind of paramortal power did she have?"

"She was an analyst like me." I paused again. "But she didn't have any magic or powers. She was a regular old mortal, as ordinarily human as they come."

Desmond drew back again, a confused look on his face.

"What? A mortal working for Section? How did she manage that?"

"Somehow, Grandma Jane found out about magic, paramortals, Section 47, all of it. So she walked into the lobby one day and applied for a job. She told them she was a psychic."

"And was she?"

I laughed. "No. She was a con artist, but the Section higher-ups bought her act hook, line, and sinker. What Grandma Jane really did was analyze *people*. She always said you could learn more by watching someone and studying their things than any real paramortal psychic could by reading someone's mind. And she was right. All you have to do is figure out what someone wants, and what they're willing to do in order to get it, and you can predict a lot about their future behavior."

"So that's how you came up with your plan to trap Trevor and Miriam," Desmond murmured. "Your grandmother taught you."

"Yep. And she taught me well."

We both fell silent again, and my thoughts returned to the suitcases sitting outside the bedroom door.

"I want to wish you luck," I said. "I know that you'll get Henrika and everyone else involved with her and the Syndicate."

"Thank you."

Thinking about him leaving made my eyes water and my chest ache, so I rolled over and glanced at the clock on the nightstand. Just after three in the morning.

I sat up. "It's late. I should get going."

Desmond reached up and cupped my face in his hand. "Stay the rest of the night. With me. Please."

My heart soared inside my chest. "Are you sure?"

"I've never been more sure about anything," he said.

Once again, I got the sense that he was talking about something else, something more, but it was an invitation I couldn't refuse, especially since I knew he would be gone tomorrow.

So I grinned, leaned forward, and lowered my lips to his again.

THIRTY-SEVEN

CHARLOTTE

The next morning, Desmond and I took a very long, hot, steamy shower together, in every sense of the word, then got dressed. He still had the clothes I had left over here when I'd been staying in the apartment, so I changed into a fresh outfit, while he put on another one of his sleek gray suits.

I sat on a barstool at the island counter while he made me a smoothie. The familiar routine made me smile, although a bittersweet ache flooded my chest. I would miss this. I would miss *him*.

"Try it," Desmond said, sliding a glass over to me. "It's a new recipe I came up with just for you."

I eyed the liquid, which was bright pink instead of the usual grassy green, but I obligingly took a sip. The taste of strawberries and limes exploded on my tongue, along with faint hints of vanilla and mint. "Wow! That actually tastes… *good*."

"See?" he teased. "I knew I could convince you to like my smoothies sooner or later."

"Smoothies aren't the only things I like about you." I waggled my eyebrows suggestively at him.

Desmond groaned. "You are killing me, Numbers."

He was killing me too, truth be told, but now that morning was here, I didn't want to let him go. So I went around to his side of the island, then slowly, deliberately hopped up onto the counter.

Desmond arched an eyebrow and crossed his arms over his chest. "Now you're playing dirty, using my own fantasies against me."

"Well, if you'd rather get to work early…"

I started to hop off the island, but Desmond moved over and braced his hands on either side of me, a hungry look filling his face.

"I'd rather be late to work," he growled.

"Me too," I whispered, leaning forward and pressing my lips to his.

And so we were.

Two hours later, I walked into the lobby of the Section building. It was after nine, which was a bit late for me, although no one seemed to notice except for Evelyn, who was sitting behind her desk as usual. I might know that she was Maestro, but she was keeping up appearances for everyone else.

Evelyn smiled. "Good morning, Charlotte."

I placed a peppermint mocha, her favorite, on the counter in front of her. "Good morning."

She raised her eyebrows. "Trying to bribe me now?"

"I was always bribing you before. I see no reason to stop now that I know you're in charge. Do you?"

Evelyn grabbed the coffee and toasted me with it. "Nope."

I grinned at her, scanned my keycard, and rode an elevator down to the third floor. I went to my desk, but I had barely cracked open my laptop when my phone buzzed, and Gia's voice filled my ear, telling me to come to her office to get my new assignment.

I grabbed Desmond's black fountain pen—which was actually an excellent pen, in addition to its hidden surveillance gear—and a notepad and went down to the fifth floor. I glanced at Desmond's desk as I walked through the bullpen, but the surface was clean and empty. He had probably already gotten his assignment and was on his way to the airport. My heart squeezed tight, but I walked by his desk, knocked on the open door, and stepped into Gia's office.

She waved me in, and I took a chair in front of her desk.

"Good work wrapping up the Redburn mission," Gia said. "We've already gotten several leads on where Henrika might be hiding."

I nodded and sat up a little straighter in my seat.

"I wanted to talk to you about your new assignment," Gia said. "First and foremost, I want you to continue your work on the third floor as an analyst. You have a great talent for seeing patterns and making connections. I want that to continue, but I also want you to work for Section in another, more hands-on capacity."

"What?" I asked.

She looked at me. "I want you to be a permanent liaison to one of the cleaners."

"Oh." I couldn't quite keep the disappointment out of my voice. Not what I'd been expecting, although I supposed it made sense, given how well Desmond and I had worked together on the Redburn mission. Section was all about maximizing talent.

Gia arched an eyebrow at me. "This cleaner specifically asked for you, Charlotte. You should be flattered."

"Actually, I'm the one who should be flattered." His low, husky voice sent a shiver down my spine. "If Numbers will agree to be my liaison."

I turned around, and there he was, leaning in the doorframe. Desmond, looking suave as always in his gray vest with his bright, rebellious, powder-blue tie. My heart lifted, but I forced myself to remain calm.

"What are you doing here?" I asked. "I thought you were leaving on your new assignment today."

"I decided to stick around D.C. a while—if that's okay with you?" He raised his eyebrows.

My heart lifted again, and this time, I didn't even bother trying to haul it back down to the ground. "Of course that's okay with me."

It was more than I'd dared to hope for, although I wondered how what we had done last night would impact our relationship moving forward. Fraternization was not exactly endorsed between Section operatives, and feelings were most definitely frowned upon. And I had all sorts of *feelings* for Desmond Percy.

Desmond sat down beside me. He winked at me, and I winked back. Then we both turned toward Gia again.

She handed each one of us a folder. "The two of you have been assigned to track down Henrika Hyde, question her for information on the Syndicate, and then eliminate her. Right now, the two of you will work here, out of the D.C. office. We still don't know the full extent to which we have been compromised, so you two are on your own. At least until we've cleared some more people to join you. But for now, you report only to Maestro and me. You don't tell anyone else what you're working on. As far as everyone else knows, it's just business as usual. Understood?"

"Understood," Desmond and I said in unison.

"Good. Then you are dismissed. Happy hunting."

Gia turned back to the other files and folders on her desk, and Desmond and I got up and left her office.

We both dumped the files on our respective desks in the bullpen, then headed out to the dead zone on the fifth floor. At this rate, we should just set up a couple of desks and chairs out here and call it our new office.

"You didn't have to stop chasing Henrika or your revenge because of me," I said, wanting to clear the air. "I knew that last night was just a one-time thing. I don't expect you to give up your mission for me. I know how important avenging Graham and your fellow agents is to you."

Desmond shook his head. "I was always planning to stick around, Numbers. Even before last night."

Surprise jolted through me. "You were?"

He nodded. "Those suitcases you saw were me moving some more things into the apartment—not my leaving. Turns out the best way to avenge Graham is to have someone with a big brain on my side. And I can't think of anyone with a bigger brain than you, Numbers." He grinned. "Besides, I have a feeling you're going to need my bodyguard skills again. You have a tendency to piss people off."

I snorted. "And you don't, Dundee?"

His grin widened. "Guilty as charged."

"And what about…" I gestured back and forth between us.

"Us?" He arched an eyebrow. "I've been *very* happy with us so far."

I sighed. "You know what I mean. Us working together will only complicate matters, the other *us*, as it were."

Instead of looking concerned, he smiled. "Here's something you should know about me—I like complicated, especially when it comes to us. Don't you?"

I couldn't stop an answering smile from spreading across my own face. "I *adore* complicated."

He nodded. "Then it's decided. We'll hunt down the bad guys and be complicated together along the way. And if Section doesn't like it, then too bad. So, shall I escort you to your desk, Ms. Locke?"

Desmond held out his arm to me, and I stepped forward and threaded my arm through his. "Yes, you may, Mr. Percy."

Then arm in arm, each of us beaming at the other, we left the dead zone to get to work and face our enemies and our future—together.

ABOUT THE AUTHOR

Jennifer Estep is a *New York Times*, *USA Today*, and internationally bestselling author who prowls the streets of her imagination in search of her next fantasy idea.

In addition to her **Section 47 series**, Jennifer is also the author of the **Crown of Shards, Gargoyle Queen, Elemental Assassin**, and other fantasy series. She has written more than forty books, along with numerous novellas and stories.

In her spare time, Jennifer enjoys hanging out with friends and family, doing yoga, and reading fantasy and romance books. She also watches way too much TV and loves all things related to superheroes.

For more information on Jennifer and her books, visit her website at www.jenniferestep.com or follow her online on Facebook, Goodreads, BookBub, Amazon, Instagram, and Twitter. You can also sign up for her newsletter.

Happy reading, everyone! ☺

OTHER BOOKS BY JENNIFER ESTEP

THE SECTION 47 SERIES
A Sense of Danger

THE CROWN OF SHARDS SERIES
Kill the Queen
Protect the Prince
Crush the King

THE GARGOYLE QUEEN SERIES
Capture the Crown

THE ELEMENTAL ASSASSIN SERIES
FEATURING GIN BLANCO

BOOKS
Spider's Bite
Web of Lies
Venom
Tangled Threads
Spider's Revenge
By a Thread
Widow's Web
Deadly Sting
Heart of Venom
The Spider
Poison Promise
Black Widow
Spider's Trap

Bitter Bite
Unraveled
Snared
Venom in the Veins
Sharpest Sting
Last Strand

E-NOVELLAS
Haints and Hobwebs
Thread of Death
Parlor Tricks (from the Carniepunk anthology)
Kiss of Venom
Unwanted
Nice Guys Bite
Winter's Web

THE MYTHOS ACADEMY SPINOFF SERIES
FEATURING RORY FORSETI

Spartan Heart
Spartan Promise
Spartan Destiny

THE MYTHOS ACADEMY SERIES
FEATURING GWEN FROST

BOOKS
Touch of Frost
Kiss of Frost
Dark Frost
Crimson Frost
Midnight Frost
Killer Frost